"Oh, you have a tree

Ivy turned back to Mitch with a teasing grin. "It appears there's a bit of playfulness in you after all."

"I hate to disappoint you, but that swing was already there when I moved in." He regretted the words as soon as he saw the disappointment flash across her face.

She fisted a hand on her hip, looking quite severe. "You mean to tell me that you've never once even sat in that swing."

"Guilty."

"Well, that's downright wasteful."

He waved a hand toward the swing. "Feel free."

"Well, there's no time like the present." With a saucy smile she started across the lawn. Ivy set the swing in motion, soaring high and laughing aloud.

Mitch leaned against a porch support, crossing his arms and enjoying the view.

As he watched her it occurred to him that perhaps her presence in his once quiet household was going to change his life more than he'd considered.

But it was too late to go back now.

What troubled him more was that he didn't want to.

Winnie Griggs
and
Noelle Marchand

Lone Star Heiress
&
The Runaway Bride

LOVE INSPIRED
INSPIRATIONAL ROMANCE

LOVE INSPIRED®
INSPIRATIONAL ROMANCE

Recycling programs for this product may not exist in your area.

ISBN-13: 978-1-335-50823-2

Lone Star Heiress & The Runaway Bride

Copyright © 2020 by Harlequin Books S.A.

Lone Star Heiress
First published in 2014. This edition published in 2020.
Copyright © 2014 by Winnie Griggs

The Runaway Bride
First published in 2012. This edition published in 2020.
Copyright © 2012 by Noelle Marchand

This edition published by arrangement with Harlequin Books S.A.

For questions and comments about the quality of this book, please contact us at CustomerService@Harlequin.com.

Love Inspired
22 Adelaide St. West, 40th Floor
Toronto, Ontario M5H 4E3, Canada
www.Harlequin.com

Printed in U.S.A.

CONTENTS

Winnie Griggs is the multipublished, award-winning author of historical (and occasionally contemporary) romances that focus on small towns, big hearts and amazing grace. She is also a list maker and a lover of dragonflies, and holds an advanced degree in the art of procrastination. Winnie loves to hear from readers—you can connect with her on Facebook at Facebook.com/winniegriggs.author or email her at winnie@winniegriggs.com.

Books by Winnie Griggs

Love Inspired Historical

Texas Grooms

Handpicked Husband
The Bride Next Door
A Family for Christmas
Lone Star Heiress
Her Holiday Family
Second Chance Hero
The Holiday Courtship
Texas Cinderella
A Tailor-Made Husband
Once Upon a Texas Christmas

Visit the Author Profile page
at Harlequin.com for more titles.

LONE STAR HEIRESS

Winnie Griggs

He shall choose our inheritance for us.
—*Psalms* 47:4

To my awesome agent Michelle
and my fabulous critique partners Connie and Amy,
who all, at various points, helped me talk through
some of the tough spots I encountered while
writing this story. Thanks for your willingness
to listen, offer terrific suggestions and most of all
your belief in and enthusiasm for this story.

Chapter One

Texas
June 1896

"This doesn't look good."

Ivy gently set the hoof back down on the grassy road and patted the mule's side. "No wonder you're limping, Jubal—it 'pears like you've picked up a honey of a stone bruise."

The mule turned around to nip at her, but she avoided him easily enough. Although Jubal might be ornery at times, he usually wasn't mean. Unfortunately, these weren't usual circumstances.

Maybe she shouldn't have set such a demanding pace this past day and a half, but she'd hoped to make it to Turnabout in two days' time. A woman traveling alone for this distance, even if she was dressed as a boy, was vulnerable to gossip and worse.

But it looked as if she was doomed to spend another night on the trail.

"Not that anyone's gonna notice we're late," she told Jubal, "since no one is expecting us exactly. I'm just anxious to find out what the mysterious inheritance is that this Drum Mosley fellow is holding for me."

Ivy gave the mule's side another pat as he brayed out a complaint. "I wish there was something I could do to make you feel better." They were a day-and-a-half's ride from home and headed in the opposite direction. It had been several hours since they'd seen signs of people or habitation, so she figured they'd be better off pressing forward. "Guess we'll just have to get by as best we can."

She turned to her other traveling companion, also of the four-legged variety. "Well, Rufus, I guess I'll be walking the rest of the way alongside you."

The dog barked in response and she rubbed his head, comforted by the feel of his shaggy coat and the trusting look in his eyes.

"Let's hope we find a homestead with neighborly folks who won't mind strangers bunking in their barn." She straightened. "At least there's lots of good foraging to be had this time of year."

She took off her straw hat and wiped her forehead with her sleeve. It might be the first week in June, but the summer heat had already set in.

How far had they come since they'd started out at dawn yesterday? Other than a couple of short breaks, they'd only stopped when darkness made it unsafe to travel last night. They broke camp at daybreak this morning and she estimated it was getting on to four o'clock now. Surely they were getting close to Turnabout. Which meant it would be time to exchange her britches for a skirt soon.

She glanced down at Rufus. "Whatever this inheritance is, it sure better be worth all this trouble. 'Cause we could really use some good luck about now."

She patted Jubal's neck. "Wouldn't it be something if we could return home with enough money to rebuild the barn and buy a new milk cow? That would sure make Nana Dovie's life a lot easier."

Grabbing the reins, Ivy looked the mule in the eye. "I know you're hurting, but we need to make it a little farther before dark."

She moved forward and lightly tugged. To her relief, Jubal decided to cooperate. She glanced down the narrow, deserted road as she absently swatted a horsefly away. They hadn't seen so much as a fence post or wagon rut since before noon. Apparently this shortcut to Turnabout wasn't well used. But surely they'd spot *some* sign of civilization soon.

Not one to enjoy long silences, Ivy shared her thoughts aloud. "It's been a wearisome day and you two have been great companions. Don't think I don't appreciate it. In fact, I have a special treat for each of you that I'll hand out as soon as we stop for the night."

She glanced at Rufus, padding along beside her. "It would be nice if you and I ended up with a barn or shed to sleep in tonight, don't you think?"

Not that she minded camping out—that's what they'd done last night and, other than fighting off some pesky mosquitoes, they'd managed just fine. But those gray clouds gathering overhead would likely bring rain before morning and she didn't relish the idea of getting soaked.

But as Nana Dovie always said, worrying was like doubting God. If you truly believe He's in charge, then you have to trust He'll work everything out for the best.

Of course, it never hurt to let Him know what you'd like to have happen.

"Mind you, Lord," she said respectfully, "I know we can use a bit of rain to settle the dust. It's just that I'm not sure that sheet of canvas I brought along will keep out more than a spit and a drizzle, and I'd rather not have a mud bath. If You could help me find a dry place to sleep, it would be most welcome."

She glanced over at the mule. "And please help Jubal heal quickly. Amen."

Ivy smiled down at Rufus. "Now, whatever happens, we'll know He has it in hand."

An hour later, she frowned up at the overcast sky. The clouds had thickened like clabbered milk and the heavy air clung to her skin like a damp petticoat. And they still hadn't come across any signs of civilization. Jubal's limp was more pronounced now—she couldn't in good conscience push him further today. She had to let the injured animal rest.

"Well, boys, as Nana Dovie says, when you don't get the thing you prayed for, it don't mean God ain't listening. It just means the answer is either *no* or *not now*. So it looks like we're going to spend another night under the stars. And this is as likely a spot as any."

Mitch Parker sat comfortably in the saddle, soaking in the morning sunshine and peaceful surroundings, letting all the stress of the past few weeks dissolve away. It had rained most of last night, but the rhythmic pattering on the cozy cabin roof had added to the serenity.

And today had dawned bright and warm—perfect weather for the first full day of his vacation. The leaves on the trees had that special shine they always had after a rain and the only sounds were those of the birds and insects. He might even take out his sketch pad later.

School was out for the summer, giving him a welcome break from his teaching duties. But more than that, he was ready for a break from Hilda Swenson. The persistent widow and mother of three had made him the target of her attention for the past several weeks and seemed oblivious to his hints that he wasn't interested. She was a flibbertigibbet of the highest order—something he had no patience for. And her determined pursuit was playing havoc with the quiet, well-ordered life he'd strived so hard to build for himself and was determined to maintain at all costs.

He never wanted to go back to what he'd once been. Nor did he want to be a husband again, not after the tragic outcome of his marriage.

His rebuffs of the widow's overtures would obviously have to be more direct in the future—a confrontation he wasn't looking forward to. Thus his decision to slip away to a friend's cabin for a week or so.

Mitch shook off those thoughts. He'd deal with that unpleasantness when he returned to Turnabout. This week was for relaxing and regaining that all-important sense of control over his life.

And this back-of-beyond cabin had been just the place to do it. He was grateful to Reggie Barr for giving him the use of it. In a way, it was a homecoming. The cabin was where he'd spent his first night in this part of the world, two years ago. Reggie had been a stranger then, but had held his fate in her hands. Now he counted her and her husband, Adam, amongst his closest friends.

He'd made it to the cabin yesterday afternoon, in

time to get some fishing in. Fishing, reading and sketching, and no people around. Yes, this was going to be a fine week indeed.

Just before he'd left town yesterday, Reggie had told him he could find some mulberry trees north of the cabin. So now he was heading that way, hoping to gather a generous amount of the fruit, and curious to explore a different section of the woods. Perhaps he'd find inspiration for some of the sketching he planned to do.

A bark echoed through the trees, catching Mitch's attention. What would a dog be doing out here? It was a four-hour ride from Turnabout and as far as he knew, no one lived out this way. Then again, maybe someone had settled here recently. He grimaced at that thought. He hoped whoever it was wasn't the gregarious type—he wasn't in a sociable mood.

But he was getting ahead of himself. A dog didn't necessarily mean there were people around. The animal could have wandered all this way on his own.

Mitch slowed Seeley, then pulled the horse to a stop. Maybe he should turn around and return to the cabin. If there *were* people up ahead, there was no sense in inviting an acquaintance. Perhaps if he refrained from intruding on them, they'd return the favor.

Then he reluctantly set Seeley in motion again. If he *was* going to have neighbors, it was best he meet them at a time of his own choosing rather than have them arrive on his doorstep when he wasn't prepared. He could also drop a hint or two that he valued his privacy.

As Mitch neared the spot where the dog's bark had come from, he heard a human voice as well, though he couldn't make out the words. Well, that answered that—there *were* people out here.

He peered through the woods and spied a youth standing on a log, plucking mulberries from a tree. It appeared someone besides him had designs on the berries.

Mitch quickly scanned the surrounding area, looking for the other members of the lad's party. There was a scruffy-looking dog and a mule, but no sign of either a homestead or other people.

The dog spotted him first and began barking furiously.

"Goodness, Rufus, what's gotten into you? Is it another squirrel?" The youth turned to look and, as he caught sight of Mitch, his eyes widened and his foot slipped, losing its purchase on the log. His arms flailed as he attempted to catch his balance. The youth's hat went flying and the appearance of a long untidy braid had Mitch quickly revising his initial impression.

A moment later, *she* was flat on her back on the ground.

And not moving.

Nightmare memories of another fallen woman whooshed through Mitch with the force of a flash flood. He vaulted from his horse, his heart pounding like a mad thing trying to escape his chest.

Not again. God wouldn't be so cruel as to make him relive such a tragedy a second time.

Would He?

Chapter Two

In a matter of seconds, Mitch knelt beside the all-too-still form, checking for signs of life. When he saw the rise of her chest, his frenetic heartbeat slowed slightly. But he refocused immediately. He needed to find out just how badly she was hurt.

His breath caught for a moment as he spotted reddish stains on her shirt and hands. But a heartbeat later he realized they came from berries, not blood.

Why was she out here alone, and why was she dressed as a boy?

He shoved those thoughts aside—there would be time later for those questions, once he'd made certain she was okay.

It was his fault she'd fallen. He hadn't intended to startle her, but that didn't absolve him of the fact that he had. He of all people knew that actions often had un-anticipated consequences. He also knew his imposing size could make strangers uncomfortable at the best of times. For a lone female who wasn't expecting him—even one dressed as a boy—his arrival must have been a shock.

She stirred and he turned his attention to her face, only now taking in her physical appearance. Her nose and cheeks were dusted with a liberal sprinkling of freckles, giving her a youthful look. Her still-closed eyes were partially covered by a fringe of reddish-brown hair that had escaped her braid. He absently brushed the tendrils away from her face and was rewarded with a grimace and a soft moan, welcome signs that she was regaining consciousness.

"Easy," he said, still uncertain of her condition.

She started at the sound of his voice, and her eyes flew open, regarding him with wide-eyed confusion and uncertainty. The deep clover-green of her irises startled him momentarily. They were the most amazingly intense eyes he'd ever seen.

"Are you hurt?" He kept his voice calm, trying not to further alarm her.

"I don't... My head hurts, but I think I'm okay."

She made as if to sit up, but he placed a hand on her shoulder, gently restraining her. "Easy now. Take a minute before you move around too much."

She gave him a peevish frown. "I *need* to sit up— the ground's wet."

That's what she was worried about? Probably still addled from the fall. "I understand, but let's check you out first."

The suspicion in her expression deepened, and she attempted to put more distance between them. "I can check my own self, thank you."

Though her words were assertive, her tone was slurred and she seemed none too steady. He didn't want to agitate her further, however, so he nodded.

"All right, but if you insist on sitting up, at least

let me assist you." He placed a hand at her elbow and
helped her up, keeping close watch for signs of injuries or weakness. Once he was sure she wouldn't fall
over again, he eased back on his haunches, ignoring the
dampness seeping through the knees of his pants, trying to maintain a nonthreatening pose.

As soon as he moved back, she pulled a knife from
somewhere and had it unsteadily pointed at his chest.
"If you're thinking to rob me, mister, you should know
I don't have much worth stealing, but what's mine is
mine."

The dog, alerted by her tone, stiffened and bared its
teeth at him.

"Whoa, there." Mitch threw his hands up, palms
out, trying to assure her he wasn't a threat. The knife,
while not especially large, looked sharp enough to do
some damage. And although he was quite certain he
could take it from her with little effort, he didn't want
to do that unless he had to. "I just want to make certain
you're okay, nothing more." She placed her free hand
on the dog's back, but he had no illusions she was restraining him.

"I'm talking about before that. Why were you sneak-
ing up on me that way?"

"I didn't *sneak up* on you. I *happened* on you while
looking for the mulberry trees. My apologies if you
were startled."

She blinked those amazing eyes as if trying to clear
her vision, and the trembling in her hand grew more
pronounced. Was it due to pain? Or weakness?

"Are these trees on your place?" she asked. "'Cause
I didn't mean to trespass."

Trespassing should be the least of her worries right

now. He didn't like the slur that had crept into her voice. Time to be firm, for her own good. "We can discuss all that later. Right now I need to know if you're badly hurt."

She still didn't lower the knife, though the effort seemed to cost her. But her left hand moved from the dog to the back of her head. "I... My head—" She pulled her hand back and stared at it as if it belonged to someone else.

It was stained with blood.

Mitch bit off an oath. "You *are* hurt. Let me have a look." He moved in closer, and she quickly raised the knife to block him, swaying slightly with the effort. Her dog let out a warning growl.

This girl had more spunk than sense. "I'm only trying to take a look at your injury—that's all. You're bleeding and it's not something you can tend to yourself."

Without a word, she nodded, her gaze never leaving his face.

Keeping his moves slow and smooth, he shifted to get a better look, ignoring the knife that unsteadily tracked his movements. A patch of blood on the back of her head stained her hair, matting it against her scalp. The wet, muddy ground she'd been lying on hadn't helped matters any, either. He tried gently parting the hair but couldn't see much beyond the blood.

He moved to face her again, and realized she'd closed her eyes. Had his ministrations hurt her?

But a moment later her eyes opened with obvious effort and her gaze held a question.

"I'm going to get my canteen so I can clean this up and get a better look. Try not to move."

She nodded wearily, then winced. "There's a shallow creek just beyond those trees." Her voice sounded strained and pain shadowed her expression.

He gave her what he hoped was a reassuring smile, crossed his fingers that she'd be all right until he returned, then sprinted back to Seeley.

Snatching up his canteen and the small cloth bag he'd intended to put the berries in, he quickly headed back, only detouring once when he saw her own canteen amongst her things.

Mitch pulled out his handkerchief as he knelt beside her again. Her hand was back on the dog's neck, but now she seemed to be using it for support rather than restraint. Not a good sign. Still, her stoicism and ability to keep her wits under the circumstances was commendable.

"I'll be as gentle as I can," he said as he wet the cloth.

She tried to raise the knife again. With a sigh, he wrested it from her in one quick move, then set it carefully out of her reach.

He regretted the spark of fear he saw in her eyes. "I'm sorry—" he kept his tone matter-of-fact "—but I can't have you hurting either yourself or me while I'm focused on fixing you up."

She watched his every move, and he saw the caution and uncertainty she was trying to hold at bay.

"I guess I should introduce myself," he said, hoping to distract her. "Mitch Parker, at your service."

"Ivy Feagan." She offered her name reluctantly, then he heard a quick intake of breath as he dabbed at the cut. She indicated the dog. "This here is Rufus." Her voice had a note of challenge in it.

Good. He preferred bravado to fear. "Glad to meet

you. By the way, did you get to sample those mulberries before I interrupted you? I hear they're exceptional."

She answered affirmatively, then fell silent again. There were no indications she was hurting, other than an occasional hitch in her breathing when he touched a particularly sensitive spot. When that happened, she'd start talking, mostly rambling thoughts, as if to hide her reaction.

Despite her unfocused chatter, he found himself admiring her. She didn't complain, or dissolve into hysterics or cower—all of which would have been understandable reactions given the situation. Instead, she maintained a stoic demeanor. He'd known men who would have acted with less restraint in these circumstances.

It took all the water in his canteen, but he finally had the area clean enough to see the cut. It was a nasty-looking gash, but the bleeding had almost stopped.

He rinsed his now-soiled handkerchief, then squeezed out as much water as he could. He folded it into a thick pad, then gently covered the injury. "Do you think you can hold this in place for a few moments?"

She obediently placed a hand over the pad. He picked up the cloth bag, quickly removed the drawstring and held it up to show her. "I'm going to use this to tie the bandage in place. Okay?"

"Okay."

He secured the pad, then leaned back to study his work. With the ties dangling over her left ear, she would have looked comical if the situation weren't so serious.

"That will have to do for now." He met her gaze and frowned. He didn't like the paleness of her skin. Her freckles stood out in stark relief, her eyes looked huge and the rest of her face had a pinched look. And he could tell she was struggling to stay focused. What should he do now?

"How bad is it?" Her wariness was still evident, but he thought he also sensed the beginnings of trust.

He chose his words carefully—he didn't want to alarm her unduly. "You've lost some blood. I imagine you're going to have a whopper of a headache for the next several days, but I've seen worse." Much worse. "But right now we need to see about getting you someplace where you can rest and be tended to properly." He strived to keep the worry from his tone. "Do you have friends nearby or a place I can take you around here?" *Please let her say yes.*

"No." Her single-word answer offered no clue as to why she was out here on her own. And that disconcerting wariness was back in full force. He couldn't really blame her for her caution—in fact he rather admired her for it. But she shouldn't have been placed in the position of fending for herself this way.

He tried again. "Is anyone traveling with you?"

"Only Rufus and Jubal."

Rufus was the dog, but who was Jubal? "Do you know where Jubal is?"

"Jubal is my mule—" Her face suddenly drained of any remaining color and her eyes fluttered closed.

Mitch managed to catch her before her head hit the ground again.

He quickly assured himself she was still breathing, and to his relief, her eyes fluttered open. As soon as she realized her position, she struggled to push him away. "What—"

He reached for her canteen and held it up to her. "You fainted. Here, drink this."

She quieted and took the canteen, raising it to her lips. Her gaze never left his.

After a few sips, she handed the canteen back, but he shook his head. "You need to drink it all," he said firmly.

She stiffened at his tone, but after a heartbeat obediently drained the canteen.

What in the world was he going to do with her?

If he had a wagon, he'd transport her directly to Turnabout and hand her over to Doc Pratt. But there was no wagon, and in her current condition, she'd never be able to sit in the saddle for the four-hour ride to town. Even if she could, she probably shouldn't.

That left him with only one option. Whether he liked it or not, he'd have to temporarily abandon his plans for solitude. "I suppose you'd better come with me to my cabin, where you can rest until you're feeling better." He only hoped she could sit in the saddle long enough to get that far.

"Thank you," she said, her suspicion obvious, "but that's not necessary. Once I rest a bit I'll be able to get on with my journey."

He knew bluster when he heard it. But he tried to navigate around her caution carefully. "Nevertheless, I'm responsible for your fall and the least I can do is share my shelter and my food with you."

She appeared to be wavering. Hoping to tip the scale in his favor, Mitch retrieved her knife.

She tensed as apprehension flared in her eyes.

He quickly held the knife out to her, hilt first. "You can hold on to this if it makes you more comfortable."

He only hoped she didn't decide to skewer him with it.

* * *

Ivy accepted the knife, wondering just how much she could trust this stranger. His size was certainly worrisome—he wasn't just taller than Goliath. He also had the broadest shoulders she'd ever seen.

Still, he'd been nothing but kind and helpful. Surely if he'd meant to harm her he'd have done so by now. And despite what she'd said, her inability to stop shaking or keep her thoughts focused was worrisome. Perhaps a hot meal and a dry place to rest would cure that. "I suppose I can rest at your cabin as well as I can here. But just for a little while."

He smiled approvingly and she decided he looked much less intimidating when he smiled. In fact, you might say he looked downright handsome, in a bigger-than-life kind of way. It was mighty tempting to let go of her worries and let this man handle them. And right now she was having trouble remembering why she shouldn't.

"Good." He nodded to his left. "I'd like to move you to that tree over there so you have something to lean against while I gather your things."

Move her? She wasn't sure she could stand and make it more than a couple of steps right now, even if he helped her.

But before she could respond, he gave her a stern look. "You appear none too steady and I wouldn't want to have to deal with you falling again."

She could see where he might feel that way, and to be honest, he had good reason. But she had a better idea. "I'll just lean against Rufus instead." She gingerly rearranged herself to demonstrate. And loyal Rufus allowed her to prop herself against him, just as she'd known he would.

She wished he would just get on with gathering her things so she could close her eyes and relax for a minute or two. But she had the nagging feeling she'd forgotten something important.

He studied her a moment, then stood. "I'll only be a few minutes and then we'll be on our way."

As soon as he turned away, she closed her eyes. Then she suddenly remembered what it was she needed to tell him and her heavy eyelids lifted reluctantly. "Mr. Parker."

He turned and took a step back toward her. "Yes? Is something wrong?"

"It's about Jubal. You should know, he turned up lame yesterday. It's why we're camped here." She hoped he'd show Jubal the same kindness he'd shown her.

His expression tightened, but he nodded and continued on his way.

Ivy watched as he made quick work of collecting her few items. For a big man, he moved with surprising grace.

She closed her eyes again. Sometime later she heard Mr. Parker talking, though she couldn't quite make out the words. His tone was soothing and a bit distant.

Prying her eyes open, she watched him approach Jubal. The mule eyed him suspiciously, ears flicking forward. Gradually, though, the animal relaxed, and by the time Mr. Parker attempted to stroke his nose, Jubal seemed ready to eat from his hand.

Satisfied, Ivy let her lids fall shut again.

"Miss Feagan."

The voice seemed much closer this time and when she opened her eyes he stood over her, a worried look on his face. His horse stood just behind him.

"I'm okay," she assured him. "Just resting my eyes."

If anything, the concern in his expression deepened. "This is Seeley. He's a well-behaved horse with an easy gait. I know you're probably not feeling up to a ride, but the cabin isn't far and I don't know of any better way to get you there."

She tried to focus on the animal. He was big—probably had to be to carry such a rider. But how did the man expect her to mount? "I can ride, but getting into the saddle might be tricky."

His lips quirked up at that but he nodded solemnly. "I think we'll be able to work that out." He offered his hand. "Do you think you can stand for just a moment if I help?"

"Of course." At least she hoped so.

He placed his hand under her elbow and gently guided her into a shaky standing position. Unfortunately, her legs felt more like limp rope than bone and muscle. If he hadn't been supporting her she probably would have toppled over. Still, if she could get a good grip on the saddle and he formed a stirrup with his hands, she might be able to—

Before she could complete the thought, he'd scooped her up in his arms.

Caught by surprise, her arms reflexively slid around his neck. "What in blue blazes do you think you're doing?" The man, for all his well-meaning kindness, was much too high-handed for her liking.

He hefted her, pulling her unsettlingly closer against his chest. "I'm helping you into the saddle."

The ease with which he lifted and held her was impressive. She wasn't a petite woman, but he made her feel almost dainty. And the sensation of being held in such a way was unnerving. Though, strangely, she felt completely safe.

He looked down at her uncertainly. "It would be best if you rode astride rather than sidesaddle."

Ivy shrugged, or at least what passed for a shrug in her current position. She shook off her irritation at the same time. This was merely an expedient way of getting her on the horse, nothing more personal. "It's my preferred method of riding, anyway."

He stared into her eyes, and she felt the full power of his gaze. He seemed to be gauging her strength and her resolve. Would he find her wanting?

As she stared back, the flecks of gold in his deep brown eyes drew her in with surprising intensity.

She finally blinked and the connection—if it had ever been there—disappeared.

He cleared his throat. "Once I get you up there, do you think you can keep your seat?"

"Of course." She'd have to, wouldn't she?

Was he really planning to *lift* her bodily into the saddle?

As if in answer to her question, he did exactly that. Mr. Parker kept a supportive hand at her waist until she'd grasped the saddle horn and swung her leg over.

"How are you feeling?"

Was he concerned for *her* or just for the trouble her passing out would cause?

She'd felt dizzy for a moment, but that had settled into a merely foggy sensation. "I'm fine." Then she frowned. "How are you planning to travel?" Would he try to climb up behind her? How did she feel about that?

"As I said, it's not far. I'll walk."

He turned the horse and led it toward Jubal, but his

gaze rarely left her. It was disconcerting to be the focus of those very direct brown eyes. He quickly tied Jubal's lead to his horse's saddle then moved to her left. She noticed Jubal only carried a saddle, and realized he'd loaded her things onto his own horse. It was more kindness for her animal than she'd expected.

"Still doing okay?" he asked.

She forced a smile. "I'm ready when you are."

"I'll be right here at your side. If you start feeling the least bit faint, let me know. Better to delay us than to risk your falling over."

She nodded and he patted the horse's side and clicked his tongue to set the animal in motion.

As they headed down the road, Ivy smiled drowsily at the thought of what an odd procession they made. She was in the lead on his horse, he walked on her left, Jubal followed on the right and Rufus alternately led and padded alongside.

The pounding in her head was amplified with each step the horse took, but she was determined not to worry her self-appointed caretaker more than necessary. She *would* remain conscious and she *would* stay in this saddle until they reached this cabin of his.

Because the alternative wasn't only dangerous and inconvenient.

It would also be altogether mortifying.

Chapter Three

Mitch kept a close eye on his injured charge as they traveled back to the cabin. He hadn't been fooled by her assurances that she was okay. He'd seen the tremble in her hands, the glaze of pain in her eyes, and the way she fought to maintain focus. The sooner he got her to the cabin, the better. But jarring her too much wouldn't do, either. He only hoped she had enough sense to let him know if she needed to stop.

The trip, which had taken only twenty minutes on his way out, took nearly an hour on the return. He paused their little caravan a few times to give her a rest from the jarring movements and make her drink some water, but otherwise he kept them moving at a slow, steady pace. At least there was no sign of fresh blood seeping from underneath her bandage. Perhaps the worst really *was* over.

Throughout that endless trip he tried to keep her talking, to make certain she was both conscious and aware. Fortunately, talking seemed to be something she enjoyed. Not that they had a coherent conversation.

She mostly rambled and his contribution was limited to an occasional question whenever the pauses drew out.

Mitch learned she came from a small town called Nettles Gap and that she lived with someone she called Nana Dovie. He also learned the life history of her dog and her mule, and what great companions they'd been on this trip.

She continued to assure him she was all right whenever he inquired, but by the time he called for the third rest stop he could see she was starting to droop. So when the cabin finally came into view he wanted to shout, "Hallelujah."

"Almost there," he said bracingly.

She straightened and he could almost see her gather her strength as she squinted ahead.

He directed Seeley right up to the front porch before he called a halt. "Now you're going to have to let go of the saddle horn and slide right down into my arms. Don't worry, I'll catch you."

To his surprise, she displayed none of the suspicion she'd exhibited earlier. Perhaps it was because she was exhausted and hurting, but he hoped it was at least partly because she had begun to trust him.

A moment later, she'd half slid, half fallen into his grasp. And for the second time he thought how nice she felt in his arms, how he wanted to protect her from harm.

"If you'll set me down, I can walk from here."

He ignored her and headed up the steps. She didn't argue further, which in and of itself worried him. After a bit of tricky one-handed maneuvering, he got the door open without jostling her too badly, then carried her inside and set her on the sofa.

"I'm going to check your bandage. It won't take but a minute, then you can lie down."

Without a word, she slumped against the cushion and closed her eyes.

He watched her a moment. She looked so vulnerable, so achingly brave as she tried to hold herself together. His hand moved to brush a lock of hair from her forehead, then stopped just short of its goal. His hand slowly withdrew, as if it had a mind and conscience of its own.

This burgeoning awareness of her as more than a person in need of aid was dangerous and had to be smothered before it could go any further.

He turned and moved to the counter, ready to put some distance between them.

Ivy focused on remaining conscious, at least conscious enough to not fall over. She didn't want to get blood and dirt all over his furniture. There were probably all sorts of other things she should be worried about, but for now the only thing getting through her foggy mind was the longing for the promised bed and the chance to sleep undisturbed.

She didn't realize Rufus had followed them inside until he nudged her leg with a worried whine. She placed a hand on the dog's head without opening her eyes. "I'm okay, boy. Just need to rest for a bit."

Sometime later—she wasn't sure how long—Mr. Parker returned. "Now, let's have a look." She felt the tug as he removed the cloth pad that had stuck to the blood.

"How does it look?" she asked.

"The bleeding's stopped. I'm going to put a clean

bandage on it and then let you rest while I cook some soup."

As he pressed the cloth against her head a moment later, Ivy marveled at what an amazingly gentle touch he had for such a big man.

Then he was done. She opened her eyes to see him examining his work. He made a small adjustment to the bandage, then met her gaze. "Ready for your nap?"

She'd *been* ready. But she'd rather not be carried again. It was a mite too unsettling. "Yes. If you'll lend me a hand and show me the way, I'd prefer to walk."

He frowned, but finally nodded.

Good to know he wouldn't just ignore her wishes willy-nilly.

He placed a hand at her elbow and helped her up. Then, slowly, led her to a door next to the fireplace.

Leaning on him more than she cared to admit, Ivy stepped inside a cozy bedchamber. As soon as she was seated on the edge of the bed, her rescuer knelt down and unlaced her boots.

She studied his bent head, strangely entranced by the whorl of hair at the top. What would he do if she reached down and touched it? She stopped herself just short of acting on that thought. What was wrong with her? That knock on the head must have affected her more than she thought.

When he'd removed both her shoes, he hesitated a moment, then went to work removing her socks. The sensation of his hands on her skin sent little tingles through her that caught her unawares.

She must have made an inadvertent movement because he glanced up.

"Sorry if that was uncomfortable," he said as he stood.

She wasn't sure how to respond so said nothing.

He studied her uncertainly, and she wondered if he was worried about putting her to bed. But before she could reassure him that she could take it from here, he turned, suddenlike, and marched to a chest across the room. He came back with a bundle that he shoved at her.

As she took it, she realized it was a nightgown. But whose?

He rubbed the back of his neck, looking extremely uncomfortable. "I thought you might want to change. I don't think Reggie would mind if you borrowed this." He turned and quickly moved to the door.

Once there, however, he paused. "I'll leave this open just a crack. If you need anything, call out."

He smiled as Rufus padded in. "It appears you'll have company."

As he left, she had two completely unrelated thoughts. The first was that it was kind of him to allow her dog inside the cabin.

And the second was, just who was Reggie and what was she to him?

Mitch unsaddled, then fed and watered both Seeley and Miss Feagan's mule. He patted the mule's side as the animals dipped their heads in the feed trough. Jubal's limping had gotten more pronounced the farther they'd walked. It would be best if he was allowed to rest for a couple of days before they set out again. Which meant a trip to town would not be on tomorrow's agenda, not unless they left the animal behind.

Which posed another problem. Miss Feagan's presence had become more than just an intrusion on his privacy. Now he had her reputation to worry about.

Of course, one could say that a woman who traveled alone in these backwoods probably wasn't terribly concerned with her reputation, but he didn't know the full story on that. Nor was that an excuse for him to treat the issue lightly.

There was nothing he could do to salvage the situation—it wasn't as if he could snap his fingers and make a chaperone appear. He'd just have to do what he could to make her comfortable and hope for the best.

On the way back to the cabin, Mitch noticed the stack of firewood was low, so he grabbed the ax from the shed and spent the next twenty minutes replenishing the pile.

Wiping his face with the tail of his shirt, he decided a quick dip in the lake to cool off and clean up wouldn't be amiss.

He quietly entered the house, wanting to check on the patient before he got out of hailing distance. He pushed her bedchamber door open just enough to look inside. The dog, lying beside the bed, lifted its head to stare at him. He stared back, keeping his demeanor impassive, and after a moment the dog lowered its head again. However, the animal's watchful gaze never left Mitch's face.

Miss Feagan, on the other hand, didn't stir. She lay on her side under the covers with that thick mahogany braid of hers mostly unbound. He watched her a moment, assuring himself she was sleeping and hadn't passed out again.

In sleep her expression lost most of the hardness that suspicion and pain had given it. With her hair flowing over her shoulder and that generous sprinkle of freckles, she had the look of a schoolgirl. The guilt he'd felt for his part in her fall washed over him again. Along with something protective and tender.

He wanted to find whoever was responsible for her and give them a piece of his mind for allowing her to end up in this situation. She deserved better.

Then Mitch remembered something he'd heard once about head injuries, something about not letting the injured party sleep too deeply. He hated to rouse her, but he'd hate it even more if he didn't and she got worse.

He squeezed her hand while he said her name. He had to do it three times before her eyes opened.

She glanced up at him, obviously disoriented. "What is it?"

"Nothing important. Go back to sleep."

With a nod, she closed her eyes and snuggled down deeper into the pillow. He pulled out his pocket watch and noted the time. He'd repeat the process every thirty minutes for the next several hours, just to be safe.

Mitch started to ease back out when he spotted the pile of dirty clothing she'd left on the floor. She'd need something clean to wear whenever she recovered enough to leave the bed. He crossed the room under Rufus's watchful gaze, gathered up the discarded clothing, then left, pulling the door behind him until only the barest crack remained.

Pausing just long enough to give the soup simmering on the stove another stir, he headed back out.

Ivy frowned as a soft *woof* intruded on the peace of her sleep. Rufus did it again and she reluctantly gave up on trying to sink back into oblivion.

"What is it, Rufus?" Even to her, her tone sounded

petulant. Then she saw Mr. Parker standing in the doorway and her cheeks heated.

"Sorry if I disturbed you," he said. "I was just checking to see if you were ready for some soup. If you'd
rather continue sleeping, though, the food will keep
until you're ready."

She eased herself up against the pillows, wincing at
the throbbing of her head. "Actually, food sounds good."
Her cheeks heated again as her stomach loudly echoed
those sentiments. She certainly wasn't making a very
good impression. "If you give me a minute to collect
myself, I'll join you at the table." She wondered if there
was a robe in that trunk he'd pulled the nightgown from.

But he shook his head. "You stay put and I'll fetch
you a bowl."

Before she could argue, he changed the subject.
"How's your head?"

"Better." Not exactly a lie. The throbbing had eased.

From the corner of her eye, she spotted her knife
resting in easy reach on the bedside table. It was likely
his way of trying to reassure her that she had nothing
to fear from him, and her heart softened a little more.
He really was a very kind, honorable man. She was no
longer worried about his intentions, even though she
was still at his mercy.

He stepped closer. "Mind if I check?"

It took her a moment to realize he was referring to
her injury, and she turned to give him access to the
back of her head. As he bent nearer to study the bandage, she felt suddenly shy and vulnerable. Both feelings were foreign to her and that made her edgy and
unsettled. It didn't help that as he checked the bandage,

his hands brushed against the nape of her neck and she shivered in reaction.

It was just an aftereffect of her fall, she told herself.

He stilled. "Sorry. Did I hurt you?"

"No." She tried to keep her tone light. "I guess I'm more woozy than I'd thought."

"Understandable." He straightened and stepped back. "I'll get that soup. Food and rest are what you need."

He was right—that was all she needed. Then she'd be back to her old self.

She tried to shake off those earlier feelings as she settled more comfortably and watched him exit. Better to focus on the savory smell wafting in from the kitchen. If the aroma was any indication, he was as good a cook as he was a caretaker.

Rufus plastered his front paws onto the mattress. "Hello, boy. I guess I haven't been very good company the past—" She paused. How long *had* she slept? Ivy glanced toward the window and frowned at the lengthening shadows. It had obviously been more than an hour or so.

Then her brow furrowed as hazy images of him repeatedly checking in on her floated at the edge of her memory. Had that really happened? Or had she dreamed it?

When he returned a few minutes later carrying a steaming bowl balanced on a tray, she edged up straighter. "How long was I asleep?"

"About six hours."

"Oh, my goodness. You must think me an awful slugabed."

"Rest is the best medicine at times like this."

As he helped her settle the tray onto her lap, she inhaled appreciatively. "Smells good."

He gave a small smile. "Only because you're hungry. I don't usually cook for anyone but myself and I make no claims that it's more than passable."

"I'm sure you're being too hard on yourself." She picked up the spoon, then frowned when he pulled up a chair. "Aren't you going to eat something, too?"

"I ate earlier. I'll get more later." He settled back in the chair. "I thought I'd keep you company, if that's okay?"

What was he up to?

Then she took herself to task. She had to stop being so suspicious of menfolk—not everyone was a mean-spirited polecat like Lester Stokes. Mr. Parker was nice and seemed to expect nothing in return. He probably just wanted to make sure she didn't faint into her bowl while she ate.

She tasted a spoonful, then smiled. "As I suspected, this is a good sight better than merely passable."

He spread his hands as if to dispute her words but didn't say anything.

Feeling the need to fill the silence, she asked after her mule. "How's Jubal doing after that long walk here?"

"He's had some feed and water, and now he and Seeley are grazing." He met her gaze squarely. "As for the hoof, I think you were right about the stone bruise. I let him soak it in warm water to try to draw out the infection, but he's going to need a couple days' rest, I'm afraid."

Poor Jubal—she hoped she hadn't done him permanent harm. But this also meant more delays. Nana Dovie would be worried if she didn't hear something from her soon. But that wasn't Mr. Parker's fault. "It was real nice of you to be looking out for him. And me, too, of course."

"And how are you feeling now that you've had something to eat?"

The way he looked at her one would think he actually cared about *her,* not just the trouble she was causing. "Much better." She deposited her spoon in the now empty bowl. "That nap and this meal have fixed me right up." No need to burden him with her aching head and shaky feeling.

But Mr. Parker didn't look convinced. "You shouldn't attempt anything that requires effort today. You need to give yourself time to heal."

Be that as it may, Ivy certainly didn't intend to spend what was left of the day in bed.

"Mind if I ask how you came to be out here alone?" he asked.

She took a sip from her glass, trying to decide how much to tell him. She wasn't much on sharing her personal business with strangers, even kind-hearted ones. "I've got business to take care of over in Turnabout. And this shortcut seemed the fastest way to get there."

"You said you were from somewhere called Nettles Gap? How far away is that?"

"Don't know how many miles, exactly, but I set out at sunup the day before yesterday."

He stiffened. "Two days alone on the road."

It was nice of him to be concerned, but she was perfectly capable of taking care of herself. "I wasn't really alone," she said, trying to reassure him. "I had Rufus and Jubal with me. And I took precautions."

But his frown deepened. "By precautions I assume

you mean that getup you were wearing and that knife you pulled out of your pocket."

He made it sound as if her efforts had been ineffective at best.

"And a dog and mule are hardly adequate escorts for a young lady. Wasn't your family at all concerned about your safety?"

Ivy blinked. Hadn't anyone called her a lady in a long time.

But she quickly pushed that thought away. He could talk about her precautions all he wanted, but *no one* was going to lay blame at Nana Dovie's door.

"Nana Dovie cares about me something fierce— don't you be thinking she doesn't. But she wasn't in any condition to come with me." No, sir, she wasn't about to let anyone speak ill of Nana Dovie, not even someone who'd been as nice as this gent.

But he didn't seem to take offense. "You mentioned this Nana Dovie before. Who is she?"

"Her name's Dovie Jacobs, and she's sort of my mother."

His brow went up. "Sort of?"

How to explain? "When you get right down to it, Nana Dovie isn't exactly blood kin. But she's family just the same. She took me in and raised me when my folks passed on. I was just a babe at the time."

"Sounds like a special lady."

Ivy nodded, pleased he'd understood. "And now that she's getting on in years and needs someone to take care of her, I aim to do my best to return the favor."

"So what was so important that you had to leave her side and set out alone?"

Ivy stiffened. "You sure do ask a passel of nosey questions."

Mr. Parker grimaced. "My apologies for prying. I'm afraid I've been cursed with a curious mind. I suppose that's why I became a schoolteacher."

She leaned back, diverted by this bit of information. "You're a schoolteacher? I guess that means you have a lot of book learning." That didn't surprise her much—he seemed like the educated type.

His lips quirked up at that. "I do like a good book."

She narrowed her eyes. "Are you making fun of me?"

"Not at all. I wouldn't dare."

Not certain how to respond to that, she took another sip from her glass.

This time he broke the silence. "You didn't answer my question."

"What question?"

"Why are you traveling to Turnabout?"

He was like a hound on a scent—he just didn't give up.

"I learned a few days ago that I might have an inheritance waiting there. And I aim to find out, 'cause if I do, I plan to sell whatever it is so Nana Dovie and I can pay off some debts and make some purchases we sorely need."

"I see."

It was time for her to ask a few questions of her own. "Are you familiar with Turnabout?"

He nodded. "I've lived there two years now."

"You mean this cabin isn't your home?" A heartbeat later, she realized she should've figured that out when he said he was a schoolteacher. He'd need to live in a town where there were actual schools and students, not out in the woods.

"This cabin belongs to friends of mine," he explained. "They let me borrow it for a few days."

"Oh." Her mind made a totally irrelevant connection. "Then this Reggie whose clothes I'm wearing…"

"Is the owner of this place."

So, Reggie wasn't his wife, then.

Not that that was important.

"And speaking of that," he continued, "I still think you should take it easy today. But if you do decide you want to sit out on the porch, you'll find more of Reggie's clothing in that chest. Oh, and your saddlebags are on top of the trunk if you need any of your own things."

"Thank you. But how far away is Turnabout?"

"It's about a four-hour ride from here."

She glanced toward the window. How much daylight was left?

As if reading her mind, he gave her a stern look. "Don't even think about trying to travel today. Even if you were up to it—which I very much doubt—your mule is not. Besides, it'll be dark in less than three hours."

She blew a stray tendril of hair off her forehead in frustration. He was right, of course. But that didn't make it easier to accept.

"I want you to know," he said, looking decidedly uncomfortable, "that I am an honorable, God-fearing man. You're perfectly safe in my company and I plan to spend the night outside so you can sleep without worry about your reputation."

As if that would stop any true gossipmonger's tongue from wagging if word got out. "I appreciate you trying to do what's proper and all, but there's no need for that, considering the circumstances." It said a good deal about him that he was worried about propriety and her feelings, but if he only knew how unnecessary that really was…

Not that she planned to enlighten him.

"Nevertheless, I feel it's important that we attend to all the proper social conventions while we're out here."

She'd be hanged if she'd let him make her even more beholden to him. "If you're going to be that muleheaded about it, then I should be the one sleeping outside. After all, your friends loaned this place to you, not me. I'm the intruder here."

He stiffened as if she'd insulted him. "If you think I'll allow that, then you must have a very low opinion of me."

Have mercy, the man could certainly look intimidating when he got up on his high horse. Not that such tactics would work on her. "I just think it's silly to worry about such things at a time like this. If it makes you feel better, Rufus can sleep in here with me and be my chaperone. Why, I'll even bar the door."

He stood. "I think I'll get a bite to eat. Would you like more soup?"

Did he take her for a simpleton? "Mr. Parker, now you're the one who's sidestepping the question. Do I have your word that you'll sleep under this roof tonight?"

His lips compressed and he was silent for a long moment. Then he nodded.

Ivy leaned back, reassured.

She might not know him well, but she knew in her gut that he was absolutely a man of his word.

* * *

Mitch sat at the table, absently eating his soup. If temperament was any indication, Miss Feagan was definitely regaining her strength. She was quickly turning into one of the most independent-minded, strong-willed, intriguing women he'd ever met.

But there were pros *and* cons to that. While she might make interesting company, she would also need watching to make certain she didn't take on more than she could handle.

He'd been pleased to see color back in her cheeks. And her hands had almost been steady as she'd ladled up the soup. So physically it appeared she really was on the mend.

That just left the *other* issue.

He stood and stepped out onto the porch, frustrated by the situation. He wouldn't sleep in the house with her, of course. But that was just for his own conscience. If word got out that they'd been here alone overnight, she'd be just as ruined as if he'd spent the night in her room.

He had trouble believing she was as unconcerned by the situation as she would have him think. Perhaps she was just being pragmatic. Or perhaps she wanted to relieve him of any guilt he might be feeling.

Or perhaps it was just that she recognized as much as he did that, other than giving them clear consciences, his sleeping outside wouldn't do much good if word of their situation got out.

Whatever her reasons, however, he intended to adhere to the proprieties as much as possible. A clear conscience was something to strive for. The promise he'd made was to sleep under the roof, and he would keep his word—the roof covered the porch, as well.

Besides, it wasn't just *her* reputation at stake. As a schoolteacher, it was important that he keep his own conduct above reproach.

What a tangle.

There'd been a time when he would have prayed for direction, but that time had long passed. He and God had stopped communicating with each other some time ago. Ever since that tragic night over two years ago.

The night he'd killed his wife and unborn child.

Chapter Four

Thirty minutes after Mr. Parker left her room, Ivy had had enough of lying about in bed. She looked down at Rufus as she threw off the covers and swung her legs over the side of the mattress. "I think exercise and fresh air are just the things to make me feel better."

But first she had to find her clothes. She glanced around. Where were they? The garments had been muddy and damp. They'd also absorbed wet-dog smell from Rufus. Mr. Parker had probably decided to get the messy things out of the cabin and she couldn't say she blamed him.

Ignoring Mr. Parker's suggestion that she help herself to his friend's clothing, Ivy turned instead to her own bag. As she crossed the room, she was pleased to find she wasn't nearly as wobbly as she'd been earlier. It took her a bit longer to change than usual, but she did it and carefully placed the borrowed nightdress over the back of the chair.

She wished she had a mirror so she could see how she looked. Then she grimaced—maybe it was better that she didn't. She likely looked a fright with her hair all a mess and her fingers stained from the berries. She pulled the comb from her saddlebag and tried to remove the worst of the tangles without disturbing the bandage. Then she quickly plaited a loose braid and let it fall down her back. With the bandage around her head, there wasn't much else to be done with it. Besides, Mr. Parker had already seen it in much worse condition so it wasn't as if this would shock him further.

Taking a deep breath and giving Rufus a pat, Ivy stepped out of the bedchamber. Her rescuer wasn't anywhere in sight. She paused a moment to study her surroundings—she hadn't been in any shape to pay attention when she'd first arrived.

To her right was a large fireplace. It was clean and tidy with wood stacked nearby. Facing the fireplace was the sofa she'd rested on when she'd first arrived. Thankfully she saw no signs of blood or dirt. There was a cozy little kitchen and a dining table across the room. The curtains at the windows and the apron hanging on a peg by the door spoke of a woman's touch. Off to one side, a ladder led up to a small loft tucked in under the eaves.

On the opposite side of the common room was a curtained-off area. Another bedchamber, perhaps?

Rufus padded out the open front door and she heard him give a friendly woof. A masculine voice returned the greeting. Well, that solved the mystery of Mr. Parker's whereabouts.

When she stepped outside, she was greeted by the sight of her missing clothing draped over the porch rail. A closer look showed that the pieces weren't just airing out but were clean.

Had he actually done her laundry? She wasn't normally missish, but the thought of him doing such a personal thing for her sent the warmth climbing up her neck and into her cheeks.

"Miss Feagan. What are you doing out of bed?"

She started at the sound of his voice. The sight of her clothes and thoughts of what it meant had momentarily made her forget she wasn't alone.

Mr. Parker sat off to her right in a ladder-backed chair. He had a large pad of paper in his lap, a pencil in his hand and a frown on his face.

She quickly collected herself—his washing her clothes likely meant nothing more than that he liked everything around him to be all neat and tidy.

Besides, the question about what he was doing with that oversize pad of paper was much more interesting.

And a much safer focus for her thoughts.

As soon as Mr. Parker saw her glance at his paper, he closed the pad, set down his pencil and stood. "Are you sure you should be up so soon?"

Was it just worry for her well-being that put the edge in his tone, or was she intruding? Choosing to believe the former, Ivy brushed his concern aside with a wave of her hand. "I'm feeling much better, thank you. And Nana Dovie always says, sunshine and fresh air go a long way toward healing an ailing body."

Ignoring his frown, she changed the subject. "Thank you for taking care of my clothes—seems I just keep getting deeper into your debt."

His expression shifted as he rubbed the back of his neck. "I just tossed them in the lake when I went down to wash up earlier. It didn't take much effort."

She could tell he'd done more than soak her things— they'd had a good scrubbing. But she let it pass and instead sat in the rocker next to his chair. Then she pointed to his pad of paper. "Please don't let me stop you from finishing whatever it was you were working on."

He sat back down. "It's just some idle sketching—nothing that can't wait."

This man was full of surprises. Intrigued, she leaned forward. "Mind if I look?"

He hesitated, then shrugged. "Help yourself."

She took the tablet and flipped it open. Then her eyes widened. She was looking at a perfect likeness of a hummingbird hovering over a morning glory. It was done all in pencil, but he'd somehow managed to capture the movement of the bird and the early morning dewiness of the flower with simple lines and a bit of shading.

She turned the page and found yet another remarkable work. It was his horse, contentedly grazing near an old wooden fence. A dandelion was bent by a breeze that had teased some of the fluff from the stalk. Again, the level of detail he'd managed to capture with just a pencil was remarkable.

When she turned the page yet again, she found an unfinished drawing. It was the view from the porch. The railings and support post were in the foreground, and beyond that was an open area and then a stand of brush and trees. A quick glance verified that he'd faithfully captured the image of the tree line up ahead.

She turned and found him watching her closely. Was he worried about her opinion? "These drawings are *very* good."

Such God-given talent was surely a treasure to be nurtured and shared. He should be displaying them proudly, not trying to hide them away.

This Mr. Parker was definitely a puzzle—one she was coming to wish she had time to figure out.

Mitch had watched her closely as she studied his work. He rarely showed his sketches to anyone—it was only a hobby, after all, and much too personal to share casually.

Not that he cared much what others thought.

But her genuine smile of delight was oddly gratifying. "Thank you. It's just something I do to pass the time." He took the sketchbook and set it on the table, then changed the subject. "Are you hungry? There's more soup on the stove."

She shook her head, then went right back to the subject of his sketches. "Do you ever draw people?"

Was she hinting that she wanted him to sketch her? "Not often."

"So you do sometimes," she pressed. "I'd love to have you sketch Nana Dovie."

That surprised him. "You might do better to get a photograph. Reggie, the lady who owns this cabin, is a photographer and her work is quite good."

She wrinkled her nose consideringly. "I think I'd rather a sketch. Photographs seem so stiff." Then she sighed. "Not that it matters. Nana Dovie would never travel this far for something she'd think was nonsensical."

She looked around then, obviously done with the subject of his artwork. "Where are Jubal and your horse?"

"Around back."

"And where does that trail lead?" she asked, waving to her left.

"There's a small lake about three hundred yards

down that way. It's where the water I've been using comes from, and there's good fishing there, too."

Her eyes lit up. "Is there a spare fishing pole around here?"

"Several. They're in the lean-to out back."

"I'm pretty good with a pole and a hook," she said with a hopeful glance his way.

"Perhaps tomorrow you can try your luck."

Her sigh had a note of disappointment, but she grinned. "Luck has nothing to do with it."

He returned her smile. "I look forward to seeing if the reality matches the boast."

"Challenge accepted." Then she stood. "Please, continue with your drawing. I'm going to plop down in that chair over in the sunshine and just enjoy the fresh air for a bit."

Mitch opened his sketchbook as she settled into her chair. She ruffled the fur on her dog's neck. When the mutt ran off, she leaned back and watched him, laughing and talking to the animal as if he could understand her.

Mitch tried to lose himself in his drawing again, to transfer the essence of the view before him onto the page. But the sound of Ivy's laughter, the sight of her blissful enjoyment of her surroundings, was making it surprisingly difficult to do much of anything but look at her.

Ivy watched Rufus sniff the ground, obviously picking up the scent of some critter or other. It was nice out here—warm but with a breeze to stir her hair. She heard the rat-a-tat-tat of a woodpecker in the distance. The sun slipped out from behind a cloud, and she closed her eyes against the sudden glare. Rufus barked from what seemed like far away, and she wondered if he'd treed a squirrel. She heard buzzing and wondered idly if it was a bee or a deerfly. But it wasn't really worth the effort to open her eyes to find out.

A moment later, someone cleared his throat right above her, breaking the stillness of the afternoon. Her eyes flew open to focus on Mr. Parker, standing beside her, his sketchbook in hand. Had he finished his drawing already?

Then she noticed the shadows had lengthened and she was no longer in full sunshine. The heat rose in her cheeks as she saw his amused glance. Despite the fact that she'd thought herself well rested, she'd fallen asleep again.

"You must think me a real lazybones."

He smiled. "You have good reason to rest." He reached down to help her rise. "Why don't we head back inside? If you're not hungry or tired, I can pull out a checkerboard, if you feel up to a game."

She took his hand, accepting his assistance. "You'll soon learn I rarely back down from a challenge."

With a smile on his face, Mitch let her precede him back into the cabin. The woman was intriguing. She was certainly unpredictable. And seemingly unflappable.

And totally unlike any woman he'd met before.

Shaking off that thought—an exercise he seemed to be doing a lot of lately—he dug out the checkerboard and set it on the table.

As she sat across from him, he raised an eyebrow in challenge. "I assume you know how to play."

She grinned. "It's been a while, but I think I remember how it goes."

Miss Feagan proved to be an aggressive player, approaching the game with more verve than strategy. He won the first two games, though they were by no means runaway victories. Those defeats didn't seem to dampen her enthusiasm, however. She merely grinned and vowed to get him next time.

He stood. "Before you try again, why don't we eat?"

She grinned. "I came close to beating you just now. Are you by any chance wanting to fortify yourself before facing me again?"

He couldn't remember the last time anyone had taken that teasing tone with him. But he found he rather liked it. "I was thinking I needed to give you an opportunity to sharpen *your* wits so you'd have a fighting chance."

"Ha!" She put her hands on her hips and glowered melodramatically. "That sounds like a challenge. I demand we play a third game so I can defend my honor as a checker player."

"After we eat." He moved toward the stove. "There ought to be just enough soup left for each of us to have a nice bowlful." She stood, but he waved her back down. "Keep your seat. This won't take but a minute."

She ignored him. Naturally. "Don't be silly." She crossed to the counter. "The least I can do is set the table. I assume the dishes are kept in here." She opened the cupboard, then reached inside.

A moment later Mitch saw her sway unsteadily, and he quickly crossed the space between them. "Whoa, there." He took her elbow and put an arm around her shoulders. "Are you okay?"

She gave him a shaky smile. "Just got dizzy for a moment."

"That does it." He led her firmly back to the table.

"I want you to sit here and not get up again until it's time to turn in."

"Don't be silly. It was just—"

"No arguments." He pointed to the chair. "Sit."

She stared at him mutinously for another heartbeat. Then she relaxed and gave him a pert grin. "I suppose," she said, sitting with exaggerated care, "that if you insist on waiting on me, I should just let you."

His lips quirked at that, and he gave a ceremonious bow. "At your service, m'lady."

Ivy propped her elbows on the table and watched as Mr. Parker went back to the stove. He certainly was a puzzle of a man. Big as a grizzly but graceful a wolf. All prickly and proper when it came to matters of propriety but able to take her teasing with good humor and even give it back to her at times. Able to carry heavy loads—like a fully grown woman—and with those same hands he could draw the most amazing pictures. And for all his stern exterior, she was beginning to believe he was soft as a mossy creek bank on the inside.

Maybe not such a puzzle after all—he was just a good man.

Rufus padded over and she reached down to pat his head. "Hello, boy. Getting restless, are you?" She glanced up at her host. "Has he eaten anything today?"

Mr. Parker turned and frowned down at Rufus. "I gave him a bit of pemmican and some broth earlier."

She should have known he'd take care of her dog. He ladled the soup into two bowls. "I suppose the mutt can have anything left in the pot when we've eaten our fill tonight."

He carried one of the bowls to the table and set it in

front of her with a stern look. "I expect you to eat all of it. You need to keep your strength up."

Without waiting for her response, he turned to fetch his own bowl.

Normally she'd get her back up at being ordered around, but she found herself smiling instead. He was being outlandishly high-handed, of course. But she also knew she'd scared him with her momentary light-headedness and this was likely how he dealt with it.

A moment later, he rejoined her at the table. As he settled into his seat, she met his gaze expectantly. "Would you like to say grace?"

Mr. Parker stilled and something she couldn't read flitted across his expression. Was he not a praying man?

But then he bowed his head. "Dear Lord, we thank You for providing this food we are about to partake of, and for the blessings You have bestowed on us this day." He paused a heartbeat, then added, "We also ask that You restore good health to Miss Feagan."

"And to Jubal, as well," Ivy interjected quickly. "Amen."

Mr. Parker echoed her amen, then picked up his spoon. Before taking a bite, he glanced her way. "Earlier you mentioned you *might* have an inheritance waiting for you in Turnabout. If you don't mind my asking, what did you mean by *might?*"

"Reverend Tomlin got a letter a few days ago that said if Robert Feagan's daughter was still alive then there was an inheritance waiting for her in Turnabout. And I'm Robert Feagan's daughter so I just figured I'd head on over to check it out."

"Just like that?"

She shrugged. "I've never been one to let others

make decisions for me." She grinned. "And I'm also not very patient. Nana Dovie says it's one of my biggest faults."

"And the letter didn't give you any other details?"

"No, and I'm more than a tad curious." Then she realized he might be able to fill in some of the blanks for her. "Do you know a man named Drum Mosley?"

"Only well enough to exchange greetings. He owns a large ranch outside of town. Is he a relative?"

Something in his tone made her think he knew more than he was saying. "No. But it seems he knew my father. According to the letter, he's been holding something in trust on my father's behalf and if I can prove I'm my father's child, he'll turn it over to me, whatever *it* is."

"My condolences on the loss of your father."

She shrugged. "Thanks. But he passed on when I was just a babe, so I didn't know him."

"Drum's expecting you, then?"

"Don't know about that."

"You didn't send a response to his letter?"

"I figured there wasn't much use since I'd get there at about the same time as a letter." She grimaced. "Or at least I would have if I hadn't run into these delays." She'd had enough of talking about herself. She'd much rather learn more about him. "Tell me something about yourself."

"Anything specific you'd like to know?"

"Do you have any family?"

"I have two sisters."

"Older or younger than you?"

"Both are younger."

She imagined he'd make a fine older brother, al-

ways there to look out for his little sisters. "I've always
wished I was part of a larger family," she said wistfully.
"Don't get me wrong, I couldn't ask for a better person
than Nana Dovie to raise me, but it always seemed kind
of lonesome out in the country with no other young'uns
to play with."

She dipped her spoon back in her bowl. "So, how
often do you get to see them?"

"Not often. They're both happily married. Erica, the
elder of the two, married a doctor and they moved to
San Francisco. They now have four children—three
girls and a boy. Katie, my baby sister, married an Ital-
ian concert pianist, of all things, and spends much of
her time in Europe. They have three little boys."

"Oh, my goodness, your family is scattered all over
creation. No wonder you don't see them often."

"We keep in touch with letters."

"What about your parents?"

"They've both passed on."

So he was an orphan, too. "I'm sorry." She hesitated
a moment, then plunged in with a more personal question. "And you never married?"

From the way his expression immediately closed off,
she knew she'd overstepped. "That was rude—forget I
asked. Sometimes I speak before I think."

"I married once. She, also, has passed away."

Now she *really* felt bad. Obviously it still stirred up
painful memories. "I'm sorry," she said again, feeling
the words were entirely inadequate.

"I appreciate your sympathy." He stood. "Looks like
you finished your soup. Would you like another serving?"

He obviously wanted to put some distance between

them, and she didn't blame him. "No, thank you—I'm full." She stood, as well. "I should probably check on Jubal before it gets dark.".

But he shook his head. "I'll take care of that. Why don't you feed Rufus?"

"I appreciate your concern, but I'm perfectly capable of taking care of my own animal."

"Then take care of your dog."

She bit her tongue, trying to remember that, despite his bossiness, he meant well. She gave a short nod.

For tonight, she'd hold her peace. But come tomorrow it would be a different story.

Mitch added a couple of buckets of water to the trough.

He'd felt like a fraud earlier when he'd said grace, especially when he'd looked up afterward to see the soft approval in Ivy Feagan's eyes.

Though he went to church services regularly and attended meals in friends' homes, where prayers were offered, it had been a long time since he'd truly prayed himself, much less done so publicly. But he did believe in the Almighty and he'd felt strangely reluctant to refuse her request.

The words had come naturally to him, as if riding a horse again after a long convalescence.

Had God, knowing his heart, been offended by his prayer?

Which, for some reason, brought his thoughts around to that moment when Ivy had asked him if he was married.

It had taken all of his control not to react as the painful memories returned. Sweet-tempered, turn-the-other-cheek Gretchen, the woman he'd vowed to cherish and protect, hadn't deserved the violent, senseless death that had been her lot. And he may not have actually pulled the trigger, but her death was as much his fault as if he had.

He could never forgive himself for that.

Mitch pushed away those fruitless thoughts and focused on Jubal. He firmly nudged the animal, forcing him to take a few reluctant steps, and studied his gait. It was quickly apparent that the mule would indeed need more time before he could make the trip to Turnabout.

"Sorry you had to make that long walk this morning, but it couldn't be helped." He gave the animal a handful of oats and patted his side. "But I'll make you as comfortable as I can while you recover."

He dug out another scoop of grain and turned to Seeley. "Here you go." He stroked the animal's nose. "You didn't think I'd forgotten about you, did you?"

As he tended to the animals, his thoughts drifted back to Miss Feagan's mention of that possible inheritance. The conversation had raised as many questions as it had answered. If her father had been dead for all these years, then why was she just now hearing about her inheritance?

And it was even stranger that Drum Mosley was involved. The man had a reputation as a penny-pincher. Mitch couldn't picture him voluntarily giving away any of his holdings. Then again, he vaguely remembered hearing that Drum had taken to his sickbed recently. Perhaps the rancher was getting his affairs in order.

Whatever the case, it was none of his business. As soon as he could get her to Turnabout, his involvement in her affairs would be over.

He picked up the water bucket and headed back to the cabin, ignoring the little voice inside him that whispered his involvement in Miss Feagan's affairs was actually just beginning.

When Mitch returned to the cabin, the dishes had been cleaned and put away, and the checkerboard set up for another game.

"I see you've been busy," he said with what he considered commendable restraint. He should have known she wouldn't take it easy.

She waved toward the game board. "Didn't want anything standing in the way of my getting my revenge."

"Are you sure you wouldn't rather turn in? I wouldn't want you to suffer yet a third defeat."

"That does it. Sit yourself down and prepare to eat those words."

And to his surprise, she actually won.

Mitch found himself smiling as she crowed about her victory. Then he started collecting the checkers. "I believe I'd better quit while I'm ahead. And dusk settled in while we weren't looking, so it's time to call it a night. It's been a long day and we both could use some rest."

She grimaced. "All I've done today is rest."

But since she followed that statement with a broad yawn, he had no compunction in insisting. "Is there anything you need before you retire?" he asked as he stood.

Miss Feagan shook her head. "I'll be fine, thank you. Good night." She crossed the room then paused and eyed him suspiciously. "You *do* remember you promised not to sleep outside, don't you?"

He'd hoped she wouldn't bring that up again. But maybe it was best that she knew his plans so she could speak honestly if questions came up later. "What I *promised* was to sleep under this roof. I'm going to drag the mattress from the other bed out to the porch. It's a nice night and I'll be quite comfortable." He raised a hand to stop the protest already forming on her lips. "My mind is made up."

She crossed her arms, glaring at him, frustration etched on her face. "It just doesn't seem right."

"Still, the decision is mine so you'll just have to accept it."

She glared a moment longer, then lifted her hands in surrender. "Have it your way."

As she turned to her room, he called out, "Take Rufus with you."

Just before she closed her door, Mitch thought he heard her mutter something that contained the phrase "more stubborn than Jubal."

He grinned as he wrestled the unwieldy mattress out the front door. She certainly wasn't bashful about speaking her mind. But at least she was smart enough to know when arguments were useless.

His smile faded as he stretched out on the mattress and stared out at the stars. If he was being entirely honest with himself, despite his desire for solitude, he hadn't really minded her presence here today. Which was troubling.

Because he had to hold himself apart. He couldn't risk hurting someone else the way he'd hurt Gretchen.

Chapter Five

As Ivy settled into bed, she marveled at how the day had turned out to be so different from what she'd imagined when she woke this morning. She'd been worried about Jubal's hoof and whether or not she'd be able to stretch her provisions if they were delayed much longer. And now, here she was, a roof over her head and a warm, dry bed to sleep in, plenty of provisions to carry her through and a proper place to let Jubal rest and heal.

And befriending Mr. Parker was an unexpected blessing for sure. Even though he was something of a stiff-necked gent at times, his concern for both her physical well-being and her reputation was touching. She no longer found his size intimidating—rather it was comforting to know that so much strength was tempered by restraint and kindness.

And as much as she considered herself independent, knowing there would be someone in Turnabout she could turn to if the need arose was also very comforting.

Lord, despite these unexpected delays, You've sure been kind to me. Of all the folks who could have hap-

pened across me out here, You sent the most honorable
man I've ever met. Thank You for that grace.
Amen.

By the time Ivy rose the next morning she could hear
Mr. Parker moving around in the kitchen. The smell of
coffee brewing had her rushing through her morning
ablutions to join him.

When she opened the door, he looked up with a
smile. "You're just in time for breakfast."

"Smells mighty good."

He shrugged. "It's nothing fancy—just hardtack biscuits and strawberry preserves. But I softened the biscuits in the skillet with a little bacon grease."

"Apologies not necessary—it sounds like just the
thing."

He gave her a searching look. "How are you feeling today?"

"Much more myself, thanks." She refused to let him
mollycoddle her today. "The smell of coffee was sure
nice to wake up to."

"It's ready if you want to help yourself. The cups are
on that shelf next to the window."

She crossed the room and reached for the cups.
"Want me to pour you some, too?"

He nodded as he set the dish of warm biscuits on the
table. "Thank you."

Ivy carefully carried the nearly full cups to the
table and took her seat. He seemed cheerful and rested
today—maybe sleeping on the porch hadn't bothered
him as much as she'd feared. "I hope the mosquitoes
didn't pester you too much last night."

"I managed to sleep through it."

His dry tone made her wonder if he was downplaying the amount of aggravation he'd experienced.

After they said the blessing, she slathered some jelly on her biscuit. "I should be up to that four-hour ride to Turnabout today."

He gave no outward reaction, but she could tell he had reservations. Not surprising—did the man ever do anything spontaneously? But she would've thought he'd be glad to get rid of her by now.

Mr. Parker took a sip of coffee before responding. "I checked on Jubal when I got the wood for the stove this morning. He needs at least one more day's rest before he undertakes that long trip."

She tried to rein in her disappointment. "Of course I don't want to push him if he's not ready. I'll take a look at him after breakfast and decide."

His left brow rose. "Does this matter in Turnabout require your immediate attention?"

She waved dismissively. "That's not it. This inheritance thing has waited more than twenty years so another day or two won't make much difference." She rubbed her cheek. "But Nana Dovie's going to worry if she doesn't hear from me soon. I promised to send her a telegram when I got to Turnabout so she'd know I'd arrived safely."

He nodded. "I see." Then he studied her a moment longer. "This Nana Dovie means a great deal to you. I can hear it in your voice when you speak of her."

Ivy nodded. "She's the only family I have," she said simply.

"And how will she react to not having heard from you yet?"

"Nana Dovie's not one to panic easily," she said. "We discussed this trip before I left, and much as I'd hoped to make the trip in two days, we both knew it might take longer. But if she doesn't hear from me by tomorrow, she'll fear the worst." Ivy hated the idea of putting the only mother she'd ever known through such needless worry.

"Don't worry—we'll send word as soon as we're able."

Ivy found it interesting that he'd said "we" and not "you."

"There's something else. Nana Dovie doesn't leave the farm, ever, so she'll have to wait until the reverend pays a visit to send an inquiry."

She saw the flicker of speculation in his eyes at her statement, but he didn't press. She was coming to appreciate his tact.

He stood and carried his dishes to the counter. "Then it's best we plan to leave first thing in the morning."

It wasn't ideal, but perhaps Nana Dovie wouldn't start imagining the worst before then. She followed him to the counter with her own dishes. "So you think Jubal will be ready for the trip by then?"

"We'll get to town tomorrow, one way or the other."

"What do you mean by that?"

"Why don't we wait and see what tomorrow brings?"

Was he being deliberately evasive?

Before she could ask for an explanation, he changed the subject. "Now, Miss Feagan, do you prefer to wash or dry?"

She grabbed a dishrag. "Wash." She dunked a plate in the basin, which already contained fresh water. "And don't you think, all things considered, there's no need for you to continue to refer to me as Miss Feagan? The name's Ivy."

Predictably, he raised a brow. "*All things considered,* I think it best we stick to the formalities."

She refused to back down. "Hogwash. You've bandaged me, bodily lifted me onto your horse, removed my shoes and stockings, practically tucked me in—you even did my laundry, for goodness' sake. Standing on ceremony at this point is just silly."

Mitch stiffened and she hid a grin. He probably didn't get called silly very often.

He accepted the clean plate and rubbed it with extra vigor. "*Miss Feagan,* we'll have enough speculation to deal with when we ride into town together from this all-but-forsaken backwoods. Any overfamiliarity we show with each other will just intensify that scrutiny."

She sighed melodramatically. "I've *never* met such a fusspot before." She'd deliberately used that word, knowing it would get his back up. And she was right.

She quickly spoke up again before he could protest further. "If you feel that strongly, why don't we compromise? While we're alone, we use first names. When we get to town, we get all formal and particular again. After all, I don't expect to be in Turnabout more than a couple of days."

He frowned but finally nodded stiffly. "Very well."

She rewarded him with a broad smile as she handed him another plate. "Good to see you can unbend on occasion."

That earned her a startled look and then the hint of a sheepish grin.

Five minutes later, Ivy patted Jubal's side sympathetically as Mitch set the animal's hoof down and brushed his hands against his pants. Unfortunately, she agreed with his assessment—Jubal was in no shape to make that trip today. She only hoped one more day would improve his condition enough to let them get under-way again.

As they strolled back to the front of the cabin, she looked at the trail thoughtfully. "You did say there was a lake out that way, didn't you?"

He nodded. "Thinking about going fishing?"

She hesitated a moment. He was so straightlaced—would he think her indelicate if she told him what was on her mind?

Then again, he'd likely already figured out she wasn't a prim and proper miss. And the urge to get clean *was* almost overwhelming.

She tilted her chin up. "Actually, if you don't mind, I'd appreciate a chance to take a bath."

He didn't so much as blink. "Of course. Gather what you need and I'll show you the way."

Relieved that he hadn't argued with her, she nodded and all but sprinted up the porch steps.

In addition to a change of clothes, she grabbed the borrowed nightdress and the sheets from the bed. Might as well do laundry while she was bathing.

When she stepped outside, she discovered Mitch had towels and a bar of soap. He also had his sketchpad.

That last gave her pause. "Just what is it you aim to do with that?"

"While you're occupied at the lake, I thought I'd search out a spot to do some sketching."

Of course. He was probably tired of playing nurse-maid to her and was ready for some privacy of his own.

He insisted she hold his arm for steadying support as they walked down the trail. That and the slow pace he set had her rolling her eyes. Even Rufus didn't stay beside them for long—within a few minutes he'd scam-pered ahead to explore on his own.

Ivy wasn't used to being treated as if she were fragile and she'd never cottoned much to being mollycoddled. But she had to admit, at least to herself, that it wasn't altogether unpleasant to have someone so concerned for her well-being.

In fact, it made her feel special.

When the trail finally opened to reveal the lake, her eyes widened, trying to take everything in at once. Everywhere she looked there was something to delight the eye. The sun glinted across the water like crystals from a chandelier. Colorful dragonflies darted here and there A pair of turtles sunned on a half-submerged log as a hawk skimmed the air high overhead.

She turned and touched his arm. "It's perfect. And the water looks so inviting—I can't wait to wade in."

He glanced at her hand on his sleeve and she quickly removed it, embarrassed by her impulsive gesture.

But his expression didn't change. "Then I'll leave you to it. And don't worry. It's not deep on this end, and it's entirely private." He took a step back. "I'll be up the trail just a little ways, close enough to hear if you call. Take whatever time you need."

Ivy watched him until he rounded a turn. Then she began unbraiding her hair. If she had to be stuck somewhere while Jubal healed, this was not a bad place to be.

And the company was quite nice, as well.

In fact, if she weren't in such a hurry to get back and check on Nana Dovie, she wouldn't mind the delay at all.

Mitch found a comfortable spot and settled on the ground with his back against a tree. He heard her break out in song and smiled at her slightly off-key but enthusiastic rendition of "Shall We Gather at the River?" as he opened his sketchbook.

Even injured, she was the most attack-life-head-on woman he'd ever met. Now that she was feeling better, she was definitely a force to be reckoned with. It was exhausting just being around her.

And strangely exhilarating, as well.

Did she really think him a fusspot? He wasn't exactly certain what that was, but it definitely didn't sound flattering. He had to admit, if only to himself, that it had been her name-calling that had made him give in on the subject of using first names. Was he so easily manipulated?

But the smile she'd given him when he capitulated had seemed strangely compelling. It had been quite some time since anyone had looked at him with such unabashed approval.

Shaking off the thought, Mitch took up his pencil and waited for inspiration. Normally he had no trouble finding a subject, but for some reason today was different. He finally settled on the image of the turtles sunning down by the lake.

Forty-five minutes later, Mitch looked up to see Ivy approaching. Her still-damp hair was loosely braided and she carried a load of wet laundry. The smile on her face reflected satisfaction and her eyes sparkled.

Her pleasure was infectious.

Closing his sketchbook, he stood and moved to meet her.

"Sorry I took so long," she said, "but the water felt absolutely wonderful and I didn't want to get out." She nodded toward his sketchbook. "Did you get any drawing done?"

"I did." He set his pad and pencil down. "Here, let's swap. I'll take those wet things from you and you take my sketch pad."

To his surprise, she didn't argue, but merely said thank you as she surrendered her load of soggy laundry.

Then he discovered why. As soon as she retrieved his pad, she opened it and studied the image inside. "It's beautiful. You have such a wonderful God-given talent."

Ivy certainly had a way about her.

"I see why you like coming here," she said, interrupting his thoughts. "It's such a marvelous place."

"It's only my second visit, but I'm enjoying this visit more than the first." He was definitely enjoying the company more than he had that first time.

She gave him a questioning look. Then her gaze sharpened. "Aren't those blackberries?"

Mitch followed the line of her gaze. "What do you know, a few end-of-season stragglers."

She was already moving toward the brambly vines, and before he could so much as blink, she had popped one in her mouth. She closed her eyes and tilted her chin up. "Mmm."

He watched, captivated by her expression of pure bliss. He couldn't have moved if his boots were on fire.

She opened her eyes again.

"You should try some of these. They're really good." Then she looked contrite. "Oh, your hands are full. Allow me."

She plucked a couple of berries and held them up to him. Without a word, he opened his mouth. Their eyes locked and she froze with her hand inches from his lips. Her eyes widened and her breath hitched. They were so close, he could count the freckles on her nose if he tried. He knew he should step back, but for the life of him he couldn't do it. But closer, oh, yes, he could move closer with very little effort.

Then Rufus returned and Ivy took a step back.

Mitch silently berated himself. The temptation to kiss her had caught him unawares, surprising him with its swift intensity. But that was no excuse. He should have had tighter control of himself. What would have happened if Rufus hadn't interrupted them?

He'd assured her he was an honorable man, that she had nothing to fear from him. Did she still believe it?

Did *he?*

His earlier thoughts about enjoying her company had come back to haunt him. For the first time since Gretchen's death he'd let his guard down enough to take pleasure in a woman's company. And look what had happened.

What was it about Ivy that she could get under his skin so easily?

Then he focused on her again.

Her cheeks were a becoming shade of pink, her expression reflected confusion. He felt a cad for having done that to her.

She turned to greet her dog, giving them both an opportunity to gather their composure.

He knew offering an apology would only make matters worse. His best course of action was to get things back on an easy, comfortable footing.

He cleared his throat. "What do you say we try out those cane poles? I've a hankering for some fried fish for lunch."

"That sounds like fun." She stood. "I seem to recall I'm supposed to show you how it's done."

He was relieved to see she'd already recovered some of her spirit. "Is that a challenge?"

"Yes, sir, I do believe it is."

Ivy arranged the wet laundry on the porch railings. As soon as they'd made it back to the cabin, Mitch had disappeared around back to fetch the poles.

She wasn't sure what had happened back there, but she *was* fairly certain it had been her fault. And she'd hate to think she'd done anything to make him think less of her. What on earth had she been thinking, offering to *feed* him those berries?

Mitch reappeared carrying a pair of cane poles and leading his horse.

She nodded toward Seeley. "Are you going somewhere?"

"Since we're headed to the lake, I thought I'd refill the water barrel."

She frowned. "You use your horse for that?"

"Yep."

Puzzled, she watched as he maneuvered Seeley so the animal was backed up to the barrel. She moved closer and discovered the barrel sat on a low wooden platform outfitted with wheels. "How clever."

"Reggie's husband built it. It has a harness so you can hitch a horse for easy transport."

She nodded appreciatively. "That would definitely save lots of time and effort hauling buckets of water."

"That's the idea." Mitch started fitting his horse with the special harness. "I figure, once I fill it, Seeley can graze until we're done fishing."

He had the horse hitched in short order and then they retraced their steps to the lake.

"If I help you fill the barrel," she offered, "it'll get done in half the time."

"No need—I've got the job in hand and it won't take long."

She knew he was mollycoddling her again, but before she could protest he picked up the small spade he'd brought along.

"I'll dig some worms for you so you can start fishing while I fill the barrel."

"No need," she said, mimicking him, "I've got *that* job well in hand."

That nudged his brow up a notch. "You plan to collect your own worms?"

"Of course." It wasn't as if she'd had anyone around to do it for her back home.

"And bait your own hooks?"

He seemed even more surprised at that. She supposed it wasn't the most ladylike of tasks. But she refused to apologize for it. "It's like threading a needle."

That teased a grin from him. "I suppose that's one way of looking at it."

She watched surreptitiously as he scooped water with the pail and dumped it into the barrel. His very broad, solid back was to her. She didn't figure there was much as could stand against a man with a back like that. Especially one with as good a heart as Mitch seemed to have.

That combination of strength and heart was mighty attractive in a man. A woman would be lucky to have a man like Mitch looking out for her.

For a heartbeat she recalled that moment on the trail, how the light in his eyes had deepened as he'd stared at her and everything else had seemed to fall away. Then she gave her head a shake and quickly turned to bait her hook.

As she dropped her line in the water, she noticed a slight tremble in her hands.

As they cleaned their catch at the water's edge, Ivy argued that her five fish to his three clearly indicated she was the better fisherman. He insisted it was more about the quality of the catch and his three easily out-weighed her five.

Ivy enjoyed their spirited discussion—it was the kind comfortable friends would have. And she hadn't had a friend like that in a long time, thanks to the outcast status Lester Stokes had foisted on her.

When they arrived back at the cabin, Ivy left Mitch to tend to Seeley while she went inside with the fish. Poking around in the kitchen, she found cornmeal, salt and a small crock with bacon grease. She also found a jar of pickled tomatoes—just the thing to go with pan-fried fish.

By the time she had all the fixings for their meal gathered up, Mitch had returned. "Thanks again for taking care of the animals," she said.

He merely nodded. For a schoolteacher he certainly wasn't talkative. Was he this way in his classroom, too?

Then he waved toward the stove. "I can do the cooking," he said. "You've had an active morning for someone still recuperating." His serious expression lightened as he gave a lopsided smile. "I'm not much of a cook, but I *do* know how to fry fish."

She shook her head. "It's *your* turn to sample *my* cooking."

He didn't argue further, but she felt him watching while she worked. As she added cornmeal and seasoning to the fish, she asked, "You said you're a schoolteacher—is drawing one of the things you teach your students?"

"No."

It was like squeezing tears from a rock to get him to elaborate on anything. "Why? I reckon there's some who'd enjoy those lessons more than reading and 'rithmetic."

"But reading and arithmetic, along with geography, history and literature, are the more important things for them to learn."

"You know all those subjects?" she asked.

"I know *something* about all of them. What I don't know I find in the books I teach from."

She glanced over her shoulder. "So you draw, fish, rescue injured travelers and have a lot of book learning. That's quite a list of talents."

He gave that crooked smile again. "You make it sound more impressive than it is. I have faults enough to offset those talents, believe me."

She turned the fish in the skillet. Was he just being modest or did he think so little of himself? "Have you always lived in Turnabout?"

"No, I moved there about two years ago."

"Where did you live before that?"

"Pennsylvania, near Philadelphia." His tone implied the topic was off-limits.

Which, naturally, piqued her curiosity. She decided to see if coming at it sideways would make him more forthcoming.

"Philadelphia—that's over on the East Coast, isn't it? Seems like that's a far piece from here."

Some of the tension she'd heard in his voice eased. "About fourteen hundred miles."

She looked at him over her shoulder. "Oh, my stars, you traveled all that way? Whatever for?" She couldn't even imagine such a distance, or why someone would cross it to come here.

But his expression had closed off again. "I was ready for a change, and moving all the way to Texas seemed like a good start."

It appeared she'd gotten too close to whatever it was

he didn't want to talk about. Time to drop the subject—
she owed him that courtesy at least. Did it have something to do with his deceased wife? Had grief put that
bleak shadow in his expression? Or was it something
more? She was human enough to be curious.

Very curious.

Mitch didn't want to think about his life back in
Philadelphia, much less discuss it. He'd rather forget
that period of his life.

As if he ever could.

"How are those fish coming along?" he asked.

"Just about done."

He crossed the room to get the dishes and set a couple of plates in easy reach for her. Then he filled a pair
of glasses from the jug of water he'd brought inside.
In short order they were seated and ready to dig into
their meal. "This is quite good," he said after taking
his first bite.

Her cheeks pinkened in pleasure. "Glad you like it.
Nana Dovie used to do most of the cooking at our place.
Lately, though, she's been insisting I do more of it."

He saw the slight furrow of her brow. "And that worries you?"

"It's as if she's trying to prepare me for life without her."

"Perhaps she's merely preparing you for when you
marry and have a kitchen of your own to manage."

Her expression closed off. What nerve had he struck?
Didn't she dream of marriage the way other females
did?

She made a noncommittal sound and focused on eating. Then she pointed her fork at him. "Have you always liked to draw?"

"I suppose."

"Did you take lessons?"

"No, just trial and error."

"Were you a schoolteacher back in Philadelphia?"

She certainly wasn't shy with her questions. "For a time. Then I bought a farm and worked that for a while." Which brought him back to memories he didn't want to relive.

He speared another bite of fish and changed the subject. "When you're not traveling long distances to claim an unspecified inheritance, what do you enjoy doing?"

"Working in the garden," she said without hesitation. "And I'm good at it, if I do say so myself. Nana Dovie says I have the greenest thumb she ever did see."

Mitch let her continue to talk about gardening for the rest of the meal, only occasionally commenting or asking a question when she paused. Later he insisted she nap while he stepped out onto the porch with his sketch pad. But he didn't pick up his pencil. Instead he stared at the tree line, focusing on nothing in particular.

Thankfully that near-kiss on the trail didn't seem to have affected her trust in him. Which was a good thing, of course.

So why was he staring off into space, wishing things could be different?

Chapter Six

"What's the verdict? Can Jubal travel today?"

Ivy wasn't certain which answer she wanted Mitch to give. Yesterday had been just downright enjoyable. After her nap, Mitch had taken her to a beautiful meadow and she'd brought armloads of wildflowers back to the cabin, filling jars and pitchers with them and setting them all around. She could tell Mitch was amused by it all, but not in an unkind way.

She'd give a lot to have just one more day in this idyllic spot. But she had obligations that she couldn't fulfill here.

"Ideally, he could use another day of rest," Mitch answered, "but I know you're worried about Nana Dovie. So I think, if we take it slow and easy, he can probably make it to Turnabout without experiencing much of a setback—as long as you're not riding him."

Ivy was puzzled. "Are you saying I should walk?"

"There is another option." His tone was carefully neutral, his gaze assessing. "We can ride double on Seeley."

Ivy blinked, not certain she'd heard right. Was the

always-concerned-with-propriety Mitch Parker actually suggesting they ride double?

"We'll have to go slow and take frequent breaks to make certain we don't overtax either animal," he continued. "But we should still make it to town well before dark if we leave in the next few hours."

Apparently he *was* serious. She felt a sudden shyness at the thought of that long ride together.

He must have sensed her hesitation. "It's your choice. We can wait until tomorrow if you prefer."

This was no time for missishness. Ivy shook her head. "Not at all. But do you think Seeley can carry us both that far? I don't want to pamper Jubal at your horse's expense."

"Seeley will be fine, especially at the pace we'll be setting."

"Then that's what we should do. I'll sure feel better once I've sent that telegram to Nana Dovie." And surely he wouldn't have suggested this if there were anything really improper about it.

He nodded, his expression still unreadable.

They set to work and made preparations to leave. And all the while, she kept telling herself not to be such a nervous twit about the upcoming trip.

When they finally closed the door on the cabin, Ivy had the strangest feeling she was leaving a special haven, a place where nothing more troublesome than hungry mosquitoes had been able to touch them.

But now it was time to head back into the real world and face whatever challenges awaited her. If only she had a little more time alone with her white knight—

She shook that thought off before she could complete it—she should focus on practical considerations, not daydreams and foolishness.

Mitch led the animals to the front of the cabin, and Ivy approached Jubal and petted his nose. "Sorry to press you back into service so soon, but we'll go as easy as we can."

When she stepped aside, Mitch attached Jubal's lead to Seeley's saddle. Then he faced her. "I think this will work best if I ride in front."

She nodded, that shy feeling returning. Hopefully Mitch didn't seem to notice anything unusual in her demeanor. He turned and mounted in one quick, fluid motion; then he nudged Seeley, prompting the horse to move next to the porch steps. Ivy took his hand and was in the saddle almost before she could give it much thought. She'd changed into the britches again, deciding that would be the easiest way to do this. She'd change back into more ladylike clothing before they reached town.

"Wrap your arms around my waist," Mitch said. "I assure you, it won't restrain or hurt me."

Ivy hesitated. That meant she'd be all but embracing him for whatever time it took to get to Turnabout. Despite the fact that Lester had succeeded in convincing the folks back in Nettles Gap that she was a fallen woman, it was a familiarity she hadn't ever experienced before.

But this was a purely practical accommodation, driven by necessity. Besides, if Mr. Fusspot saw no problem with the arrangement, it had to be perfectly respectable.

She took a deep breath and did as he'd instructed.

Her arms didn't come close to reaching all the way

around his broad chest. Not that she tried. Instead, she held herself stiffly upright, trying to leave a bit of space between them.

"Relax," he said gently. "I won't let you fall. And it's going to be a long ride."

She was relieved that he thought she was only worried about falling, though his words and his tone did ease some of her tension. She shifted, tightening her hold and allowing herself to lean against his broad back.

"That's better." He gathered the reins. "Ready?"

"Ready." She supposed *better* was one way to describe it. Very safe and altogether too cozy was another.

With a click of his tongue and a slight movement of his knees, her white knight set his steed in motion.

Ivy was obviously on edge. Was she uncomfortable with this enforced closeness? For all her apparent independence, Mitch sensed she was still naive and innocent in many ways. Which was as it should be.

The best way to put her at ease was to get her mind focused elsewhere. And it wouldn't be a bad thing to find something for him to focus on besides the feel of her pressed against his back, either.

"Tell me about your Nana Dovie. What's she like— as a person, I mean?"

"Oh, my, that's a tall order. Let's see, if you were just to look at her while she's resting, you wouldn't think there was much to her. She's a little woman, not quite five feet tall and skinny as a possum's tail. But, like a banty rooster, she can be very forceful when she needs to be, and she can turn a grown man into a stammering schoolboy with just a look."

He felt Ivy relax against him a bit more as she talked.

"But that ain't to say she's mean or vengeful or anything like that," she explained. "It's just that she's not afraid to give you the benefit of her opinion. She's God-fearing and generous, and stands up for what she feels is right, even if it means she has to stand alone. And she might not have much book learning, but she's the wisest person I know."

"She sounds like quite a woman." And very like Ivy herself.

Ivy nodded in agreement. "I owe her everything I have and am. That's the main reason I have to see this thing through, and as quickly as possible."

"We're working on that. How did you come to live with her?"

"She was a friend of my ma's and also a midwife. She was there when I was born and when my ma died. When my pa died a few days later, she took me in."

He hadn't realized she'd been orphaned so young. No wonder Ivy was so loyal to the woman. "So the two of you run a farm on your own?"

"It's not a big place. We have a nice-size garden and some chickens…and a goat."

He sensed there was something she'd left unsaid. "No other livestock?"

"We used to have a milk cow, and a horse, too. But…" He felt her shudder as she paused. "But four months ago the barn burned down and we couldn't get the animals out in time."

Sympathy washed through him. "I'm sorry. That must have been hard to watch."

"I've never felt so helpless and heartsick in my life. Both Buttercup and Homer were more than just farm animals—they were like pets. It's the one and only time I've seen Nana Dovie cry."

She shuddered again and he had to fight the urge to stop the horse and take her in his arms to console her. But he didn't have that right. Instead he tried to turn her thoughts to other matters. "Did you rebuild your barn?"

"Not yet. That's one reason I'm so anxious to see what this inheritance business is all about. We need a new barn and new animals. As it is, we had to borrow—"

She stopped talking abruptly, as if afraid she'd said too much. "Sorry, didn't mean to rattle on about my troubles."

"I don't mind." In fact, he wished she felt comfortable sharing more. Exactly how deep in debt had they gotten? "After you send your Nana Dovie that telegram, what's your next move going to be?"

"I figure I'll go see Mr. Mosley and show him my proof that Robert Feagan was my father. You said he has a ranch outside of town. Is it on our way?"

"I'm afraid not—it's about a forty-five-minute ride to the other side of town. I'll get a wagon from the livery and escort you there."

She didn't say anything. Had he overstepped by inviting himself along?

Instead of pressing her, he moved on. "Before we do any of that, though, I intend to have Dr. Pratt take a look at that injury of yours."

She was quick to respond. "There's no need. My head feels much better."

No matter how much she protested, it wasn't a point he intended to give in on. "That's for the doctor to decide."

"You sure can be mighty bossy." There was a grumpy note to her voice that succeeded only in making him smile.

"I prefer to think of it as determined," he said dryly.

She made a rather indelicate noise at that.

He chose to ignore it. "Do you have a place to stay while you're in Turnabout?"

"I assume there's an inn there."

"There's a hotel called The Rose Palace."

"Sounds fancy."

He shrugged and found he liked the way she reflexively tightened her hold. "I wouldn't describe it as fancy, but it's clean and comfortable."

"Then that's all I need. Besides, I won't be staying long."

Strange how talk of her leaving needled him. "Just ride in, claim your inheritance and head home again."

"Of course." She sounded happy about it. "The sooner I get back to Nana Dovie, the better."

And why would she stay?

"Miss Jacobs is lucky to have someone like you to care for her."

"I'm the lucky one." Then she sighed. "Though I have to learn not to be such a worrier. As Nana Dovie reminds me, God has everything under His control. And He can make all things work for good, even if we don't see it at the time."

Mitch shifted. There was a time when he'd shared that belief. But where had the good been in Gretchen's senseless death? Where had God's mercy been when those bullets were flying?

"Is something wrong?"

Apparently his silence on the matter had caught her

attention. He pasted a smile on his face in the hopes it would lighten his tone. "We've been on the road for about an hour. Time to stop and give the animals a rest."

It wouldn't hurt to put a bit of distance between them, as well.

Ivy realized he hadn't answered her question. She noticed he often tried to sidestep when her questions got too personal.

She didn't want to press too hard, though. Besides, she was more than happy to climb down and stretch her legs.

As soon as she had her feet on the ground, she moved to Jubal. "How are you doing, old friend? I promise when we get to town I'll find you a nice place to rest with lots of comfy straw. And I'm going to get you the juiciest apples I can find."

"Speaking of feed…"

She turned to see Mitch untying the food sack from the saddle.

"I think I'll have a bite to eat," he said. "How about you?"

They ate some berries and hardtack and shared water from his canteen to wash it down, as they stood in companionable silence.

When they were done, Mitch reattached the food sack, then quickly mounted up. As soon as he was settled, he reached down to her. With an ease that still surprised her, he lifted her into the saddle.

Once they were on their way, Ivy took stock of how far they'd traveled and where the sun was in the sky. "We're not going to make it to town in time for me to see Mr. Mosley today, are we?"

"Probably not."

"At least I'll be able to send that telegram. The rest can wait until morning."

He cleared his throat. "You will undoubtedly encounter Reggie and Adam, the couple who own the cabin, while you're in town. When you do, I know your first tendency will be to thank them." He turned enough to give her a stern look. "But it would be best if you refrained."

"But—"

He faced forward again. "If we're going to hide the fact that we were alone out there for two days, then we must keep silent about *every* aspect of our time there."

Really, he could be like an old biddy hen with her chicks. Only she wasn't a helpless little hatchling. "I don't plan to lie to anyone."

"Neither do I. It's just best we don't volunteer any information unnecessarily. Surely you don't want to burden my friends with keeping our secret as well, do you?"

That gave her pause. "I hadn't thought of it that way." Perhaps she'd been selfish in her thinking. "Very well, we'll do this your way."

But the thought that this decision would come back to haunt them wouldn't let her go. These were his friends so she would bow to his wishes. But it had been her experience that secrets had a way of coming to light.

And when they did, feelings would be hurt and trusts would be broken.

Chapter Seven

Ivy discovered yet another reason to be grateful Mitch was with her. Thanks to his familiarity with the area, she was able to don her skirt before they reached the first farmhouse. And when they did reach that first farmhouse, Mitch, who seemed acquainted with the family living there, convinced them to loan him a wagon.

So when they finally rolled into town, they did so with at least a smidgeon of the propriety Mitch so diligently strove for. Of course, with Seeley and Jubal tied behind and Rufus riding on the floor between them, a smidgeon was the best they could hope for.

As further proof of that, several townsfolk along the sidewalks were eyeing their little procession curiously. Not that she blamed them. The makeup of their group was unconventional, and she was a stranger who'd arrived out of the blue with the town's schoolteacher.

She tried to ignore the stares and instead focus on the town itself. Turnabout was larger than Nettles Gap. The street they were on had businesses lining both sides. She spotted a barbershop, a boot store, an apothecary and others whose signs she missed. Mitch finally stopped the wagon in front of a redbrick building with fancy double doors that were propped open. The gold-lettered sign above the entrance read The Rose Palace Hotel.

"Here we are," he announced unnecessarily.

"Shouldn't we go to the livery stable first and see Jubal settled in?"

"Better to get your things unloaded first so we don't have to carry them through town."

He dismounted, then helped her down. After hitching the horse to the rail, he retrieved her things and then glanced down at Rufus. "I don't believe animals are allowed inside. Will he be okay out here?"

Ivy nodded and stooped so that she was practically nose to nose with Rufus. "I need you to stay out here and guard Jubal." She ruffled his fur with both hands. "We won't be gone long."

The animal responded with a couple of yips and Ivy gave him a final pat before she stood and met Mitch's gaze. "He'll be fine," she said confidently.

His raised brow indicated he was skeptical, but he nodded and escorted her inside.

Ivy looked around as they entered the lobby. There were faded red velvet chairs and large potted plants arranged near the stairway. The front desk was made of a rich-looking wood that had a high polish to it and there was an ornate brass bell on the desk.

Mitch might not think of this place as grand, but it was nicer than anyplace *she'd* ever been. Would her meager funds cover her stay?

He ushered her to the desk and greeted the bespectacled man standing there. "Hello, Edgar, I have a customer for you—Miss Ivy Feagan. Miss Feagan, this is Edgar Crandall."

It appeared they were back to formal address, which she should have expected, given their earlier agreement to adhere to the proprieties once they were among his friends.

The clerk gave her a friendly smile. "Welcome to The Rose Palace Hotel, miss. Always glad to have fresh faces around here."

Ivy doubted her face was very fresh right now, but she returned his smile. "Thank you. This seems like a mighty fine establishment."

The man's smile broadened at her compliment. "We take a lot of pride in this place." He opened a ledger. "Now, let's see if we can get you fixed up. How many nights will you be staying?"

Ivy hesitated. "I'm not sure."

But the man didn't so much as blink. "We'll just leave that open-ended for now." He pointed to a blank line in the ledger. "If you'll just sign here."

She did as he asked, and by the time she'd finished the man was holding out a key. "I've put you in room three. Turn right at the top of the stairs and it'll be the second door."

Ivy reached for her bag, but Mitch was ahead of her.

"Allow me." He waved her to the stairs and she had no choice but to go along unless she wanted to make a scene. She was very aware of his presence behind her as she climbed. When they reached the room she'd been assigned, he finally handed over her bag. "Take whatever time you need. I'll wait downstairs. The livery is on the way to the train station, where the telegraph office is, so we can take care of both of those things when you're ready."

With a nod and a promise not to take long, Ivy opened the door. The room was slightly larger than her bedchamber back home. The furnishings consisted of a bed, a dressing table and mirror, two chairs, a bed-side table and a stand that held a basin and ewer. More than adequate for her needs.

She was pleased to see fresh water in the ewer and a clean towel nearby, so she took a moment to wipe some of the travel dust from her face and hands.

She had to admit, having someone as solicitous as Mitch to smooth the path for her entry into town was quite nice. It was clear he intended to make sure she was comfortably settled rather than just wash his hands of her right away.

She hoped this resumption of formal terms of ad-dress didn't dampen any other part of their friendship. She headed downstairs with a spring in her step.

As promised, Mitch was patiently waiting for her when she returned to the lobby. And when they stepped outside, the ever-faithful Rufus was waiting, as well. "I just thought of something," she said as he handed her back up into the wagon. "Where's Rufus going to spend his nights?"

Mitch stared at the dog a moment, then climbed up beside her. "I suppose he can stay at my house."

"You'd do that?" His offer surprised her more than anything he'd done so far. She didn't think he even liked Rufus.

He shrugged. "He doesn't seem to be much trouble."

Ivy was touched by his gesture, more than she knew how to say.

When they arrived at the livery, Mitch introduced her to Fred Humphries, the owner.

"Glad to meet you, miss." Mr. Humphries turned back to Mitch. "You're back in town early, ain't you?"

Mitch shrugged. "My plans changed." Then he changed the subject. "Miss Feagan's mule here has come up lame. We were hoping you'd take a look at it."

Mr. Humphries examined Jubal's hoof, then declared it to be healing nicely and promised to apply a special poultice he had for such injuries.

Then they walked to the train depot. Ivy quickly dictated the telegram she wanted to send to Nana Dovie and was pleased when Mitch didn't argue over her insistence that she pay for this herself.

But as soon as they stepped outside, his high-handedness returned. "Our next stop is Dr. Pratt's office."

"That's not necessary. It's hardly even tender anymore."

"Nevertheless, I insist."

She rolled her eyes, but his expression remained set. She finally decided it would be easier just to get it over with.

Along the way they passed a building with a sign that caught Ivy's eye and she stopped in her tracks—The Blue Bottle Sweet Shop and Toy Store. She turned to Mitch in delight. "Is it really a store that sells nothing but sweets and toys?"

He nodded, a hint of amusement on his face. "There's a tea shop inside, as well."

She couldn't help herself. "Can we go inside?"

"Yes." He gave her arm a little tug to get her moving again. "*After* we see Dr. Pratt."

She resisted the urge to stick her tongue out at him, but it wasn't easy.

When they reached the doctor's home, where he apparently had his office, an older woman with a friendly smile answered his knock. "Why, hello, Mitch." She opened the screen door wider. "I thought you were going to be gone for several more days."

Did everyone in town know his plans?

Mitch removed his hat. "Good afternoon, Mrs. Pratt. I hope I'm not disturbing you, but I have a young lady here who needs to see your husband."

"Of course, come right on in. Grover's still back in the clinic."

As they stepped inside, Ivy turned back to Rufus. "Wait here, boy. We won't be long."

Rufus obediently sat on his haunches and watched her with tongue hanging out.

Mitch made the introductions. "Mrs. Pratt, this is Miss Ivy Feagan. She's in town on business." He turned to Ivy. "Miss Feagan, this is Mrs. Pratt, the doctor's wife."

Ivy extended her hand. "Pleased to meet you, ma'am."

Mrs. Pratt took Ivy's outstretched hand and gave it a pat. "It's nice to meet you, too, dear. I hope there's nothing serious ailing you."

"Oh, no, ma'am. Mr. Parker is just being a bit of a worrywart."

Mitch cleared his throat. "Actually, Miss Feagan fell and ended up with a nasty cut on the back of her head. She claims to be feeling better, but I thought it best your husband look at it."

"Quite right. Always better to be safe than sorry. Come along back to Grover's office."

Ivy resisted the urge to roll her eyes Mitch's way as they followed the woman down the hall. This was a total waste of time, but they were here because Mitch was concerned for her welfare, and as misguided as that concern might be, she couldn't fault him for it.

In fact, it felt quite nice to have someone so squarely in her corner for a change.

Mitch sat in the outer office as Dr. Pratt examined Ivy. The examination seemed to be taking quite some time, but according to his pocket watch it had only been fifteen minutes. He supposed if she could read his thoughts she'd call him a fusspot again, but it was only natural to worry when someone had been injured.

As soon as Dr. Pratt opened the door, Mitch stood. "How is she?"

The physician closed the door behind him. "She's got quite a knot on the back of her head, but I don't think there'll be any lasting effects. With a head injury, the first twenty-four hours are usually the trickiest and it seems we're beyond that."

Mitch felt an immense sense of relief—he refused to think that it might be out of proportion for the situation.

He ignored the questioning look the doctor gave him. "Are there any special instructions for her care?"

Before Dr. Pratt could respond, the door opened and Ivy stepped out.

"What did I tell you?" Her tone held a triumphant note. "Doc here says I'm right as rain."

Dr. Pratt gave a stern *humph*. "That's not exactly what I said, young lady. I said there should be no lasting effects. You should take it easy for the next few days, just to be safe." He wagged a finger. "And if you feel the least bit dizzy, I want you to come back to see me right away."

"Yes, sir."

Now that that was settled, Mitch brought up another topic. "By the way, I heard Drum Mosley had taken ill. How is he doing? Miss Feagan is here specifically to see him."

The doctor's expression turned somber. "I'm sorry to be the one to deliver the bad news, but Drum passed away yesterday." He gave Ivy a sympathetic look. "Was he a relative or friend of yours?"

She shook her head. "No. I just had some business to discuss with him."

Ivy was doing a good job hiding her disappointment, but Mitch could see what a blow this news was.

He cleared his throat, reclaiming Dr. Pratt's attention and giving her time to collect herself. "I suppose Carter is handling the estate?"

The doctor spread his hands. "I'd assume so. As Drum's only relative, it makes sense he'd inherit it all."

Mitch glanced at Ivy. When she held her peace, he straightened. "Thank you for your assistance, but we should be going now."

"You make certain you do as I said and take it easy."

Ivy nodded. "Thank you, Dr. Pratt. I will."

"And I'll hold her to it," Mitch added.

Mitch insisted that Dr. Pratt put the bill on his tab, countering Ivy's protest with a stern reminder that the visit had been undertaken at his insistence. A moment later they were back out on the front porch. As soon as the door closed behind them, Ivy bent to pet Rufus's head.

"Who's Carter?" she asked without looking up.

"Drum's nephew. He's helped Drum manage the ranch for a number of years now," Mitch added.

He kept a close eye on her, trying to figure out what she was thinking, but she didn't meet his gaze. Instead, she straightened and started down the walk.

She brushed at her skirt. "Would Drum have confided in him about my father?"

"I honestly don't know. But we can certainly speak to him and find out."

She cast him a sideways look. "We? You still want to go along?"

"Of course." Did she think he would abandon her at this stage? He felt a certain responsibility for her—after all, he *had* been responsible for her fall.

She was quiet a moment, but her chin seemed the slightest bit higher and her step a little lighter. Was she pleased to know he was sticking around? "Perhaps I should talk to this Mr. Barr person first," she said.

Mitch nearly missed a step. "Adam's involved in this?"

She gave him a puzzled look. "Yes, I believe his first name *is* Adam. Do you know him? He sent the letter on Mr. Mosley's behalf."

Mitch nodded. "He's one of the men who traveled here from Philadelphia with me. And he's married to Reggie, the lady who owns the cabin we stayed at."

"Oh." She looked at him uncertainly. "I hadn't realized he was *that* Adam. Then I guess he's trustworthy."

"Absolutely." It made sense Drum would have enlisted Adam's assistance. Adam had worked as an attorney before he came to Texas, and folks still turned to him when they needed legal advice.

"Come on, I'll take you to meet him. It's probably best you and he discuss this before we pay Carter a visit."

"Do you think we should just drop in on him without an appointment?"

"We're not going to his office—he'll be at home for the evening. And he won't mind. Besides, I need to let Reggie know I'm no longer at the cabin, anyway."

He glanced at the dog padding along beside them. "But we should drop Rufus off at my place first."

She nodded, but her mind was apparently on his earlier statement. "You said Mr. Barr was *one* of the men who traveled from Philadelphia with you. How many were there?"

"There were two others—four of us in total."

"You must have been really good friends to just up and leave your homes, and move here together."

"Actually, we didn't know each other before we planned the trip." And they hadn't gotten along very well at first, either. That had been a very uncomfortable trip.

Ivy paused a heartbeat, staring at him in confusion. Then she started walking again. "Four gentlemen from Philadelphia all decide to travel way out here to Turnabout the same time? Sounds like one whopper of a coincidence."

"There was no coincidence. You see, we had a common acquaintance—Reggie's grandfather, as a matter of fact—who pulled us together for a unique business opportunity." The opportunity being to participate in a marriage lottery for Reggie's very unwilling hand.

And the less said about that, the better.

She nodded. "So y'all went into business together."

He could see why she'd be confused, but he really wasn't at liberty to reveal the whole story. And to be honest, he wasn't sure he'd want to even if he were.

"No. We've all gone our separate ways. Adam married Reggie shortly after we moved here and now he manages the bank and gives legal advice on occasion. Everett runs the local newspaper and married Daisy, who runs a restaurant. And Chance and his wife, Eve, run that toy and candy shop you saw earlier." He spread his hands. "And I'm one of the town's two schoolteachers." Did that sound as anticlimactic next to the accomplishments of the other three as he thought it did?

"Do you consider these men your friends *now?*"

He didn't have to think about that one. "Of course." The four of them had had their differences during the trip here and during those tense days when they had been waiting for Reggie to make her decision.

To be honest, during that trip his mind had been more on his reason for leaving Philadelphia than on what company he was in. Gretchen's death, and his guilt, had been fresh then. Getting close to anyone had been beyond his abilities.

But in time the four men and Reggie had forged a mutual respect and friendship.

But he hadn't allowed anyone to get really close since he'd moved here. He wasn't certain he even knew how any longer.

Ivy wondered if Mitch knew how telling his words had been. Each of the men who'd traveled here with him had found love and established a family. Each one except him.

That didn't make sense. Mitch was a tall, handsome man with a strong sense of honor and a good heart. Any girl would be lucky to have him for a husband.

Which was not an appropriate topic for her to dwell on.

As soon as Mitch pointed out his house, she studied it with interest. It was a white two-story structure, very simple and plain in design. It was just the right size, she decided—small enough to be cozy, but large enough so he wouldn't feel cramped.

It was a bit stark, though. Unlike many of the homes they'd passed, there were no swings or rockers or even benches on the front porch. The yard appeared well maintained, but there were only a few bushes flanking the front gate—no flowering plants or flashes of color. No woman's touch.

The fence guarding his yard was wooden, about waist high, and it seemed sturdy enough to hold Rufus, as long as the dog didn't want out very badly.

Mitch stepped forward to open the gate. "Let me get a bowl of water for the mutt and then we'll head to Adam and Reggie's place." He paused, then added, "Perhaps it would be best if you waited here with Rufus. I'll just be a minute."

She nodded—this was likely another of his attempts to protect her reputation. But despite his stiff-necked tendencies, he'd been thoughtful enough to take time to get Rufus a bowl of water.

Then she saw his front door and she couldn't help the grin that spread across her face. Unlike the stark formality of the rest of his place, the door was painted a deep apple-red. Perhaps Mitch wasn't quite as reserved as he tried to pretend.

True to his word, Mitch returned a few minutes later. He set a large pan on the porch, then closed the front door behind him.

Ivy bent down and rubbed the dog's ears. "Okay, Rufus, there's plenty of water and lots of room to run around. You be good and don't make Mr. Parker sorry he volunteered to keep you."

The dog followed them as far as the gate, then sat on his haunches as she closed him in. For a moment, Ivy worried about abandoning him in a strange place. Then he caught sight of a squirrel and took off, chasing the animal across the yard and around to the back of the house.

She smiled. He'd be fine.

"I like your door," she said as they started down the walk.

His only reply was a noncommittal *"Hmm,"* but she thought she detected a slight self-conscious wince.

Deciding not to tease him further, she contented herself with asking questions about the town.

Finally, he waved a hand. "That's the Barr home just up ahead."

The Barr home was a two-story white structure, larger than Mitch's, with a nice-size lawn and some well-cared-for rose bushes brightening up the front porch.

"Remember, don't mention the cabin," Mitch reminded her. "And no first names."

Ivy nodded, trying to ignore the spurt of exasperation at his stern warning. Did he think she would be so indiscreet?

But a bit of irritation was a small price to pay for all he'd done for her. Having Mitch introduce her to Mr. Barr would make her meeting with the man less awkward than it might have been otherwise.

And she clearly needed all the help she could get, now that Drum Mosley was dead. She still couldn't wrap her mind around that and what it meant for her. Had her chance to claim a windfall inheritance died with him? Had she made this long, trouble-plagued trip to Turnabout for nothing?

She certainly hoped Mr. Barr had some answers for her. But knowing he was a friend of Mitch's already inspired her with confidence that things would work out.

And if they didn't, well, having Mitch in her corner was still a win any way you looked at it.

Chapter Eight

Mitch placed a hand at the small of her back as they turned up the front walk.

She drew comfort from his touch, suddenly feeling unaccountably nervous. Not only was her access to that mysterious inheritance on the line, but these people were Mitch's friends and she didn't want to do or say anything that would embarrass him.

A lady with vivid blue-green eyes and coffee-brown hair answered his knock.

"Mitch." The woman opened the screen door, concern in her expression. "I thought you planned to stay at the cabin for another four or five days. I hope nothing's happened." Then she noticed Ivy. "Oh, hello."

As Ivy stepped forward, Mitch smiled reassuringly. "Don't worry, nothing untoward happened. My plans just changed."

Ivy smiled at the woman. "That was my fault, I'm afraid."

"Reggie, this is Miss Ivy Feagan." Mitch turned to Ivy. "Miss Feagan, this is Regina Barr."

Reggie smiled a greeting. "Pleased to meet you. And

I'm dying to hear how you changed Mitch's plans. But first, come inside so we can speak more comfortably."

"Call me Ivy, please. And I'm very glad to meet you, too."

When Ivy entered she found herself in a warmly furnished entryway. The hat rack and hall table had both seen better days, but the wood had a lovely glow to it. The oval mirror above the narrow table had an ornately carved frame, and was flanked by lovely photographs.

Before Ivy could take in any more, Reggie gave her arm a friendly pat. "As I said, I'm very interested in hearing how you managed to pry Mitch away from his vacation."

Mindful of Mitch's concerns, Ivy chose her words carefully. "I was on my way here from Nettles Gap and ran into a bit of trouble. My mule came up lame and then I fell and bumped my head. Mr. Parker stumbled on me, so to speak, bandaged me up and offered to escort me to town." She gave Mitch a teasing look. "I think he was afraid I'd hurt myself further if he'd didn't keep an eye on me."

"How chivalrous of him." Reggie eyed Mitch thoughtfully, then turned back to her. "You say you bumped your head—I hope you weren't badly hurt."

Ivy waved dismissively. "I bumped my head, but I'm okay now. Even Dr. Pratt says so."

"Well, that's a relief."

Mitch cleared his throat. "Actually, the other reason we're here is that Miss Feagan has some business to discuss with Adam."

"I see. Well, Adam is right in here." She stepped aside as they reached the open doorway to a parlor, where a man was watching a toddler play on the floor.

He stood as soon as he saw them.

"Adam, Mitch brought a new friend of his round to see us," Reggie said. "This is Ivy Feagan. Ivy, this is my husband, Adam."

Mr. Barr's eyebrow went up momentarily at the introduction, and Ivy wondered if he'd recognized her last name. But he merely nodded politely. "Miss Feagan."

"Nice to meet you, Mr. Barr."

The toddler started fussing and Reggie scooped her up. "And this little doll is our daughter, Patricia." She gave the child an affectionate squeeze, then turned to her guests. "Patricia and I will leave you to your business with Adam. But I warn you I will be back later for that chat."

Reggie exited, closing the door behind her, and Ivy took a seat on the sofa while Mitch sat on a nearby chair.

Mr. Barr glanced from her to Mitch. "May I inquire how you two are acquainted?"

Mitch gave him the same story they'd relayed to Reggie earlier.

Then Reggie's husband turned to Ivy. "I assume you're here in response to the letter I sent out on Drum Mosley's behalf."

Ivy nodded. "I understand Mr. Mosley passed away yesterday."

Mr. Barr nodded. "He'd been quite ill for some time." Then he eyed her curiously. "What is your relationship to Robert Feagan?"

"He was my father."

"I see."

Mitch leaned forward. "What are Miss Feagan's options now? Does she need to take this up with Carter?"

Rather than answer the question, Mr. Barr asked Ivy

a question of his own. "How much do you know about your father's relationship with Drum Mosley?"

"I didn't even know there *was* a relationship. I was just a few days old when my pa died. The lady who raised me, Dovie Jacobs, couldn't remember much, either. When your letter came, she thought on it a bit. All she could remember was that my pa was setting up a new home for us when he got word about my ma taking ill. But it all happened so long ago, she doesn't remember much else." Ivy leaned forward with her hands clasped together. "Do *you* know the story?"

"Only what Drum shared with me."

"And that was?"

Mr. Barr leaned back and rubbed his jaw. "Drum requested you bring proof that you are who you say you are. Do you have that with you?"

"It's back at the hotel with my things."

"May I ask what it consists of?"

"I brought a letter from Nana Dovie, the midwife who delivered me. And I have my ma's Bible that has her name in it, along with a family tree that goes back three generations." She started to rise. "I can fetch them if you need to see them."

Mitch placed a restraining hand on her arm. "I don't think that's necessary." He turned to Adam. "I'll vouch for her. If she says she has them, then she does."

Ivy was touched by Mitch's trust.

Adam gave a short nod. "Then that's good enough for me. At least as far as telling you this part of the story."

What did that mean?

"Nine days ago, Drum sent word that he needed to see me. It seems that, once he knew he was nearing the end of his life, he had a crisis of conscience and wanted to make sure his affairs were in order. He wanted my advice on how to right a wrong that may or may not have been committed twenty-one years ago."

"Something to do with my pa?"

"Yes."

Ivy felt a fluttering beneath her breastbone. She would finally learn what this was all about.

"From what Drum told me," Mr. Barr continued, "back in their younger days, he and your father worked together on a number of cattle drives. They became friends and decided they were tired of working for others, so they agreed to buy a parcel of land together and develop their own ranching operation."

"They were partners?"

Mr. Barr nodded. "They pooled their money and bought a parcel of land just outside of Turnabout. They spent the first year just getting the land ready. Then they borrowed heavily to purchase a bull and a few dozen head of cattle to establish their herd."

Her father had been a cattle rancher. "Where was my ma all this time?"

"According to Drum, your mother stayed in Nettles Gap. She had a delicate constitution and your father didn't want to bring her here until he'd built a proper house for her. He and Drum had just about put everything else in motion when he learned she was expecting. So he and your mother decided to wait a little longer so she could be with folks she knew and felt comfortable with until the child was born."

Ivy found this story fascinating—she hadn't heard any of it before now. The puzzle was finally starting to make sense.

Mr. Barr looked at her with a kindness she hadn't

expected from a near stranger. "Do you know the circumstances around your parents' passing?"

"Nana Dovie told me I came too early and that my ma died in childbirth. Not long after, my pa died of grief."

When she was younger she'd thought dying of grief was romantic. Later, she'd wondered why her pa hadn't decided to stick around for her sake—didn't he love her, too? And come to think of it, how did one die of grief, anyway?

She suddenly became aware of Mitch's strong presence beside her, quietly supportive as she absorbed this new information about her parents. She gave him a quick smile, then turned back to Mr. Barr. She wasn't sure she wanted to hear the answer to her next question, but it had to be asked. "What was Mr. Mosley's version of my pa's story?"

He shifted slightly, but nodded. "Something similar. After your father buried your mother, he returned here and threw himself into his work. Drum said that all he could get out of him was that your mother had passed and that the baby wasn't expected to live."

She winced at that. "Nana Dovie *did* say it was touch and go for a while as to whether I would live." But why hadn't her father stuck around to find out?

"At any rate, your father died a few days later when he fell from his horse."

It wasn't grief, then. Or maybe it was grief that made him careless. She supposed she'd never know. "So what does all this mean?"

"As for the particulars of Drum's will, that should wait until I have both you and Carter together. I had planned to speak to him after the funeral tomorrow.

Perhaps you should come as well so we can attend to the matter properly."

"We'll be there," Mitch said before Ivy could answer.

He was being high-handed again, but in this particular case, she couldn't say she minded. She nodded. "I'd like to pay my respects." After all, even though she'd never met him, Drum Mosley had given her a glimpse into who her parents had been.

Mitch spoke up again. "What else can you tell Miss Feagan about her prospects?"

Mr. Barr turned to speak to her directly, which she appreciated. "I can tell you your father and Drum had a formal partnership agreement, which stated that if either of them died without a direct heir, then their share of the property would go to the other partner. As far as Drum knew, your father had no direct heir remaining, so he assumed ownership of the entire ranch. And no one came forward to challenge his claim."

Did that mean she *did* own some land? "What made Mr. Mosley decide to check his facts now?"

"I think he always wondered in the back of his mind if Robert's child had really passed away. But he ignored those niggling doubts and continued to build on, and profit from, the ranch." He rubbed his chin. "Then, as I said, facing his own mortality forced him to reevaluate."

Mitch leaned forward. "Does Carter know about this?"

"When last we spoke, Drum instructed me that no one, including Carter, was to know about this unless an heir stepped forward. So unless he changed his mind, I'd say no."

Before she or Mitch could ask anything further, Mr.

Barr leaned back. "Now, I'd prefer to defer the rest of this discussion until we meet with Carter tomorrow."

Ivy nodded. "Of course. And I appreciate you taking the time to tell me this much."

As if she'd been waiting for her cue, Reggie reentered the parlor with a now smiling and cooing toddler. She hefted the child on her hip. "I've waited long enough. Surely your business is complete by now."

Mr. Barr stepped forward and gave his wife a peck on the cheek. "So impatient. But yes, we're done."

"Well, then, Mrs. Peavy tells me supper is ready." She turned to Ivy and Mitch. "And I insist you join us."

"That's mighty kind, ma'am, but I wouldn't want to intrude," Ivy said.

"First of all, I'll have none of this 'ma'am' fustiness—it's Reggie. And second, there's more than enough for two guests, and it will give me a chance to visit with you properly. Besides, I want you to meet our son, Jack, as well as Mrs. Peavy and her husband, Ira, who live here, as well."

Mitch spoke up before she could refuse again. "Thank you, we accept."

Reggie smiled. "That's better." She handed the toddler over to her husband and linked her arm through Ivy's. "Now, I want to hear all about how you and Mitch met."

Ivy sent a quick glance Mitch's way, unsure how to reply to that. He immediately came to her rescue.

"When Miss Feagan fell, I got to play white knight to her damsel in distress."

"A white knight, was it?" Reggie grinned. "I always thought there was hero material inside you—you just needed the right circumstances to bring it out." She cut a quick glance Ivy's way. "Or the right person."

Ivy's cheeks warmed at that and she quickly turned the conversation in a different direction. "Mr. Parker tells me you're a photographer. That sounds like an interesting skill to have."

Reggie accepted her change of subject. "I enjoy it. Stop by my studio while you're here and I'll show you some of my work." Then she tilted her head. "Speaking of which, how long are you planning to be in town?"

"I'm not sure. It depends on how long it takes to settle this business with Mr. Mosley."

"Well, we'll do our best to make certain you want to stay for a nice long visit."

"Thank you, but I left Nana Dovie—that's the woman who raised me—on her own and I don't like to be gone for too long."

Reggie patted her arm. "In that case, I suppose we'll have to wish for a speedy and happy conclusion to your business here."

As Ivy thanked her again, she cast a quick look at Mitch, the man who'd stood by her ever since he'd first stumbled upon her, and had helped her in more ways than she could count.

Would he miss her when she left?

Because she had a feeling she would definitely miss him.

As Mitch walked Ivy back to the hotel, he saw the lamplighter starting his rounds on Second Street. It was hard to believe they'd left the cabin only this morning.

"The Barrs seem like real nice people," Ivy said.

"They are."

She paused for a moment, then added, "Like you."

She thought he was nice? He wasn't sure how to respond to that. So he changed the subject. "How are you feeling about all of these new details you're learning about your parents?" She'd been uncharacteristically silent on the subject.

"It was unexpected, of course. But after thinking on it a bit I find it fills in a lot of gaps for me. I just wish I would've made it here before Mr. Mosley passed on. It would have been really nice to speak to someone who knew my pa so well."

So she was more focused on her father than on the legacy he'd left her. The way her mind worked never ceased to surprise him.

"I appreciate all you've done to help me," she continued, "but I don't want you to feel like you have to keep going out of your way on my behalf. There's no need for you to go out to Mr. Mosley's ranch tomorrow if you want to head back to the cabin and finish your vacation."

Was she tired of his company? He found himself strangely reluctant to step away. "You don't think I'm going to come this far and not be there when the end plays out, do you?"

"Well, if you're sure it's something you *want* to do…"

"It is."

A yawn escaped her as they arrived at the hotel. She gave him a sheepish look. "I'm sorry. I—"

"No need to apologize. You've had an eventful day. A good night's sleep will do you a world of good." He escorted her just inside the lobby. "I'll see you in the morning."

"Thanks again for taking care of Rufus."

"All I did was pen him up in my yard."

She rolled her eyes at him, then turned serious. With a vulnerable smile that tugged at all his protective instincts, she placed a hand on his sleeve. "In case I haven't said it enough, I'm truly grateful for everything you've done for me these past few days. And I don't just mean tending to my injury." She waved her free hand. "I didn't realize just how unprepared I was. You've made this whole situation unbelievably easier for me."

Then, as if embarrassed by her own seriousness, she dropped her hand and gave him a tongue-in-cheek smile. "I guess there are some benefits to your being such a fusspot, after all."

And with that she turned and moved quickly to the stairs.

Mitch walked the three blocks to his house down quiet, dusk-shadowed streets, a smile tugging at his lips. He still wasn't sure what to make of this teasing affection she treated him with. No one had dared do that since he and his sisters were in the schoolroom.

Then he sobered. They'd managed to avoid any sort of gossip, salacious or otherwise. But the real test would come tomorrow, once word of his return and the new visitor to town got around.

He turned into his yard, bending down to absently scratch an enthusiastic Rufus behind the ears.

Would they really be able to pull this off and remain unscathed by gossip?

And if not, what would he do about it?

Ivy settled into bed, exhausted.

Last night she'd been at the cabin, with Mitch out on the porch. He was so thoughtful, so uncomplaining.

Of course, he probably would have done the same for any female in her situation. Still, it had made her feel special. Which could be dangerous, given that she'd be returning to Nettles Gap soon.

She rolled over, wondering what tomorrow would bring. Hard to believe her father had been a landowner all those years ago, but if Mr. Mosley had been willing to acknowledge it then it must be true. Were her money woes truly over?

She stared at the ceiling. Better not to count on that just yet, though. If Mr. Barr was right, Mr. Mosley's nephew didn't know about her or her claim yet. The poor man had just lost his uncle—how would he react to her claim?

Whatever happened, she was glad she'd be facing it with Mitch at her side.

Chapter Nine

The next morning Drum's funeral was held on the ranch at the Mosley family cemetery. Once it was over and the attendees had offered their condolences to Carter, folks began drifting back to their carriages and wagons, leaving the gravediggers to complete their job.

Adam and Reggie were among the last to speak to Carter, and afterward Adam gave Mitch a subtle signal that they should proceed to Carter's house. Then Adam handed Reggie up into their carriage to send her back to town on her own before climbing into the carriage Mitch had rented from the livery.

Mitch eased the carriage into the procession slowly exiting the cemetery, but rather than turning onto the road to town, he followed Adam's directions and took the fork that led to the ranch house.

Ivy looked around. "How big is this place?"

"Around fifteen hundred acres, I believe," Adam said.

"Mercy me! I can't believe my pa owned part of this."

Mitch wondered if it had sunk in yet that soon, she would, too.

When they pulled up in front of the house, Carter was waiting on them. "You said we needed to talk about the estate," he said distractedly. "Can we make this quick?"

Adam took the lead. "We'll do our best. But first, let me offer my condolences once again on the loss of your uncle."

Carter nodded acceptance. "Thank you."

"I believe you already know Mitchell Parker."

Carter gave a short nod. "The schoolteacher, right?"

Mitch returned his nod, not sure he liked the man's impatient tone. "That's correct." He drew Ivy forward. "And this is Miss Ivy Feagan."

Carter touched the brim of his hat in acknowledgment. "Miss Feagan," he said, looking slightly puzzled.

It was clear to Mitch that Carter didn't recognize Ivy's last name, which meant Carter didn't know about Drum's plans. How would he react when he heard the story?

Carter had already turned back to Adam. "I assume you need to talk to me about Drum's estate." He gave Adam a puzzled look. "Though I'm not sure why. I've seen Drum's will and it looks pretty straightforward to me."

Adam indicated the folder of papers he held. "There's been a change. Drum called me out here a little over a week ago and asked me to revise his will."

That definitely sharpened Carter's attention. "Revise it how?"

"For one, he named me executor." Adam nodded toward the house. "It might be best if we go inside to discuss this."

Carter nodded, then paused. "Not to be rude, but why are these two with you?"

Mitch stiffened and touched Ivy's arm protectively.

But Adam's expression never changed. "Miss Feagan is here at my invitation because this affects her, too. And Mitch is here as her friend and adviser."

Her friend and adviser—Mitch liked that.

Carter's frown deepened and he gave Ivy a speculative look. But a moment later he turned without comment and led them into the house. They walked through a short hallway and entered a room that appeared to be an office.

Drum's nephew took a seat behind the desk and waved them to the other chairs. Mitch seated Ivy, and he and Adam sat on either side of her.

"So, let's get to it," Carter said. "What are the terms of this new will?"

Adam folded his hands over the file in his lap. "First, I need to give you some history. Have you heard of Robert Feagan?" When Carter shook his head, Adam gave a quick rundown of the partnership agreement, Drum's actions after Mr. Feagan's death and his recent crisis of conscience.

Mitch watched Carter, noting his deepening displeasure. Apparently Carter was getting an idea of where the conversation was headed.

When Adam finished his story, he pulled a paper from the file. "Drum amended his will to indicate that if Robert Feagan's child had survived, and could prove her paternity, she was entitled to a portion of the estate."

Carter's posture was fence-post stiff. "If all this were true, Uncle Drum would have told me."

"Your uncle didn't want to say anything to you until

he learned whether the heir was still alive." Adam's tone and expression remained businesslike. "I assure you, there is no subterfuge here—he did amend his will. He also instructed me to tell you that you would find his copy of the will folded in the pages of his Bible."

Carter made no move to verify the presence of that copy. "Uncle Drum is barely in the ground and already someone is trying to stake a claim on this place."

"I'm truly sorry for your loss," Ivy said softly. "And I agree the timing ain't the best. But, and I mean no disrespect by this, the timing is your uncle's, since he only recently contacted me."

How did she manage to sound so understanding, Mitch wondered, when faced with blatant hostility?

Carter stared at her a moment without responding, then turned back to Adam. "What if I wanted to contest the will?" he asked.

Mitch stiffened at this hint that Drum's nephew would attempt to keep Ivy's portion of the estate from her.

Adam, however, merely pulled out another document. "That's your right, of course. But Drum gave me his copy of the partnership agreement between himself and Robert Feagan. So, whether he added Miss Feagan to his will or not, she has a legitimate claim on the estate."

Carter's jaw tightened and his brow drew down, narrowing his eyes. "I've heard Uncle Drum talk about the early years of the ranch. That agreement, if it's legitimate, was drawn up when this place was barely more than rock-strewn dirt and scrub, and the herd that ran here could be contained in a small pen."

"Be that as it may, Miss Feagan still has a rightful claim."

"Rightful." Carter looked as if he wanted to spit the words. "There's been a lot of blood, sweat and tears poured into this place over the past twenty-one years, and Robert Feagan—" he cast a quick, hostile look Ivy's way "—not to mention his heirs, had no part in any of it. To my way of thinking there's nothing *rightful* about her claim."

Before he or Adam could respond, Ivy leaned forward. "Mr. Mosley, I understand why you would feel that way," she said, her tone surprisingly polite, "and I sure don't expect you to split this place down the middle. I'm willing to talk about a more reasonable arrangement."

Her words didn't seem to appease the man. He glared at her a moment, then turned back to Adam without responding. Mitch felt Ivy stiffen and he didn't blame her.

"How do we even know she is who she says she is?" Carter demanded. "After all, from what you've told me, this Robert Feagan didn't expect his daughter to live."

Mitch couldn't hold his peace any longer. "Because she's not a liar," he said. "And because your uncle would never have sent that letter if he hadn't believed there was a chance she was still alive."

Ivy gave his arm a quick touch, then turned back to Carter. "I brought a letter from the midwife who delivered me, and I also brought my mother's family Bible."

The man made a sharp, dismissive gesture. "Folks can be bribed to write whatever they're told to, and that Bible could have been acquired another way." He leaned back in his chair. "Seems to me we really don't have much more than her word to go on."

"I didn't bribe anyone," Ivy said indignantly. "And that Bible came straight from my ma—Nana Dovie said so and she's as honest as a baby's cry."

Again Carter ignored her. "You're the lawyer, Mr. Barr. What options do I have to fight this?" He narrowed his eyes. "Or maybe I shouldn't ask you since you're obviously on her side."

Adam remained unruffled. "I have no problem answering objectively. As I said, your uncle named me executor of the estate, and my only interest is to see that his wishes are carried out. If you want to fight Miss Feagan's claim, then you'll need to take her to court and let a judge decide the case."

Carter nodded decisively. "Then that's what I'll do. We can both take our chances with the judge."

Adam put the papers back in the folder. "That's your right, of course. I'll write to the circuit judge and let him know we have a case for him the next time he comes through."

He met Carter's gaze evenly. "Of course, right now, the will states Robert Feagan's heir gets half the *original* estate, which was five hundred acres. Your uncle tripled that since his partner's death. If you take this to court, you run the risk of having the judge divide the whole thing right down the middle."

The man blinked uncertainly, but then lifted his jaw. "I'll take my chances."

Ivy rubbed her chin. "How long will all this take?"

Adam turned to her. "I believe Judge Andrews is due back through here in about three weeks."

"Three weeks!" Ivy plopped back in dismay. "I didn't plan on sticking around that long."

Carter shrugged. "Suit yourself. You can always go back where you came from and drop this whole matter."

Mitch had had enough of the man's rudeness. "She's staying. And we'll see what the judge has to say when he looks over the proof she brought with her, and learns how your uncle cheated her out of her inheritance for twenty-one years."

Carter narrowed his gaze. "Tell me again what your role is in all of this, schoolteacher. Are you maybe looking to snag a rich wife?"

Mitch surged to his feet, ready to defend both his and Ivy's honor. But Adam stood as well and placed a hand on his shoulder, holding Mitch's gaze for a long moment, bringing him back to his senses.

When his friend finally turned to Carter, Mitch cast a quick glance Ivy's way and saw her puzzled expression.

Before he could do more than offer her a tight smile, Adam was speaking again.

"I understand this has come as a shock to you," his friend said with his unblinking gaze now focused on Carter, "especially on top of your uncle's passing, but there's no need to toss around insults."

Mitch said a silent amen to that. "I think it's time for us to take our leave." He had to get out of here.

"I agree." Adam looked at Carter levelly. "Think over all I've told you and look over your uncle's will for yourself. Then decide if you really want to pursue this course of action. In the meantime, I'll contact Judge Andrews."

"I don't need to think about it."

Mitch held himself very still. The fact that he'd nearly lost his temper a moment ago had shaken him to the core. He'd thought he'd come a long way in getting that beast inside him under control—apparently it still had the capability to slip its chains when provoked.

He couldn't let that happen again.

Not ever again.

A few minutes later, Ivy leaned back against the seat of the carriage, trying to gather her thoughts while Mitch drove and Mr. Barr sat behind them. She'd been shocked by the accusation Mr. Mosley had flung at Mitch, and equally surprised by the vehemence of Mitch's reaction. The last thing she'd wanted was to bring trouble to this man who'd shown her such kindness.

Perhaps she should do as Carter wanted and just drop the whole thing. Not much good ever came from getting something for nothing, anyway.

Then again, there was still the matter of how Nana Dovie would pay her debts. And it sure would be nice to have a milk cow again.

She took a deep breath. Here she went again, trying to figure things out on her own. That wasn't the way to tackle this at all. She bowed her head and closed her eyes.

Dear Lord Jesus, I sure am all discombobulated by this. It seems wrong to come all this way and then not see the matter through, especially when this whole out-of-the-blue windfall seemed to be the answer to our prayers. But I sure don't want to put material things above friendship, or above Nana Dovie's welfare.

And another thing to consider is that I don't have the money to stay in that fancy hotel for three weeks— I barely have enough to stay three nights.

So please, help me figure out what I should do.

She kept her eyes closed a few moments longer, letting her thoughts settle.

It was several minutes before she realized a heavy silence had fallen. This wouldn't do. She turned to Mitch. "Thank you again for accompanying me today and for speaking up on my behalf. I'm sorry if it caused you any discomfort."

Mitch nodded without taking his gaze from the road. "No need to apologize. I'm just sorry you were subjected to that."

His voice was tight, controlled. Was he still upset over the man's accusation? Of course it was ridiculous to think he might be interested in *marrying* her, whether for money or not. Surely Mitch didn't think anyone would take that accusation seriously?

Though the idea of marriage to the man beside her wasn't something she'd look amiss on. Assuming he was interested, which he obviously wasn't.

Quickly squashing that line of thought, she decided to steer the conversation onto a safer track. "Mr. Mosley's reaction isn't hard to understand. He just lost his uncle and now a stranger comes along and stakes a claim on a place he's been led to believe is rightfully his. And I think it hurt his feelings that his uncle confided in Mr. Barr and not him."

"Feelings! You're being too kind."

She gave Mitch a reproving look. "There's no such thing as being *too* kind. And all I meant was that I don't suppose anybody could rightly blame him for not taking the news well."

Mitch made a noise that was neither agreement nor disagreement. "Adam, how good are Carter's chances of winning his challenge in court?"

Mr. Barr rubbed his chin. "Unless he can throw serious doubt on Miss Feagan's status as Robert Feagan's daughter, her claim should stand. The fact that I have in writing that Drum himself admitted to not having followed up at the time of his partner's demise will work in her favor."

Ivy spoke up, irritated that they were talking about her as if she weren't sitting right here. "He does have a point about all the work he and his uncle poured into that place. What little I've seen of it, it looks like a mighty nice spread with a fine house. I wouldn't want to take anything that wasn't rightfully mine."

Mitch snorted. "Nonsense. Keep in mind, Drum thought you had a right to a share of the place."

Ivy stiffened. He didn't need to sound so superior. "I only meant—"

Mr. Barr cleared his throat. "Why don't we wait until the judge hears the case and validates your claim to worry about all of that?"

Mr. Barr was right. She twisted around to face him. "Can you explain how this is supposed to work? I mean, if the judge says my claim is legitimate, then do Mr. Mosley and I just sit down together and figure out how we want to divide up the estate?"

"That's one way to do it." His tone was carefully neutral. "Or if that doesn't seem feasible, the judge can appoint someone to mediate the process."

Ivy nodded and faced forward. This was all getting so complicated. And she still felt a bit like a circling buzzard. She wished Nana Dovie were here so they could talk it over.

Which brought up the issue that had been niggling at

her since talk of this three-week delay came up. Could she leave Nana Dovie on her own that long?

"What's wrong?"

How did Mitch know she was worried? Was she so easy to read?

"I was just thinking three weeks is a much longer time than I'd planned to be away." She turned to face Mr. Barr. "Is there any way to speed this up?"

He gave a regretful shake of his head. "I'm afraid the judge's schedule is pretty well-set. And as important as this is to you and Carter, it would take something much more significant to have him alter his normal circuit route."

"I see." Not the answer she'd wanted but about what she'd expected.

Mitch gave her a quizzical look. "Getting homesick?"

"I've never been away this long before." Not quite an answer, but hopefully it would satisfy him.

Truth to tell, she was actually enjoying her time here more than she'd expected. She'd seen new sights and had new experiences in the short time she'd been away. And folks around here didn't treat her like a leper the way they did back home.

Of course, another part of the reason she was enjoying herself was sitting right next to her.

Best not to dwell on that, though.

Chapter Ten

By the time Mitch dropped Mr. Barr at his home, it was nearly noon and Ivy was no closer to figuring out her next move than she'd been when she'd left the ranch. She wasn't one for giving up just because things got difficult, but she also wasn't sure this was a battle she really should be fighting.

Once they'd delivered the carriage back to the livery, Mitch gave her a searching look. "Come along, we can have lunch at Daisy's while we discuss what happens next."

So he wasn't ready to wash his hands of her just yet. Suddenly feeling her mood lighten, she raised a brow. "Daisy's?"

"Daisy Fulton runs a restaurant here in town. The hotel's food is okay, but Daisy's cooking is much better."

She grinned. "Then lead on."

As they strolled along the sidewalk, Ivy paused to admire a frock in the window of a dress shop. It was simply made, out of a pretty blue-and-yellow fabric. But the touches of lace at the collar, yoke and cuffs gave it a special-occasion look.

"Thinking about getting a new dress?"

Ivy cut him a quick smile. "Nana Dovie has a birthday coming up and I would love to get that dress for her. But she'd give me such a scold if I did."

"Why?"

"Because there are more practical things to spend our money on."

"My sisters always believed birthdays were a time to forgo the practical and indulge in the frivolous."

Ivy grinned. "I think I'd get along very well with your sisters."

"I think you would, too."

The half smile with which he delivered those words did something funny to her insides.

Before she could form a response, someone stepped out of the dress shop. The woman looked to be in her fifties, and had dark hair and a solid build. Her gaze darted with keen interest between her and Mitch, and she approached them with an eager smile.

"Why, hello," the woman said to Mitch. "And good day to your friend, as well."

Was it her imagination or did Mitch stiffen slightly?

Mitch nearly groaned. Eunice Ortolon was a well-meaning woman, but she was also the most notorious gossip in town. If there was a secret to be ferreted out, Eunice was the one to do it. He only hoped Ivy wouldn't say anything to put her on the scent.

He touched the brim of his hat. "Mrs. Ortolon, allow me to introduce you to Miss Ivy Feagan." He turned to Ivy. "Mrs. Ortolon runs the town's boardinghouse."

Ivy gave a neighborly nod. "Pleased to meet you, ma'am."

"So you're the young lady who rode into town with

Mr. Parker yesterday." She didn't wait for a response before rushing on. "I saw you at the funeral this morning but didn't have the opportunity to say hello. Was Mr. Carter a relative of yours?"

Mitch held his breath. How would Ivy respond?

"No, ma'am. He was an old friend of my father's."

Of course—the perfect answer.

Mrs. Ortolon nodded sympathetically. "How very kind of you to travel here to attend his funeral. Did you have to come far?"

"I came from Nettles Gap."

That raised the woman's brow a bit. Was she wondering why Ivy hadn't arrived by train? Mitch took Ivy's elbow. "If you will excuse us, we were headed to Daisy's."

"Of course. Enjoy your meal."

As they walked away, Mitch imagined the woman's eyes boring into their backs.

"She seems very friendly," Ivy said, though her tone was tentative. "She must make a very good boarding-house proprietor."

"She does run a very tidy and comfortable place." Mitch believed in giving credit where credit was due. "I stayed there for a few weeks when I first moved to Turnabout. All four of us did." That's when he'd learned the woman had a talent for extracting a juicy bit of blather from the most unwitting of sources. She wasn't malicious, just drawn to gossip like a bee to nectar.

Still, it would be best if he kept Ivy away from Eunice Ortolon—and any other gossips—as much as possible.

Ivy studied the colorful sign above the door proclaiming the establishment to be Daisy's Restaurant. It had a charming little daisy dotting the *i,* and somehow it made her feel welcome. This was going to be another eagerly anticipated first for her—she'd never eaten in a restaurant before.

When they stepped inside, Ivy was further delighted. The place was decorated with a sunny, playful brightness reflected in everything from the yellow walls to the flowery curtains. And if the aromas were any indication, the food would be every bit as good as Mitch had promised.

As for Daisy herself, she was as down-to-earth and friendly as the flower she was named after.

While they were waiting for their meal, Daisy's husband, Everett, popped in to talk to Daisy for a minute, and she brought him over for introductions. It turned out that her husband, who spoke with a slight accent, was another of the men Mitch had traveled from Philadelphia with.

After the couple moved away, Ivy asked Mitch about the accent.

"Everett was born in England," Mitch explained. "He didn't move here until his adolescence."

"Oh, my. I thought Philadelphia was a far piece from here, but he crossed an ocean." It certainly put her two-day trip—that had turned into four—into perspective. "What's that over there?" She indicated the wall that was lined with bookshelves, and fronted by a small desk and cabinet.

"That's Abigail's circulating library."

"Is it normal to have a library inside a restaurant?"

"Not usually, but Everett's sister, Abigail, moved here and decided she wanted to open a library, so Daisy gave her a section of the restaurant to use. It's become a popular spot."

Ivy had enjoyed reading while she was in school, but she hadn't had the opportunity to do much since. Maybe she'd give it another try while she was here.

Then she paused. She was acting as if her staying here had already been decided. And that was far from true.

"You're worried about your Nana Dovie, aren't you?"

Ivy met his gaze, surprised by his ability to read her. "Much as I'd like to see this through, I just don't like the idea of leaving her alone for so long."

"Is it because you believe she needs someone to look after her?"

Ivy grinned. "She'd get a switch after me if she ever heard me say so. But, for all that she's determined to do for herself, she's getting on in years and I worry about her not having someone to help with the chores and just generally keep an eye on her."

"You said the preacher was checking in on her while you were gone. Would he be willing to continue doing so for the next few weeks?"

His questions and tone were logical, but she thought she detected a hint of concern just below the surface. Or maybe that was just wishful thinking. "More than likely, but that's not the same as someone being there all the time."

"I agree it's not ideal, but it is workable. Other than your concern about her well-being, is there another reason you're reluctant to delay your departure?"

She hesitated, not wanting to appear vulnerable or pitiful. But there was no getting around the facts, and after all he'd done for her, he deserved the truth. She absently stabbed a green bean with her fork, dragging it across her plate.

"I don't have the wherewithal to pay for a stay of three weeks."

* * *

Mitch mentally chided himself as he saw the color rise in her cheeks. He should have realized her dilemma. "I'm certain Reggie would let you stay in her guest bedroom," he offered quickly. But his words didn't have the desired effect.

Ivy stiffened. "You shouldn't go speaking for her. She hardly knows me. And besides, it's bad enough I slept in her bed down at the cabin and wore her clothes without being able to thank her. I won't take advantage of her generosity knowing that I already have an unpaid debt she isn't even aware of."

Mitch quickly looked around. He knew she was distracted by other concerns, but a slip of the tongue like that could cost her dearly. Thankfully no one appeared to be paying attention.

"Even if all that wasn't an issue," she said, waving a hand dismissively, "I still don't like the notion of leaving Nana Dovie alone for so long. No, I figure the best thing for me to do is to head back to Nettles Gap in the morning."

He took hope from the fact that she didn't sound happy about it. "You're going to just give up your claim?"

"I can always return here when it's closer to the time for the judge to show up."

Mitch didn't approve of that plan at all, but he didn't stop to analyze why. "Think this through. What if the judge comes early? His schedule isn't always precise. If that should happen, you risk missing him altogether and allowing Carter to present his case without you there."

She rubbed her chin. "I hadn't thought of that. I wouldn't want to stand the judge up."

Seeing she was weakening, he pressed his advantage.

"Exactly. Even though your case is strong, there's no telling how he might rule if you're not here to counter Carter's arguments."

"I suppose, if I decided to stay and plead my case, the preacher could keep a close eye on Nana Dovie for me." Then she sighed. "But none of that matters if I don't figure out how to pay my way."

They were back to that. "If you're absolutely set against staying with Reggie, there are other people here in town who'd provide you with a room. I can ask around."

She speared him with a glare. "I won't go begging, or let you do it for me. I've always been one to pay my way or I do without."

"You do know that pride is a sin, don't you?"

She lifted her chin. "Only false pride."

He hid a smile and let her comment pass. "Fortunately, I think there's another option."

"And that is?"

"You could rent a room in someone's home for much less than what the hotel costs."

Her suspicion didn't appear to abate any. "I told you, I won't live on charity—not yours or anybody else's."

"That's not what I'm suggesting. Eileen Pierce, a young widow, put the word out a month or so back that she'd be willing to take in a boarder so she could have some extra pin money."

Ivy looked at him as if trying to decipher an ulterior motive. "A month ago. And nobody's taken her up on the offer? Is there something wrong with it, or just not much call for rooms around here?"

Mitch chose his words carefully. He wanted to let her know what she'd be walking into without being judgmental of the young widow. "She's not the most popular individual in these parts. Not for any reason that would put you at risk, I assure you. But there are things in her past some folks still hold against her."

Just after Mitch had arrived in Turnabout two years ago, Eileen's husband, who'd embezzled money from the local bank, had committed suicide when it had become obvious his guilt would be discovered. Many in town blamed his downfall on his young wife's extravagant tastes and spending habits.

But Mitch wasn't one to give credence to gossip. Nor was he one to spread it. Though to be fair, the woman's withdrawal from everyone after the tragedy hadn't helped her cause.

To his surprise—and relief—Ivy didn't press for details. Instead she seemed to brush right past the issue. "When it comes down to it," she said matter-of-factly, "most of us have things in our past we wish we could change."

He added a silent amen to that. But there'd been a hint of poignancy in her voice that piqued his curiosity. "Including yourself?" he asked before he could stop himself.

She gave him a that's-off-limits look. Then, instead of answering, she took the conversation back to its original focus. "Anyway, I prefer to form my own opinion about folks."

"Very commendable," he said quickly, embarrassed by his prying. But he was even more curious about what she might be hiding than he had been before. Not that it was any of his business. "If you're agreeable, then," he said, following her lead, "I'll take you round to Mrs. Pierce's place and introduce you. The two of you can take it from there and work out the details."

Her brows went up. "You mean now?"

"Of course. I assumed you wanted to get this settled right away."

He also didn't want her second-guessing her decision to stay.

When she still hesitated, he gave her a challenging look. "I thought you said Mrs. Pierce's reputation didn't bother you."

"It's not that." She rubbed her neck absently. "The thing is, even if she only charges half of what the hotel does, it'll still cost me money I don't have."

Ivy said this with more frustration than embarrassment. She was the practical sort, he'd give her that. And she'd already made it clear she'd never accept a gift of money from him, or even a loan.

But perhaps there was another way he could both help her and keep an eye on her during her stay. "Are you opposed to taking a job while you're here?"

Her eyes lit up and her shoulders straightened. "Not at all. In fact, I'd be mighty grateful to have a chance to earn my way." She leaned forward eagerly. "Are you saying you know of something like that?"

"I certainly do."

It didn't take Ivy but a moment to figure things out. When she did her smile faded and she sat back with a thump. "You're talking about working for you, aren't you?" Irritation colored her tone.

But Mitch was ready for her resistance. He put on his haughtiest expression. "I assure you, if you take this job, you won't get any special treatment just because you know me. I'll expect you to earn every cent I pay you. There's a *real* house to clean and *real* meals to cook, and I have high standards for both." Which was absolutely true.

He'd never before considered hiring anyone, though.

His home was his private retreat, a place where he could insulate himself from the world. Very few individuals— very few friends—had ever stepped across his threshold. And that was just the way he liked it.

Or at least the way he needed it to be if he was to maintain his distance. But this situation called for extreme measures. *And* it was just for a few weeks. Afterward, he could slip back into his solitary routine and things would return to normal.

Although he wasn't so sure how he felt about "normal" anymore since Ivy Feagan had burst into his life and reminded him how intriguing the unconventional could be.

Ivy knew he was waiting for her answer, but she wasn't sure what to make of his offer, which still smacked of a handout. She didn't have a lot of choices, though, not if she wanted to remain in town until the judge arrived. And despite her worries over leaving Nana Dovie alone, she found she really did want to stay.

Besides, as long as she put in an honest day's work, kept it strictly businesslike and didn't accept more pay than was reasonable, she supposed it didn't really matter what his motives were.

Of course, she could—and should—question her own motives in ignoring her better judgment and taking him up on his offer.

"I don't expect any kind of special treatment," she warned.

He held up his hands. "Understood. We can work out the details after you settle the matter of lodging. Shall we head over to Mrs. Pierce's now?"

He'd certainly changed the subject fast enough. Was

he hiding something? Deciding to trust him, she nodded, and in a matter of minutes they were on the sidewalk.

Once they'd settled into a comfortable stroll, Ivy said, "Tell me about this Mrs. Pierce. Not about her past," she added quickly. "Just in general what sort of person she is, so I'll know what to expect."

"I thought you liked to form your own opinions?"

Surely that wasn't a hint of amusement in his tone? "I'm not looking for judgments on her character. I only meant things like is she chatty or quiet, more down-to-earth or highfalutin, does she have a sense of humor— that sort of thing."

"Of course. Let's see, before her husband's death she was quite social, loved to throw and attend parties, wore stylish clothing and surrounded herself with beautiful things. Since her husband's death she's become more reserved and keeps to herself more often than not."

Sort of like him. Had his wife's death affected him in the same way it appeared to have affected Mrs. Pierce?

"As for her stylishness," he continued, "even though her husband has been gone nearly two years now, she still wears black."

"She must have loved him very much." That was the sort of love she hoped to find one day—the forever kind. It was the reason she'd spurned Lester's advances, the start of all her troubles. Still, if she could find that kind of love, the hardships of these past five years would have been worth it.

"I didn't know either of them well" was his only comment. There was something in his tone, though, that made her think perhaps he didn't view it as romantically as she did. Had something in his own marriage affected his views?

"That's it, up ahead," he said, pointing. "The three-story brick one with all the flowers in the yard."

Ivy studied the house with interest. It was an impressively large structure with white columns supporting the front porch. Did Mrs. Pierce live in this huge house alone?

But what really caught her eye was the lovely flower garden. She identified rosebushes, irises, snapdragons, lilies and camellia bushes. And there were others she'd never seen before. Despite what Mitch had said about the widow, Ivy found herself immediately predisposed to like this Mrs. Pierce. A woman who took such pride in her garden had to have a good heart.

Mitch escorted her to the front door without sparing so much as a glance for the flamboyant array of colors, and twisted the ornate brass doorbell.

The chimes echoed musically inside the house, and a moment later, the door opened. Her first impression of Mrs. Pierce was that she was an elegant, slender woman who seemed very poised. She oozed sophistication, from her impeccably arranged dark blond hair to the hem of her black silk skirt.

"Good afternoon, ma'am," Mitch said. "I hope we're not disturbing you."

She gave him a smile that was more polite than warm. "Mr. Parker. To what do I owe the pleasure of this unexpected call?"

"Please allow me to introduce you to Miss Ivy Feagan."

Ivy stepped forward, and the widow studied her with an unreadable expression, then dipped her head regally. "Miss Feagan."

"I'm pleased to make your acquaintance, ma'am.

And to answer your question, I've come to inquire about renting a room from you."

There was a flicker of surprise and something Ivy couldn't quite identify in the widow's expression. "I see." She stepped back. "Please come inside where we can discuss this more comfortably."

Ivy was a little disconcerted by Mrs. Pierce. She'd never before encountered anyone who was so closed off. But she took hope from the fact that the widow hadn't dismissed them.

Once they were inside, Mrs. Pierce ushered them into a parlor that was sparsely but impeccably furnished. As she waved them to a seat, she focused on Ivy. "You're the young woman who rode into town with Mr. Parker yesterday afternoon, aren't you?"

Ivy resisted the urge to shift, instead returning the woman's gaze without blinking. "I am."

"Tell me what you're looking for."

"Of course. It turns out my business here in Turnabout is going to take longer than I'd planned. Unfortunately, I don't have the funds to stay at the hotel for that long."

From the corner of her eye, Ivy noticed something akin to a wince flash across Mitch's face. Had it been indelicate to mention money?

She refocused on Mrs. Pierce. "When Mr. Parker remembered you'd wanted to rent out a room at one time, I figured I'd pay you a visit."

"I see. Since you mentioned finances, I would need to know that you can meet your obligations. And that would mean payment by the week, in advance."

Ivy's heart sank. Would the meager funds she still had cover the first week's payment? Before she could ask what the rate would be, Mitch spoke up again.

"You do understand that Miss Feagan will be expecting to pay significantly less than she would at the hotel or boardinghouse."

"What exactly do you mean by 'significantly less'?"

He named a figure that was about a third of what she was paying at The Rose Palace.

Mrs. Pierce frowned. "That is somewhat less than what I had in mind."

Ivy spoke up before Mitch could speak for her again. "I would be willing to perform some chores around the place to make up the difference."

Mitch frowned. "You'll hardly have time to be a housekeeper here if you're performing the same function for me."

His speaking for her was getting to be annoying.

Mrs. Pierce eyed them both speculatively. "So you'll be working for Mr. Parker while you're in town?"

"I will." Ivy left it at that. "And I'm certain I could manage a few added responsibilities in exchange for my lodging. Assuming you're agreeable."

Mrs. Pierce folded her hands in her lap. "As I said, I was hoping to get a little more for the room. After all, it hardly seems worth the trouble of having a stranger in my home for such a pittance. But perhaps we can work something out along the lines you suggested. If you were to, say, do my laundry once a week, that might be acceptable."

Mitch frowned, but Ivy nodded. "Agreed. I can take care of your wash at the same time I do mine."

Mrs. Pierce inclined her head graciously. "Very well. And may I ask how long you're planning to stay?"

"I'm hoping to wrap up my business in about three weeks, but it might be a little longer." She smiled hopefully. "Does this mean you'll lease me the room at that rate?"

"Before I agree, I have some very specific rules for any boarder staying with me that you need to know about."

"And those are?"

"I guard my privacy very jealously, so you would need to respect the boundaries I set. You would have access to your room, this parlor and the kitchen—not any other area of my home. The rest of the rooms are strictly off-limits unless I specifically invite you inside."

If the woman's tone was any indication, there would be no such invitation forthcoming.

She cast a meaningful glance Mitch's way. "Visitors must be entertained on the front porch, not inside the house, and only during daylight hours."

"That won't be a problem," Ivy responded. "Since I'm a stranger here, I don't expect to have callers. And besides, I'm going to be working as Mr. Parker's cook and housekeeper so I won't be around most of the day."

Mrs. Pierce nodded approval. "You would also be expected to care for your own room and linens, and provide for and cook your own meals. I will be your landlady, not your maid." She lifted her chin. "Those are my terms and they are not negotiable."

Her list was restrictive, but fair. "Those terms are perfectly acceptable."

"Then we have a deal."

Ivy shot a quick, triumphant glance Mitch's way.

"How soon would you like to move in?" Mrs. Pierce asked.

"This afternoon, if possible."

The widow nodded. "That's acceptable. Give me four hours to get things in order and then the room is yours." She stood, sending a clear signal that they were dismissed. "And please have your first week's rent with you when you return."

Ivy nodded and shook hands with the widow, sealing the deal, then made her exit, closely followed by Mitch.

As they stepped onto the sidewalk, he frowned at her. "I think we could have negotiated for a deal that wouldn't have included you becoming her washerwoman."

It was sweet of him to want to champion her, but the widow had dealt fairly with her. "It's a fair arrangement." she responded calmly. "As long as I'm happy with it, I don't see where you have any cause to complain." Then she had another thought. "If you're thinking it'll interfere with my work for you, I give you my word it won't."

He gave a dismissive wave. "That thought never even entered my mind."

She relaxed, encouraged by his show of faith. "Looks like I have four hours to fill until I move," she said, firmly changing the subject. "Which is good, since there are a few things I need to take care of."

"Such as?"

At least his grumpy frown had faded. "I need to send a telegram to Reverend Tomlin about continuing to keep an eye on Nana Dovie while I'm gone. Because if he's unable to do that, none of the rest of this matters."

He nodded. "We'll head to the depot first."

"And after that, I should look in on Jubal again." She grimaced. "I also need to arrange for extended stabling." Another expense she hadn't planned for.

"Don't worry," he said. "Fred's fees are quite reasonable." He tugged on his cuff, cutting her a knowing look. "And I suppose after that you'll want to check in on Rufus."

"He *has* been alone all day and he's not used to being penned up."

He raised a hand. "No need to explain. You probably should get a look at my place while you're there anyway. That way you can see what you're in for."

Ivy had to admit, to herself at least, that she was looking forward to seeing what the inside of his house looked like. Would his walls be covered with his sketches? Would there be pictures of his sisters and his late wife?

Would there be anything at all to give her insights to other parts of his personality?

He'd probably be irritated by her interest in learning more about him, but it was his own fault for being so intriguing. A girl couldn't be blamed for wanting to get to know her own personal knight in shining armor a bit better, could she?

Besides, what could it hurt? She'd be leaving here soon enough and when she did they'd likely never see each other again.

For some reason, that thought dimmed the sunshine of her day just a smidge.

Chapter Eleven

As they approached The Blue Bottle—the building that housed that intriguing sweet shop Ivy had noticed yesterday—a woman and three young boys stepped out onto the sidewalk. Each child had a parchment-wrapped treat in his hand.

As soon as she spotted them, the woman gave Mitch an arch smile and waited for them to draw near. "Mr. Parker, it's so good to see you. I heard you had returned to town early. I trust there's nothing amiss."

The woman was surprisingly tall and big-boned with blond hair and fair skin. She also seemed to have a particular interest in Mitch, which brought a frown to Ivy's face. Did she not already have a husband? Then Ivy mentally chided herself. This was none of her business. Just because Mitch was being kind to her didn't mean she had any sort of claim on him.

Mitch touched the brim of his hat. "Good day to you, Mrs. Swenson. Allow me to introduce my friend Miss Ivy Feagan. Miss Feagan, this is Mrs. Hilda Swenson."

Was it her imagination or was his tone even more reserved than normal?

But the woman was studying her with an oddly assessing look, so Ivy pushed aside her thoughts and flashed a smile. "Pleased to meet you, ma'am. Those are handsome children you have."

The woman relaxed slightly. "Thank you. And I'm pleased to meet you, as well. Are you in town for long?"

Was there an edge to her voice?

"About three weeks or so," Ivy answered.

"Well, I certainly hope you enjoy your stay."

"Thank you. I'm sure I will." Ivy couldn't help but notice how well matched this woman and Mitch would be. With their striking heights and complimentary light and dark good looks, they would command attention wherever they went. She felt absolutely mousy beside this woman.

Mitch placed a hand at her elbow, and it seemed to Ivy there was something sweetly protective and slightly possessive in the gesture.

And it didn't go unnoticed by Mrs. Swenson, whose eyes narrowed slightly.

"If you will excuse us," Mitch said politely, "Miss Feagan and I have business to attend to at the train depot."

"Of course."

As they moved away, Ivy couldn't help but do a bit of probing. "She seems nice. What does her husband do?"

He looked at her as if trying to determine the motive behind the question. "Mr. Swenson passed away about a year and a half ago."

"Oh. It must be difficult for her, especially with three sons to raise." Ivy couldn't blame the woman for hoping that Mitch would step in and fill those shoes.

He gave a noncommittal response and this time she let the subject drop. But that didn't mean she forgot it.

The telegram was dispatched quickly, with just a pang of guilt. And to her surprise, Mitch had been right about the stabling fees. Not only was the cost less than she would have thought, but it turned out Mr. Humphries was willing to wait until she was ready to leave town for her to settle the bill. Ivy wasn't naive enough to believe this was something he offered to every visitor—undoubtedly it was because Mitch was there to vouch for her. But his earlier comment about her pride was still uppermost in her mind. Besides, she wasn't in a position right now to look this particular gift horse in the mouth.

Ten minutes later, they turned onto the block where Mitch's house was located. As soon as Rufus spotted her, he ran to the front gate, wagging his tail furiously and barking a joyful greeting.

Ivy quickened her pace and reached the gate well before Mitch. As soon as the gate was open, the dog jumped up, planting his paws on her skirt, trying to lick her face.

Ivy laughed and ruffled his neck fur. She could always count on Rufus to lavish affection on her. "Hi, boy. I missed you, too. I hope you're behaving yourself for Mr. Parker."

Mitch rolled his eyes. "If you and that mutt are finished greeting one another, I'll show you the inside of the house."

As he opened the red door, she smiled again at the color. Someday, she'd have to get the story of that red door.

She stepped across the threshold and paused to take in the house. Her first impression was that he was indeed a very tidy, orderly man. There didn't seem to be a thing out of place. Nor was there anything of a personal nature visible from the entry.

He waved her into the parlor, and to her disappointment, the rows of books in his bookcase were the only personal touch to be seen. The curtains at the windows were a nondescript brown without ruffle or trim. The mantel over the fireplace was as empty as the walls were blank. There were no pictures, trinkets or memorabilia in sight.

Why didn't he at least display his sketches?

She itched to add some clutter and color to the place, to move a few books off the shelf and onto a table, set out a vase or two of wildflowers, replace his curtains with a less bland set.

If the rest of his house was like this, the only housekeeping she'd be doing would be a daily sweep of the floors.

She glanced at him. "How long have you lived here?"

"Nearly two years."

How could he *not* have put his own stamp on the place in all that time? She knew, deep down, this man had a flamboyant expressive streak—he couldn't draw those wonderful sketches if he didn't. So why did he work so hard to keep it bottled up inside?

"Do you have many visitors?"

"No."

She was surprised by his response. He seemed to have so many friends here. Everywhere they went he was greeted with respect.

But his expression told her not to press. "What exactly will my duties be?"

"Sweeping, dusting, mopping—that sort of thing."

"That should take me all of an hour." She couldn't accept a full day's pay for so little work.

"Don't forget the cooking. Come on, I'll show you the rest of the house."

She stepped inside the room across the hall and found two walls lined with bookcases, a solid-looking desk and a pair of comfortable chairs situated in front of a fireplace.

"Oh, I'd expected this to be a dining room."

He shrugged. "I didn't need a dining room. I *did* need a study." He waved her back into the hallway. "Shall we move on to the kitchen?"

She followed him down the hall and found herself in another very stark, almost sterile room. The kitchen, of all rooms, should be warm and inviting. Back home, it was where she and Nana Dovie spent the most time together; it was where they'd had countless talks as she'd grown up and it was where Nana Dovie had comforted her when that awfulness with Lester had happened five years ago.

Mitch, however, seemed perfectly happy with it the way it was. "The pots and dishes are stored over there," he said, indicating a cupboard across the room. Then he moved to a door set in the wall to their left. When he opened it, she saw a well-organized pantry with shelves of perfectly arranged foodstuffs.

"I think you'll find it's well stocked for someone with my simple tastes. But I'll set you up on my line of credit at the mercantile and butcher shop so you can shop for whatever you need."

She tried to match his businesslike tone. "Tell me what kind of food you like."

"Other than not caring for liver or beets, I'm easy to please."

Clearly she'd have to draw her inspiration from elsewhere. She moved to the back door. "How big is your kitchen garden?"

"I don't have one."

Ivy turned to stare at him in disbelief. "No fresh herbs or vegetables?"

He shrugged. "I get what I need from the mercantile or local farmers."

"But *every* home should have a garden. If for nothing else than the satisfaction of eating something you've grown yourself."

He seemed to find that amusing. "I haven't seen the need."

Perhaps he just needed someone to show him the way. "I know it's late to be planting, but do you mind if I put a garden in for you?" The thought of actually doing something meaningful for him lifted her spirits tremendously. Not only would she be doing work she loved, it would also help her feel as if she were actually earning her pay.

But he raised a brow. "It hardly seems worth the effort since you won't be here to reap the benefits."

He had a very flawed view of what a garden could be. "Planting things and watching them grow is *always* worth the effort."

That drew a smile from him. "Then by all means, plant." He stepped past her to open the back door. "My entire yard is at your disposal."

She stepped out onto the back porch, working out the logistics in her mind. "Let's see, it's not too late to plant a few herbs and maybe some tomatoes, peppers and beans. They'll need lots of watering and loving attention at this late stage, but if we got some hearty cuttings we could probably coax some produce from them." She eyed him. "But I would expect you to keep it going after I'm gone."

He raised his hands palms up. "I make no promises."

"If it's a matter of not knowing how to care for a garden, I could teach you."

In fact, sharing something she loved so much with him would be rather nice.

But when a shadow of some strong emotion crossed his face, Ivy realized she'd gone too far.

Mitch did his best not to let her see how his gut twisted at her simple offer. She couldn't know that he'd been a farmer at the time his world had exploded around him. He forced a smile. "Scratching in the dirt is something I'm not particularly interested in."

From the expression on her face, he could tell some harshness had spilled into his tone despite his efforts. He tried to cover with a more conciliatory tone. "But I'm not averse to you getting your hands as dirty as you like."

There'd been a time when he'd taken pride in tilling the soil and reaping the crops he'd grown himself for the family table. He could still see Gretchen smiling in triumph when she'd harvested her first ear of corn from the land they'd built their home on.

"Oh, you have a swing!"

The utter delight in Ivy's voice shook him out of his sober thoughts. She was staring at the oak tree that shaded one end of his backyard. Whoever had owned this place before him had attached both ends of a long chain to one of the sturdy branches and used a notched board for the seat.

Other than noting it was there, he'd paid very little attention to it in the time he'd been here.

She turned back to him with a teasing grin. "It appears there's a bit of playfulness in you after all."

"I hate to disappoint you, but that swing was already there when I moved in." He regretted the words as soon as he saw the disappointment flash across her face.

But she rallied quickly. "It's yours now, though. And it looks strong enough to support even you."

He was relieved to hear her teasing tone. Apparently she wasn't holding his lack of enthusiasm against him. "I wouldn't know."

She fisted a hand on her hip. "You mean to tell me that in the two years you've lived here you've never once even *sat* in that swing?"

"Guilty."

"Well, I call that downright wasteful."

He smiled at her nonsensical notion and waved a hand toward the swing. "Feel free to make use of it while you're here."

She gave him a challenging grin. "Well, you can be all stuffy and grumpy, but I like a bit of play in my life. And there's no time like the present." With a saucy smile she started across the lawn, a defiant spring in her step.

He leaned against a porch support, crossing his arms and enjoying the view.

Ivy sat on the board and set the swing in motion, soaring high and laughing aloud at the pure joy of it. She pumped her legs and threw her head back with as much enthusiasm and abandon as would any of his students during recess. Rufus followed the movements of the swing, barking encouragement and running to and fro.

As Mitch watched her, it occurred to him that perhaps her presence in his heretofore serene household was going to change his life more than he'd considered.

He watched her with her unruly braid flying out behind her and her unapologetic laughter ringing around him, and couldn't find it in himself to be sorry.

He told himself if he had any modicum of sense remaining he'd head inside. But for some reason he never followed through on the thought. It was fifteen minutes later before Ivy abandoned the swing, and even then, she did so reluctantly.

When she finally rejoined him on the porch after a quick game of fetch with Rufus, she was grinning. "That was fun. You ought to try it sometime."

He decided not to grace that comment with a response. "Have you selected a patch of ground for your garden yet?"

She surveyed his backyard. "I think that spot right there by that clump of clover flowers will work for a small herb garden. The vegetables can go next to your east fence."

He studied the two spots she'd indicated and nodded. "You have a good eye."

"I told you, I have a knack for gardening. Nana Dovie says that God gives each of us at least one thing we're good at. He gave you the ability to draw those wonderful pictures. And to open your students' minds to learning new things. I guess gardening is what He gave me."

She continued to surprise him with her homespun insights.

"Any idea where I could get some cuttings?" she asked. "It's late to be trying to plant from seeds."

He thought about that for a moment. "Reggie has a nice garden out behind her house. And her place is near Mrs. Pierce's. Perhaps after we get your things moved in, we can stop by and speak to her."

He looked at his pocket watch. "Speaking of which,

we have another two hours before Mrs. Pierce will be ready for you. Is there anything in particular you'd like to do?"

She didn't hesitate. "I can start working the ground for the garden. I've actually missed mine these past few days."

"Then by all means, till away."

"Do you have any gardening tools?"

"There were some left by the previous owner. They'd be in the toolshed. Come on, let's see what we can find."

He led her to a small outbuilding in his backyard. When he opened the door, he paused a moment to let his eyes adjust to the dim interior. He ducked his head to step inside the small room, and she followed him without hesitation.

He heard her chuckle. "Even your toolshed is organized."

She said that as if it were a bad thing. He had actually spent a great deal of time organizing this place when he'd first moved in and was quite proud of the result. There were tools of all sorts arranged on shelves or hanging from pegs. The center of the room held a couple of sawhorses, three small kegs—one with chains, one with nails and one with wooden stakes—and a lawn mower.

"What's that?" she asked, pointing.

"That's a lawn mower."

"A lawn mower?" Her nose wrinkled in question.

"I push it across the yard and it cuts the grass."

Her expression cleared. "Well, now, ain't that something. It sounds a mite easier than using a scythe."

"It is." He crossed to the wall to his left. "Here's a spade, a garden fork and a trowel." He handed them to her. "I'll grab the hoe and shovel. Is there anything else you see here that you think you'll need?"

"I'll need a bucket for watering, but otherwise I think that's it."

He waved her toward the exit. "There's a bucket on the back porch you can use. Now, let's break some ground."

"Does that mean you're going to help me?" she asked with a smile.

"I figured I'd help get the ground ready. Then you're on your own."

They started with the patch of ground she'd earmarked for the herb garden and worked side by side, digging up the sod and turning the soil until they had what looked like a proper planting bed.

Ivy sat back and admired their handiwork. Then she gave him an approving look. "I do believe you *have* done this before."

He wiped his forehead with the back of his hand. "I never said I hadn't. Just that I wasn't particularly fond of it." He grabbed the shovel and hoe and moved toward the toolshed, wishing he could push the memories away as easily.

Then he paused, struck by a startling thought. It was only now, when they were done, that the memories of his other life, the one he'd shared with Gretchen, had intruded. Up until then he'd actually been enjoying working side by side with Ivy.

He wasn't sure whether that was a good thing or not. It was definitely unsettling. And he wasn't ready to face what that might mean just yet. "I think we've done enough for today," he told Ivy. "Time to clean up and get your things moved from the hotel."

Chapter Twelve

Ivy slowly rose and trailed behind him with the hand tools, wondering at his change of mood. What was it about gardening that put that stiffness in his demeanor? No, not stiffness exactly. More like a deep sadness.

There was obviously something in his past eating at him, shadowing his happiness in the here and now. Such a kind, generous man didn't deserve to be robbed of joy that way. She ached to ask him about it, so she could help him get past whatever it was. But she didn't have that right. Not yet, anyway.

Something inside her stirred. She might only be here for three more weeks, but she planned to do everything she could in that time to discover his secret pain and help him through it.

Whether he wanted her to or not.

She owed him that much and so much more.

After they stowed the tools back in the shed, they made their way to the porch, where they poured water into a chipped basin and washed their hands and faces.

When they were done, Mitch handed her a cloth to

dry her face and took a second one for himself. "I'll help you move your things."

"Thank you, but don't feel obliged. I can manage on my own."

"Obligation has nothing to do with this," he said matter-of-factly. "I'm merely one friend helping another."

So he thought of them as friends now. That lightened her mood. She hadn't had many friends since Lester had made everyone believe the worst of her. "Then I accept your offer."

"Good. Before we head out, though, perhaps we should find something to eat. Mrs. Pierce did say you were responsible for your own meals."

Ivy knew if they went back to Daisy's he'd insist on paying again and she wasn't really comfortable with getting deeper in his debt. "Why don't I fix us up something from your pantry?"

"I hadn't intended for you to start working for me today."

"It'll be a practice run of sorts. I can get used to your stove and figure out what supplies I'll need." She gave a little smirk. "Besides, it'll just be one friend cooking for another."

His lips twitched. "Very well. I'll stoke the stove while you gather the ingredients."

Ivy stepped over to the pantry and studied the contents. Without access to perishables she'd have to get creative. And she'd definitely need to do some shopping before she fixed breakfast in the morning.

There were several jars of various vegetable preserves—had he purchased these or had friends such as Reggie and Daisy given them to him? She studied the jars and identified several kinds of beans, carrots, squash and pickled tomatoes and cucumbers. There were a few she couldn't identify without further scrutiny and she decided to ignore them for now.

On another shelf, she found sweet ingredients such as honey, jams, preserves and syrups. So he possessed a sweet tooth—good. It gave her hope that he was still open to a bit of frivolity in his life.

Then she spotted the cornmeal. Did he have molasses? Yes, there it was. She turned to him. "Do you like corn bread?"

He nodded without looking up from the stove.

"Nana Dovie has a recipe she uses for when the hens aren't laying. It looks like you have everything I need if you want me to fix up a batch."

Mitch straightened. "As long as you're eating with me, I'm game to give it a try."

She grinned. "You just want to make sure I won't feed you something I wouldn't eat myself."

"Something like that."

His tone was dry, but she saw that half smile tease his lips again.

"Fair enough." Ivy began pulling ingredients from the pantry. He crossed the room and took the sack of cornmeal and the jar of molasses from her and carried them to the table. When she had everything else she needed for the corn bread, she started looking for a mixing bowl.

He moved to help, but she stopped him with a raised hand. "You take a seat and leave me to figure things out. Like I said, consider this a dry run." She looked around. "I don't suppose you own an apron?"

He shook his head. "Sorry."

"Never mind. I can do without."

Ivy went to work. Mitch stayed in the kitchen with her, watching while she worked. He said it was so he'd be on hand if she had questions, but she got the strangest feeling he had other motives, as well.

Not that she'd let herself think on what those motives might be. That would involve a bit of wishful thinking. And a woman who was leaving town in three weeks couldn't afford to do such a thing.

Mitch watched as Ivy busied herself in his kitchen. Her movements were confident and sure, and in very little time she had the pan of corn bread in the oven.

"Now, let's see what we can fix to go with that." She moved back to the pantry, still talking to herself as she considered and discarded several options.

It was fascinating to listen to her one-sided conversation, so full of whimsy and humor. Did she have any idea how revealing of her unique outlook on life it was?

She cast a glance over her shoulder. "You must like bland food—I don't see much in the way of herbs or seasonings."

"As I said, I'm a man of simple tastes."

"Simple doesn't have to be tasteless." She turned back to his pantry and finally pulled out two jars. "Field peas and pickled tomatoes—I might be able to do something with these."

It was an unusual combination but he didn't question her. To his surprise, she poured the beans into a pot, then poured about half the jar of pickled tomatoes into the same pot, adding a bit of molasses to go with it.

Well, he'd said he was game to try anything she would eat herself. He supposed she was taking him at his word.

And to his surprise, the unusual mix of sweet and tangy turned out to be quite satisfying when taken as a whole.

Much like the woman herself.

Once the meal was over, Mitch insisted on helping her clean up.

"That's my job," she insisted.

But he was having none of that. "Not until Monday. Now, why don't you scrape these plates into that bowl on the back porch for your dog while I fill the basin with water."

Without giving her a chance to argue further, he turned and headed for the counter.

He allowed himself a small smile at the sound of her grumbling about stubborn, bossy know-it-alls, but there were no further arguments. She washed and he dried, and in no time they had the kitchen set back to rights.

As he rolled down his sleeves, he had another thought and went to the pantry. Quickly scanning the contents, he pulled out a jar of fig preserves and a tin of crackers, and held them out to Ivy. "Take these, please."

She took them with a puzzled frown. "What do you want me to do with them?"

"Since you haven't had time to do any shopping yet, you'll need something for breakfast in the morning."

She held them out to him. "That's very kind, but—"

He raised his hands palms out. "You'll be doing me a favor—Mrs. Peavy gave me the preserves, but I'm not overly fond of figs."

And without waiting for her response, he turned and moved to the door.

Why did she have to be so all-fired stubborn about accepting his help? Her constant questioning of his offers was making him have to think about the reasons he was doing this.

And *that* was making him decidedly uncomfortable.

* * *

Ivy walked beside Mitch as they headed for the hotel and tried to decide whether to be angry with his I-know-best attitude or not. One part of her wanted to just relax and enjoy the flattering attention. But the other part of her, the one that knew she would be leaving Turnabout soon, warned her not to grow accustomed to such gallantry.

She left Mitch in the hotel lobby while she went up to her room to pack her things. It didn't take long, but when she came back down she discovered Mitch had already settled her bill. And that was taking matters too far.

"Mr. Parker, I thought I made it clear to you that I didn't want to accept any charity."

"This is just a loan. I intend to hold the amount out of your first week's pay."

"Even so, you should have discussed this with me first. You can't keep going around making all these decisions on my behalf, no matter how kindly it's meant."

He nodded solemnly. "I'll keep that in mind. Do you have the money to pay Mrs. Pierce?"

Was this how he discussed matters with her? Thankfully she could answer yes to his question, even though paying Mrs. Pierce would take just about all she had left.

He nodded and reached for her bags, but she didn't relinquish them. "Thank you, but I can manage."

"I didn't say you couldn't." He gave her a don't-argue-with-me look as he plucked the saddlebag from her shoulder. "Nevertheless, I insist."

She rolled her eyes at him but surrendered the items.

"You are the most stubbornly polite man I ever did meet."

He slung the saddlebag over his shoulder and took firmer hold of the handle of her carpetbag. "Then you either haven't met many men, or they were the wrong kind of men." And with a wave of his hand, he indicated she was to precede him out of the hotel.

When they reached Mrs. Pierce's home, Ivy paused on the front porch. "I can take my bags now."

Mitch stepped up to ring the doorbell. "I've carried them this far—I can take them up the stairs for you."

"But Mrs. Pierce has asked me not to bring guests inside her home."

The door opened just then and Mitch turned to the woman in question. "I'm certain Mrs. Pierce won't mind if I come inside just long enough to deliver these things to your room. Would you, ma'am?"

Mrs. Pierce stepped aside for them to enter. "I suppose that will be acceptable," she said with a decided lack of enthusiasm.

The widow moved to the staircase, then paused. "As I said earlier, I require a week's payment, in advance."

Ivy reddened at this pointed reminder. She should have offered that up immediately. She quickly loosened the strings on her purse and carefully counted out the amount they had agreed on. Looking at her woefully depleted coin purse, she wondered once again if she was making the right choice in staying here.

Mrs. Pierce accepted the money with a regal nod, then started up the stairs. "If you'll follow me, I'll show you to your room."

As Ivy climbed, she noted the elaborately carved banisters and beautiful stained-glass window on the landing. The widow certainly had a beautiful home.

Topping the stairs, Ivy counted seven doors facing the U-shaped landing. Like those on the first floor, they were all closed. Was Mrs. Pierce hiding something? Or just keeping her new tenant out?

Mrs. Pierce led them to the door at the far end of the landing. "This will be your room. I assume it will meet your needs."

Ivy stepped inside and took everything in at a glance. The curtains on the windows were a pretty shade of green. The room was a little smaller than the one at the hotel and the furnishings were obviously odds and ends, but it was nice nevertheless. "I'm sure I'll be quite comfortable here."

Mitch set the luggage down.

Before he straightened fully, Mrs. Pierce gave him a stern look. "I believe your delivery duties are complete."

Mitch sketched a short bow. "Of course." He turned to Ivy. "I'll wait for you outside." Then he unhurriedly made his exit.

The widow turned back to Ivy. "Since you've agreed to do my wash, allow me to show you where the laundry equipment is stored."

Ivy nodded and followed her back downstairs. Laundry was actually her least favorite chore. But it was a task she had to do for herself anyway so doing it for her landlady wouldn't be much extra work.

Later, as she and Mitch walked toward the Barrs' home, Ivy reflected on how fast things were changing. She'd only met Mitch four and a half days ago, but now it felt as if he was a dear friend. She'd planned on being away from Nettles Gap for a week, and now it looked like it would be a month. In just the past few hours, she'd attended a stranger's funeral, confronted a rival for her inheritance, taken a room and a job, found a new plot of ground to cultivate and made several new friends.

"You're quiet. Is something wrong?"

She gave him a reassuring smile. "I was just counting my blessings."

"And what might these blessings be?"

"Well, you, for one."

He frowned, seemingly uncomfortable with her statement, and she felt compelled to explain.

"I could have fallen out there in the woods without help close by. Or I could have arrived in town and had to confront Mr. Mosley on my own. Instead the Good Lord sent someone—you—to help me through both situations."

Mitch shook his head. "You seem to forget, I'm the one who caused your accident in the first place. And it was Adam who did most of the talking with Carter, not me."

She tossed her head. "I stand by what I said." The man obviously didn't know how to accept a compliment. Maybe he just hadn't received enough of them. Well, she could certainly do her part to fix that.

Mitch opened the gate to the Barrs' front walk without responding.

Reggie was in her front yard, cutting blossoms from her rose bushes. After they exchanged greetings, she gave Ivy a sympathetic smile. "Adam told me things didn't go as smoothly as you'd hoped. I'm sorry for the trouble this will cause you, but I'm glad it gives you a reason to stay awhile." Then she tilted her head slightly in question. "You *are* staying, aren't you?"

Ivy nodded and smiled at Mitch. "I am. Thanks to Mr. Parker."

Reggie raised a brow in Mitch's direction. "Oh?"

"Yes, indeed." Ivy enjoyed Mitch's attempt to look bored with her bragging on him. "I was worried about making my money stretch to cover an extended stay. But Mr. Parker introduced me to Mrs. Pierce, who had a room to let, and then he offered me a housekeeping job so I'll have a way to earn some money while I'm here."

Reggie gave Mitch an assessing look. "Well, now, wasn't that nice of Mr. Parker?"

"It was much more than nice—it was providential. I've been thanking the Good Lord for putting him in my path ever since we met." Mitch gave her a stern look, and Ivy decided to relent and stop teasing him. "Which brings me to why we've intruded on your afternoon."

"I assure you it's no intrusion. You're welcome to drop by anytime—with or without Mitch." Reggie started tugging at her gardening gloves. "Is there something I can do to help you get settled in?"

"Maybe. It turns out Mr. Parker doesn't have a garden, which I view as a tragedy. So I've offered to put one in while I'm here. And I'm looking for some cuttings that will work for a late planting."

"Say no more. I can fix you right up." Reggie linked arms with her. "Come on out to my garden—I'm sure we can find what you need." She sent Mitch an airy wave. "You'll find Adam in the parlor."

Mitch was still mulling over what Ivy had said as he went to find Adam. She considered their meeting providential? He'd have thought she would've seen it as the disaster that had kept her from arriving in time to talk to Drum.

"I thought I heard your voice," Adam said, finding him standing in the hallway, lost in thought.

Hiding his embarrassment at having been caught

woolgathering, Mitch pulled his thoughts back to the present. He quickly explained why he was there and the two men moved to the back porch.

"So putting in a garden was Miss Feagan's idea?" Adam kept his eyes focused on the two women as they sat.

"It certainly wasn't mine," Mitch said dryly. "Apparently Ivy's not only a skilled gardener, but she loves it, as well." He suppressed a smile. "And because I don't share her belief that every household with a yard should also contain a garden, she thinks me little better than a heathen."

Adam was grinning now. "And she feels it's her duty to convert you?"

Mitch nodded. "With a fervent, missionary zeal." Then he sobered. "So what about Carter? He seemed dead set on fighting her claim. Is there anything she should be worried about?"

Reggie apparently said something amusing because Ivy let out a boisterous laugh, which he found enjoyably distracting. It appeared the two women were becoming fast friends.

Adam rubbed his jaw. "As long as her proof of identity is solid, there's really not anything Carter can do to negate her claim."

Mitch nodded. But he still had a nagging worry that they shouldn't rest easy just yet. Even if Ivy's case was strong, Carter could still make things very unpleasant for her. He intended to be at her side to support her, come what may.

Jack stepped out onto the porch and asked Adam to help him with a tangled string on his yo-yo. Looking at them with their heads bent over the task, Mitch felt a sharp pang of jealousy.

He turned back toward the garden, but this time he didn't see Ivy and Reggie there. He saw Gretchen, smiling as she went about her work, quietly joyful with the knowledge of the new life she carried inside her. A new life that never had a chance to flourish. It took him a long moment to pull himself together, but when Jack wanted to show him a trick with the now untangled yo-yo, he was able to respond with appropriate interest.

Twenty minutes later, Ivy and Reggie strolled back to the porch, still chattering away. Mitch smiled—chattering away seemed to be Ivy's natural state.

When the women drew close, Mitch stood. "Did you two work it all out?"

Ivy nodded. "Reggie has a marvelous garden and she's generously sharing it with us."

Mitch wasn't quite certain how he felt about that familiar use of "us." Especially with those thoughts of Gretchen and his unborn child still lingering in his mind.

"Fiddlesticks," Reggie said. "The garden needed thinning anyway and I was happy to do it. Mitch, you're lucky to have Ivy putting in your garden for you. She really understands plants—gave me a few tips for how to improve my own harvest."

Ivy's cheeks turned pink, and she smiled happily. "You have a fine garden—I just pointed out one or two things that have worked for me." Then she tucked a stray tendril of hair behind her ear. "When will it be most convenient for me to come by and collect the cuttings?"

"Since tomorrow is Sunday," Reggie answered, "how does Monday morning sound?"

"Perfect." Ivy nodded in satisfaction. "I can stop by here on my way to Mi— Mr. Parker's place Monday morning."

Mitch hoped his involuntary wince went unnoticed. Had anyone else caught her stumble over his name?

"Nonsense." Reggie waved away her offer. "Mrs. Peavy and I can harvest the cuttings and shoots Monday morning and load them up in Jack's wagon. Then Jack and Ira can pull the wagon over to Mitch's place." She turned to her son. "Can't you, Jack?"

"Yes, ma'am. My wagon can hold a whole lot."

"Why, thank you, Jack," Ivy said. "I'd be mighty beholden to you."

Then Reggie raised a finger. "That reminds me. You must join our gathering for lunch tomorrow."

Ivy's brow wrinkled. "Gathering?"

Reggie waved the question away. "Mitch can explain, but I won't accept no for an answer." She turned to Mitch. "Don't forget, it's now June so we'll be meeting at Eve and Chance's place."

"I remember."

"Of course you do—you're always so on top of things." She climbed the porch steps. "If you'll excuse me, I need to check on Patricia."

Mitch and Ivy took their leave. They were barely back on the sidewalk when Ivy turned to Mitch. "What is this mysterious gathering that Reggie insisted I should attend?"

"Remember I told you I traveled here from Philadelphia with three other men, and that it was Reggie's grandfather who introduced us to each other before we set out?"

She nodded.

Mitch chose his next words carefully, not wanting to reveal any secrets that weren't his to tell—Reggie's grandfather had sent them to Turnabout with a very specific purpose in mind, one his granddaughter had been furious to learn about.

"When we arrived here, Reggie opened her home to us and we got in the habit of taking our meals together." He suppressed a grin as he remembered what a little tyrant Reggie had been as she insisted they do so to put a good face on a difficult situation.

"Once we all settled into our new lives here," he continued, "it gradually became a once-a-week event— Sunday lunch. It's a tradition that's survived to this day—as members of the group marry and have children, or other relatives come to town, the circle has expanded, but that hasn't stopped us."

"What a lovely tradition. But if it's for the four of you and your families, perhaps I shouldn't—"

He didn't let her finish. "You heard Reggie. She would skin me alive if I showed up without you. And don't worry, the size of the group expands and contracts over time and it seems like every few weeks we seat a different number. Last Sunday we had ten adults, if you count Everett's sister, Abigail, and four children. So one more will scarcely be noticed."

"And so this Eve, who has the unlucky chore of cooking for your large gathering, is she the wife of the fourth member of your group?"

"That's right—Chance Dawson. Eve runs that candy store you eyed when you first got to town. So you'll finally get to sample her wares."

"She must be quite a cook."

"Reggie, Daisy and Eve take turns hosting, swapping up every month. This month is Eve's turn. But they all contribute something to the meal."

"Don't you ever take a turn to host?"

"As a bachelor, I'm exempt. Besides, my dining room

isn't big enough." He was tempted to explain further, but held his tongue.

They arrived at Mrs. Pierce's, and Mitch opened the front gate. She stepped forward, but rather than following, he gave her a short bow. "It's best I leave you here."

She cast a quick glance toward the house and nodded. "Mrs. Pierce's rules. Thank you again for all you've done to help me—and not just today."

She looked suddenly small and alone, and he felt as if he were abandoning her. "You're quite welcome. I'll come by in the morning to escort you to church."

She tilted her head in question. "Shouldn't I come by to fix your breakfast?"

"Sunday is your day off," he said firmly. "And I'm perfectly capable of preparing my own meals—just as I've done every day for the past two years."

She grinned. "A man of simple tastes—I remember. Well, then." She paused, as if drawing the moment out. "I suppose I'll see you in the morning."

Mitch waited until she'd stepped inside the house, then turned and started back toward home. It was getting on toward dusk and Tim would be out lighting the streetlamps in another few minutes.

It had been a very interesting day—several days, he should say. There'd been none of the peaceful solitude he'd planned to enjoy this week. And it looked like that would hold true for the next three weeks, as well.

But strangely, he didn't feel the least bit cheated.

It was undoubtedly the stimulation of having something new and unexpected to focus on.

And Ivy was definitely unexpected.

She was chatty, stubborn and indifferent when it came to propriety. She was also warm, generous and altogether intriguing at the same time. He refused to feel guilty for thinking so—after all, he was merely acknowledging the facts.

When Mitch reached his front gate, Rufus ran to greet him. The dog, no respecter of propriety either, scampered enthusiastically around him, all but tripping him up, until he gave in and stooped down to scratch the animal's neck. "Ivy spoils you. Don't expect to get the same level of attention from me." When Mitch stood, the dog raced off, then returned carrying a stick in his mouth. With a reluctant smile, Mitch accepted the offering and gave the stick a toss that sailed it across the yard.

Rufus quickly returned it to him and they repeated the game three more times until Rufus spied a squirrel and gave chase.

As Mitch entered his house, he thought again about just how much his life had been disrupted. Even when Ivy wasn't here, her dog made sure his time was no longer wholly his own.

What surprised him, though, was how little it bothered him.

Not wanting to impose on Mrs. Pierce, Ivy had gone to her room almost immediately.

Opening her window to let in some air, she spotted Mrs. Pierce in her very lush vegetable garden, watering the rows.

Her heart went out to the woman. Though she was very serene and elegant on the surface, Ivy sensed a loneliness in her.

Would she welcome an overture of friendship from her tenant?

She began unpacking her few possessions and her thoughts naturally turned to Mitch. She found it strange that he had never taken on his share of the Sunday hosting duties. His comment about the size of his dining room seemed merely an excuse. But if he didn't want to host his friends, she supposed it was none of her business.

But why did he hold himself so aloof from everyone?

His friends were nice people. *Very* nice people. And the fact that they had accepted her so quickly simply because she was his friend spoke volumes for the regard they held him in.

That feeling of being accepted was a gift—one she no longer took for granted.

Lord Jesus, I'm starting to believe You had more blessings in store for me than I ever imagined when You sent Mitch to me out in them woods. I know this won't last forever, but I promise to cherish every minute of it. And when it's time for me to return to Nettles Gap, I will lean on You to give me the strength not to mourn its loss.

But while she was here, she aimed to do what she could to make Mitch see how blessed he was.

Whether he welcomed her attempts or not.

Chapter Thirteen

The next morning, Mitch stopped by Mrs. Pierce's home to escort Ivy to church. The widow walked with them at Ivy's invitation, but when Ivy and Mitch paused to speak to Adam and Reggie, she took her leave and entered the church building alone.

After the greetings were exchanged, Reggie shifted Patricia to her other hip. "Ivy, did Mitch explain about our gathering?"

"He did, and I feel honored to be included, so long as you're certain the hostess is okay with an extra guest."

"Oh, don't worry about that—Eve won't mind." Then she glanced past Ivy. "Oh, look, there they are now."

Reggie waved the new arrivals over and Ivy was quickly introduced to Eve and Chance and their boy, Leo.

Eve Dawson was a petite woman with an infectious smile. "So you're the young lady who rode into town with Mitch and set everyone's tongues to wagging."

"Guilty. And you're the lady who runs the sweet shop."

Eve smiled. "Guilty. You'll have to stop by to sample some of my candies."

Mitch touched Ivy's elbow, as if to lend her added support. "Miss Feagan will be joining us for lunch today."

"Wonderful! It'll give us a chance to get better acquainted." Eve gave Ivy a grin. "Not only that, but it means I won't be the newest arrival at the table any longer."

"You lost that standing six months ago when Daisy's Wyatt was born," Eve's husband said. Chance Dawson was a boyishly handsome man with a charming smile and a teasing tilt to his lips. But it was obvious he only had eyes for his wife.

Eve tapped his arm with a mock pout. "*Must* you be so literal?"

Ivy was enjoying the banter and easy camaraderie the group shared, but her smile faltered when she spotted Carter Mosley from the corner of her eye. The man visibly stiffened when he saw her. Averting his eyes, he walked into the church building without a backward glance.

She had grown used to such snubs at home, but somehow, here, it stung much more.

The church bells pealed and the folks still milling about moved toward the entrance.

Once inside, Ivy spotted Mrs. Pierce sitting by herself. Impulsively, she headed directly for that pew and took the seat next to the widow, and Mitch slid in next to her.

Mrs. Pierce turned, and surprise flashed in her eyes. Then her demeanor closed off again and she gave Ivy a cool nod before facing forward again.

When the service started, Ivy discovered Reverend

Harper was quite different from Reverend Tomlin—he was a bit older and lacked some of Reverend Tomlin's stern seriousness. But he seemed equally sincere and concerned for his flock, and she found herself enjoying the service a great deal.

After the service, Mitch introduced her to Reverend Harper as they exited. The man welcomed her with a warm smile and they chatted for a moment about Ivy's plans and how she was enjoying her stay.

Before Ivy could turn back to Mitch, Mrs. Swenson swooped in on him, her three children following like a covey of quail.

"Mr. Parker, how nice to see you on this fine Sunday morning."

Mitch touched the brim of his hat. "Mrs. Swenson."

"Isn't it an absolutely gorgeous day?"

"It is." Mitch glanced back at Ivy, as if wanting her to step forward so they could leave, but Mrs. Swenson wasn't giving way.

"I baked an apple pie this morning," the woman continued. "I wondered if you'd like to join me and my sons for lunch."

"Thank you, but I already have plans." He moved back a step and firmly tucked Ivy's hand on his arm. It was all she could do not to preen.

The imposing woman eyed Ivy frostily. "Miss Feagan, how nice to see you again."

Ivy nodded with a smile. "Mrs. Swenson, what a lovely hat."

The woman eyed the familiar way Mitch held Ivy's arm as she spoke. "Why, thank you, I made it myself. How long did you say you were going to be in town?"

"About three weeks."

Mitch sketched a short bow. "If you'll excuse us, we should be on our way."

Mrs. Swenson dipped her head regally. "Of course. Perhaps you can join us some other time." She turned toward her children. "Come along, boys." Did Mitch have any idea how special he'd made her feel when he took her arm?

More importantly, what would he think if he *did* know?

Mitch breathed a sigh of relief as the woman walked away. He turned to find Ivy studying him with a speculative gleam in her eye. Ignoring her unspoken question, he asked, "Ready to head to Eve and Chance's place?"

"I need to make a quick stop at Mrs. Pierce's."

"Forget something?"

"I just need to fetch my contribution to the gathering."

"Contribution? Did you cook something?"

"No. I didn't have the proper ingredients to make anything. But I didn't want to go empty-handed, so I gave Mrs. Pierce a few coins this morning for the privilege of plundering her flower garden. I thought flowers might at least brighten the table."

"That's very thoughtful of you." And it was also incredibly generous. He knew she didn't have many coins to spare.

When they reached the Pierce home, the widow was nowhere in sight. Ivy picked up garden shears, gloves and a large basket that had been left at the ready on the front porch. She held the basket out to Mitch. "Mrs. Pierce said I could borrow this to carry the flowers in. Do you mind?"

He accepted the large wicker receptacle and then

watched her pull on the gloves while she studied the bounty of flowers with a judicious eye. "I promised I'd only thin the blooms and not strip any one section," she said without taking her gaze from the garden.

With a decisive nod, Ivy stepped forward and went about harvesting select blossoms and greenery. Mitch acted as her assistant, placing the cuttings carefully into the basket. It amused him to listen to her hold a running conversation, talking both to herself and to the flowers. Did she even realize she was doing it?

When she finally stepped back, the basket was full, yet the garden looked nearly as colorful as ever.

"There, I think that will do." She set the shears and gloves back on the porch, then smiled at him as she held out her hand. "I can take that now if you like."

But Mitch shook his head. "I've got it. Are you ready?"

With a nod, she preceded him through the gate.

As they stepped onto the sidewalk, Mitch spotted the Barr household a couple of blocks ahead of them. Both Adam and Ira carried large hampers, undoubtedly food that Reggie and Mrs. Peavy had prepared for their gathering.

"I do hope Eve has something we can put these in," Ivy said. "I didn't feel right asking Mrs. Pierce to borrow her vases."

Mitch detected a hint of nervousness in Ivy's tone. Was she worried about fitting in? He had no doubt she'd be welcomed, but he planned to do his part to make her feel comfortable.

"I'm certain Eve will have something suitable," he said.

Truth be told, he felt a little nervous himself. Hopefully his friends wouldn't read more into his escorting

Ivy into their gathering than was there. After all, it was Reggie who had issued the invitation to Ivy. He was merely providing escort.

But he had a feeling the others wouldn't see it in quite that light.

Ivy tried to calm her nerves as they strolled down the street. She saw Reggie and the rest of the Barr household up ahead but had no desire to hail them. She was perfectly content to stroll along with just Mitch for company. She glanced at him from under her lashes and couldn't help but smile. He should have looked ridiculous, this giant of a man carrying her basket of riotously arranged flowers. But instead he looked quite charming.

He shifted the basket to his other hand just then and took her elbow as they reached a street crossing.

She knew those little gestures were no more than what he'd afford any woman lucky enough to be in his company, but it still made her feel special in a way she never had before.

When they arrived at Eve and Chance's place, Ivy braced herself, hoping she wouldn't do anything to make Mitch sorry he'd introduced her to his friends.

The main doors were open wide, with the entrance barred by two swinging half doors, similar to what she'd seen on the saloon in Nettles Gap. But this was no saloon—far from it—and she liked the openness of it.

Ivy stepped inside to see the room was divided in half by a low half wall. On one side was the sweet shop. On the other side was what looked like a toy workshop. Display cases contained all manner of tasty-looking treats, and shelves were filled with wooden and tin toys.

Candy and toys—what a magical place.

Eve came bustling over as soon as she spotted them.

"There you are. We were beginning to worry that you'd changed your mind."

"Not a chance," Mitch said, holding out the basket. "Ivy just stopped to pick these for you."

Eve's eyes lit up as she accepted the basket. "Oh, how beautiful!" She turned to Ivy. "And how thoughtful. Come along to the kitchen and we'll find something to put them in."

Ivy felt a strange sense of being set adrift as she left Mitch's side. But he gave her an encouraging smile, almost as if he'd read her feelings.

Braced by that smile, she followed Eve as Mitch was drawn into the circle of menfolk arranging the tables for the upcoming meal.

When Ivy stepped into the kitchen, she found a roomful of women working amicably together. Daisy and Reggie were unpacking hampers of food. Mrs. Peavy was stirring something on the stove. Someone had spread a pallet in the far corner of the room and Abigail sat there with Daisy's baby in her lap, holding up a wooden rattle to amuse Reggie's Patricia.

"Look at the beautiful flowers Ivy brought us," Eve announced.

The women immediately gathered around to admire the contents of the basket. There were oohs and ahhs as Ivy's contribution was examined in detail.

"Wherever did you get such beautiful blooms?" Reggie asked.

"From Mrs. Pierce's garden." Then she quickly clarified. "I had her permission."

"Eileen let you pick her flowers?" Mrs. Peavy remarked. "Well, mercy me, isn't that something? That garden is her pride and joy."

In short order, Eve found a large vase and several

jars to place the flowers in. While the others went back to their cooking and babysitting duties, Ivy separated and arranged the flowers.

"You have quite an eye for that," Abigail said.

Ivy shrugged self-consciously. "I like working with plants." Then she smiled at the sixteen-year-old. "And it looks like you are very good with the children."

Abigail grinned with pixielike impishness. "It's not very difficult when you have two sweeties like these."

Ivy nodded, then went back to work on the flowers. It was so nice to be here amongst these women, but rather bittersweet, as well. She wasn't really one of them, no matter how kindly they went about including her. In a few weeks' time, she'd be leaving, after all.

"It's a bit overwhelming, isn't it?"

Ivy glanced up quickly to see Eve watching her with a sympathetic smile.

"Pardon?"

"Being thrown into the midst of such a large group of near-strangers—it can be overwhelming."

Ivy nodded, hoping she hadn't done anything to make her new friends uncomfortable.

"It's only been about seven months since I was the new person here," Eve continued. "And I remember very well how, even though everyone was warm and welcoming, I still felt like an outsider for a while."

So Eve really did understand. "You seem very much a part of the group now. What was your secret?"

Eve laughed. "I suppose marrying Chance helped."

That was no help. Marrying her way in wasn't going to happen for her. No matter how much she'd begun to contemplate the idea.

"But truly, these people accepted me into their midst before Chance ever thought about proposing."

Ivy liked the sound of that.

"There's absolutely no need for you to feel like an intruder," Eve continued. "Those four good men respect each other and are closer than they would have you believe or even admit to themselves. If Mitch thinks you belong here, then that's the only stamp of approval you need with the rest of them."

Ivy suddenly found herself wondering if Mitch had brought other women to this gathering.

Taking herself to task, Ivy reminded herself again that in three weeks she would return home and never see these people again. Even if she did end up with land in Turnabout, Nana Dovie would never leave her home and that was that.

Preferring not to dwell on the thought of leaving, Ivy lifted one of the flower containers. "Where shall I put these?"

Eve put a finger to her cheek. "I think the vase should go on the candy counter. The smaller ones would look nice on the table in a row down the middle. Hopefully our menfolk have it set up by now." She picked up one of the jars. "I'll help. I need to see if the men have finished so I can put cloths on the tables."

The men did indeed have everything set up, so while Eve spread the cloths, Ivy transported the remaining flowers from the kitchen. Almost without conscious thought Ivy glanced Mitch's way and the approving smile on his face warmed her as she worked.

"Now, isn't that a nice touch," Eve's husband said as Ivy placed the last jar of flowers onto the table. "It appears you like prettying up a place as much as Eve does." He grinned and gave a gallant bow. "Which you both do quite well just by your presence."

"Don't mind him," Eve said as she set out the napkins. "He can't help himself—flirting is in his nature."

"Alas, it's true," he said unrepentantly as he placed an arm around Eve's waist. "But who can blame me for flirting with such lovely ladies as yourselves."

Ivy smiled at his outrageous comment and realized she felt a little less like an intruder than she had earlier.

When the food was finally brought out and they were all seated, Mr. Dawson offered up the blessing, giving thanks for the food and the company gathered around the table. Then he stood and cleared his throat. "Before we dig in to this wonderful meal, Eve, Leo and I have an announcement to make." He held out his arm, and Eve stood and stepped into his embrace, then shuffled aside to make room for Leo to stand between them.

Mr. Dawson paused to place a hand on the ten-year-old's shoulder. "As of yesterday, the adoption process is complete. Leo is officially our son."

A chaotic chorus of congratulations erupted as everyone stood to surround the trio. There were slaps on the back for Chance, delighted hugs for Eve and congratulations for the boy.

She was surprised to learn Leo wasn't their natural son. Later she'd ask Mitch to tell her the story of how Leo had come to live with them, but for now she was happy to just share in their joy.

Ivy couldn't tell which member of the newly formed family looked happier. Leo's chest seemed about to burst with pride and the grin on his face could outshine the sun. But Eve's and Chance's faces shone with so much love and joy that it couldn't help but touch the hearts of any who witnessed it.

Once everyone took their places again, Ivy found herself drawn into the conversation, as if she were a long-time friend of these people. Mitch, as usual, didn't say much. But she noticed that when he *did* speak, people paid close attention.

Did he realize how much his friends respected him?

When the meal was over, everyone pitched in to clear the table. Then the men put the room back to order while the women cleaned the dishes and portioned out the leftovers.

Eve placed one of the packets in the basket Ivy had carried the flowers in. "This is for you and Mitch."

Ivy shook her head. "Oh, no, I couldn't. And I'm sure Mitch would agree. The leftovers should go to those who contributed to the meal."

She suddenly realized she'd inadvertently used Mitch's first name and nervously glanced around. Would anyone notice?

But Eve seemed more focused on the other part of Ivy's statement. "You contributed those beautiful flowers. And Mitch always contributes to the meal, though it doesn't surprise me that you didn't know. That man is more closemouthed than a stone statue."

Mitch had contributed? How?

Before she could ask, Reggie nodded. "Even though we've each told him it's not necessary, Mitch has placed a standing order with the butcher. Every Saturday, regular as clockwork, either a roast or ham is delivered to whomever is hosting that week's Sunday gathering."

Why hadn't he said something when she questioned him? But she already knew the answer—Mitch wasn't one to boast over his own good deeds.

As the gathering broke up, she studied the family groupings. Only she and Mitch were solo. Would she ever feel the joy of becoming a wife and mother? It was a cherished dream that Lester had tried to steal from her. But being with these people—with Mitch—made her dare to hope she could still have it.

She glanced toward Mitch. She knew why she was still unmarried—Lester had robbed her of her reputation. But it made no sense to her that Mitch was still single. A man such as he—kind, generous, honorable— that kind of man should have no trouble finding a wife. Moreover, a wife who would treat him as he deserved.

The only explanation she could come up with was his grief over the loss of his wife.

He looked her way and gave her a questioning glance. Had he read something of her thoughts in her expression?

She flashed a quick smile, then busied herself with retying the string that was wrapped around the food in her basket. Mitch crossed the room to take the basket from her, and she relinquished it with a thank-you, then turned to say something to Abigail before he could question her.

It seemed natural for Mitch and Ivy to leave together—after all, they'd arrived that way. But Ivy was still aware of the eyes of her new friends on them as they did so.

When they stepped out onto the sidewalk, Mitch turned to her. "I suppose you'd like to check on Rufus?"

She nodded and they turned their steps toward his place.

Rufus greeted Ivy with his usual enthusiasm, but his attention quickly turned to Mitch—or more specifically, the basket in Mitch's hand.

"Rufus! No!"

But Mitch accepted the animal's less-than-decorous attention with good humor. "You can't blame him—this food is worth getting excited over. I asked Eve to toss a bone or two in my packet so he'll get his share." He lifted the basket to her eye level. "I'll divide the rest between us. We should each get a nice meal out of it."

"Oh, no, I couldn't accept that."

"Of course you can. The ladies always send me too much—you'd think they were trying to fatten me up for something. Besides, I'm certain sharing this is what Eve intended."

Ivy took advantage of that opening. "Eve and Reggie told me you always furnish the main meat for the meal."

He shrugged. "It seems fair since I don't take a turn hosting."

"But why didn't you say something yesterday?"

"It wasn't important." Then he turned away. "While you and Rufus catch up, I'll put this in the kitchen."

Ivy absently ruffled Rufus's fur, then picked up a stick and tossed it for him, her mind still on Mitch.

The man was such a puzzle. But a puzzle she wanted to solve.

She drifted across the lawn as she played with Rufus and almost before she realized it, she found herself in the backyard. The swing caught her eye and drew her like crumbs drew a mouse.

Mitch must have heard her because a few moments later he stepped out the back door.

He crossed the yard and stopped just out of reach of the moving swing. "Your food is in Mrs. Pierce's basket whenever you get ready to go."

"Mind if I ask you a question?" she asked from her perch on the swing.

His lips curved up in a wry smile. "I find trying to stop you is a waste of energy."

She ignored that bit of teasing. "Why don't you have any of your sketches hanging on your walls or up on your mantel, where folks could see them? They're much too beautiful to keep hidden away."

His expression didn't change, but she saw a slight crease appear on his forehead. She'd come to recognize that as a sign he was about to close himself off again. "Those sketches are purely for my own enjoyment, not for display."

This time she wouldn't drop the subject. And there was only one response to such a stuffy answer. "How selfish."

He blinked, obviously caught off guard by her words. "Hardly that, since I don't ever have visitors."

No visitors? But Mitch had friends here. Good friends, if the gathering today was any indication. Didn't he see that?

"If both of those things you just said are true," she replied, "then you've only proved that the drawings *should* be displayed."

He gave her a puzzled look.

"If they're for your pleasure only, and if no one ever comes here, then it only makes sense for you to display them so that *you* can enjoy them without worry that any-one else will accidentally enjoy them, too." She hoped he caught the irony in that last bit.

"Quite a debater, aren't you." His tone was dry, but she didn't detect any irritation. Still, she wasn't sure if he'd meant the words as a compliment or not. She de-cided it didn't matter, and forged ahead.

"Have you done any sketching lately? I mean, since we left the cabin."

He nodded.

She stilled the swing and leaned forward eagerly. "May I see it?"

Something flashed in his expression—was it reluctance? Had she overstepped? But then he nodded.

"All right."

She stood, but he held up a hand. "Keep your seat. I'll bring it out here."

Was he merely saving her a few steps? Or was he guarding her reputation again? Or was he forcing her to keep her distance?

When he returned, he didn't hand over his sketchbook immediately. "It's not finished yet. I still have some shading to do."

She stood and smiled, holding out her hand. "I'll keep that in mind."

He finally handed it over and she flipped open the cover. Then she gave a delighted smile. It was a sketch of Rufus. The dog stood on two legs, front paws braced against a tree and barking at something above him. She'd seen him in that very pose dozens of times. "You've captured him perfectly!"

Mitch rubbed the back of his neck. "I thought you might like to have this one."

"You mean it? Oh, Mitch, I'd *love* to have this." Impulsively she threw her arms around him, giving him a big hug. A moment later she realized what she'd done and stepped back, horrified.

The stunned look on his face did nothing to alleviate her embarrassment.

What must he think of her?

Chapter Fourteen

"Oh, my, I mean, oh, Mitch, I'm... I'm so sorry. I don't know what—"

He'd recovered quicker than she had, cutting her stammering apology short by touching her arm lightly. "Please don't apologize. I know it was merely an impulsive gesture of thanks, and I accept it as such."

He was right, of course. That was all it had been. She'd have done the same with anyone, given the circumstances, wouldn't she? And the fact that he'd momentarily slipped an arm around her in response had probably just been reflex, too, on his part.

She tried to cover her confusion with chatter. "It's just that this is the best gift I've ever received."

He gave a self-deprecating smile. "I doubt that, but I'm glad you like it. Now let me have it back so I can finish it."

She gave it up reluctantly and he flipped the cover closed again.

Then she brushed at her skirt, not ready to meet his gaze yet, knowing her cheeks were still a bright pink.

"I should be going." She needed to get away, to take

stock of what had just happened without his very distracting presence beside her.

He gave her a long, searching look, and she had the feeling he was reading her thoughts. He finally nodded. "Of course. I'll fetch the basket and then walk you home."

"That's not necessary."

"Perhaps, but it *is* what I'm going to do. Besides, Rufus needs a walk. He's been closed up in this yard for too long."

Her hand went to her mouth. "Oh, my goodness, I should have thought of that myself. I didn't mean to saddle you with all of Rufus's care."

He shrugged. "I enjoy long walks. But, if it'll make you feel better, we can walk him together."

How could she refuse his company when he put it that way? "Of course."

At least that impulsive hug hadn't pushed him away. In fact, as far as she could tell, other than his initial startled reaction, it didn't seem to have affected him at all.

Seeing as how he was her employer, that was a good thing. So why did it leave her with a dissatisfied feeling?

Mitch still felt that impulsive hug, could feel the impact of her throwing herself at him, of her arms wrapping around his chest, of his own arm wrapping around her in return in a gesture that felt all together too right.

It had been highly inappropriate, of course. Holding her, even for so brief a moment, had opened a floodgate of emotions that he'd long held at bay. And opening that particular floodgate was a dangerous thing.

But somehow he couldn't regret that it had happened.

He hadn't realized how much he missed that kind of close physical connection.

Of course he couldn't allow it to happen again. It wouldn't be fair to Ivy.

No matter how good it felt.

But if Ivy's demeanor was any indication, he didn't need to worry about it. She'd appeared to have some very real regrets. And now she was unusually quiet, talking to Rufus in subdued tones and doing her best not to meet his gaze.

He certainly didn't want things to get awkward between them. After all, she'd be working in his home for the next three weeks.

Perhaps it was time *he* made the effort to carry a conversation.

Mitch cleared his throat. "How do you like your new accommodations?"

She glanced his way. "The room is very comfortable. Much cozier than the hotel."

She didn't expand further and there was another silence.

He tried again. "And are you and Mrs. Pierce getting along okay?" Her decision to sit with her landlady during the church service had startled him, but only for a moment. Given that she knew the widow had few friends, he should have guessed she'd show public support.

Ivy nodded. "Of course we haven't spent much time together. I mean, she's a bit standoffish, but that's her right. She doesn't know me very well yet."

Then she gave him a smile that was closer to her usual sunny expression. "We discovered we share a love of gardening, though, so I have a good feeling about how we'll get along in the future."

Gardening was obviously a touchstone for her. "Her flowers *are* nice. I think Eve really appreciated your bringing them to our gathering."

"I'm glad." Her smile widened. "Mrs. Pierce's garden is lovely. There are more flowers out back. There's also one of the largest and most varied herb gardens I've ever seen—I have no idea what some of the plants even are. And she has a luscious vegetable garden, as well."

To his relief, the awkwardness between them had all but disappeared.

Ivy absently tucked a strand of hair behind her ear. "I plan to learn what I can from her while I'm here."

"Are you sure she did it all herself?"

Ivy nodded decisively. "She was out watering it when I returned home yesterday. And this morning I saw her collecting some of the produce. Does that surprise you?"

Mitch found it difficult to picture the elegant Mrs. Pierce working in a garden. He'd thought he hadn't judged the widow, but it seemed he had. "I suppose she didn't strike me as someone who liked getting her hands dirty. You're showing me a side of her I hadn't seen before."

"Nothing wrong with getting your hands dirty. A little dirt under the fingernails can help cleanse the mind of all its worries."

"Another of your Nana Dovie's sayings?"

She grinned. "No, that's one of mine. But that doesn't make it any less true."

"I agree. And I'm glad you've found some common ground with Mrs. Pierce."

"That reminds me, I'll need at least one day off to

take care of this laundry business. I can do yours at the same time if you like, as part of my housekeeping duties, I mean."

"That's not necessary." There was no way he would add more to her workload. "I already send my laundry out. And as for a day off, you'll have Sundays off, naturally, and then whichever other day you'd like, though I'd prefer it not be Saturday or Monday."

"That makes sense. I reckon Wednesday would work best, it being the middle of the week."

"Then Wednesday it is."

As they reached Eileen Pierce's gate, Ivy straightened. "I suppose it's time I say farewell to you and Rufus."

He was guiltily gratified to hear a touch of regret in her tone. He hoped they were back to the easy friendship they'd shared before.

Now if he could just keep things that way.

Ivy stooped down to give Rufus one last goodbye hug, and Mitch had to tamp down the memory of that embrace she'd given him. What was wrong with him?

"Be good," she admonished the animal. "I'll see you in the morning." Then she smiled at him. "I'll see you in the morning, too. Thanks for a lovely day."

"You're welcome." He felt an odd reluctance to return to his empty house. "How do you plan to spend the rest of your afternoon?" he asked.

She fingered her collar. "I want to write a letter to Nana Dovie. A lot's happened since I left Nettles Gap and I know she's curious. There's so much more you can say in a letter than a telegram."

And then Ivy closed her eyes and lifted her face as

if absorbing the heat of the sun. "It's such a pretty afternoon," she said dreamily.

The unconscious innocence of that gesture, and the beauty of her smile, took his breath away.

Then she dropped her chin and opened her eyes. "I'll probably sit on the front porch to write the letter."

He hoped she hadn't noticed his momentary gaping. But she wasn't looking at him. She brushed at her skirt. "How about you?"

Was she reluctant to part, as well? He shook off the thought.

"I'll probably finish the book I started earlier this week." Strange that he hadn't thought about that book since Ivy had entered his life.

She nodded but didn't turn away immediately. "Oh, I forgot to ask—what time would you like me to show up tomorrow?"

Mitch considered that a moment. His first thought was to have her arrive at nine o'clock since he liked to have time for quiet reflection when he first got up in the morning. But then he realized that would leave her on her own for breakfast.

"I'd like my morning meal on the table at eight-thirty. Will that be a problem?" He normally ate much earlier, but he supposed he could survive on coffee until she arrived.

"Not at all. What do you like to have for breakfast?"

"Nothing fancy. Biscuits and eggs will do."

She gave him an exasperated look. "Now what kind of breakfast is that? A body needs a hearty meal to start off the day proper—especially a body as large as yours." Her teasing look made it clear she'd meant no offense.

"I'll fix your eggs and biscuits, of course," she continued, "but I'll also add meat and cheese. And some jam for the biscuits. And if I can find potatoes—"

He raised a hand. "Don't go overboard. Adding a bit of meat and some jam will be more than enough."

"All right, you're the boss, I suppose." Her words were delivered with a reluctance that amused him. "I'll shop for supplies first thing and then see you bright and early."

He nodded, waiting for her to turn and go.

But she wasn't finished. "Hopefully I'll arrive before Reggie's cuttings are delivered."

He'd forgotten about her plans for a garden. "If not, I'll see that they're unloaded properly for you."

"Thank you." She gave a little wave. "Well, goodbye."

Was he imagining the wistfulness in her voice? Mitch stayed by the gate until she reached the front porch. Then he turned and headed for his place, Rufus padding along beside him.

It was definitely going to be an interesting three weeks.

Twenty minutes later, Ivy sat on the front porch, a half-written letter on the table beside her.

She'd been worried that her impulsive gesture earlier would cause some awkwardness between them, causing Mitch to worry that she was much too forward, or that she was throwing herself at him. But it seemed that hadn't been the case. Any surprise he'd felt had been short-lived.

By the end of their walk, it appeared he was prepared to act as if it hadn't happened.

She, on the other hand, couldn't brush it aside quite as easily.

It had only been six days since she'd met Mitch, but she was afraid she might already be developing deeper feelings for him.

Which would never do. Because falling for him would only lead to heartache.

He was kind and generous and honorable—everything a girl could hope for in a husband. But he wasn't romantically inclined toward her. Which was actually a good thing, because if he ever learned all there was to know about her, he would be shocked, and perhaps worse. And she couldn't bear to see that in his eyes.

Besides, he was her employer now, and it would be best to keep things strictly businesslike between them.

No matter how *un*businesslike she felt.

And she would never, ever think about that unfortunate, but very, *very* nice embrace again.

Now if she could just figure out how to make her heart listen to common sense.

Chapter Fifteen

Ivy gave Rufus a quick pat when she arrived the next morning, but then moved briskly toward Mitch's back door. She was determined to be businesslike today. She would focus on doing a good job and earning her pay—nothing more.

She smelled the coffee as soon as she opened the door.

"Good morning," Mitch said, sitting at the table with a cup, giving her that smile that she was quickly getting addicted to despite herself. He stood and crossed the room to take the basket from her. Those gentlemanly gestures were quite addictive, as well.

"Good morning," she said briskly. "That coffee smells good."

"Help yourself. The stove is already stoked and ready for you."

She grinned. "Hungry?"

He shrugged. "I wouldn't turn down a good meal."

She'd have to make sure she got here a little earlier tomorrow. Those were chores she should be doing herself if she was going to be earning her pay.

Ivy hung her bonnet on a peg by the door, then

paused. There, on one of the other pegs, was a nicely starched apron. When in the world had he gotten it?

She lifted it from the peg and put it on, then spun around to face him. "Very nice. Thanks."

He gave a casual wave. "You can thank Daisy—it's one of her extras," he said casually, though she thought she detected a note of pleasure.

"But you're the one who got it for me, so again, thank you."

"You're welcome." Then he gave her a stern look. "You're planning to have breakfast with me, right?"

It was time to establish limits. "I don't think that's appropriate. It's important that we maintain a businesslike relationship." She was fast coming to hate that word.

He leaned back in his chair. "Now who's being overly concerned with propriety?"

She was determined to stand her ground. "I want to make certain we do this right. Remember—no special treatment."

He raised a brow at that. "You remember that first night when we ate at Reggie and Adam's home?"

She nodded, wondering where he was going.

"Didn't Mrs. Peavy, Reggie's housekeeper, sit down to eat with the family? Are you saying that was inappropriate?"

"Well, no, but—"

"No buts. If it's appropriate for the Barr household, it's appropriate for this one."

Now she was confused. She couldn't find a hole in his argument, but she was sure there was one somewhere.

When she didn't answer right away, he smiled. "I'll take that as agreement, so the matter is settled." He moved to the hall door. "I'll be in the study if you need me for anything."

Unable to come up with a response, Ivy clamped her mouth shut and went to work preparing the meal.

He sure wasn't making it easy for her to maintain her distance.

Then again, if she insisted on maintaining a strict working relationship with him, it would make it harder for her to fulfill her goal of helping him learn to let down his guard a bit and take joy in what life had to offer.

Somehow she'd have to figure out how to strike a proper balance.

And protect her own all-too-vulnerable heart in the process.

Mitch felt quite pleased with himself as he sat in his study, listening to the sounds of Ivy in his kitchen, preparing his breakfast. She'd liked the apron and he'd convinced her to share his meals. Two victories in her first ten minutes officially on the job. Perhaps he'd be able to maintain control of the situation after all.

When she called him in to eat, he tried to ignore the fact that it wasn't just hunger that hurried his steps toward the kitchen.

As with the other meals she'd prepared for him, it was simple but hearty fare. They passed the time in easy conversation, with him allowing her to do most of the talking. He found the personal glimpses of her life and character that slipped into her conversation absolutely fascinating. Her ability to laugh at herself, and to find blessings in the darkest of situations was both admirable and charming.

But there was one thing missing from her stories, something that he thought might give him a further insight as to what her life at home was like. During a rare pause, he decided to touch on it.

"It sounds like you and Miss Jacobs lead an interesting life on that farm of yours."

She nodded. "I wouldn't trade it for anything else in the world."

He ignored the little twinge he felt at that and moved on. "I assume you don't spend all your time there, though. What's life like in Nettles Gap itself?"

She shifted in her seat, as if suddenly uncomfortable. "Nettles Gap is a lot like Turnabout, only smaller. We have a church, a school, a livery and so on. The railroad bypassed us, but the stage still comes through every Tuesday, and Mr. O'Hara runs a freight wagon from the train station at Bluehawk a couple of times a month."

Was she deliberately avoiding his question? "I wasn't asking about the town's commerce, I was asking what sort of social life you have there. What do you do for fun?"

She'd forked up the last bit of egg from her plate, and now she slowly chewed her food. He had the feeling there was something here she really didn't want to talk about. Should he change the subject?

Before he could decide, a knock sounded at the front door.

Ivy quickly stood, something like relief on her face. "I thought you said you never have visitors."

"I usually don't." He stood and moved toward the hall, but Ivy stopped him with a raised hand.

"Hold on. I'm the housekeeper, remember? I should be answering the door."

He frowned, letting his exasperation show. "Nonsense. Whoever is at the door is no doubt here to see me, not you."

She fisted her hands on her hips. "That's neither here

nor there. You hired me to be your housekeeper, and I intend to do my job."

He tried another tack. "You wouldn't be trying to put off doing the dishes, would you?"

His teasing had the desired effect. She relaxed and grinned. "Maybe." Then she waved a hand in surrender. "All right, you answer the door and I'll get started on the dishes."

As Mitch headed down the hall, his thoughts returned to the strange way she'd reacted to his question. What was she hiding?

He opened the door to see Ira Peavy standing there. Behind him, at the foot of the porch steps, was Jack with a wagon crammed full of plants.

"Reggie said you'd be expecting these," Ira said with a grin. "Where do you want them?"

"By the back door, if you don't mind. I'll let Miss Feagan know you're here." He glanced down at Jack. "I think there may be a few extra buttermilk biscuits and some honey if anyone is hungry."

Jack's eyes lit up. "Yes, sir!"

When Mitch returned to the kitchen, he found Ivy energetically scrubbing a plate.

"I was wrong," he said when she looked up. "It *was* for you. Jack and Ira are here with your cuttings. They're bringing them around back."

A dazzling smile lit her face. "Oh, I'd almost forgotten! If you'll have them unload everything next to the porch I'll tend to the planting as soon as I'm done cleaning up in here."

With a nod, Mitch stepped outside, hiding a grin at the way Ivy seemed to suddenly be moving at double speed. She was obviously eager to finish her chores so she could tend to the plants. He'd tell her to let the dishes wait, but he knew she wouldn't welcome anything that hinted at special treatment.

Besides, he needed a few more moments to figure out how he was going to get her talking about her life in Nettles Gap again.

Ivy flew through her chores, listening to Mitch, Mr. Peavy and Jack chat as they unloaded the wagon. Of course it was mostly Mr. Peavy and Jack doing the talking. Good to know Mitch wasn't quiet just with her.

Then again, she sure wished he'd been less chatty when he started asking about her life in Nettles Gap. She wasn't going to lie to him, but she'd rather not be too forthcoming about certain aspects of her life there.

Better to focus on something more positive. Like the wagonload of cuttings. She was already picturing where she'd place each plant, and she couldn't wait to get started.

As soon as she'd put away the last plate, she stepped outside. The wagon had already been unloaded. Mr. Peavy and Mitch stood nearby talking and Jack was across the yard, playing with Rufus.

Ivy looked over the plants and frowned. "There must be some mistake. There's more here than Reggie and I agreed on."

"No mistake," Mr. Peavy said. "Reggie loaded this wagon herself."

Her new friend had been more than generous. There were the peppers, peas, snaps and cucumbers they'd discussed. And sage, rosemary and lavender. But there was also squash, okra, parsley, thyme, mint and a few other things she'd have to take a closer look at to identify.

"Make sure you tell her how much I appreciate this. And, if you don't mind, also let her know I plan to stop by and thank her in person as soon as I can."

"By the way," Mitch said, "I told Jack there might be some biscuits and honey left from breakfast."

"Of course." She refrained from casting a longing look at the plants and waved for the boy to follow her. "Come on inside and I'll fix you right up."

Fifteen minutes later, Ira clapped Jack on the shoulder and said it was time to go, and the two took their leave.

With a happy sigh, Ivy turned to her garden-in-the-making. She knelt, ignoring Mitch's amused expression, to look through the bounty Ira and Jack had delivered.

"Oh, look," she exclaimed. "There's even cuttings from her rosebush. We'll have to plant these near your front porch."

"If you like." There was a decided lack of enthusiasm in his voice.

She glanced up curiously. "Don't you like roses?"

"I don't *dislike* them."

Was he not certain how to care for them? "They're not really hard to nurture and they'll definitely brighten up your front yard."

Again that disinterested shrug. "I've managed just fine with a not-so-bright front yard."

Was he being deliberately contrary? She refused to let it deter her. "Wait and see. You're going to like the difference it makes."

He straightened. "I'll get the garden tools while you finish sorting the plants."

He was offering to help her again. "Please don't feel you need to join me if you've got something else to tend to. After all, this *is* part of my job now." She grinned. "The fun part."

"There's nothing else requiring my attention at the moment." He gave her a searching look. "Unless you'd rather do this alone."

Was it her imagination or was there a hint of vulnerability behind his polite question? She smiled. "Not at all. I'll be glad of the company. I just didn't want to keep you from anything important."

"You're not." He rolled up his sleeves and went to get their tools. And for the next few hours, Ivy was blissfully happy playing in the dirt. She started with the herb garden, arranging and planting the sprigs of sage, rosemary, lavender, mint, basil, parsley and thyme. Mitch worked beside her but, to her surprise, deferred to her direction on how she wanted things done.

When at last she had the final herb planted, she leaned back and admired their work. "We did a good job if I do say so myself."

"It looks like more than what I'll ever use." He gave her a dry smile. "I don't bother with herbs when I do my own cooking."

"That's because you didn't have a handy source before. You just wait—once you get used to flavoring your foods with fresh-picked herbs, you'll never want to go back to bland food again."

He shot her a skeptical look that made her laugh. "I'll get scrap timbers from the lumber mill to edge the garden with," he said.

"That'll look nice. And it's good to see you taking pride in the garden."

He raised a brow. "You made it clear you expected me to take ownership."

She grinned. "Good to know you were paying attention."

He glanced toward Rufus, who was sniffing around the edges of their plot. "What's to keep your mutt from digging all this up as soon as we go inside?"

"Rufus knows better than to dig in any garden of

mine. Don't worry. He'll let it be." Then she grimaced. "Unless a squirrel scampers through it. Then it's a whole nother story."

She stood and stretched the kinks out of her back. "Time to tackle the vegetable garden."

"Are you sure you don't want to take a short break first?" he asked.

She glanced skyward, shading her eyes with her hand. The sun had climbed higher and the day had heated up accordingly. She was a bit stiff, but not ready to quit just yet.

"The sooner those cuttings get planted, the better." She gave him a challenging look. "But if you're tired, by all means take a break. I can finish this up."

He shook his head as he reached for a carefully wrapped tomato cutting. "You, Miss Feagan, are an unrelenting taskmaster. Lead on."

Ivy loved the way he treated her as if her opinions mattered. He deferred to her judgment in this particular task, but when she asked for his opinion he didn't hesitate to give it, and his thoughts were sound. It was as though he thought of them as equals.

And he seemed to be a bit of a mind reader, as well. He brought the water bucket and dipper around periodically without being asked, as if he could sense when she was ready for a refresher, sometimes even before she'd realized she needed it herself.

A girl could get spoiled being around a man who showed that kind of consideration.

Mitch once again fetched the bucket and ladle. Looking at Ivy's flushed face, he decided she needed more than a quick water break. "Time to get out of the sun for a few minutes."

She swiped her forehead with the back of her hand, then took the dipper from him. After gulping down a nice long drink, she stood. "All right. I could stand to enjoy a patch of shade for a few minutes."

Instead of going to the house as he'd expected, Ivy headed for the oak tree and sat down on the swing, but didn't set it in motion.

He followed and leaned back against the trunk of the tree.

"I wonder what Nana Dovie is doing right now," she said dreamily.

"She's probably wondering the same about you."

"Probably." She absently scratched Rufus's ear. "She's having to take care of all the chores herself while I'm gone."

He could hear the worry in her voice and he wanted to comfort her. But he dare not risk a repeat of what had happened yesterday.

"If things work out with this inheritance," she mused, "I'll be able to do some things to make our life easier. Rebuild the barn and purchase a wagon. Get a new milk cow. Maybe even get a newfangled washing machine."

"Those are all good investments. But isn't there something you want for yourself? Maybe buy some nice clothes or take a trip?"

She looked affronted. "Are you saying my dresses aren't nice?"

Had he insulted her? "No, no, not at all," he said hastily. "I only meant—"

She laughed. "I was just teasing, I know what you meant. My clothes are just fine for the life I live. And I wouldn't want to go off traveling without Nana Dovie, and she's not one for leaving the farm."

"You mentioned that once before." He left it at that, not wanting to press.

"It's the strangest thing. She's always been something of a homebody. But when I was younger she also enjoyed her weekly trips to the mercantile and going to church. And she was always the first one to visit a family who was in need of comfort. But lately…"

Her voice trailed off and she set the swing in a lazy, dragging motion before she continued.

"Lately she hasn't been able to leave our place. She's tried—even went so far as to climb up in the wagon once or twice. It's not that she doesn't want to leave, it's that she can't seem to make herself leave. She's even stopped going to church."

So that meant Ivy was tethered to the farm, as well. As anxious as she was about returning, perhaps this time away was good for her.

The soft vulnerability of her demeanor had him once more longing to comfort her. This time it was harder to push away thoughts of yesterday's embrace. But a heartbeat later her mood had shifted as she suddenly popped up off the swing, startling Rufus into a surprised yelp.

Mitch straightened immediately. The stricken look on her face had him taking a half step in her direction.

"Oh, my goodness. I forgot to get lunch started."

Mitch relaxed. "Is that all?"

"Is that all?" She waved a hand in dismay. "It's the job you hired me for, isn't it?"

"There's nothing that says you have to cook something to prepare a meal. Many's the day I've had a cold lunch. Some cheese and fruit will be adequate. I told you, I'm a man of simple tastes."

She sniffed disdainfully. "It may be too late to cook a proper lunch, but I think I can do better than *that*."

"Be that as it may, what I'm paying you for is to do some work around here. And you've definitely earned your wages this morning," he assured her.

She nodded, then halted. "That reminds me of something I wanted to do."

He watched as she turned and headed toward the back of his lot, Rufus trotting at her heels. What was she up to?

She walked all the way to the fence where the weeds had taken over. To his surprise, she started picking wildflowers. When she had an armful, she headed back. "Aren't these beautiful?"

He looked over her bounty of posies dubiously. It was a mismatched lot that seemed composed mostly of weeds. But she had such a pleased look on her face that he found himself nodding. "What do you plan to do with them?"

"Why, brighten up your house, of course." She hefted her burden of blooms. "I suppose it's too much to hope you have a vase or two?"

When he shook his head she merely smiled. "That's okay. I can use a glass or jar. Won't it be nice to have such a happy splash of color in the house?

"Very nice indeed." But the splashes of color he was thinking about were the sparkling green of her eyes, the pink in her freckled cheeks and the soft auburn of her hair.

Being trapped on that farm was a hardship for her, that much had been obvious in her demeanor when she spoke of it. Surely there was something he could do to free her?

The fact that by doing so it might free her to live here in Turnabout was merely an incidental benefit.

By the next morning, Mitch was certain he was better prepared to keep an appropriate distance between himself and Ivy. She arrived right on schedule and went about preparing breakfast while he sat at the table with his newspaper, and the conversation was appropriately inconsequential.

He escaped to his study right after breakfast, channeling his edgy feelings into his sketching for a few hours. He was still there when he heard a knock at the front door.

"I'll get it," he called back to Ivy.

Who in the world could that be? Had Reggie decided to send additional cuttings? He'd had no visitors except deliverymen in the two years he'd been here, and now two visitors in two days? It seemed his life was changing in more ways than he'd imagined as a result of letting Ivy into it.

His smile faded as soon as he opened the door.

Hilda Swenson stood on his front porch, along with her three boys.

What in the world was she doing here?

Chapter Sixteen

"May I come in?"

Mitch opened the screen door wider, though in fact that was the last thing he wanted to do. "Of course."

His visitor turned to her sons. "Peter, keep an eye on your brothers. I won't be long."

"Yes, Momma."

As she stepped inside, she sighed dramatically. "They're good boys, but it is *so* hard on them not having a father in their lives."

Mitch ignored her very obvious hint and ushered her into his parlor. "What can I do for you, Mrs. Swenson?"

"Oh please, how many times must I ask you to call me Hilda?" Her gaze scanned the room, seeming to miss nothing. "I hope you don't think it forward of me to come calling, but now that you have a *housekeeper,*" she said, with a note of false enthusiasm in her voice, "I decided there could be no hint of impropriety. And it was something that could not wait."

"And what might that be?"

"My oldest son, Peter, will move up to your class next year. And I'm afraid his mathematical skills are not at the level they should be. Miss Whitman suggested I have him work with a tutor this summer."

Janell Whitman was Turnabout's other schoolteacher. She worked with the younger students and Mitch with the older ones. He considered her a good teacher—by the time students moved from her classroom to his they were well prepared.

"If Miss Whitman suggested it, then I'm confident that is what you should do. Would you like me to provide the names of some of my students who would make good tutors? There are several excellent candidates."

"Actually, I was hoping you would take the job."

Mitch stilled. Was she using her children to get to him?

But Mrs. Swenson seemed not to have noted his reaction. "Peter will respond much better to an adult than to a young person. I would help him myself, but I'm afraid I have no head for numbers," she said as if it were something to be proud of. "My talents are much more feminine and domestic."

Mitch tried to maintain an impassive demeanor. "Surely there is someone else in town—"

She didn't let him finish. "My boy deserves to have the very best. And who better than a schoolmaster? Since Miss Whitman will be out of town most of the summer, that leaves you."

She sat without invitation, obviously planning to stay awhile. "Besides," she added coyly, "this will give the two of you an opportunity to get to know each other before school starts. You'll find Peter is a very attentive student, eager to learn."

So why had he fallen behind? But Mitch refrained from asking that aloud. "This is what I'll do. I'll give Peter a set of problems to work on at home. I'll look over his work when he's done and assess what kind of help he needs."

She flashed a bright smile. "That sounds more than fair. Peter will benefit from the extra attention, I'm sure of it."

Mitch stood. "If you'll excuse me, I'll write down the problems for him."

"Of course. Take your time—I don't mind waiting."

Trying to ignore the victory in her voice, Mitch headed to his study. As he pulled out a piece of paper, he heard voices coming from the yard. Glancing out the window, he spotted Ivy and Rufus entertaining the three boys. He watched, enjoying the uninhibited abandon with which she joined in their play.

It was several minutes before he remembered what he'd stepped into his study to do. Turning back to his desk, he carefully wrote out the arithmetic problems. As he worked, the sound of laughter and horseplay drifted in through the window. He'd heard that same sound many a time from his classroom.

But he'd never before been as tempted to join the participants as he was today.

Mitch finally leaned back and studied the list of problems. Satisfied that it was complete, he returned to the parlor only to find his guest examining his things. Strange—when Ivy had done that, it hadn't really bothered him. But the widow's actions struck him as intrusive.

When she looked up and spotted him, she smiled as if there was nothing to be embarrassed about. "Your home could certainly use a woman's touch."

"I like to keep things simple."

She laughed and it was a very soft, feminine sound. Nothing like the boisterous joy of Ivy's laugh.

"Isn't that just like a man?" she said archly. "But if a woman ever puts her mark in here—softer curtains, flowers, a few delicate bits of bric-a-brac—you'd wonder why you ever resisted."

What would she think of the wildflowers Ivy had added to his kitchen and study?

He handed her the papers he'd brought with him. "Ask Peter to work on these and bring them back to me tomorrow." Then he remembered tomorrow was Ivy's day off. And he'd rather not be alone when the woman returned. "Make that the day after. And I would caution you not to help him."

She placed a hand over her heart. "I wouldn't dream of it." Then she fluttered her lashes. "Besides, as I said, I have no head for numbers."

Did she honestly think that made her more attractive to him? "Then I'll see you on Thursday."

Her nose wrinkled. "What's that smell?" Then her eyes widened in alarm. "My goodness, is something burning?"

Mitch sniffed the air, then turned abruptly and raced for the kitchen. He knew what had happened even before he pushed open the door. Ivy must have been distracted by the children and left something on the stove for too long.

Sure enough, when he entered the kitchen, smoke billowed from the stove grates. Grabbing a cloth, he opened the oven door and pulled out the now blackened lump of what had undoubtedly been a loaf of bread. Wanting to get the still-smoking mess out of the house, he headed for the back door, pushing it open with his hip.

Ivy glanced up as soon as he stepped outside. The

expression on her face would have been comical if she hadn't looked so stricken.

He tossed the blackened mass from the pan toward the fence. Rufus rushed over to check it out, but after one good sniff, he gave a violent sneeze and bounded away again.

Ivy approached the porch like a student caught passing notes. "I am *so* sorry—I lost track of time."

"Nothing to get distressed over. I've eaten meals without bread before—it won't hurt me to do so again."

She clapped a hand over her mouth "Oh, my goodness, the stew!" She gathered her skirts and rushed to the back door. "I hope I haven't ruined that, as well."

Mitch barely managed to get the door open for her before she raced inside. Then she halted abruptly.

Following close behind, he caught sight of what had stopped her in her tracks.

Hilda stood at the stove, stirring the contents of the pot, looking for all the world as if she were the lady of the house.

"Hello, dear." Both her tone and smile were condescending. "I hope you don't mind. I added some water to the pot to keep it from burning." She tapped the spoon on the rim of the pot before setting it on the spoon rest. "I think I got to it just in time. And I hope you don't mind but I also added a pinch of salt and rosemary to it. It was rather bland, and a worldly man like Mr. Parker surely likes flavor in his food."

"Thank you," Ivy said evenly, "but I'll take over now."

"Of course. I was just trying to help." Her smile took on a feline quality. "You seem to have been otherwise occupied."

Mitch sensed Ivy's stiffening and quickly stepped forward. "I'll see you and Peter on Thursday, then."

Mrs. Swenson turned to Ivy. "I'm sorry if my boys distracted you, my dear. When you're a mother yourself someday, you'll learn how to manage both a home and children."

Mitch took the woman's elbow and ushered her from the room before Ivy could respond. "Allow me to escort you to the door. I'm certain your sons are eager to reclaim your attention."

By the time Mitch returned, Ivy stood at the sink, scrubbing the blackened bread pan with great determination. She paused a moment to glance his way. "I'm truly sorry."

"You don't have to keep apologizing. As I said, it's really nothing to concern yourself over. I've burned more than one meal myself." He tried to shift the focus to something more positive. "You seemed to enjoy entertaining those boys."

Her expression softened. "I did. They came to the kitchen door and asked if it was okay to play with Rufus. I told them yes, but then Davey, the youngest, seemed a little afraid, so I went out to put them at ease. I'd only meant to be a minute, but then Davey asked me to push him on the swing.

"They're good boys," she continued as she returned to her scrubbing. "A little too quiet for young'uns, but they relaxed after a bit. Andy, the middle boy, really took to Rufus. They don't have a dog of their own, but it sure sounded as if they'd like to have one."

She'd make a good mother someday, he decided. A sudden image of her with a babe in her arms and a toddler at her feet flashed through his mind with the clarity of one of his sketches. The sweet tenderness of it nearly took his breath away.

"I'm not off to a very good start, am I?"

It took him a minute to focus on her meaning. "I wouldn't say that."

"You're kind, but yesterday I fed you a cold lunch and today I burned the bread to a charred lump."

He didn't like the defeat in her eyes. "Look at it this way—it hasn't been boring." He'd meant that as a bit of levity, but he realized it was true. His life had been turned upside down since she entered it, but he hadn't felt so alive in a very long time.

"I hope my negligence didn't spoil your visit with Mrs. Swenson."

There was a note in her voice he couldn't quite read. "It wasn't a social call. Her oldest son needs some tutoring."

"Peter? He seems to be a very serious youngster. Maybe a mite *too* serious."

"You could tell that from a few minutes of play?"

She shrugged. "I could see how dutifully he watched over his brothers, and how he didn't let himself relax and just have fun."

"That's typical of the oldest child in a family. I see it in my students."

She eyed him thoughtfully. "You said you're the oldest."

Was she trying to draw comparisons? "Yes. And I did keep an eye on my sisters. But Peter has the added burden of being the man of the house now that his father is gone."

"How long ago did his father pass?"

"About a year and a half ago."

She dried her hands on her apron and moved to the

stove. "Those poor boys. It must be hard on them not having a father in their lives."

"They'll manage, as others have. And there are good men in this community to serve as role models for the boys until she marries again."

She smiled. "Good men, like a certain schoolteacher I happen to know."

Mitch paused, unsure how to respond as feelings he couldn't quite identify washed over him.

She considered him a *good man?*

Ivy had been doing her best not to dwell on the poor showing she'd made in front of Mrs. Swenson.

She did have her pride, after all. But more than that, she couldn't bear the idea of letting Mitch down. And right now he looked slightly dazed. What was he thinking? She wished he would say something. But he just continued to stare at her in that unnerving way.

Trying to cover the silence, she said the first thing that came to mind, "Do you plan to help him? Peter, I mean."

He finally relaxed his gaze and rubbed his chin. "I'll help, yes, but I haven't yet decided quite how. I gave his mother a test for him that will let me know the extent of his need. Once I look over the results, I'll decide."

Relieved that their discussion was back on safer ground, Ivy nodded. "I suppose that means she'll be returning here. Do you know when?" She was eager to snatch at this chance for domestic redemption. "I want to be prepared with refreshments next time."

"That's not nec—"

"It's *absolutely* necessary. When you have visitors in this home, it's my job to help you be prepared to welcome them properly."

And that woman would not find her lacking again. She refrained from examining too closely why Mrs. Swenson in particular could get her back up this way.

"Then yes, I expect her to return on Thursday, but we didn't discuss a time."

Ivy waved that minor obstacle aside. "No matter. I'll just prepare something that keeps well."

"If it's important to you, then by all means do so."

Ivy hesitated a moment, then decided to say what was on her mind. "Mrs. Swenson seems quite smitten with you."

Mitch frowned uncomfortably. "I believe *smitten* is too strong a word."

Ivy didn't agree. But perhaps he was still mourning his late wife too much to see anyone else in that light. "You must have loved her very much."

His surprised look brought heat to her cheeks. She hadn't intended to say that aloud. "Your wife, I mean," she added hastily. "Not Mrs. Swenson."

"Gretchen was a sweet, gentle woman who deserved better than me."

"I doubt she thought so."

"Nevertheless," he said, his tone relentlessly firm, "that was it for me. I don't plan to ever marry again."

Ivy felt as if she'd been slapped. She'd always known, of course, that any kind of permanent relationship with Mitch was out of the question, that after her case with Carter was settled she'd likely never see him again.

But just because her head knew that didn't mean her heart had accepted it.

"You shouldn't slam the door on the possibility. I mean, you never know wh—"

"That may be true for others, but my situation is different. I stand by my statement, and now I'd prefer we move on to another topic."

Ivy went back to work preparing a meal from scratch. He must have loved his wife deeply to refuse to marry another.

Surely she wasn't jealous of a dead woman?

Trying to move past her own reaction, Ivy realized she'd obviously touched a very raw nerve with Mitch, but it had been illuminating. He was even more stubbornly closed off than she'd imagined. And that was no way for a person to live.

She was more determined than ever to open his eyes. Now if she could just figure out how...

Mitch had seen the hurt look Ivy tried to mask before she turned away and felt a pang of regret for putting it there. But he knew he'd done the right thing. Now there would be no misunderstanding. If she had in fact formed any sort of affection for him, she was now aware that it could lead no further than friendship.

And if that thought left a sour feeling in his gut, well, it was just what he deserved.

She was quieter than usual as she worked at the stove. He wouldn't have been surprised if she refused to sit down to the meal with him, but to his relief that wasn't the case. But all through the meal he couldn't shake the feeling that she was studying him, but to what end he couldn't imagine.

He also found himself missing her cheerful chatter. Even the leading questions that normally started her talking failed to elicit more than direct responses.

When had her babble become so dear to him?

And what was he going to do when she returned to Nettles Gap for good?

Chapter Seventeen

Ivy rose early Wednesday morning. She wanted to get started on her laundry duties before the hottest part of the day.

Doing the laundry for herself and Mrs. Pierce wasn't much more work than doing it for herself and Nana Dovie. Mrs. Pierce's clothing was of a finer quality, but surprisingly worn. Perhaps she wanted to cling to her mourning clothes as long as possible.

As Ivy worked, her mind kept replaying yesterday's conversation with Mitch. She couldn't believe such a man could feel truly fulfilled leading a solitary life. Surely, in time, he'd find a woman who could bring him joy again.

But it obviously wouldn't be her. Still, she couldn't let that stop her from her self-appointed mission to help him. It was the right thing to do.

No matter how much it hurt.

When she'd hung the final load on the line, it was nearly noon.

It would be a while before the laundry was dry enough for her to take down. Perhaps she'd head over to Mitch's place. Just to see if he needed anything. And to check on Rufus, of course. She went to the back porch, then hesitated. She could see Mitch through the screen door. He was seated at the table, sketch pad spread out. Would he welcome her presence or was he savoring his solitude?

He looked up then, taking the decision from her hands.

She was gratified to see his smile of greeting. "Well, hello. Come on in."

"Actually, I'm just taking a break while I wait for the wash to dry. I thought I'd see if the garden needed watering and maybe give Rufus a walk."

Why did she suddenly feel so shy?

To cover her nervousness, she sat on the porch steps to greet an exuberant Rufus. A moment later, Mitch joined her outside, leaning against the nearby porch support. "I watered the garden earlier. And you should be enjoying your day off, not looking for additional chores to do."

She leaned back to avoid more of Rufus's slobbery kisses. "I don't really consider gardening and taking a stroll with Rufus doing chores."

"Have you eaten lunch yet?"

"I'll get something a little later." She was certain she could find something edible on her walk with Rufus. And she was still hoarding a bit of the hardtack he'd given her a few days ago.

"I was about to head over to The Blue Bottle to speak with Chance. Why don't you join me? I'm sure Eve would be glad to see you."

"That's really not necessary. I'll need to get back to check on the laundry in a little bit." She took a deep breath. "Actually, I had another reason for coming."

"Oh?"

"I wanted to apologize for yesterday. I overstepped with my comments about Mrs. Swenson and about your wife."

His expression closed off and he was silent for a long moment. Then he straightened. "I insist you accompany me for lunch. We need to discuss your duties."

Ivy was confused. That was it? He wasn't going to acknowledge her apology? Then his words registered. Was he unhappy with her work? Or had her prying questions yesterday brought on his dissatisfaction? Or was it a combination of both? "Of course."

As they strolled toward The Blue Bottle, Ivy kept waiting for Mitch to speak up on whatever he wanted to discuss with her, but instead he seemed more interested in learning how her morning had gone.

By the time they reached their destination she realized she'd done most of the talking.

Mitch held the door as she stepped inside. She was very careful not to brush against him as she passed, but even so his closeness was highly distracting. It was getting harder and harder to deny her feelings.

Eve was transferring chocolate treats from a tray to a display stand on the counter. Chance sat at a workbench across the room, painting a wooden train.

"Mitch, Ivy—welcome!" Eve set the tray down and wiped her hands in the folds of her apron. "Can I interest you in something sweet?"

Mitch nodded a greeting. "Everything smells so good. Why don't you fix us a cup of whatever tea you have today, along with some of those fancy sandwiches you make."

Eve's brows lifted in surprise, but she recovered quickly. "Of course."

Then she turned to Ivy. "Just have a seat and I'll bring that right out."

Based on Eve's reaction to Mitch's request, Ivy gathered he didn't normally order tea and sandwiches. Was he doing all this for her benefit? And when was he going to let her know what he wanted to discuss with her?

As Ivy took her seat, she noticed Mitch and Chance deep in discussion. She couldn't hear what they were saying, but from the hand gestures Mitch was making, it appeared he was describing something he wanted Chance to build.

As she watched, she couldn't help but compare the two men. Chance was boyishly handsome with a ready smile and deep blue eyes. He always seemed relaxed and ready to enjoy whatever life tossed his way.

On the other hand, there was nothing boyish about Mitch. He was mature, impressive, solid. He exuded responsibility and dependability. There was something so admirable, so attractive in the quiet strength that was a natural part of him, and the control and grace with which he wielded that strength.

And while there might be some who preferred Chance's sunny good looks, she personally was partial to a man whose face reflected character and control, and whose manner suggested authority without being overbearing.

As soon as Eve stepped out of the kitchen, Mitch and Chance wrapped up their business.

Eve placed a cup of tea in front of Ivy, and a plate of daintily cut sandwiches on the table. "Today I have a peach tea. And two kinds of sandwiches—cheese and apple, and a chopped egg and vegetable mix."

It all sounded quite exotic to Ivy.

"Perfect," Mitch said as he joined them and took his seat.

Eve returned to the counter to finish unloading her tray of bonbons, leaving Mitch and Ivy to their tea and sandwiches.

Mitch picked up one of the tiny sandwiches, then moved the plate closer to her. "Help yourself."

She obediently took one and nibbled on it, watching Mitch surreptitiously. He should have looked silly with that dainty cup and tiny sandwich in his huge hands. But he seemed completely at ease and entirely unself-conscious.

"Is something wrong with your sandwich?"

His question brought the heat to her cheeks as she realized she'd been staring rather than eating. "No, it's quite good." She took a large bite to prove her point and followed it with a sip of the delicious tea.

She turned to Eve. "You'll have to teach me how you make this tea. I'd like to fix some for my Nana Dovie when I go back to Nettles Gap."

Eve smiled. "Of course. Stop by whenever you have a few minutes and we'll brew a pot together."

Still very aware of the man sitting at her elbow, Ivy kept her gaze on Eve. "Where's Leo?"

"Ira took Leo and Jack fishing this morning. They're not back yet so either the fish are biting well and they don't want to quit, or they're not biting and they don't want to give up."

The talk of fishing put her in mind of the fishing she and Mitch had done back at the cabin, and she couldn't resist a quick look his way.

Sure enough, he was watching her with a smile.

"Ivy enjoys fishing, too," he said. "Even digs her own worms and baits her own hook. Or so she tells me."

"Is that so?" Chance said. "Maybe when Eve teaches her to make that tea, she can teach Eve to fish."

Eve shook her head firmly. "I'll cook 'em, but I'll leave the catching to those who enjoy it."

Chance gave an exaggerated sigh, then smiled. "I suppose I'm still getting the better end of that bargain."

Eve blushed prettily under his smile, but gave a sassy toss of her head. "That you are."

A pang stabbed Ivy as she watched the affectionate exchange between them. She was very happy for them, of course, but it was hard to realize she would likely never experience that same closeness and intimacy with anyone. No one in Nettles Gap would look twice at her, and moving away from there was not an option.

This time, she resisted the impulse to look at Mitch. Instead, she focused on her food.

When they finally took their leave, Ivy decided she'd waited long enough. "You said you wanted to talk about my duties?"

"So I did. Do you know how to sew?"

That wasn't at all what she'd expected. "Depends what you mean by sewing. I can mend and patch just about anything. And I can make up a new piece of clothing if I have a pattern to work from. But I'm not very good at fancy work."

"How about curtains?"

Her spirits rose immediately. Was he ready to add some color to his place? "Of course. As long as you want something simple without ruffles and such."

He gave her a dry smile. "Definitely no on the ruffles."

"Are you planning to replace all the curtains or just some?"

"Neither. I want to add curtains to the kitchen window."

Ah, well, that was a start. "Do you already have the fabric?"

"No, but I'm sure we can find something at the mercantile."

He'd said *we.* If he really was willing to let her help select it, maybe she could talk him into something colorful. "I did notice they have a nice selection." She was already imagining a print of some sort with a bright blue as the prominent color.

"Shall we go take a look?" he asked.

"I probably should be getting back—"

"It won't take long, and there's no time like the present."

She was surprised by his insistence. "All right, I suppose the laundry *could* probably use a few extra minutes to dry."

When they arrived at the mercantile, Mitch placed a hand lightly at the small of her back and guided her down one of the aisles. Ivy was certain it was a reflexive gesture, totally impersonal and meant to be polite rather than affectionate.

But her reaction to it was anything but impersonal.

The table where the bolts of fabric were stacked was at the far end of the store and she remained acutely aware of the protective warmth of his touch the entire way. The walk seemed to take forever and end too quickly at the same time.

As soon as they reached the fabric table, Mitch stepped away from her and reached for a bolt near the top of the stack. "What do you think of this one?"

She tried to focus on the fabric. It was a tan-and-brown plaid with a thin maroon stripe providing the only hint of color.

She stifled a grimace. There was nothing inherently wrong with it, but she'd had something a little brighter in mind. "Perhaps something with a little more color."

To her relief, he didn't seem insulted. "Which one would you recommend?" Then he gave her a stern look. "No flowers."

She laughed, and the smile he gave her warmed her right down to her toes.

However was she going to make it through the rest of her time in Turnabout with her heart unscathed?

Mitch watched as Ivy studied the bolts of fabric. He hadn't been able to resist the urge to touch her, even if it was just to put a protective hand at her back.

He'd have to watch that in the future. Ivy was the last person he wanted to mislead.

She studied the bolts intently, as if it were a decision of utmost importance. He decided he liked the way her nose crinkled and her lips quirked up on one side when she was mentally working through a problem.

She fingered a yellow print covered with white flowers and then another that had white-and-yellow polka dots on a green background.

To his relief, she dismissed both of those and continued looking. With a triumphant grin she pulled out a bolt of blue gingham. Grabbing a corner of the fabric, she turned to him with a smile. "How's this?"

He pretended to study it critically. "It's not neutral, but I think I can live with it."

Mitch had turned to signal Doug Blakely, the owner of the mercantile, that they needed help when another customer walked in. To his chagrin, it was Hilda Swenson and her boys.

The widow caught sight of him at the same time, and her expression brightened. She immediately headed his way. "Mr. Parker, how nice to see you. Are you doing your shopping, too?"

When she spied Ivy, her expression slipped for just a moment, but she recovered quickly. "Miss Feagan. I thought you were off on Wednesdays."

Now, how had she learned Ivy's schedule?

"I am. I'm just helping Mr. Parker pick out some fabric for kitchen curtains."

"How very nice." The widow glanced at the fabric Ivy had picked out. "Oh, my dear, surely you're not thinking of going with that gingham."

Mitch started to protest, but Ivy spoke up first.

"I know it's not the most colorful of prints, but I'm trying to keep in mind that this is for a bachelor's home."

So she'd picked up on his more conservative tastes, had she?

Mrs. Swenson nodded. "Of course. But just because men don't appreciate florals doesn't mean we must choose something dull." She stepped past Ivy and dug through the bolts stacked on the table. She finally pulled out one from the bottom of the pile. It had alternating stripes of red and blue separated by narrower strips of white.

"This one is much brighter and still has a masculine look to it, don't you agree?"

Ivy nodded. "You're right, this is a much better choice. I don't know how I missed it."

The woman preened. "I'm just more familiar with the offerings here." She glanced Mitch's way. "I confess I'm always on the lookout for ways to make my home cozier and more welcoming. Mr. Blakely lets me know when he has something that might interest me."

Mitch cleared his throat. "I think the fabric Miss Feagan selected is fine."

Ivy, however, disagreed. "But this one Mrs. Swenson found will work out much better than the gingham."

Before Mitch could respond, Mrs. Swenson spoke up again. "If your duties keep you too busy to sew, I'll be happy to make these curtains for Mr. Parker. Mr. Swenson used to say I was quite the seamstress. He took pride in showing off my domestic talents." She lifted her chin proudly. "And of course I make most of the clothes for myself and the boys." She fanned out one side of her skirt, inviting them to admire it.

"That's quite kind of you," Ivy responded, "but I consider this part of my job and wouldn't feel right letting someone else take care of it."

"But I—"

Mitch had had enough. "That's indeed a generous offer, but as I'm in no hurry, I'm certain Miss Feagan can work it into her schedule."

With a disappointed smile, the widow nodded. "Of course. But the offer stands if that changes." Then she tightened the strings on her purse. "Now, I'll leave you to finish making your purchase. And I'll see you tomorrow to discuss Peter's tutoring needs."

Later, when they stepped outside, Mitch offered Ivy an apologetic grimace. "I'm sorry if Mrs. Swenson's interference upset you. She can be overbearing at times."

"Not at all. She means well and she was right about the fabric." She hefted the parcel in her hands. "This piece is much better than the one I selected." She gave him a curious look. "I would think you'd be flattered by the attention. She's a handsome woman with a number of nice qualities that would make her a fine wife for some lucky man."

"She'd be better served to turn her attention elsewhere. I've tried to make my disinterest as clear as I can without being outright rude."

They stopped in front of Mitch's house and he opened the gate. Ivy handed him the fabric as Rufus raced to greet her.

She finally straightened. "Thank you for the tea and the company, but it's time I headed back. In this heat, I'm sure at least part of the laundry has dried."

"Of course. I'll see you in the morning."

Ivy started to turn away, then paused. "By the way, would you mind if I spoke to Mrs. Pierce about purchasing produce from her garden? She's harvesting more than she can use, and I like the idea of picking it fresh myself."

"Not at all. Tell her to keep tabs on the amount and I'll pay her once a week when I pay you."

Mitch watched Ivy walk away, surprised once again at her thoughtfulness. First her tactful handling of Hilda's interference and now this scheme to help Mrs. Pierce out.

He slowly headed for his backyard. He'd actually enjoyed their little shopping expedition today. Strange how even the most mundane tasks took on a sense of adventure when he was able to view them through her eyes.

He was going to miss that when she was gone.

That and much more than he cared to admit, even to himself.

Chapter Eighteen

Mitch was working on a sketch of Ivy seated on the swing when a knock at the door sounded the next morning, and he reluctantly put down his pencil. This time, he had no doubt as to who it was.

He wasn't happy at the interruption. It had been a long time since he'd had any interest in sketching a person, but he could see already that this sketch was going to be his finest work to date. If he could just capture her smile…

But before he could get up, Ivy appeared in the hallway and gave him a very firm look. "I'll get it."

With a smile, he settled back in his chair. She'd shown up at his kitchen door this morning with a determined look in her eye. She'd made quick work of breakfast and then shooed him away, saying she had baking to do and didn't want to be distracted.

He'd heard her humming and talking to herself for the past few hours and it had influenced his sketching, infusing the figure coming to life beneath his pencil with a joyous abandon.

"Mrs. Swenson, good day to you." Ivy's words carried clearly to him, and he smiled at her formal tone. "I believe Mr. Parker is expecting you. If you and your boys will have a seat in the parlor, I'll let him know you're here."

Mitch put away his sketchbook as he waited for her to appear in the doorway, which she did almost immediately.

"Mrs. Swenson has arrived."

"So I heard."

She gave him another stern look. "I'll have refreshments ready in a few moments."

He knew it would be useless to tell her not to bother, so he merely nodded. He would let her have her moment, even if it might give Hilda Swenson the impression she was welcome here.

He straightened the papers on his desk, then headed to the parlor.

As soon as he stepped into the room the widow gave him a beaming smile. She sat on the sofa and her three boys occupied the other seating in the room.

He decided to remain standing for the moment.

"Peter, hand Mr. Parker your papers, please," she instructed.

The boy solemnly complied.

Mitch smiled down as he accepted the papers, trying to put the youngster at ease. "Thank you, Peter." He didn't like the idea of discussing the boy's work in front of his siblings. "Perhaps Peter and I should step into my office to review this."

"Oh, there's no need for that. I'm sure his brothers can learn from whatever you have to tell Peter."

Before Mitch could insist, Ivy returned carrying a tray loaded down with two teacups and a platter of sandwiches similar to what they'd had at Eve's place yesterday.

"I thought you might enjoy a bit of refreshment while you have your discussion." She set the tray down on a small table next to the sofa, then turned to the two younger boys. "If you'd care to join me in the kitchen, I just took a tray of cookies out of the oven and need someone to taste them." Then she turned to Mrs. Swenson. "If it's okay with your mother, that is."

Mrs. Swenson graciously gave her permission and the two younger boys hopped up, eager to follow Ivy.

Before they exited, Ivy turned to Peter. "Don't worry. There'll be cookies left when you're done with your business here." Then she turned and ushered Peter's brothers out the door.

Had she overheard his request for more privacy with Peter? Or was she just intuitive when it came to the feelings of others?

Mrs. Swenson recaptured his attention as she reached for a teacup. "It was very charitable of you to hire Miss Feagan as your housekeeper," she said complacently.

Charity had had nothing to do with it, but he didn't feel the need to explain himself. "She's earning her wage."

"I'm certain she is. And she's providing a nice woman's touch to your place." She glanced at the wildflowers Ivy had placed on the mantel this morning. "In fact, I predict that you'll miss all these little niceties once she leaves."

Mrs. Swenson met Mitch's gaze head-on, as if she was intentionally reminding him that Ivy would be leaving soon. Mitch made a noncommittal sound, then turned to Peter. "Before I review your papers, why don't you tell me which parts of this test gave you the most trouble?"

Twenty minutes later, Mitch had finished his assessment. Peter seemed to have grasped all but a few of the basic principles. And the boy had meticulously detailed his computations, so it was easy to see where he'd gotten off track.

Mitch put a hand on Peter's shoulder and turned to the boy's mother. "There's no need to be concerned. Peter has a good understanding of the basics, and I think just a few sessions will set him on the right path."

Mrs. Swenson nodded. "And you'll work with him?"

He glanced down at the boy. "I'll be happy to."

"Then we should discuss payment."

Mitch frowned. "That won't be necessary. As I said, it won't take more than a couple of sessions, and I consider this part of my role as his teacher."

"Then at least let me bake something for you."

"That won't be—"

"Nonsense. I must repay you somehow. And I do so love to bake. Mr. Swenson used to say I was quite the dessert maker."

Apparently the late Mr. Swenson had seen no wrong in his wife. "I'm certain you are. But I have a cook so—"

Again she interrupted his protest. "I won't take no for an answer. Now, which days would be best for you to work with Peter?"

Mitch decided the sooner this was over, the better. "Let's plan on tomorrow and Saturday."

"Perfect."

"And it would be better if I saw Peter alone."

Her expression fell.

"It will allow him to focus solely on his work," he said smoothly. "I'm sure a good mother such as yourself can understand how important that would be."

The bit of praise from him seemed to restore her good humor. "Of course."

Mitch stood. "I won't keep you." He smiled down at the boy. "And don't worry, Peter. We'll have you tackling these math problems with confidence in no time."

Mrs. Swenson stood, as well. "I'm certain Peter will be grateful for your attention. I'll just fetch my other two boys and we'll be on our way."

Mitch wasn't at all sure Ivy would welcome Mrs. Swenson into her kitchen again. "Why don't I fetch them for you?"

She ignored his offer and moved toward the doorway. "No need. I know the way. Besides, I'm sure Peter is eager for the treat your housekeeper promised him."

He found her insistence on referring to Ivy by role rather than name irritating. When they reached the kitchen, Mrs. Swenson paused on the threshold so abruptly Mitch almost bumped into her.

"What is going on in here?" The widow's voice vibrated with outrage.

Mitch stepped past her and had to hide a grin.

Both boys stood on upside down crates around the table. They wore aprons made of large dish towels and were stirring the contents of a large bowl. Flour was everywhere, including the boys' faces and clothing. Ivy stood beside them, a damp cloth in her hand, and it appeared she'd been laughing just prior to their arrival. As for the boys, they were watching their mother with identical guilty expressions.

Ivy, still looking amused, spoke up first. "Don't

worry. It's only flour." She gave the boys approving smiles. "Andy and Davey volunteered to help me make up a fresh batch of cookies. Unfortunately, the flour canister tipped over and a breeze from the window did the rest. My fault entirely." She began wiping the younger boy's face. "I'll have them cleaned up in no time."

Mrs. Swenson marched over, took the cloth from Ivy and began vigorously wiping her son's face. "And just what were my sons doing wearing aprons and mixing cookie dough?"

Ivy frowned uncertainly, as if unsure why the widow was angry. "I apologize if you disapprove. I assure you I wouldn't have let them do anything that—"

Mrs. Swenson cut her off. "Baking is not a skill my boys should be taught, nor do they need to be clothed in an apron. Baking is women's work."

"Quite the contrary," Mitch said, his voice deliberately cold. "Where I come from, some of the finest and most respected pastry chefs are men."

Mrs. Swenson's expression of righteous indignation faltered for a moment, but she recovered and rounded on Ivy again. "Be that as it may, I will thank you to refrain from assigning my sons work of any sort."

It took everything Mitch had not to cross the room and stand between Ivy and Mrs. Swenson's misguided tirade. His desire to protect her—and everything about her that was joyous and charming and thoughtful—was nearly overwhelming.

Ivy held her tongue with difficulty.

Yes, the woman was only being protective of her

children, but her response seemed out of proportion to the offense.

She'd appreciated Mitch's ready defense and while a part of her felt the woman deserved a bit of a set down, she did understand that the woman was only being protective of her children. And it wasn't right to argue with her in front of her sons.

Ivy took a deep breath, reminding herself that she was an employee in this house, and needed to act accordingly. "Please accept my apologies, Mrs. Swenson. Of course I should have asked your permission before allowing your sons to help me. But you can be proud of what polite, helpful boys you're raising here."

The widow seemed to collect herself and gave a short nod. "Thank you. And I'm certain you meant well. I'm sorry if I was abrupt."

With the truce now having been called, quick work was made of getting the children cleaned up. Ivy handed Peter his promised treat and the Swensons finally made their exit.

Ivy went to work scrubbing down the table. To her surprise, however, Mitch returned to the kitchen after he saw his guests out.

She paused long enough to meet his gaze. "Was she still angry?"

"I think she'll get over it."

Was that a glint of amusement in his eyes?

She tried to remain contrite. "I should have thought it through before I invited the boys to help."

"Perhaps. But based on the condition of the kitchen, I'd guess they were enjoying themselves."

Her grin broke through. "That they were."

"And I daresay, Mrs. Swenson may think twice before she brings them here to suffer under your influence again." He gave her a mock frown. "Which is such a shame."

This time she laughed out loud. "You, sir, are not fooling anyone."

He grabbed the broom and helped her finish cleaning up the mess, whistling as he went.

Ivy thought she'd never heard a finer bit of music.

As they exited the church together on the following Sunday, Everett called Mitch over to discuss something about a story he was working on. Ivy waved him on, secretly pleased that he'd glanced her way before leaving her side.

She was looking forward to again having Sunday lunch with Mitch's friends, people she was beginning to think of as her friends, too. She'd once again made arrangements to purchase flowers from her landlady's garden, and was trying to decide whether she should go on and take care of that or wait for Mitch when Mrs. Ortolon approached her.

"How are you this fine Sunday morning?" she asked Ivy.

"I'm doing quite well, thank you. And you?"

"My rheumatism is acting up, but I can't complain," she said with a long-suffering sigh. Then she gave Ivy a sympathetic smile. "But what about you? I understand that you'd fallen and injured yourself when Mr. Parker found you. I hope you've fully recovered."

"Yes, ma'am." Ivy glanced toward Mitch, thinking what a fine hero he made.

"Well, it's unfortunate that you were hurt all the

same. But I must say, that aside, it sounds like a very romantic way to meet."

Ivy nodded, smiling at the memory of those two days at the cabin. "He *was* quite heroic. Bandaged my head, then just lifted me up and plopped me onto that great big horse of his like I didn't weigh more than a pup." She smiled at the memory. "He made me ride while he walked all the way to the cabin. He even cooked me a broth and tended to my mule."

The woman's sharp intake of breath brought Ivy's gaze quickly back around.

"The cabin?" The woman's eyes had narrowed. "I thought Mr. Parker found you on the trail back to town."

The warmth rose in Ivy's cheeks as she realized her slip. Mrs. Ortolon watched her like a child eyeing a new toy.

What had she done?

This was exactly what Mitch had warned her about.

Ivy scrambled for a way to divert the woman's suspicions. "Actually, I was on my way here, but when Mr. Parker found me I wasn't far from the cabin so he took me there first to tend to my cut and let me rest for a bit. Then we came on to town."

Strictly speaking, that sequence of events *was* correct. So why did she feel as if she'd just told a fib?

"Of course."

From the look on her face, Ivy could tell the woman wasn't going to let the matter drop.

Mrs. Ortolon watched her closely. "I believe that wagon you two rode into town on came from the Morrisons' place just outside of town."

"Yes, ma'am. They generously loaned it to us when Mr. Parker told them of our situation."

"Isn't Reggie's cabin quite some distance from the Morrisons' place?"

Ivy didn't like the speculative gleam in the woman's eye. She wished Mitch were here to extricate her from this mess.

As if he'd heard her unvoiced plea, Mitch appeared at her side. "Mrs. Ortolon, how nice to see you."

"Thank you. Miss Feagan and I were just having an interesting conversation on the circumstances of your meeting."

Mitch's expression didn't change and his demeanor remained unruffled, but Ivy could sense tension in him.

"Yes, it was quite fortuitous. But if you'll excuse us, Miss Feagan and I are meeting friends for lunch."

As they moved away, Ivy cast a guilty glance his way. "I'm sorry. I'm afraid I may have let more slip than I intended to."

"What exactly did you tell her?"

Ivy quickly related the conversation. When she was done, Mitch grimaced.

"I'm so sorry."

"You aren't the first to let a secret slip to that woman. She can sniff out gossip like a buzzard scents carrion." He let out a heavy breath. "What's done is done. The question now is, what do we do about it?"

Ivy worried at her lip. "Do you really think it's that bad? I mean, she doesn't know anything for certain."

"That won't matter. She'll relay what she knows and follow it up with 'surely you don't think they…' or 'far be it from me to surmise, but…' And before long the damage will have been done."

Ivy didn't like the set, tight-jawed look on Mitch's face. She liked even less that she'd put it there. If he was right, then this development didn't just affect her—there would be repercussions for him, as well. And it was all her fault. She'd done to him what Lester had done to her, though in her case it hadn't been deliberate.

How could she have been so careless?

Chapter Nineteen

Mitch remained silent as he escorted Ivy to Mrs. Pierce's home. But his mind was churning furiously, trying to process what Ivy's slip of the tongue meant for the two of them. There was a small chance, of course, that nothing would come of it. But he needed to be prepared for the worst. He needed to prepare *Ivy* for the worst.

And come what may, he would make sure she didn't suffer for this. Even if it meant he had to go back on his vow to never remarry. Surprisingly that prospect didn't bother him as much as it would have a mere week ago.

He placed his hand on the gate to Mrs. Pierce's front walk, but didn't open it. He waited for Ivy to meet his gaze, but she didn't seem inclined to do that anytime soon.

"Ivy," he said gently, "we need to talk about this."

She finally looked up, and the regret in her eyes was almost his undoing. "I'm so sorry," she said. "You warned me, but I didn't take it seriously enough."

He touched her arm. It was supposed to be a gesture of comfort, but he felt something more pass between them. "It's not the end of the world. If the worst happens, I promise to step up and give you the protection of my name."

She withdrew her arm from his hold. "I wouldn't dream of asking you to make such a sacrifice."

By the tone of her voice and the injured pride in her expression he realized he'd flubbed his offer. "I truly wouldn't mind."

She opened the gate, her posture stiff. "I know you mean well, but there's no need. Now, let me take care of the flowers so we can be on our way." And with that, she marched toward the porch.

Mitch rubbed the back of his neck. What now? How could he make this right?

"Ivy, I'm sorry if—"

"You've nothing to apologize for. It was an honorable gesture. But we both know how you feel about getting married again, so you'll be relieved to know I release you from all responsibility."

Was she wielding the garden shears with just a little more vigor than necessary? "Will you please just put that down and talk to me face-to-face for a moment?"

She ignored his request. "There's nothing further to say. And we don't want to keep your friends waiting."

And no matter how much he tried, she refused to budge from her position.

It was a quiet walk to The Blue Bottle.

As soon as they stepped inside, it was obvious from the sympathetic looks that everyone had already heard the rumors.

Ivy excused herself and scuttled off to the kitchen as if she couldn't get away from him fast enough.

Mitch watched the kitchen door close behind her,

his frustration curling his hands into fists at his sides. Surely there was something he could do to fix this.

He turned to find all three of his friends regarding him with sympathy. He grimaced. "How bad is it?"

Adam answered first. "Reggie was approached by two different people who heard second-and thirdhand that you and Ivy spent time together at our cabin."

"Mrs. Ortolon was flitting around the churchyard like a bee in a flower garden," Chance added.

"It was entirely innocent," Mitch explained through his clenched jaw. "She was injured and her mule had come up lame. We had no choice."

"We never thought otherwise," Adam assured him.

The other two men nodded agreement, and Mitch felt some of his stiffness ease. He thanked them with a nod and rubbed his jaw. "I plan to do the right thing, of course," he said. "I'm just having trouble convincing Ivy that marrying me *is* the right thing."

Everett clapped him on the back, and Mitch remembered that the newspaperman had once been in a similar situation when Eunice Ortolon had discovered an unlocked door that connected his apartment to Daisy's.

"She hasn't had time to think it through," his friend said in that clipped British accent of his. "Give her time. She'll come around."

Mitch certainly hoped Everett was right.

Ivy stepped into the kitchen, tightly clutching the basket of flowers. What sort of reception would these women give her? If they turned cold or distant, she wasn't sure she could bear it. In fact, it might be best for everyone if she just found an excuse to leave now, before things got awkward or uncomfortable. If she said she felt ill, that wouldn't be a lie—her stomach was tied in knots so tight she'd never be able to eat a bite anyway.

But the women were so unbelievably supportive she almost broke down and cried right there.

Immediately she was engulfed by her friends. Mrs. Peavy took the basket of flowers, Reggie led her to the table and Eve placed a warm cup of tea in her hands.

What should she say? Explanations tumbled around in her mind, chaotic thoughts out of sequence and incomplete. What came out was "It wasn't Mitch's fault."

"Of course it wasn't." Eve patted her hand. "And I'm sure it wasn't yours, either."

"Nothing happened."

"You don't have to explain yourself to us." Reggie took the chair beside her. "We know Mitch is honorable, and we can see what high regard he has for you."

Mitch held her in high regard?

She looked at Reggie. "I stayed two nights at your cabin and borrowed some of your things—I'm sorry I didn't tell you sooner."

Reggie waved a hand dismissively. "Don't give that another thought. I'm just glad it was there when you needed it."

Why were these women being so nice? Would they feel the same if they knew her whole story?

Daisy placed a hand on her shoulder. "You look like you could use a bit of fresh air. Why don't we step out back for a moment?"

Ivy frowned, not certain why Daisy had issued the unexpected invitation, but she saw something in the woman's eyes that convinced her to accept the offer.

They walked in silence for a moment, and then Daisy

spoke up. "I understand how you're feeling, because something very similar happened to me."

Ivy shot her a disbelieving look. "What do you mean?"

"I mean Everett and I were the subject of some rather unpleasant gossip, and were more or less backed into a corner where we had to announce our engagement."

"How awful. But, I mean, it seems obvious you two love each other."

Daisy's smile softened. "Very much. Only it wasn't so obvious then, and I didn't much cotton to the idea of marrying someone who didn't really want to be married."

So Daisy *did* understand. But then again, Daisy wasn't dragging a sullied past into the marriage with her. "Thank you for sharing that with me."

"I told you because I don't want you to lose heart. I've seen the way Mitch looks at you, and you at him. The two of you are good with and for each other."

Ivy wished that were true. "Thank you, but this is more complicated than it appears. We're friends and that's as far as it *can* go. I'll be returning to Nettles Gap in a couple of weeks and then Mitch can get on with his life."

"I don't believe that will be as easy for him as you think."

Ivy's heart fluttered at that. But much as she wanted to believe it, she was sure Daisy was mistaken. Besides, what was the use? There were too many obstacles in their way. And now this.

She mustered a smile. "We ought to be getting back. It'll be time to set the table by now."

Daisy touched her arm lightly. "Please think about

what I said. And no matter what you decide, remember that you have friends here."

There was no further mention of the gossip, and the meal proceeded as it had the previous Sunday. But this time Ivy studiously avoided looking Mitch's way.

She couldn't keep him from her thoughts, though. She remained acutely aware of his every movement, his every word. And try as she might, she couldn't forget what Daisy had told her.

Later, as they left The Blue Bottle together, Ivy nervously waited for Mitch to say something. Would he press her to marry him again, or had he accepted her refusal as the out he needed?

When they reached the crossroad where they would normally turn to go to his home, Ivy halted. "Perhaps I should leave you here."

He frowned down at her. "We need to talk. The sooner we settle this matter, the better."

"I consider it already settled."

His frown deepened. "Do you really want to have this discussion here on this street corner?"

She glared at him. She was not going to let him bully her into giving in. "I certainly don't think it advisable for us to have it inside your house right now."

His jaw worked for a moment, and then he nodded. "Agreed. We can have our discussion as we walk Rufus." He arched a brow. "Assuming that's acceptable?"

She supposed she couldn't put him off forever. She gave what she hoped was a regal nod. "It is."

No sooner were they following an exuberant Rufus out the front gate than Mitch said, "We must announce our engagement immediately."

Well, at least he wasn't beating around the bush. "We'll do no such thing."

"I understand that this isn't the ideal arrangement for either of us, but there's no other solution. You may think you don't care about your reputation, but believe me, when everyone starts whispering and staring, you'll change your mind."

"I won't." She took a deep breath. It was time to be totally honest. "And I'm not guessing. I've already been through that, and I know exactly how it feels."

He stopped in his tracks. "What do you mean?"

She turned to face him, her gaze locked to his with all the intensity she could muster. "My reputation was already shredded five years ago."

Mitch saw the pain behind her brave facade. Who had hurt her? He suddenly wanted to find whoever was responsible for that haunted look in her eyes and make him pay.

They were passing the deserted school yard, and he led her to one of the swings. He leaned against a tree and waited for her to explain.

She finally met his gaze. "Aren't you going to ask me what happened?"

"Only if you want to tell me. But I know whatever happened, you were wronged."

He saw her eyes fill with tears then, but she didn't allow them to fall. Instead, she nodded and pushed the swing into a lazy rocking motion. "I'd like to tell you about it."

"Then I'm honored to listen."

"When I was sixteen, a young man decided to court me. To this day, I'm not really certain why. He was quite prominent in our community—the son of the mercantile owner—and several girls had made it clear they would welcome his advances. The thing was, I didn't share his feelings and tried to tell him so. But he apparently thought I was just being coy."

Mitch thought of his situation with Mrs. Swenson. But how much worse must it have been for her?

She wrapped her arms around the ropes holding up the swing. "Finally, at one of the town dances, when he was being particularly insistent, I made my feelings very clear, telling him in no uncertain terms just how I felt. Unfortunately, the encounter was not as private as I'd thought and Lester felt humiliated."

So this cad's name was Lester.

"Lester couldn't accept what I'd done—not when I'd so inadvertently but thoroughly stomped on his pride. So he figured out a way to get even."

Mitch hadn't even heard what the cad had done and already he was ready to throttle him. It was probably just as well the oaf wasn't in striking distance.

"We had a goat that liked to wander off. He never went far, but one day I had trouble finding him and ended up going farther into the woods than I'd realized. Then I found the animal tied to a tree. Before I could do more than wonder what was going on, someone placed a bag over my head and tied my hands behind my back. Then, without saying a word, he forced me to walk what seemed a long ways. The more I struggled, the tighter his grip on my shoulder."

She rubbed her shoulder, as if reliving the experience. Mitch's hands fisted helplessly at his sides, but, sensing she needed to keep going, he didn't say anything.

"He finally stopped and then pushed me to the ground. I struggled to get back on my feet, more afraid than I'd ever been in my whole life, wondering what would happen next. But nothing did. I couldn't hear anyone, and because the sack was over my head, I couldn't see anything, either. I finally realized he'd just abandoned me there. I stumbled around for a bit, then somehow managed to get that sack off."

That was his girl, resourceful even when scared out of her wits.

"Whoever had tied me up was long gone. But I had no idea where I was. I didn't have any choice but to start walking. After about twenty minutes, a stranger found me. At first I thought it was the person who'd tied me up and I started running from him. But he caught up with me and was very kind. Said he'd been out hunting when he spotted me. He untied me and helped me find my way back to town."

She stopped, but he had a feeling there was more to the story, so he bided his time without responding. But it was very hard not to pull her into his arms then and there.

"We came out of the woods in a spot near the Lowells' farm. They were having a barn raising and most of the town was there. It was late evening and folks were gathering up their things. I was so relieved to see familiar faces I almost sobbed."

She paused for a long moment. "And just as we cleared the woods, the man who'd rescued me pulled me into a tight embrace and gave me a kiss, right on the lips. I could hear the gasps even from a distance."

He wanted to gather her into his arms and give her

what comfort he could. But not here in the open. He'd be doing her no favors if he did that.

"He finally stepped back," she continued, "gave my cheek a pat, then turned and marched back into the woods, leaving me to face everyone alone. I knew I looked a sight—my dress was dirty and torn, my hair in wild disarray." Her expression turned grimmer still. "And then I saw Lester, smirking at me, enjoying my disgrace. And I knew—deep in my heart, I *knew*—that he had planned the whole thing."

She pushed the swing in motion again. "After that, my reputation was in shreds. Everyone believed the worst. I was shunned by most everyone in town." She looked up at him. "So you see, there's no need to worry about my 'good name,' because I haven't had one in a very long time."

Everything inside Mitch was wound tight enough to explode. He could barely breathe right now the need to avenge her was so strong. If the cowardly little weasel had been in Turnabout, there was no telling what he would have done. But right now he had Ivy's feelings to consider. And he was more determined than ever to give her the protection of his name. "Perhaps that's true in Nettles Gap, but not here."

She smiled sadly. "I think the events of today paint a different story."

"Not if you marry me. Even if it's an in-name-only arrangement, if you move here you'll have a fresh start and friends who will welcome you into their midst."

She firmly shook her head. "That's a very generous offer, especially given your feelings about getting married again."

Was that what was holding her back? He should

never have told her how he felt, even if he'd thought at the time he was protecting her.

Or maybe he'd just been trying to protect himself.

"Besides, once this case is resolved I'll be headed back to Nettles Gap."

"But you don't have to—head back to Nettles Gap, I mean. Once the judge settles this case you'll own land here. Why not move here where you can get a fresh start? Turnabout is a really good place for that."

"I told you, Nana Dovie won't leave home, and I won't leave Nana Dovie."

It seemed they were at an impasse. "Then at least marry me before you go. You can return to Nettles Gap as my wife. That should change your standing in the community."

For a moment he thought she would agree, but then she shook her head. "Thank you, but I can't."

"Can't? Or won't? You need to take emotions out of this and be reasonable."

"I *am* being reasonable. When I marry, it's going to be for love. Otherwise, everything I've gone through the past five years has been for nothing."

Mitch had no response to that. The fact that her words indicated she didn't love him was irrelevant.

So why did he feel this stab of disappointment?

Brushing that thought aside, he tried again. "If you can't do it for yourself, then do it for me."

"What do you mean?"

"I don't want to be known as a man who won't take responsibility for his mistakes."

She winced, then straightened. "I think your reputation is strong enough to survive this, especially once I'm gone." She lifted her chin. "But if you're really worried, I can make it obvious that you asked and I refused."

"Will you do it to save me from the advances of women like Mrs. Swenson?"

At least that won him a grin. "Coward. I'm afraid you'll have to find another way to deal with the women who are attracted to you." She stood and brushed at her skirt. "Now, I think Rufus has chased enough squirrels for the afternoon."

"We're not through with this discussion."

"I am. At least for today." She whistled for Rufus and began to walk away.

Mitch shook his head and followed the frustrating woman.

Ivy held herself together by sheer willpower. She was doing the right thing, so why did it hurt so much? For all his support and kindness, Mitch had never once mentioned love.

She didn't know why she'd thought he might—perhaps it was Daisy's comments that had planted that idea in her mind. But it was now crystal clear that he was proposing marriage out of a sense of obligation and nothing more. He wanted to protect her and that was admirable, but it wasn't the same as love.

The problem was, she now realized, *she* loved *him*.

There it was, plain as the sun in the sky and every bit as big. She loved him, and because she did, she couldn't allow him to sacrifice himself for her.

No matter how sweet the thought of a life with him sounded.

Mitch walked her to Mrs. Pierce's house and left her at the front gate. She could tell he was unhappy with her decision, but there was no help for it. And after she'd returned to Nettles Gap, he'd realize she'd been right.

The first thing Ivy did when she stepped inside the house was seek out her landlady, whom she found doing some stitchwork in the parlor.

"I suppose you heard the whispers," she said without preamble.

Mrs. Pierce looked up from her stitchery. "I don't indulge in idle chitchat much these days." There seemed to be a wealth of meaning in her words.

Ivy took a deep breath, drew her shoulders back and met the woman's mildly curious gaze. "They're saying that Mr. Parker and I spent time together at the cabin before coming into town."

The widow set the cloth and needle on the sofa, and then folded her hands in her lap. "And did you?"

Ivy tilted her chin up. "I was injured and Mr. Parker didn't have a way to get me into town right away."

"So that means yes."

Ivy gave a short nod. It was hard to tell what the woman was thinking. "If you want me to move out, just say the word."

"What you did or did not do is none of my concern so long as you continue to pay the rent and follow my rules."

Some of the rigidness left Ivy's spine. "Of course."

"Will you be continuing to work for Mr. Parker?"

"For now. We want to go on as before."

"I see." Mrs. Pierce picked up her sewing again. "If, by some happenstance, you find yourself no longer able to work for Mr. Parker, I may have some work for you myself."

Ivy was both surprised and touched by the out-of-the-blue offer. "What kind of work?"

"I hear you are making curtains for Mr. Parker's kitchen, so I assume you can sew."

Ivy nodded.

"I have decided it's time to add a bit of color to my wardrobe again. But none of my older gowns fit as they should. I need someone to take them in for me."

"I would be more than happy to help you with that task in the evenings."

"Then we will come up with a price per garment that we can agree on and adjust your weekly rent payment accordingly."

"Mrs. Pierce, I meant I would be glad to help you as a *friend*."

The woman paused midstitch for just a heartbeat. Then she nodded. "Thank you."

"If you like, you could select several pieces now and we could take a look at what needs to be done."

The woman rose gracefully from the sofa. "I suppose that would be acceptable." She moved to the doorway, then paused and glanced back at Ivy, her demeanor cool. "And afterward, perhaps you would care to join me for supper." Her expression softened. "And please, call me Eileen."

"I'd be honored."

Ivy watched Eileen leave the room. This had definitely been a day of emotional highs and lows. She'd let slip the secret that brought her and Mitch under judgmental scrutiny. But then God had used the opportunity to show her what good friends she had in the women who were part of the Sunday lunch gathering.

Mitch had tried to convince her to marry him and in

doing so had made it clear that he didn't love her. But she had discovered that she loved him, and though it was a bittersweet realization, it was one she still treasured.

And now she had this new opportunity to crack through the wall Eileen Pierce had built around herself and forge a friendship.

Dear Lord, I'd hoped this little vacation from everyone looking down their nose at me would last while I was here. But I did this to myself so I don't have any call to be complaining. Thank You for giving me a passel of blessings to help offset the trials. Please help me to focus on those blessings, and to make my peace with the trials.

And chief among those blessings was Mitch. No matter the outcome, she would never be sorry for this time she'd had with him.

And she still had to find a way to help him. On top of everything else, she had to make sure this gossip didn't hurt him.

But how?

The next morning, Ivy did her best to hold her head up and smile as she walked through town. She hoped for the best but braced herself for snubs.

The first few people she encountered seemed more uncertain than affronted. She received tentative smiles and nods in return for her greetings. She saw a couple of women on the other side of the street whispering behind their hands, and she tried to convince herself they were talking about something besides her.

Then, as she passed Daisy's restaurant, Abigail stepped out onto the sidewalk. She linked her arm through Ivy's with a smile. "Mind if I walk to the mercantile with you? I need to pick up some flour for Daisy."

"Of course." Had this been Abigail's idea or had Daisy put her up to it? Regardless, Ivy was grateful for the show of support. Especially when they arrived at the mercantile to find Mrs. Ortolon there talking to two other ladies.

The conversation came to an abrupt stop when they entered. Abigail ignored it all, and keeping her arm firmly locked with Ivy's, she approached the counter and greeted the proprietor as well as Mrs. Ortolon and her friends.

Ivy almost felt sorry for them. Abigail was relentless in her cheerful chatter, giving them no choice but to respond or seem churlish. When they parted company, Abigail gave her a very tight, very public hug. "Don't forget you have friends here," the girl whispered. And then she was gone.

Buoyed by that encounter, Ivy had no trouble keeping a smile on her face as she walked the rest of the way to Mitch's.

She arrived to find him standing outside talking to two young men.

He immediately waved her over. "I'd like to introduce you to Calvin and James Hendricks. I've hired them to paint my house and shutters."

Both youths tipped their hats respectfully in response to her greeting, then turned back to their work.

Ivy frowned. Mitch's house didn't really need painting. Maybe she'd had some influence on him and he'd decided to add some color. She leaned forward, eager to check out the paint cans, then dropped back on her heels in disappointment. It was stark white, the same color as his existing walls.

She shook her head. "While you're going to all of this trouble, might I suggest you at least think about painting your shutters red to match your door."

Mitch studied his house for a moment, then nodded. "Good idea." He turned to the older of the young men. "Calvin, we may need another can of the red paint."

Calvin saluted with his paintbrush. "Yes, sir, I'll take care of it."

As Ivy watched this exchange, it suddenly hit her— Mitch had hired the Hendricks brothers not because he had a pressing need to paint his home, but to serve as very visible chaperones for the next few days.

She didn't know whether to be grateful or irritated. Then she decided she was a little of both.

As she climbed the back porch steps, she mentally reviewed her basket of groceries and what she could remember of the pantry contents and decided it would stretch to feed two additional people who would likely have hearty appetites after working out in this heat all morning. She'd decided last night that one way to try to help him was to get him to talk about his wife. It was an understandably touchy subject for him, but she needed to understand, and she also felt it would be good for him to share his hurt, as well.

She just had to find the right time....

Mitch watched as Ivy dusted the bookshelves. She seemed unusually pensive this afternoon. Was the gossip taking its toll on her? Perhaps it was time to renew his efforts. "So, have you been thinking about what we discussed yesterday?"

She didn't turn around. "It would be hard not to."

Her dry tone gave nothing away. "And are you ready to see reason and admit marriage is the best course of action? I assure you, I *will* let you go your own way afterward if that's what you want."

She was silent for a long moment, and he wished she would turn around so he could see her face. Finally, she did.

"I told you, when I marry, it will be for love."

There was a finality in her tone that seemed to slam the door on the subject. But it was the words themselves that struck him hard. She was saying she wouldn't marry him because she didn't love him.

Not that he was looking for love from her. It was just, well, didn't she feel even the least bit of affection?

"Do you mind if I ask you something personal?"

There was something in her tone that told him he wouldn't like the question. Still, he couldn't bring himself to deny her, so he gave a short nod.

"What was your wife like?"

Mitch kept his expression carefully neutral, but it took some effort. "The first word that comes to mind when thinking of Gretchen is *gentle*. She was a very sweet, very delicate woman."

Ivy nodded. "You must have loved her very much."

Mitch straightened a few papers on his desk, not meeting her gaze. He had cared for Gretchen, very much. But—

He realized Ivy was still waiting for his answer. "Everyone who knew Gretchen loved her." He moved a stack of papers on his desk by a half inch. "And she loved me, right up until the day she died, though I never did quite figure out why."

"I know why." Her soft words caught him by surprise and he glanced up quickly.

She reddened and turned back to her dusting. "That's why you're so set against getting married again, isn't it? You're still in mourning and don't want to go through the pain of losing someone again." She shot him a look over her shoulder. "But that's the wrong way to look at it. If you don't let yourself love again, it's true you might never again hurt as deeply, but you'll never find joy, either. And that would be very sad."

"I've asked you to marry me, haven't I?"

"Because you feel like you must, not because you want to."

"Why does that matter?"

She shrugged. "Because it does."

He hesitated a moment. She'd bared her soul to him yesterday. Now it was his turn. "You're wrong."

That earned him a startled look.

"About the reason behind my decision to not marry again," he explained. "It's not because I mourn Gretchen so deeply. It's because I killed her."

Chapter Twenty

Ivy wasn't certain she'd heard right. "By accident, you mean."

His lips compressed in a hard line. "It was a deliberate action on my part that led to her death."

Just as she'd thought. "Then you didn't kill her. You just feel responsible for whatever happened." She crossed the room to stand in front of his desk. "Tell me what happened."

He raked a hand through his hair. "Gretchen didn't believe in violence, not for any reason, not even in self-defense. She believed one should always turn the other cheek, no matter what. And I tried to live that way, for her sake."

"Tried?"

"Pacifism doesn't come easily to me. But I was successful, for a time. Then one of our neighbors, a fellow named Early, started a feud over land boundaries. And no matter how much Gretchen pleaded with me to just give in, I wouldn't do it. I'd worked that land with my own two hands and I intended it to be a legacy to my children someday."

"It was your right to stand up for what was yours."

Mitch continued as if she hadn't spoken. "The dispute escalated. I took Early to court and won my case. I was quite proud of myself. I'd managed to hold on to my land without resorting to violence."

He made a sound that was full of self-derision. "But the man's son decided to ignore the judge's orders and began tearing down fences. Before I could do anything about it, he broke his neck when his horse threw him. Unfortunately, it happened on my property. When I carried his body back to his father, he didn't believe it was an accident."

How awful that must have been—for all parties.

"No matter how I tried to explain, Early blamed me. That night he came riding onto my place all drunk and wild-eyed and ready for blood. Gretchen begged me to stay inside, but I stepped out with my rifle. There was a gunfight and a stray bullet found its way into the house and killed Gretchen."

His gaze finally met hers again and she was shocked at the bleakness she saw there. "She was carrying our baby at the time," he said dully.

Jagged shards of horror pierced Ivy's heart at the thought of what he'd gone through. She came around to his side of the desk and took both of his hands. "Oh, Mitch, I'm so sorry. That must have been terrible for you." She squeezed his hands. "But her death was *not* your fault."

"Wasn't it? If I had done what Gretchen wanted, if I had turned the other cheek and not taken him to court, Gretchen and the baby would still be alive."

"You can't know that for sure."

"Their chances would certainly have been better."

"But what would have happened to you?"

"Me? I would have been poorer, but I imagine I would have survived, as well."

"Physically. But if you had done as your wife wished and let that neighbor run roughshod over you, it would have eaten away at the part of you that needs to take care of your family and build a home that is safe and secure. It would have made you feel less of a man and more than likely affected the way you viewed your relationship with your wife."

He gave her a self-mocking smile. "Don't you believe in turning the other cheek, in reserving vengeance for the Lord, the way it says in the Bible?"

"There is a time and place for that. But there is also a time to stand up and defend yourself and your loved ones. And yes, that's biblical."

He didn't seem entirely convinced.

"Mitch, have you prayed about this?"

"I haven't come to terms with God on this matter yet." He said this almost defiantly, as if trying to shock her. "I went a little crazy for a while. Nearly killed Early and did some property damage." His lips twisted in a grimace. "It should have been me who died that night, not Gretchen."

"Don't you dare say that. Don't even think it. God left you here for a reason—don't try to second-guess Him. It's hard when we lose our loved ones, but we've got to trust that God is in control and that He loves us." She saw a flicker of doubt in his eyes. "He *does* love you," she said firmly. "There's nothing you can do that He won't forgive, if you just ask Him to."

Mitch pulled his hands from hers and stood. "If

you'll excuse me, I think I'll go see how the Hendricks boys are doing." And with that, he strode from the room.

Ivy stood there for a long time after he'd gone, her heart breaking for him. The story he'd related had been truly heartrending—to have lost not only his wife but his unborn child in such a manner—how had he borne up under such pain? That was a terrible burden to carry all on his own. No wonder he was afraid to give his heart again.

But his thinking was flawed. Somehow she had to make him see that.

It had become her new goal.

Later that afternoon Ivy answered a knock at Mitch's door to find Carter Mosley standing there, hat in hand.

"Miss Feagan, could I speak to you for a few minutes?"

She opened the door. "Of course. Come in."

Mitch stepped out into the hall. "Who is it?" Then he saw Carter and his eyes narrowed. "Is there something I can do for you?"

"Actually, I came to speak to Miss Feagan."

"Perhaps you should wait to do your talking when the judge arrives."

Ivy held up a hand. "No, it's all right. I'd like to hear what he has to say."

Mitch crossed his arms. "Then I hope the two of you won't mind if I sit in."

"Not at all." Carter fingered the brim of his hat. "Look, I know I wasn't very civil last time we spoke, and you have every right to be angry, but I'm sorry for that and I hope you'll hear me out now."

Mitch waved an arm toward the parlor. "Let's talk in here."

As soon as they took their seats, Carter began. "I won't lie. I didn't believe your story. And I'm afraid I acted badly." He gave her a penitent look. "For that, you have my apologies."

Ivy relaxed. "Of course. You were grieving your uncle's death and it was unfair of us to spring that on you so quickly."

He nodded acceptance of her forgiveness. "I didn't leave it there. I sent one of the hands, a man I respect, to Nettles Gap to check things out and learn what he could about you."

Ivy tensed again. Surely he had heard about her ruined reputation. Would he spread the stories here to enforce the current gossip?

"Sonny talked to a number of people there," Carter continued. "And he learned that you are exactly who you say you are, Robert Feagan's daughter."

"And?" At least the story about what Lester had done to her wouldn't come as a surprise to Mitch.

"*And,* after reading the papers my uncle left me, including a journal, I'm withdrawing my objections to your claim. I'd like us to settle this matter without going to court."

Ivy blinked. It was impossible to believe his man hadn't heard the gossip from Nettles Gap. Why hadn't he brought it up? But Carter was watching her with something very akin to neighborly sympathy. Was silence on the matter his way of strengthening his apology?

"I'd like that, too," she said with a more genuine smile.

Mitch leaned forward. "What sort of settlement did you have in mind?"

"Something that will be fair to all parties, that will honor Uncle Drum's wishes. We can work through the details when we get down to drawing up the paperwork." He stood. "I need to get back to the ranch, but with your permission, I'll set up an appointment with Mr. Barr for later in the week. Hopefully we'll be able to work things out to everyone's satisfaction in very short order."

Ivy accepted his outstretched hand and shook it. "That's my hope, as well."

"Once we determine what portion of the estate you're entitled to," Carter said diffidently, "I hope you'll consider letting me buy you out."

Ivy smiled. "Of course. And I want you to know that I don't intend to take advantage. My pa didn't put all the hard work into the place that you and your uncle did, so I'm not looking for an even split."

Ivy was thrilled that they wouldn't be going to court. And the thought that she would have money to bring back to Nana Dovie…

But her joy was short-lived. Because she was just now realizing that the sooner she and Carter settled, the sooner she'd be on her way back to Nettles Gap. And away from Mitch.

Mitch listened to the rest of the exchange without comment. It appeared things were going to work out to Ivy's satisfaction. And while he was happy to see she wouldn't be going through a contentious legal battle, he wasn't as happy about what that meant. Once they met with Adam this week, there'd be nothing left to hold

her here. She'd be free to return to Nettles Gap and her
Nana Dovie…without marrying him.

He couldn't let her do that. He had a responsibility
here, and a reputation of his own to protect. After all,
what parent would want their child's teacher to have a
questionable reputation?

He had to convince her to marry him. He simply had
to. He was just being practical, after all.

But from somewhere deep inside, a voice whispered,
Coward, over and over.

The next morning, instead of Abigail accompanying
Ivy to the mercantile, Reggie "happened" to be going
in the same direction. They met Jack and Ira outside
the newspaper office and Ivy picked up Mitch's newspaper. And once again, Ivy felt deep gratitude for the
new friends she'd made in Turnabout.

Once she arrived at Mitch's place, she greeted the
Hendricks brothers and invited them to share in her
planned lunch of pan-fried chicken and gravy with garden vegetables, then headed inside to fix breakfast for
Mitch.

She handed him his newspaper, glad he would have
that to occupy him while she cooked breakfast. Perhaps
it would keep him from renewing his arguments for why
she should marry him before she left.

Ever since she'd realized yesterday that she only had
a few days left in Turnabout, the time seemed to be
speeding by much too quickly. By the end of the week
she'd be headed back to Nettles Gap. For just a moment
she'd had a wild urge to send word to Carter to delay
their meeting with Adam.

But this little interlude had to end sometime, and

perhaps it was better that it happen quickly. Now that the story of their time at the cabin had come to light, it would be less awkward for Mitch if she were no longer around as a reminder.

He could go back to his normal routine. She prayed, however, that he wouldn't isolate himself so much in the future and that, someday, someone would come along whom he could love enough to share himself with.

Someone sweet, gentle, delicate.

Someone, obviously, unlike her.

Just before lunch, there was a knock at the door. As Ivy bustled to answer it, she grinned. For a man who "never had visitors," he certainly had received his share of callers lately. Perhaps things were changing for him.

She opened the door and her smile, along with everything inside her, froze.

"Hello, Ivy."

Lester Stokes, the man who'd ruined her life, stood there, smiling like a fox facing a cornered rabbit.

Chapter Twenty-One

For a moment Ivy couldn't speak. What in the world was Lester Stokes doing in Turnabout?

"Well," he said in that cocky drawl she hated, "aren't you going to invite me in?"

Ivy made no move to step aside. "What are you doing here?"

She saw a flash of irritation in his eyes, but his smile never faltered. He stepped closer. "I really think it would be best—"

He halted abruptly, and Ivy realized Mitch now stood behind her.

He must be an intimidating sight to a bully like Lester Stokes.

"Care to introduce me to your friend?" Mitch's tone was mild, but Ivy suddenly felt as if nothing bad could touch her.

"Of course. This is Lester Stokes." She felt Mitch's subtle stiffening.

"Lester, this is Mr. Mitch Parker, my employer."

Mitch stepped forward and offered his hand to Lester. "Are you an acquaintance from Nettles Gap?"

Lester quickly withdrew his hand. "That's right. Ivy and I grew up together."

Lester gave Ivy a meaningful glance. "If you have a few minutes, I need to talk to you." He cut a quick glance Mitch's way. "On a personal matter."

Mitch leaned against the doorjamb with folded arms, apparently oblivious to Lester's hints.

Lester frowned in annoyance, then turned back to Ivy.

"I'm afraid I have bad news about Miss Jacobs."

Ivy's heart stuttered painfully, her mind dishing up all sorts of awful possibilities. "Is she all right?"

"She fell and hurt herself. Doc says she shouldn't be alone until she heals. My ma is with her, but I thought you should know as soon as possible."

"Yes, of course." She turned to Mitch, her thoughts racing. "I'm sorry. I need to go to her."

"Tell me what I can do to help."

Lester spoke up before Ivy could. "Everything is taken care of. I've already booked a return passage on tomorrow's train. And my sister, Dory, is with me—she's at the hotel right now—so Ivy shouldn't feel any discomfort with our traveling together."

Ivy's mind was awhirl with disjointed thoughts of things she needed to take care of before she left and images of a hurting Nana Dovie needing her. She should never have stayed away so long. "My meeting with Carter and Adam—"

"I'll let them know to reschedule."

"Tomorrow is laundry day—"

"I'm certain Mrs. Pierce will understand."

"Rufus and Jubal—"

"Ivy." Mitch took her hands, forcing her to focus on

his words. "Don't worry. I'll watch over your animals until you return. And I'll see that those who need to know, do. As for your housekeeping duties—" he gave her a crooked smile "—I'll manage to cook my own meals and care for my own house just fine."

She took a deep breath, drawing strength from his supportive presence. "Thank you."

She turned to Lester and was surprised by the furious look in his eyes. Was he so bothered by the fact that she'd found a friend and champion in Mitch?

"Thank you for bringing me the news. I'll be ready to leave when the train pulls in tomorrow."

Mitch eyed Lester critically. "I wonder why you didn't send a telegram. Miss Feagan could have already made it to Nettles Gap by now."

Ivy frowned. In her concern over Nana Dovie, she hadn't thought things through. Mitch was right—why *had* he come? And why Lester, of all people? He'd be the last person who'd want to do her any favors.

"I thought it best Ivy receive such upsetting news from a friend rather than a telegram," Lester said. "And I didn't want her to have to make the trip alone."

Since when did Lester consider himself her friend? Then Ivy took herself to task. Carter was proof people could change. Perhaps this was Lester's way of making up for past wrongs.

"I know this has come as a shock," Lester continued. "Why don't I escort you to your lodgings so you can rest?"

"Thank you, but if I do that I'll just go crazy worrying. It's best I keep busy." She started to untie her apron. "And I should send Nana Dovie a telegram to assure her I'll be there tomorrow."

"I'll take care of that for you," Lester said quickly. "And I'll come by when you're done here and take you to supper. I'm certain Dory will appreciate your company."

"You don't need—"

"I insist." Lester gave Mitch a terse nod, then turned and left before Ivy could protest further.

Mitch didn't like this—something about Lester Stokes's story seemed off.

Once Ivy closed the door, he crossed his arms. "Is this the same Lester you mentioned once before?"

Ivy nodded.

Mitch's hands fisted at his sides. Just the thought of what that snake had put Ivy through was enough to make him throw his vows of nonviolence to the winds. "Then I don't want you traveling with him tomorrow. I'll escort you to Nettles Gap myself."

She placed a hand on his arm. "Thank you. But that won't be necessary. Lester is obviously trying to make amends, and with Dory tagging along, I'm sure he'll be on his best behavior."

"I'm not so sure his motives are as benevolent as you appear to believe."

She waved away his concerns. "I'll be fine. I'm not a naive sixteen-year-old any longer. If Lester does resort to some of his old tricks—which I highly doubt—I can take care of myself."

"Be that as it may—"

"Please. There's enough gossip circulating about us as it is. How do you think it will look if you follow me back to Nettles Gap?"

"How it will look is not my primary concern."

She gave him a teasing smile. "I never thought I'd hear those words from Mr. Propriety himself." Then she moved past him toward the kitchen. "Now, lunch should be just about ready. Would you ask Calvin and James to get washed up and join us?"

Mitch watched her head down the hall, frustration almost smothering him. No matter how much he reasoned or cajoled, she still refused to marry him. And now she was leaving in the morning. She'd return, of course, once Miss Jacobs was better. But only to complete the negotiation with Carter. After today, he wouldn't have her to himself, or even in his life again. Order and peace would be restored.

And he couldn't garner even a speck of enthusiasm for that prospect.

The next morning, Ivy settled into her seat on the train and stared out the window. Mitch stood on the platform, Rufus at his side, watching as the train pulled away. Perhaps it was best this way, for them to have this clean break now, before the gossip could do any more damage.

But there was no denying how much she was going to miss Turnabout.

And Mitch.

When the train turned a curve and the town finally disappeared from sight, Ivy sat back and smiled at Dory beside her. "Thank you again for coming here with your brother."

The girl glanced nervously toward Lester, then gave Ivy a shy smile. "You're welcome. It was a chance for me to see someplace other than Nettles Gap."

Lester, who sat across the aisle from them, stood. "Dory, change seats with me. Ivy and I need to talk."

Something about Lester's tone raised Ivy's hackles. "What about?"

Lester didn't answer her until he was comfortably settled beside her. "First, I wanted to put your mind at ease. Miss Jacobs is not injured—in fact, as far as I know, she's as healthy as the day you left her."

Ivy stiffened, her relief quickly followed by anger. Lester Stokes had fooled her *again*. But before she could say anything, he pressed on.

"I just needed a good excuse to get you back to Nettles Gap with minimum resistance and fuss."

Icy spider legs scuttled up her spine. "Why?"

"Because of your inheritance, of course."

How did he even *know* about that? Surely Reverend Tomlin hadn't said anything.

"Someone came to town last week looking for information on you and your pa. I convinced him to tell me what was going on. Imagine my surprise when I found out that you're going to be a prominent landowner soon."

"So?"

"So, you're going to marry me, and as your husband, I'm going to gain control of that land."

Marry him? Ivy was so astonished she hardly knew what to say next. "What makes you think for even a minute that I'd consent to such a thing?"

"Because I'm not going to give you much choice. I can call in your precious Nana Dovie's loan if you don't."

Ivy blanched, then recovered. It was Lester's father who held the note on their place. And he was a much fairer man than Lester had ever been. Besides, that would soon be a moot point. "If my claim holds, it won't matter. I'll be able to pay the loan without any trouble."

"But not before we've already repossessed the farm. There are ways to delay the judge's arrival. And there are also ways to throw doubt on your claim to be who you say you are. Oh, you'll win your case eventually, but think of the damage that can be done by the time you do."

She stared at him defiantly. "I don't need to wait for the judge. Carter Mosley and I have discussed settling this between us."

Some of his confidence seemed to slip. "You haven't signed any papers yet, have you?"

"No, but I gave my word—"

"Then it's not too late to back out. From what I can tell, you have a claim to half of the whole estate."

"But that's not what I agreed to. And with this offer from Carter, I should be able to get matters settled quickly, so there's nothing for you to hold over me." Surely he couldn't force her hand.

His expression turned ugly. "You think not? Do you really believe you can get matters settled and have money in hand before I evict Miss Jacobs?"

She hesitated and he grinned triumphantly. "I've heard how she can't leave her place. I hear she gets agitated and downright hysterical if she tries. I wonder how it will affect her if the sheriff comes by to toss her out?"

"You might be that cruel, Lester Stokes, but I don't think your father is. Especially if I tell him about the money I'll have shortly."

"My parents are on a business trip. He left me in

charge until he returns, which may be as much as a month from now."

Ivy felt trapped, but struggled not to show it. "How can you do this? You already have so much."

His face twisted. "I have nothing—it's all my father's. Gaining control of that land means I won't have to live under his thumb anymore."

The dark determination in his expression scared her. "What if I just sign over a part of my inheritance to you?"

He seemed to think about that for a minute, then shook his head. "I know you've gotten cozy with that boss of yours. No doubt he'd help you find some way to wiggle out of the deal. No, the only way to be certain is for us to get hitched."

Ivy frantically tried to come up with a way out. How could she marry Lester after she'd spurned Mitch, saying she'd hold out for a love match?

But if she didn't, Nana Dovie would lose her home, and worse. She couldn't bear to think what it would do to that dear lady if she were forced to leave.

Nana Dovie had made many, many sacrifices to raise her, and now it was time for Ivy to return the favor, no matter how distasteful the task before her might be.

"Nana Dovie must never, under any circumstances, learn why I'm doing this."

His face contorted into a triumphant smirk. "Agreed."

Chapter Twenty-Two

Mitch knelt in the garden, pulling weeds. Rufus lay nearby with his head forlornly resting on his front paws. It had been two days since the train had carried Ivy away, but it felt more like two months.

Mitch could barely stand to be inside the house. It seemed too quiet, too empty.

He felt empty.

He sat back on his haunches and stared at Rufus. "What's happening to me? I never considered myself melodramatic before."

The dog gave a halfhearted bark.

"Don't worry, she hasn't abandoned you. She'll be back in a few days to meet with Carter and Adam. Which means I'll have one more shot at getting her to see reason."

Rufus set his head back down on his paws, watching Mitch with doubtful eyes.

"I don't understand why she's so resistant to the idea of marrying me. I know she's been hurt, but given our situation, compromises must be made."

He stabbed at the ground with the trowel. "If I can

put my feelings aside and enter into marriage again after vowing I never would, then surely she can do the same."

He pointed the trowel Rufus's way. "And as for this matter of holding out for a love match—" Mitch slowly lowered his arm. "Perhaps, if she married me, love would come with time."

This time Rufus's bark was more enthusiastic.

Mitch gave him a wry grin. "One thing you do have going for you is that you're a good listener."

Suddenly the dog lifted his head, an alert look on his face. A moment later he was up and racing to the front yard.

Did they have company? Had Ivy returned already?

Mitch followed the dog in long strides. He rounded the corner to see not Ivy but Zeke Tarn from the train depot. Swallowing his disappointment, Mitch slowed his step.

Zeke descended the porch steps. "Oh, hi, Mr. Parker." He held out a telegram. "This just came for you."

Mitch's pulse kicked up a notch. He pulled a coin from his pocket to give Zeke, then stepped inside before he allowed himself to open the telegram.

It was from Dovie Jacobs.

And it contained a single line:

IVY NEEDS YOU.

Mitch pulled the buggy to a stop and studied the place. According to the farmer he'd passed on the road about a mile back, this was Dovie Jacobs's farm.

He smiled at the profusion of flowers bordering the fence and porch. Ivy lived here, all right.

Rufus jumped down and ran to the house, barking with tail-wagging enthusiasm.

Mitch followed, his pace nearly as hurried. That cryptic telegram had proven what Mitch already knew in his heart: he should never have let Ivy go with that snake—the man was nasty business. If he'd done anything to hurt Ivy—

The door opened before Mitch reached it, and he found himself facing a petite gray-haired woman with sparkling green eyes and gnarled hands resting on top of a walking stick.

He removed his hat. "You must be Ivy's Nana Dovie."

She'd been studying him with a piercing gaze. Then she smiled. "And you must be her Mitch."

He gave a short bow, liking the sound of "her Mitch." "Yes, ma'am, and I'm very glad to meet you. I came as soon as I received your telegram." He tried to look past her into the house. "Where's Ivy?"

"In town." She frowned at him. "You're almost too late."

His disappointment in not seeing Ivy gave way to concern. "Too late for what?"

"To stop the wedding."

Mitch felt as if the breath had been knocked out of him. "Ivy's getting married?"

"She is. To that weasel Lester Stokes."

"She loves him?" He refused to believe such a thing.

The woman snorted. "Ivy has more sense than that. But that's what she tried to have me believe."

He studied her, noting her firm stance. "So his report that you were injured was just a ruse."

"I'm healthy as a horse." Then her eyes narrowed. "Is that how he got her to come home with him?"

Mitch nodded. "It's why I let her go." He should have listened to his gut.

"That was a mistake."

"Yes, ma'am, it was." He tried to rein in his impatience. "Do you know the real reason she's agreed to marry him?"

"I have a good idea."

He waved a hand toward the two rockers on the porch. "Then let's talk."

Ivy shifted in the saddle. The horse she rode belonged to Lester's family. She didn't like the idea of being beholden to him, but he'd insisted, saying her borrowing it would go a long way toward making the community believe they were serious about their marriage.

The two of them had spent the morning with Reverend Tomlin making arrangements for the ceremony, which was to be held at Ivy's home tomorrow morning. The preacher had wanted them to wait until Lester's folks returned, but Lester had brushed that concern aside. He'd used Ivy and Nana Dovie's financial situation as an excuse, and assured the clergyman that they would schedule a second ceremony when his parents were available.

Reverend Tomlin had shot her several concerned looks throughout the discussion, but she'd done her best just to smile and let Lester do the talking.

And all the time her mind was desperately trying to find a way out of this mess, as it had been ever since Lester had made his twisted proposal.

A part of her wished she'd accepted Mitch's offer of marriage—he might not love her either, but at least he respected her. For one heartbeat of time, she thought about sending for him—her white knight who always seemed set on rescuing her.

But she discarded the thought almost immediately. Not only would it not be fair to *him,* but the thought of his coming to resent her later was unbearable.

If only Nana Dovie weren't so tied to this place, she'd let Lester have the farm and take her someplace where they could both make a fresh start.

Like Turnabout.

But, as Nana Dovie liked to say, if wishes were fishes…

As their small farm came into sight, Ivy frowned. Whose carriage was that?

She nudged the horse into a faster gait. It wasn't the reverend; she'd just left him. And no one else, other than an occasional peddler, ever came out here. Was Nana Dovie okay?

Then a familiar figure came bounding out the front gate. Rufus!

Her pulse kicked up a notch. There was only one explanation—Mitch was here.

But why? Could it be that he'd missed her as much as she'd missed him?

As soon as she arrived at the house, Ivy slid from the horse's back and smoothed her skirt. Then she paused to make certain her bonnet was on straight.

Taking a deep breath, she headed inside. She found Mitch sitting at the kitchen table with Nana Dovie, sipping a cup of coffee.

He stood as soon as she entered, and the sight of the warm smile on his face was almost enough to make her fling herself into his arms. Instead, she merely smiled.

"What are you doing here?"

"Ivy Kathleen, what kind of question is that?" Nana

Dovie gave her a stern look. "And he's here because I sent for him."

"Nana!"

"You didn't think I would let you marry that bully Lester Stokes without doing something about it, did you?"

Ivy cast a quick, embarrassed glance Mitch's way. She couldn't believe Nana Dovie was involving him in all of this. She turned back to her. "It's all settled. Reverend Tomlin will perform the ceremony here tomorrow morning. It'll just be us, you and Dory."

Please don't let Mitch still be here. She couldn't bear the idea of him watching her marry Lester.

"There's not going to be a wedding."

She blinked at the absolute certainty in Mitch's voice. "Listen, Mr. high-and-mighty Mitch Parker, you can't just walk in here and give me orders."

"You told me once that you would only marry for love. Do you love Lester Stokes?"

"Who I love or don't love is none of your business."

"So you don't love him. That means you're being coerced. Perhaps the fact that his father owns the note on this place has something to do with that."

"Don't you *dare* offer to pay that note. I won't be taking charity from you or anyone else."

"Ivy Kathleen!" Nana Dovie looked truly shocked. "Didn't I teach you what a terrible sin pride is? And that ingratitude is nearly as bad?"

"Yes, ma'am."

"Besides, last time I looked it was my name on the deed to this place. Don't you think it should be my decision as to whether or not to accept an offer of help?"

"But—"

Nana Dovie patted her hand. "I know, dear, you're

just trying to help and be very brave in the process. But I can't let you do that for me. And no, I'm not taking Mr. Parker's money."

"Then what—"

"I'm taking you both away from here." Mitch's tone brooked no argument.

"But—" Ivy turned and took the older woman's hands. "Nana, I can't let you do this."

"I've held you back for too long. That stops now." She smiled in satisfaction. "The way you described Turnabout, I think it's going to be a mighty nice place to set down new roots."

Ivy was afraid to let the hope building inside her unfurl. She looked from Mitch to Nana Dovie and back to Mitch, trying to make sense of it all.

Mitch gave her a reassuring smile. "Miss Jacobs and I discussed several things we think will make this trip smoother for everyone."

"Such as?"

This time Nana Dovie spoke up. "There's a medicine I know how to mix up that helps a person relax, relax so deeply they sometimes fall into a deep sleep. I'll take this medicine tomorrow just before we leave, and with any luck I won't even notice I've left home until I wake up in Turnabout."

Ivy wasn't convinced. "You've told me yourself that medicines can be tricky—different people react differently. How do you know it'll work?"

"Because I've tested it on myself. Don't look so shocked. I've wanted to take you away from here ever since Lester spread those lies about you five years ago. I just didn't have anywhere to take you before now."

Ivy stepped up and gave her a fierce hug. "Oh, Nana Dovie, I love you so much."

The woman waved her away. "Now, you two have important roles to play if we're going to make this work. First, I'm not certain I'll be able to get around very well, if at all."

"Don't worry, ma'am, I'll see that you get where you need to go, with nary a hair out of place."

Ivy smiled up at him, remembering the ease with which he'd carried her.

"And I'll also need a place to stay when I get there," Nana Dovie continued. "A nice, quiet room where I can be alone whenever I want to."

"I'm sure Eileen Pierce will rent us another room at her place. And if not we can share mine until we can make other arrangements." Then Ivy looked around. "But this house, all your things…"

"They're just things, child. What's important are the people and the memories—and those we bring with us. We'll find new things when we settle in this new place."

She stood. "I'll hear no more arguments. Now, you two go to Arnold Hemp's place. He'll be willing to take on the animals we've got here along with the tools and equipment for a fair price. Tell him he can also have whatever produce from the garden he can cart off, but he has to get it all before noon tomorrow."

She walked them to the door. "Don't spend a lot of time dickering with him, but make sure you get enough to stake us for the next couple of weeks." She gave Ivy a look that, on a younger woman, would have been called sassy. "After that, I expect you to use that in-heritance of yours to take care of my needs." Then she made shooing motions. "Now off with you. There are preparations to be made."

Mitch helped Ivy into the wagon, savoring the luxury of having her beside him again.

Once she'd given him directions to Mr. Hemp's farm, he set the wagon in motion, trying to figure out how to say all he was feeling. He didn't want to mess it up this time.

"I'm sorry Nana Dovie asked you to come all the way here." She stared straight ahead.

"I'm not."

She turned to study him.

He tried for a light tone. "Rufus missed you."

She nodded, then faced forward again.

He cleared his throat. "We both did."

This time, when she turned to face him, there was a curious mix of hope and doubt in her expression. But she finally gave him a soft smile. "I missed both of you, too." She shifted slightly. "I'm sorry for being so rude earlier."

"You've been carrying a lot on your shoulders the past few days."

"Still, I owed you better than that. Thank you for riding to my rescue yet again."

"It was my pleasure." Did she have any idea how deeply he meant those words?

"I can see Nana Dovie likes you."

"The sentiment is returned. She's quite a lady."

"I hope she knows what she's doing."

Mitch placed a hand over hers. "Have faith."

Her gaze flew to his. Was it a reaction to the touch or his words? He was pleased when she didn't pull her hand away. Instead, she repositioned it so that their palms touched and their fingers intertwined.

At that moment, she could have asked him to carry the world on his shoulders and he would have gladly attempted to do it for her.

Chapter Twenty-Three

It was difficult to convince Mitch to leave Nettle's Gap without confronting Lester. But Ivy had finally gotten through to him. She thought, more than anything else, it had been his memory of the consequences of ignoring another woman's entreaty that finally did the trick.

To her great relief, the trip to Turnabout went surprisingly well. Nana Dovie slept through most of it.

There *was* a bit of trouble at the train station when they tried to board. The conductor suspected the elderly woman was ill and at first refused to allow her on the train. But after a long discussion, and a bit of money changing hands, the man relented and Mitch was allowed to carry the slumbering woman aboard.

When they arrived in Turnabout, Mitch marched all the way from the train station to Eileen Pierce's home carrying Nana Dovie. With Ivy and Rufus flanking him on either side, they attracted every bit as much attention as they had when Ivy had first arrived in town beside him on that borrowed buckboard.

Mrs. Pierce, unruffled by their unannounced appearance on her doorstep, seemed pleased to be able to earn income from a second boarder. Within minutes of their arrival, a slowly awakening Nana Dovie was comfortably ensconced in the room next to Ivy's.

Afterward, Ivy walked Mitch as far as Eileen's front door.

He took her hand. "I'll see that your things are delivered from the depot. And I'll send word to Carter that you're back and ready to settle your business with him as soon as possible."

"Thank you." She didn't withdraw her hand, and neither did he.

"And don't worry about Rufus, he's welcome to stay with me again."

She grinned. "I'd better watch it or he'll start thinking he's your dog."

He gave her hand a slight squeeze. "I know this isn't the right time for a long discussion on the matter, but I hope you'll reconsider my offer of marriage. Especially now that you're moving into the community permanently."

"Thank you, Mitch. You'll never know how much it means to me that you care so much." She gently tugged her hand free. "But as I said before, barring blackmail, I intend to hold out for a love match."

Her little attempt at humor didn't elicit so much as a smile.

"Aren't friendship and respect strong enough emotions to base a marriage on?" he asked.

Was that what he felt for her? "Not for me. Because I know what love feels like. And I want someone to feel that for me."

He went very still. "There's someone you love?"

She nodded. Why was it so hard to say the words?

"With all my heart. But he doesn't feel the same for me." She touched his cheek. "So while I will always cherish his friendship and respect, marrying him would eventually break my heart, knowing he doesn't return my feelings."

And with a quick kiss to his cheek, she turned and raced back up the stairs, feeling a bittersweet triumph.

She'd just told Mitch Parker that she loved him.

Mitch stood on Eileen Pierce's front porch, too stunned to move. His heart pounded so hard he could hear it thrumming in his ears. She loved him? For one shining moment, his whole being thrummed with exultation.

Then he sobered. This changed everything. A businesslike arrangement was one thing. It was safe and practical and had purpose—namely her protection.

But love—that was messy, complicated. If she loved him then he could disappoint her, fail her. Even if he loved her in return.

Who was he kidding? There was no *if* about it—he loved her, had loved her long before he'd allowed himself to admit it.

But knowing it didn't give him the right to act on it. Not with his history.

Perhaps she was right to refuse him.

Over the next few days, Ivy and Carter reached an agreement on how to split the ranch, and in the end, Ivy found herself the recipient of more money than she'd ever thought to see in her lifetime. While it wasn't a fortune by some standards, and Carter would be paying it off to her over a course of several years, she was confident it was enough to find a place for her and Nana Dovie to start their new lives.

Word reached them that Lester had not taken their leaving well. He had, in fact, set a torch to their house—his house, she supposed—in a fit of anger.

Nana Dovie took the news in stride, surprising Ivy with the prediction that he'd probably regret his actions once his pa returned home.

And despite Mitch's fears, mainly due to the support of his circle of friends, Ivy was not ostracized. While there were some who would always give in to the urge to whisper and gossip, for the most part Ivy was made welcome throughout the town.

But there was one welcoming smile she missed. She'd barely seen Mitch since she'd told him of her feelings four days earlier.

Had she made a mistake?

"Where is Ivy?" Mitch stood, hat in hand, on Eileen Pierce's front porch.

Nana Dovie, who was shelling a bowl of peas, eyed him as if she could read his secrets. "Out back in the garden," she finally said.

Of course. Where else would she be? "Thank you."

Before he could step away, she spoke up again. "There's something different about you today. You're carrying yourself with a sense of purpose. Does this mean you've finally come to your senses?"

He didn't pretend to misunderstand. "Yes, ma'am. I only hope I'm not too late."

She waved him away. "Well, what are you waiting for? Go tell her how you feel."

He nodded and jammed his hat back on his head. "Yes, ma'am."

Mitch marched around the house, trying to figure out just what he'd say. He still hadn't settled on the right words when he caught sight of her.

She spotted him at the same time, and the welcome smile on her face gave him hope.

"Mitch, hello. Come see the size of these tomatoes."

"Very nice. But it's you I'm here to see."

Something flashed in her eyes and he prayed it was love. "Is there something I can do for you?"

"Yes. You can marry me."

She frowned, and this time it was sadness in her eyes. He winced, knowing he was the one who'd put that there.

She turned away, tugging another tomato from the plant. "Please, I've told you how I feel. Let's not go through it again."

"No, we haven't been through *this* before. I *want* to marry you. Not because I feel I have to. Not because I feel responsible for you. But because I *love* you."

She shook her head vehemently, not turning around. "Stop. I know you think this is the right thing to do, but I can't bear it." She turned to face him and he was almost undone by the pain glistening in her eyes. "You're a good man, but you have to accept that you can't fix every problem—the gossip has all but died down, the inheritance is settled, Nana Dovie and I are happier than we've been in a long time. And much of this is thanks to you."

She took a deep breath. "As for what I said the other day, I probably shouldn't have said anything. I'm happy to have you as a dear friend. So please, don't throw yourself on your sword over this."

"You're not listening." He took hold of her arms. "I. Love. You."

Her eyes searched his face and he hoped she could see what he truly felt.

"But I thought you never wanted to marry again."

"So did I. Then you came into my life, and everything changed. I've fought it for as long as I can. I may not deserve you but I've finally realized I can't go on without you."

Ivy was afraid to believe what she was hearing, though she very much wanted to. This had to be just another way he'd found to *help* her, whether she wanted that help or not.

"But I'm not the kind of woman you're drawn to— I'm not gentle or delicate."

"True. In fact, you're the most stubborn, down-to-earth, speak-your-mind female I've ever met. And you're also strong, generous, spirited, courageous and sensitive to the hurts of others. You'd willingly sacrifice yourself in marriage to a wretchedly cruel and selfish man to save your dear friend's refuge. And you are quick to extend grace and forgiveness to those who have wronged you."

The look in his eyes as he uttered those beautiful words chipped away at her resistance. Could he really mean what he was saying?

His hands slid down her arms, his fingers twining with hers. "What you are is the woman I love. And you're absolutely right. This community has accepted you so there's no reason that you have to marry me. Except that I'll be totally and completely lost without you."

He gave a crooked smile. "Marry me so you can bring color and life to my home, which seems so unbearably empty without you. Marry me so you can enjoy that swing in my backyard that seems so forlorn now. Marry me to tend to my garden and decorate my yard with riots of flowers. But most of all, marry me because I love you with all that I am."

He traced the line of her jaw with a finger as tears slid down her cheeks.

"I love you, Ivy Kathleen Feagan. I've been every kind of fool and I'm so sorry it took me this long to realize it. But I promise to say those words to you every day for the rest of my life, if you'll let me."

This time there was no doubting the truth. It was there in his words, in the slight tremble of his fingers, in the ragged emotion shining from his eyes.

She lifted a hand to his cheek. "Oh, Mitch, I love you so much. It would make me very, very happy to spend the rest of my days as your wife."

With that, he pulled her into a hug and twirled her around. Then he set her on the ground again and very gently bent down to give her a kiss. A kiss that promised he would love, protect and cherish her, now and forever.

He was her hero, the man who would fearlessly slay all of her dragons and quietly make all of her dreams come true.

Epilogue

Mitch studied his new bride across the expanse of Eileen Pierce's backyard, not caring if his expression reflected how hopelessly smitten he was. He still couldn't quite believe Ivy was well and truly his at last.

The wedding service, which had been held at Mrs. Pierce's place so Nana Dovie could comfortably attend, had ended nearly an hour ago and it seemed as if he'd barely been able to say two words to Ivy since. He tried to tell himself to be patient—after all, he had the rest of his life to spend with her—but he decided he'd been patient long enough. Excusing himself from the discussion with Dr. Pratt and Sheriff Gleason, he circulated through the crowd with purpose, closing in on his bride.

After a half dozen stops to accept congratulatory slaps on the back, Mitch finally made it to her side. The warm smile with which she greeted him set his pulse racing. He leaned forward and kissed her cheek, then whispered in her ear, "What do you think, Mrs. Parker—is it too early for us to make our exit?"

Her low, throaty laugh had him wanting to tug her to him for a proper kiss.

But before she could give him an answer, Reggie ap-approached. "There you are. I'm ready to take photographs of the happy couple if you'll spare me a few minutes."

Ivy shot him an apologetic look and squeezed his hand before turning to Reggie. "Of course. Just tell us what to do."

"I'm set up right over there." Reggie led the way to the flower-bedecked arch where they'd recited their vows earlier. Along the way, Ivy squeezed his arm and nodded off to her left. "I do believe Mrs. Swenson has found a new object for her affection."

Mitch glanced in the direction she'd indicated and smiled. Mrs. Swenson was engaged in conversation with Carter Mosley of all people, and the two seemed to have more than a passing enjoyment of each other's company.

A few moments later, Reggie was fussily posing Mitch and Ivy while some of the guests drifted over to watch. At last, Reggie was satisfied and she took two photographs—one with just the two of them, and one with Nana Dovie between them.

"I wish your sisters could have come," Ivy said. "Then we could have a true family photograph."

"They're eager to meet you, as well." Mitch dropped a kiss on the top of her head. "We'll plan some trips soon." He knew his sisters were going to love Ivy, and she them. But he hadn't wanted to wait a moment longer than he had to for the wedding.

His plans to lead his bride away were foiled yet again when Reggie stopped him. "If you don't mind, there's one more photograph I'd like to take. And this one's for me."

Mitch raised a brow. "You want a picture of me and Ivy?"

"Not exactly." She turned and glanced to the folks gathered behind her. "Adam, Everett, Chance—you three come over here and stand next to Mitch."

Adam raised a brow. "What are you up to?"

Reggie took Adam's hand, then looked at the four men. "I remember when you all first arrived here two years ago—and I know we didn't see eye to eye back then. But this town is the better for all of you being here, and I am, too." She pitched her voice so only they could hear. "I'd like to have a picture of my three would-be grooms, and my one true love, to hang on my wall."

As Mitch stood shoulder to shoulder with his friends, he thought again how they'd all set out to find fresh starts here in Turnabout.

What they'd found was so much more than any of them had ever expected—a community that welcomed them in with open arms. And more importantly, good women to cherish and be cherished by, and to build their lives and futures with.

He met Ivy's warm gaze and thanked God again for not giving up on him when he'd given up on himself, for leading him here to Turnabout and for bringing Ivy into his life to show him how to love and laugh again.

The flash of Reggie's camera released him from his pose and he marched toward his wife and captured her hand in his. "Time to go," he said.

She laughed. "Is everything ready?"

"The hamper and bags are already in the carriage."

"What about the fishing poles?"

"They're there, as well."

"And you're sure Reggie doesn't mind us borrowing her cabin."

"She insisted. After all, I never did get in that week I'd planned on."

"I hope you're not looking for peace and quiet this time out."

"No, ma'am. This time I'm looking for excitement and adventure." He grinned. "I even have the materials to construct one fine tree swing. Ready?"

She nodded, and hand in hand, they slipped away, together, the way Mitch intended them to be forever.

* * * * *

Noelle Marchand is a native Houstonian living out her childhood dream of being a writer. She graduated summa cum laude from Houston Baptist University in 2012, earning a bachelor's degree in mass communications and speech communications. She loves exploring new books and new cities. When she's not scribbling out her latest manuscript, you may find her pursuing one of her other passions—music, dance, history and classic movies.

Books by Noelle Marchand

Love Inspired Historical

Bachelor List Matches

The Texan's Inherited Family
The Texan's Courtship Lessons
The Texan's Engagement Agreement

Unlawfully Wedded Bride
The Runaway Bride
A Texas-Made Match

Visit the Author Profile page at Harlequin.com for more titles.

THE RUNAWAY BRIDE

Noelle Marchand

Bear with each other and forgive one another if any of you has a grievance against someone. Forgive as the Lord forgave you. And over all these virtues put on love, which binds them all together in perfect unity.
—*Colossians* 3:13–14

Dedicated with love to my sister by blood,
Ashley Marchand, and my sisters in spirit,
Cynthia Rouhana and Erika Gutierrez.
Also, to my mother, Juanita Marchand,
for her continued encouragement.

Chapter One

Peppin, Texas
August 1887

"Lorelei Wilkins, will you take this man to be your lawfully wedded husband, to live together after God's ordinance in the holy estate of matrimony? Will you love, honor and keep him, in sickness and in health: forsaking all others, keeping only unto him so long as you both shall live?"

Lorelei's eyes widened as she stared silently at Reverend Sparks. Did he have any idea how formidable those words sounded? If she was making a mistake, it would be irreversible. Yet, he stood there waiting. Waiting—just like the man beside her who'd gone through the trouble of slicking back his hair, shining his boots and donning a fancy shirt. She glanced at her groom. Lawson Williams swallowed nervously.

"I…" Her gaze slipped to Lawson's best man. Sean O'Brien's green eyes watched her carefully. He was probably wondering if she was going to prove that his suspicion about her had been right all along. Hadn't he secretly warned Lawson not to court her? Some secret. She'd heard the words he hadn't intended for her ears two years ago, and they reverberated in her thoughts even now.

"You're making a mistake. Lorelei isn't the kind of girl you can count on. She's always been flighty and insincere. If you aren't careful, you'll end up with a broken heart."

She turned back to Reverend Sparks. "Will you repeat the second question?"

Nervous laughter spread through the church behind her, but she listened carefully as he repeated. "Will you love—"

He continued, but that one word was all she needed to hear. Would she love Lawson, as a wife should love her husband, for as long as the two of them lived? She couldn't do this to herself, and she certainly couldn't do it to Lawson…because the answer was no.

Shaking her head, she took a halting step backward. Gasps tore through the air as she lifted her white skirt and ran down the aisle she'd just marched up. The doors of the church burst open with a bang, and light flooded the sanctuary as she tripped quickly down the stairs onto the lawn. Gasping in quick hard breaths, she only escaped a few feet before she heard footsteps behind her.

"Lorelei!" a strident voice called.

She ignored it. Pressing the back of her hand to her lips, she felt the lump of her engagement ring. A hand caught her arm. "Lorelei?"

She swung around to face her intended. "I can't. I can't do this. I'm so sorry, Lawson."

His handsome face noticeably paled. "What do you

mean you can't do this? We're getting married today. Right now."

She swallowed. "It isn't right."

"What are you talking about?" Painful silence lingered in the air until he stepped toward her. "I thought you loved me."

"I do love you, Lawson, but not in the way a woman should love the man she's going to marry. I wish that I did," she said sorrowfully, then tilted her head to survey him carefully. "Do you love me like that, Lawson? Can you honestly tell me that you do?"

He turned away from her and dragged his fingers through his hair before he met her gaze again. His answer was halting, almost inaudible. "No."

She pulled in a deep breath and tugged the ring from her finger. "Then this shouldn't belong to me."

His eyes filled with resignation as he took it from her. He allowed her a curt nod before he walked back toward the church where his best man waited on the steps. Her gaze caught only briefly on that figure before she turned away.

She'd barely made it to Main Street when her delicate white boots began to pinch her feet. She allowed herself a grimace as she leaned against the wall of Maddie's Café and rustled through the satin overlay and layers of tulle to reach her shoes.

"If you wait here, I can get the buggy and drive you home."

Her heart stilled at the sound of Sean's voice. She gritted her teeth. "No, thank you. I'll walk."

"Now, Lorelei—" His deep voice drawled.

Her blue eyes lifted to meet his suspiciously. "Why are you here?"

"Lawson asked me to see you home."

Frowning, she rooted around for the other shoe. "I don't need anyone to see me home."

He lifted an imperious brow, and she barely kept from rolling her eyes. She knew what that meant. Sean was Lawson's best friend. If Lawson asked him to see her home, then Sean would see her home out of respect for his friend's wishes even if he couldn't stand her. No doubt he saw it as his duty, and if that was the case Sheriff Sean O'Brien would never back down.

"Fine," she bit out. "We'll walk." She handed him her boots a little too forcefully, then lifted her skirts out of the dust as she crossed Main Street. It lacked its usual bustle since most of the town was still at the church waiting for word about her wedding. Still, there were plenty of folks around to gape at her, so she darted into the alleyway behind the post office to hide from their curious eyes. She ignored her companion as she led him through the alleyways to the residential area of town. Finally, Lorelei stopped on the stairs of her family's porch and faced Sean to murmur, "Thank you for walking me home."

He frowned and crossed his arms as he surveyed her. "I think you're making a mistake."

He always did. A vague cloud of disappointment settled over her at his disapproval, but she'd come to expect it. For so long she'd waited for her feelings for him to change. They had. They'd gone from a desperate unrequited yearning to a hollow ache. She wasn't sure that counted as progress. She hid her feelings with an impudent tilt of her head. "And I'm supposed to care what you think because…?"

His eyes flashed with annoyance at her decidedly

rude tone. She didn't wait for his response. Instead, she stepped into the house and closed the door firmly behind her. Leaning against it, she lifted her shaking hands to cover her face as the impact of what she'd done finally began to settle in. She didn't regret her decision to call off the wedding. She just could not believe she'd let it go this far. At least she'd done the right thing in the end.

Of course, the town wouldn't soon forget the day a bride hauled up her skirts and dashed out of the church rather than finish the ceremony. Facing her parents when they arrived home would be hard. Facing Lawson in town in the days to come would be harder. And facing any more of Sean O'Brien's disapproval would be hardest of all. She shook her head. Somehow she had to get away from the memories, the murmurs and the men.

"Well, why shouldn't I?" she whispered to the empty house. She was already packed and ready to leave for the honeymoon to her great-aunt's house in California. The train ticket was in her reticule. There was no reason not to go. She'd change out of her finery, and if her parents weren't home by the time she was done, she'd just write them a note. Either way, she was leaving—now.

She could only hope that distance would do what time had failed to accomplish by ridding her of whatever feelings she had left for Sean O'Brien once and for all.

The late-afternoon sun burst through the nearby window to gleam off the metal star on Sean's dark green shirt. He heaved a sigh, then tapped his pencil on the paperwork in front of him to expend his frustration and anger. His mind kept replaying the scene that had taken place at the church that morning. How dare Lorelei walk out on his best friend like that? The couple had been together for almost two years, despite his original prediction that the relationship wouldn't last more than six months. He'd started to think Lorelei might not be as impulsive, unpredictable and flighty as he'd imagined. She'd proven him wrong—again.

He'd spent the past several hours sorting out the mess Lorelei had made of the wedding so Lawson wouldn't have to. Lawson had been abandoned by his parents as a child and forced to drift from town to town in order to survive. Sean's family had taken him in when he'd shown up in Peppin at age fourteen. Several months later, Doc and Mrs. Lettie had adopted him, but Lawson had stayed close to Sean and his family. They were practically brothers as far as Sean was concerned. His friend of ten years didn't deserve the treatment Lorelei had just dealt him.

Lorelei Wilkins had been a thorn in Sean's side since grade school days when she'd informed the whole school that they would get married one day. He'd been annoyed then, but by the time he'd turned nineteen the idea hadn't seemed so awful. Lorelei had become the belle of Peppin. She could have had any guy in town, but she'd made him think he was the one she wanted. Nothing had been said between them, but he'd started to plan for her. He'd left his family's farm and accepted the position of sheriff to save up enough money to provide for her. He'd even carved a pitiful wooden promise ring.

He'd waited for the perfect moment to express his intentions. Then, just when the time seemed right, she suddenly chose his best friend. She'd become Lawson's girl practically overnight, and Sean had finally gotten a glimpse of her true character—impulsive, unsteady and completely unreliable. He hadn't said a word to anyone about her betrayal. Instead, he'd pretended she hadn't just landed a punch to his heart that would leave him reeling for years.

He realized his pencil was tapping in cadence with the ticking of the nearby clock and threw it aside. He'd be better off pacing the streets than sitting at his desk. He was just pushing his chair aside when the door flew open. Richard Wilkins, the president of the town's only bank and Lorelei Wilkins's father, stepped inside with Lawson right behind him.

Sean's eyebrows lifted at the grim looks on the men's faces. He settled back into his chair, then motioned them to the seats across from him. He gaze bounced between their worried eyes questioningly. "What's wrong?"

Richard settled into his chair with a dejected slump. "Something has happened to Lorelei."

Sean frowned. "Is she hurt?"

"No." Lawson shook his head. "She's gone."

Sean's stomach dropped to his boots with a surprising amount of dread. He stared at the men. "You mean she's dead?"

Richard abruptly straightened in his seat. "Of course not, boy! She just up and disappeared while we were all shutting down the wedding and packing up the reception."

Sean sighed. That was exactly the kind of stunt Lorelei would pull in a situation like this. Nevertheless, he readied his notebook and grabbed a pencil. "She couldn't have gone far. How long has she been missing?"

Lawson shot a glance at Richard. "Well, she isn't missing exactly."

The pencil hovering over the notebook hesitated as

he glanced up at the men across from him in confusion. "Then y'all know where she is?"

"No," Lawson said just as Richard said, "Yes."

Sean lowered his pencil in tempered exasperation. "Well, which is it?"

"My daughter has run away."

"You mean she truly ran away, as in she's left town?" At Richard's nod, Sean frowned. "Are you sure?"

"I'm sure because she left this." Her father handed him a folded piece of paper.

He studied the written note carefully. "She says she wants a new life for herself and is going to live with her great-aunt in California."

"Keep going."

"She begs you to let her go and—" he glanced up sharply to meet Lawson's gaze before continuing quietly "—and not to send Lawson."

Lawson nodded firmly. "That's why we chose you."

"You chose me," he echoed as a sense of foreboding filled his chest. "To do what?"

"To bring her back." Lawson swallowed. "Not to me, of course, but to her parents."

Richard cleared his throat. "I'd go myself but my wife says I'd just end up letting Lorelei have her own way like I always do. As much as I hate to admit it, the Lord knows Caroline is probably right. That's why you've got to do it."

Sean leaned forward to set his arm against the desk. "Listen, I'm sorry, but I am not the man for this job. I'll tell you what I can do instead. I'll send my deputy—"

Lawson laughed skeptically. "Jeff Bridger? He's the only man in town who's gotten lost walking down Main Street."

"His sense of direction isn't that bad anymore," Sean protested. "I've been working with him and he has definitely improved."

"I'm glad, but do you really think I'm willing to trust that man to find my daughter, let alone bring her back? Besides, I think you're a little confused here." Richard's fierce gaze told Sean he wasn't to be trifled with. "This isn't about you, Sheriff. This is about my daughter, who, as a citizen of Peppin, deserves your protection just like everyone else. She has no chaperone. She has no supplies and hardly any money. She's a target for every charlatan from here to California."

Sean cleared his throat as he tried to regain control of the conversation. "I understand that, Mr. Wilkins, but I can't just leave town for several days to run after your daughter. I have a job to do here."

"Actually, that seems like a good job for Jeff." Lawson crossed his arms. "After all, the man can't get lost just sitting in an office, can he?"

"I guess not." Sean stared at the men before him with a mixture of bemusement and dread.

Lawson shifted forward in his chair. "Sean, I would go myself but you read the note. We both know it isn't safe for her out there. Why, she's never even traveled before. She needs protection. I know she and I aren't going to get married, but that doesn't mean I don't care about her. I'm asking you to protect her not only because she's a citizen of our town but for my sake, because I can't."

Sean pulled in a fortifying breath to push aside his misgivings. His voice filled with resolve. "I'll leave first thing tomorrow morning. It will take that long for me to pack and coordinate things with Jeff."

Relief painted Richard's face with a smile. Lawson

reached out to shake his hand. Sean didn't bother to hide his frown. All he could hope was that he'd be able to head her off before she made it to California. It'd be a dandy of a fight to bring her all the way back to Peppin if she was already settled with her great-aunt. Nevertheless, he'd taken an oath to protect the people of this town, and it would take more than one particularly troublesome female to keep him from fulfilling that promise.

Lorelei eyed the gingerbread style white-and-green boardinghouse dubiously. She had no idea what she was going to do. She barely had enough money in her pocket to buy herself a meal and certainly not enough for the rest of the trip to California. She wasn't even close to the Texas state line—any of them. She still seethed when she thought of that horrible man on the train. How dare he take off with her reticule?

She had to own that it was partially her fault for being thoughtless. She should have hidden most of her money in her boot or corset instead of leaving it all in her reticule for some villain to ride off with. It wouldn't have been such a setback if the train went straight to California from Peppin. Unfortunately, she was supposed to transfer to another line. How could she do that when she didn't even have money for a ticket?

She needed help, and she didn't want to go to her parents for it. She was a grown woman on a trip of her own undertaking. She'd figure this out somehow, then write her parents from California to tell them exactly how wonderful her new life was. If this didn't work, then fine, but she at least had to try to do it on her own first. She entered the bustling boardinghouse and went over to the woman who seemed to be checking people in.

"Welcome! I'm Mrs. Drake and I have a room all ready for you. May I have your name please?"

"Lorelei Wilkins, but I'm not here for a room exactly—"

"Wilkins," the blonde woman repeated then smiled. "You're from Peppin, aren't you?"

"How did you know?" she asked with a bit of trepidation. Surely news of her wedding hadn't spread this far that fast.

The woman tossed a dismissive hand. "Oh, I've visited family in Peppin once or twice during the past several years. I heard of your family while I was there. Perhaps you know mine. My aunt and uncle are Joseph and Amelia Greene."

Lorelei easily placed the family connection. "Yes, I know them. My mother is friends with your aunt."

The woman's face lit up. "Isn't that wonderful?"

"Yes, it is," Lorelei said with a smile as she realized it probably wouldn't be wise to mention that Mrs. Greene also had a reputation of being the town gossip. "As I was saying, I've run into a problem and I hope you might be able to help me. I was taking the train to meet my elderly great-aunt in California—"

"California!" Mrs. Drake frowned. "That's quite a ways to travel alone."

"Yes, well, I placed my reticule in my lap where I was sure no one would dare take it, but when I awakened it was gone. I'm sure that man sitting across the aisle stole it. To think he got close enough to steal my money and I never even felt it!"

"How unnerving! I'm sorry, dear, but what can I do?"

"I thought perhaps you might let me work for you

so I can pay my room and board. It would just be until I'm able to get more money somehow."

"I wish I could." Suddenly the woman froze with some sudden thought. "Do you like children?"

"What?"

"I know of a job for you if you like children but— Oh, what time is it?" Mrs. Drake popped open her small pocket watch. "We just might be able to catch them."

"Catch who?"

"The children." The woman rounded the desk to survey her carefully. "Yes, I think you'll do perfectly. Is that your only bag?"

Lorelei glanced down at her traveling bag. "Yes."

"Good. You won't take up much room." Mrs. Drake grabbed her hat from the stand and opened the door. "Come on. We have to run to catch them."

Lorelei followed her out the door and down the porch steps at a trot to keep up with her rapid pace. "But, Mrs. Drake, I really don't understand. Where are we going? Who are these children and what sort of job is it?"

"I'm sorry. I get rather scattered when I'm in a rush." The woman darted across the street with Lorelei at her heels. "The position is with a traveling preacher and his wife. They are very good friends of mine. James takes his family with him on his circuit once every few months or so. They're going with him this time. Usually the young woman down the street goes with them to help see to the children, but her father is sick so she can't go. James and his wife, Marissa, couldn't find anyone else on short notice."

"So I'm supposed to replace their neighbor?" Lorelei asked breathlessly.

"Yes, if we can catch them. They were supposed to

be leaving now," Mrs. Drake said. "Watch that hole in the road."

Lorelei veered away from the hole just in time to save herself from a sprained ankle. "You said he's a traveling preacher. Where are they traveling?"

"That's the beauty of it, Miss Wilkins. They're going farther west. Not to California, mind you but— Oh, there's the wagon. Help me wave it down."

Lorelei lifted her free hand to wave at the retreating covered wagon. The little boy who was practically hanging out the back of the wagon waved back with a grin, then turned around. He must have yelled something to his parents because the wagon pulled off the road and stopped. Mrs. Drake caught Lorelei's arm and led her around the wagon to meet an attractive young couple. They listened patiently to Mrs. Drake's breathlessly halting explanation and introduction.

Marissa Brightly smiled down at Lorelei, though her brown eyes showed compassion. "I'm so sorry this happened to you, Miss Wilkins, but I can't help feeling this is all part of God's plan."

"It certainly is. We'd be delighted to have you join us," James said. "I know that you want to get to California as soon as possible, but we are heading farther west and would be glad to pay you a small salary. Once you have the financial ability to continue your journey, we would send you on with our blessing."

Marissa leaned forward. "Please, say you'll come."

Lorelei bit her lip for a moment, then smiled. "I suppose I will. I have nothing to lose and I think I'll enjoy traveling with you very much."

"Good," James said with a satisfied nod. "Let me help you into the wagon."

Lorelei thanked Mrs. Drake for her help, then followed James to the back of the wagon where the little boy she'd seen earlier peeked out from the large hole in the canvas. "Pa, is she coming with us?"

"She sure is," James answered as her traveling bag disappeared inside. "Move out the entrance so she can get in, Hosea."

Once inside, Lorelei glanced around to take stock of her surroundings and froze. "Are *all* of these children yours?"

"Yes. Starting with the oldest, there is Henry, Julia, William, Hosea and Lacy. Children, Miss Lorelei will be traveling with us. Mind her as you would your Ma and I. I'll leave y'all to get acquainted."

Each child lifted a hand when their name was called as though their father was taking attendance. They stared at her as she found a seat near the rear of the wagon on a cushioned wooden chest. She stared right back at them. Five children. She was going to be taking care of *five* children. She hadn't even had any siblings growing up. What was she going to do?

The wagon started abruptly, and she fell off her seat onto the wagon floor. A few stifled gasps echoed under the canvas roof as the children waited for her reaction. They looked so shocked that she burst out laughing. That somehow gave them permission to, as well. As they laughed, relief settled into her bones just as tentatively as she settled back on her seat.

She was on her way again after only a momentary delay. Although her trip had been a disaster in some ways, it had been successful in its main goal. She'd barely thought about Sean since she'd left Peppin and certainly wouldn't have a chance anytime soon, now that she was surrounded by five children. She tried not to wonder if he even cared that she'd left or what he thought about possibly never seeing her again. He'd probably been indifferent, or worse: relieved.

No, though the decision had been made on the spur of the moment, she knew she'd made the right choice in leaving. She only wished she'd made that decision sooner. If she hadn't wanted so badly to prove she wasn't a flighty, insincere heartbreaker, she might have done the right thing with Lawson a long time ago. She should have trusted her instincts from the beginning instead of spending so much time overthinking things. Usually her first thoughts on a subject were clearest anyway. She shook her head. That was in the past. She could finally look forward to a future without Sean's distracting presence. In the meantime, it seemed she had a job to do.

The chortles finally died down enough for her to ask, "Who wants to play a game?"

All five hands eagerly went up. She grinned. Her new life without Sean O'Brien was going to be a cinch.

There she was—Lorelei Wilkins. Sean slid from his mount, then put a calming hand on Jericho's nose to keep him quiet as they crept through the woods toward the banks of the river. He ought to walk right out into the open and give her a piece of his mind. That's what he'd been planning to do for the two days it had taken to find her. Now that he'd found her, he decided to take a moment to gather himself.

Through the green veil of leaves, he could see her peaceful expression as she sat innocently reading under a nearby weeping willow. He noticed the soft smile at her lips and the dark curve of her downcast lashes.

For some reason only one thought came to mind—she hadn't married Lawson. Relief lowered his tense shoulders for an instant before he frowned. It shouldn't matter to him that she was no longer engaged. It *didn't* matter to him. The relief he felt at seeing her came only because it meant his task was nearly complete, and he'd soon be able to return home. Nothing more.

He gave a dutiful nod and began moving toward her. Suddenly she tossed her book aside. The soft hum of a melody drifted through the air as she practically danced into the river. He froze, befuddled yet transfixed by the sight. Her well-trained soprano arched over the quiet woods into the first lilting verse of "Beautiful Dreamer." He was barely aware of leaving Jericho to walk quietly toward the woman wading in the thick expanse of river until he stood at its banks.

She hadn't noticed his approach since her eyes were closed, so he tipped back his hat and crossed his arms to stare at her. Now, this was a side of Lorelei he'd never seen. Oh, sure, she sang at church occasionally but never with such passion. He'd seen her smile a hundred times but never with such freedom. Apparently, a weight of some kind had been lifted from her shoulders…and placed squarely onto his. His jaw tightened in aggravation.

His horse neighed. Lorelei froze. Her lashes flew open. Their eyes met. He heard her breath escape her lungs in a startled gasp as she instinctively backed away from him. Her blue eyes changed from alarm to dismay, then she stepped back one too many times and disappeared into the clutches of the racing river.

Chapter Two

Lord, have mercy, it's Sean O'Brien! Water swirled above Lorelei's head as she tried to reconcile the man she'd just seen with the fact that she'd traveled all those miles to leave him behind. No, it couldn't have been Sean. It just couldn't. She'd been enjoying the first break she'd had after two days of caring for five exuberant children when she'd heard a sound like quiet footsteps. She'd ignored it, but then she'd heard that neigh. She'd opened her eyes never expecting to see *that man* standing on the bank of the river looking for all the world as though he'd been there for hours.

Her lungs began to hanker for air. Lorelei tried to swim to the surface to satisfy them. She also wanted to make sure her imagination wasn't playing tricks on her, but her heavy skirts dragged her downward, subjecting her to the twisting, turning pull of the current. She careened through the water and away from the bank. Panic filled her. She fought the urge to gasp in air, knowing it would only drown her. Her thoughts began to muddle together. *What a foolish way to die!*

Suddenly an arm encircled her waist. A body came

alongside hers and pulled her upward. With one last thrust of energy, they surfaced. Lorelei gasped for air. She met Sean's vibrant green eyes as he held her tightly to his chest.

"Don't let go," he commanded abruptly. She was too spent to argue, so she allowed him to pull her to the riverbank. The water gave way to solid ground. They both collapsed on the grass-covered banks. She turned her face toward him and found that they were only inches apart, but she didn't have the strength to remedy the situation.

His arm lay across her stomach barring her from flight. He made no effort to remove it. Instead, they stared at each other as they both took in gasping breaths. A few days' worth of golden stubble covered the base of his jaw and met just above his mouth. A slight sunburn trailed down the bridge of his nose drawing more attention to his unsmiling lips. Hints of gold and light hues of green shimmered in his eyes like the sunlight reflecting off of a slow-moving creek. Despite the disapproval she found there, her heart gave a familiar thump.

What was he doing here? He couldn't be here of his own volition. That would be too unbelievable. More likely, he had been sent by her father to bring her home. Well, that was not going to happen. She would not stand passively by as he wrecked her plans. She glared at him.

The dashes of his dark gold brows lowered into a frown as he rose onto his elbow to look down at her with a maddening smirk and finally spoke. "The good news is you made it out alive. The bad news is you didn't get away."

"I wasn't trying to get away. You frightened me by appearing out of nowhere. I responded as any normal person would." Somehow she found herself lifted into his arms as he stood and swept her up to his chest. She kicked her feet. "Put me down. What are you doing?"

"You're in no condition to walk."

"Yes, I am. Put me down. What is wrong with you?" She could count on one hand the number of times he'd purposefully touched her. Now, he wouldn't let her go. She kicked her legs again. "I said, put me down!"

"Hold on, you wildcat—"

A warning shot rang through the air. Lorelei screamed. Sean froze, then whirled around to face his adversary. She peered through her wild chocolate-colored curls to get a glimpse of Pastor James standing broad-legged and determined. He cocked his gun again and aimed it at Sean. "You heard the lady. Put her down."

The tone of his voice was deadly. Not at all what she expected from the gentle man she'd gotten to know over the past several days. She bowed her head so neither man could see the smile that curved her lips. She allowed her body to completely relax even as she felt Sean's arms tense beneath her legs and arms. He carefully lowered her legs to the ground but trapped her against his side in a one-armed embrace entirely too close to be proper.

This man was determined to meddle with her head. She was too smart for it this time. She wouldn't let his protective instincts or plain orneriness put ideas in her head or a silly feeling like hope into her heart. He could hold her as uncomfortably close as he liked, but from the looks of James's rifle, this situation was about to become just as uncomfortable for Sean. She vowed to enjoy every moment of it.

* * *

Sean kept Lorelei tucked against his side so close he could feel her shaking. Was she shivering from her plunge in the river? The water hadn't been that cold. Perhaps she quaked from fear after nearly drowning to death. He glanced down at her and found the answer in her mirth-filled eyes. She was laughing at him.

He narrowed his eyes to stem her mirth, but that only seemed to increase it. She dropped her head so the preacher couldn't see her smile as her body continued to shake in silent suppressed laughter. Annoyance led his hand down to his revolver. It probably wasn't any good as water-soaked as it was, but it was nice to have some reassurance while staring down a shotgun. He widened his stance to stare at the man intent on defending Lorelei from him. "Look, I don't know who you are or how this is any of your business, but the only protection this woman needs is from herself."

That got her riled up. She gave a pretty fierce little growl for a woman her size and in her situation. He tried to fight back his smirk but wasn't quite successful.

"I am Pastor James Brightly and that woman is under my care. I insist you release her this instant."

"This instant, huh?" Sean glanced down at Lorelei. Her dark blue eyes stared back at him, making him realize there was a lot of sanity in doing just what the preacher commanded. He let go of her. She took a few wavering steps away from him but somehow managed to stand on her own.

The preacher waved his shotgun. "Now, be on your way."

Sean shook his head. "Oh, no. I've been searching for this woman for days. I'm the sheriff of the town where she lives. I'm not trying to hurt her, but I'm not leaving until she and I have a little talk, Preacher."

"Lorelei, is this true? Do you know this man?"

He met her gaze squarely. He watched her tilt her head thoughtfully as she considered her next step. He could almost read the thoughts running through her head. All she had to do was tell the preacher that little two-letter word. If she did, he'd be dodging bullets and receiving a nice little prayer for safe travel courtesy of the preacher. Her smile grew.

He frowned at her. "Oh, come on, Lorelei. I just saved your life. The least you could do is save mine."

Her expression changed to one of reluctant resignation. "I know him, Pastor James, but I'd also like to know what he's doing here."

Sean hid his relief when the preacher lowered the rifle to his side. Lorelei didn't bother to hide her disappointment when the two men shifted into a less combative stance. She frowned at him. "Well?"

"You know very well why I'm here." He shook his head like a wet dog, then pinned her with a look. "Your father and Lawson sent me to bring you home, and that's exactly what I'm going to do."

Lorelei stiffened. "Oh, no, you won't!"

"Oh, yes, I will." He stepped closer to her. "Do you have any idea how worried your parents are right now?"

"I left them a note."

"That only compounded their fears. They knew that you were traveling alone with very limited finances, no supplies and hardly any idea how to get to California, let alone reach your great-aunt's estate." He caught her arm, hoping to somehow transfer a little good sense. "Anything could have happened, Lorelei!"

She wrenched her arm from his grasp but lowered her voice. "Don't you think I've realized that?"

"Then come home with me."

She crossed her arms. "No. Not when I'm so close to getting away from—" she seemed to catch herself and changed the sentence "—getting to California."

"Have you looked at a map lately? You aren't even close to making it out of Texas."

Her hand made its way to her hip. "I will. Marissa and James are paying me a fair wage. As soon as I have enough saved up, I'll take the train."

"Alone? Haven't you been preyed on enough?" He nodded in response to her suspicious look. "I know all about your reticule being stolen. That just proves I'm right. A young woman traveling without protection will warrant the attention of every outlaw and charlatan from here to California."

"I'll be careful."

"That's not enough."

"Well, it will have to be enough because I'm certainly not leaving with you!" She flipped her wet hair away from her face and stormed off.

He'd nearly forgotten the preacher was still there until the man spoke. "Do you know why she ran away?"

"I know enough to say she should stop this foolishness and go home. Like I said, I'm Peppin's sheriff, it's my responsibility to keep the town's citizens safe—even when they're being too pigheaded to see sense."

James nodded patiently. "I understand that you're trying to do your duty, but that is her choice to make. You can talk to her about it, but you can't force her to return. In the meantime, you may want to think more carefully about trying to bring her back to the situation that was uncomfortable enough to make her leave."

Sean hid a grimace at the preacher's advice. There was nothing wrong with the situation Lorelei was in that she hadn't caused. His job was to find her and bring her home. Her parents were supposed to deal with her after that. Somehow he didn't think the esteemed Pastor James would find his reasoning particularly favorable, so he kept his mouth shut and nodded in agreement. He needed a place to sleep after all and a way to keep an eye on Lorelei since she had gotten into the habit of disappearing.

The leaves of the towering oak tree quivered above Sean's head as he placed his Stetson over his face. Four days he'd waited for Lorelei to come to her senses. It seemed as if she was just sliding deeper into her joyous little cloud of insanity. He could hear her now. She was playing with the children in the gurgling brook and having a wonderful time while he tried to cool his temper and not let the sound of her laughter set his teeth on edge.

He was glad James decided to give his family a day of rest from traveling. Sean was pretty tired himself. He figured this was the perfect time to craft a plan to change the mind of a stubborn young woman bent on getting herself to California. If he didn't figure out something soon, he'd be stuck trailing her halfway across the country.

The ground beneath his back seemed to sway slightly. He caught his breath. This couldn't happen. Not here. He needed to ward off the panic now before it got worse. Nevertheless, his heart began to quicken into a familiar staccato rhythm.

The first time he'd noticed that beat had been the night of the storm that had taken his parents' lives. At ten years old, he'd lain awake in bed listening to the wind howl past his window and trying to fight the sense of foreboding that gripped him. Somehow he'd known they wouldn't come back. The next morning brought news of the accident, and with it the entire world had turned on end for him and his two sisters. He'd tried to step up and be the man of the house, but at such a young age there was so much that he couldn't do to help his eighteen-year-old sister, Kate, manage the farm, besides try to keep eight-year-old Ellie out of trouble.

The next two years had passed with him in such a state of stress that he would lie awake at night listening to his rapid heartbeat pound in his ears thinking for sure it would burst from his chest. He never told anyone that, especially not his sisters. To them, he'd remained stalwart and dependable until his brother-in-law Nathan had stepped into their lives.

The burden had suddenly lifted from Sean's shoulders, and he'd thought that would be the end of the waves of panic that occasionally took over. It wasn't. Even now he could feel his breath shortening. It always did when he found himself in a situation like this where he could do nothing but wait. He forced himself to pray.

Lord, You know I'm trying to be patient, but I need to get back to Peppin. This isn't what I bargained for when I agreed to bring her home. Help me change her mind. It took a few minutes for his body to settle down. Relief filled him. He shouldn't have another one for a

while now. He'd just go on as if it hadn't happened...
like always.

He slowly felt himself leaning toward sleep. Suddenly a small fountain of water poured over the sides
of his hat and settled around his ears before soaking
into the ground. Letting out an exaggerated roar, he sat
up. His Stetson tumbled to the ground, and Sean found
himself face-to-face with a six-year-old. Hosea stood
in what would have appeared to be paralyzed terror if
not for the delight sparkling in his round eyes. His hand
clutched a large tin cup now emptied of the water he
must have carried from the nearby brook.

Sean quickly surveyed the situation and realized that,
while Hosea may have been the culprit, he was only a
small part of a much larger plot. Watching with just as
much glee were the rest of the children and one very
naughty nanny.

Time seemed to stop for the seconds it took Sean to
slowly rise to his feet. Perhaps that was simply because
all the children froze when he pinned them with a calculating stare. Then his gaze caught hers. His smile said
one thing. William yelled it. "Run!"

Suddenly the world was a blur of motion. Hosea tried
to make a break for it, but Sean was too fast for him.
He scooped the boy under his arm like a sack of potatoes. Henry managed to evade his grasp, but Sean
lifted William with his other arm and spun the boys
around just enough to make them deliciously dizzy before he set them down. He repeated the process with
Julia and Lacy.

Meanwhile, Lorelei casually meandered in the direction of the camp. She should have moved faster, but

she couldn't help lingering to watch the sight before her. Sean was always so serious, so stern—it was fascinating to watch him grinning and playing with the children. It wasn't fair of him to look quite that...handsome. Not when she was trying so hard to ignore him.

Too late, she realized she'd missed her chance to escape. Her opponent caught sight of her and stalked toward her. He smiled predatorily. "Sending the children to do your dirty work, is that it?"

She widened her eyes innocently. "Now, Sean. It was all in fun."

"Was it?"

She glanced around for help, but the children had abandoned her to stagger laughingly toward camp. "Sean, don't..."

Sean swept her into his arms and spun her in a tight circle. She let out a small scream that lasted from the first rotation until he set her feet back on the ground. Her eyes finally opened to focus on his. The trees continued to sway perilously behind him. He gave her a pointed look. "There. Now, we're even."

"That's what you think," she muttered and tried to step around him, but he refused to release her.

"That's what I know. Unless you want me to haul you back to the Peppin jail for assaulting an officer." He gave a low whistle. "Now, there's an idea."

She glared at him. "Oh, why won't you just go away?"

He leaned toward her, meeting her challenge with his own. "You'd like that, wouldn't you?"

She pushed away from his chest, then wiped her suddenly wet hands on her skirt. "Yes, I certainly would."

"Tough." His green eyes captured hers. "You won't

get rid of me until I drop you and your problems back in your father's lap. I gave him my word—and Lawson, too—which means I'm going to stick to you like glue."

"You mean fleas," she muttered as she brushed past him and walked back to camp. She wouldn't let it bother her that nothing short of a promise to her father and his best friend would tempt Sean to stick close to her. She hated being his *duty,* and he certainly didn't want her to be anything else, so the smartest thing for her to do would be to stay as far away from him as possible.

True to form, he followed her back a few minutes later and took a seat near the campfire to whittle as she helped Marissa prepare supper. She ignored him and was grateful when Marissa struck up a conversation. "Tell me more about Peppin, Lorelei. It sounds like a charming town."

"There really isn't much else to say," she said as she felt Sean's gaze resting on her. "It's small but not stiflingly so. The people are friendly and really care about you. There is always something going on, so you're hardly ever bored. You can just go to the mercantile or the café to find someone to talk to or about, in some cases. It's just a normal everyday Texas town. The only thing special about it are the people."

"It sure is a good town," Sean said wryly. "I guess that's why most people are content to stay right where they are."

Lorelei refused to meet his gaze. She'd never said Peppin wasn't a good town. It was her home. Nothing would change that. She'd only left to get away from Sean, and that hadn't done any good. Why, she could do a better job avoiding him in Peppin than she could in this wilderness. So it was decided. She was going home. She dreaded the victory she knew she'd see in Sean's gaze when she told him, but it couldn't be helped. She'd tell him tomorrow.

Sean ignored Lorelei's quelling stare as he propelled her through the evening shadows that painted everything in dark smudges of color. The Brightlys must have made very close ties with the people in this area. An inordinate amount of them were still around more than an hour after the service was over. Lorelei stopped short at the sight of the large crowd of people waiting to speak with the Brightlys. "I can wait until these people leave."

He shook his head. "I'm not going to give you that much time to change your mind. Besides, we'll both need our sleep. We're leaving at first light."

She rolled her eyes. "I know. You keep saying that."

"That's because I like the way it sounds," he said in satisfaction. Placing a hand on her back, he guided her forward until they took their place at the front of the line.

"You're going to get us shot," she whispered.

"This will only take a minute," he said loudly enough for the others in line to hear. "I'm sure the Brightlys won't mind talking to their children's nanny for a moment."

A short while later, with James and Marissa's undivided attention, he announced, "Lorelei has finally agreed to let me escort her home. We'll be leaving at first light."

"You're leaving?" Marissa asked in alarm.

Lorelei shot him a glance that told him exactly what she thought of his blunt way of telling the couple. "I'm afraid so. I'm so sorry! I know this leaves you in a lurch."

"We told you that you could leave whenever you liked. The problem is that the two of you would be traveling without a chaperone," James stated gravely.

Sean shrugged. "It isn't ideal, but it can't be helped."

Marissa shook her head. "You have to think about Lorelei's reputation."

"Her reputation," he echoed with frustration, then glanced over his shoulder at the milling crowd that was shamelessly listening in.

"Maybe we should stay after all, Sean," Lorelei suggested, her determination wavering. "Just until we reach the next town with a train station. Then we won't have to worry about traveling unchaperoned."

"No," he said a bit too abruptly. "That could take days and days. We have to get back to Peppin. Perhaps one of the parishioners would be willing to act as our chaperone."

"I'll do it!"

Sean jumped in surprise at the quick response. He was still searching for the origin of that almost musical voice when a woman stepped forward to claim it. She didn't look anything like he thought a chaperone would. She was probably older than his mother would be if she'd lived but had pulled her mousy brown curls back with a girlish ribbon.

She stepped forward again which drew his gaze downward. His eyebrows rose. The woman was wearing pants or some female variation of them. Bloomers—Sean remembered his sister Ellie calling them. They were tucked into her high buckled leather boots.

Pastor James shifted uneasily beside Sean. "I don't think we've met, ma'am."

"The name's Miss Elmira Shrute. I've been traveling and came back to visit family." The woman's smile seemed friendly enough. "I'm about ready to head out though, so I can go with you. I assume the position would be paid?"

Sean glanced at Lorelei. Her reluctant expression turned doubtful. She cleared her throat daintily. "The little money I have, I'm going to need for traveling. Perhaps someone else would be willing…"

Her words were drowned out by a general murmur stating the opposite. Sean caught snatches of phrases like, "children to feed," "farm to run" and "pure foolishness." He grimaced.

Lorelei shifted slightly closer. "Well, what are we going to do?"

He glanced back at Miss Elmira. "I could pay you two dollars."

The woman grinned. "That works for me. When do we leave?"

"Sean, I'd like a brief word with you," Pastor James said as he took a step backward and led Sean away from the crowd. "I have to advise you against this. I've never met that woman before, but I know of her family. They don't exactly have the best reputation for being honest in their dealings with folks."

Sean frowned. "I appreciate your concern, but I'd be taking a chance with anyone I hired. Lorelei has agreed to go back with me, and I've got to get her moving before she changes her mind or gets a notion to take off on her own again. Miss Elmira may not be my first choice, but she is the only option."

"It's your decision and I respect that." Pastor James gave a reluctant nod. "Do what you have to do. Just keep an eye out for trouble."

They walked back to the crowd. Sean met Lorelei's inquiring look with an affirming one of his own. His shoulders relaxed from the tension he hadn't even realized was there. Things were finally going according to plan. Like Pastor James advised, he'd keep an eye out for trouble. It wouldn't be hard to do since he knew exactly what it looked like—a dark-haired beauty with the knack for getting under his skin in all the wrong ways.

"Lorelei, wake up. We've been robbed." Sean's words filtered through her consciousness, rousing her with a start.

Lorelei pushed the mass of dark curls from her face. Her hairpins had disappeared and Miss Elmira had refused to part with even one of her ribbons to help out a bedraggled fellow traveler. After two days of traveling, the woman had turned out to be as mean as she was peculiar. Lorelei realized Sean knelt at her side, so she propped herself on her elbow and frowned at him. "Was anyone hurt? Is Miss Elmira all right?"

"If I had to speculate, I'd say Miss Elmira is feeling pretty good right about now." He crossed his arms and glared out into the woods. "James was right about her. She must have taken off in the middle of the night, and my wallet went with her."

"*Miss Elmira* robbed us?" She glanced around to find her valise, but it was gone.

"Yes, and it's a little unsettling because she must have touched me to get my wallet and I never even felt it. In fact, I've never slept so deeply in my life. You don't think that tea she gave us…"

"At this point, I wouldn't put it past her," Lorelei said with a stifled yawn. "At least she left your horse."

He nodded. "She had her own horse. Besides, horse thieving is a hanging offense."

"What do we do? Should we go back to the Brightlys?"

Sean moved toward the fire he'd built and poured himself a cup of coffee. "I'm sure they've moved on by now. It would take longer to catch up with them than to simply keep going to the nearest train station."

"But we don't have any money!" She threw her bedroll aside and began to pace. "I suppose I could ask my father to wire us some once we get to town. That's probably the only option."

"I was kind of hoping you might say that," he admitted.

She sighed as she sank down onto a log across from him. "I can't believe I've been robbed twice since I left Peppin. What is *wrong* with this world?"

He glanced at her over his steaming cup. "An impulsive young woman ran off to California alone. That's what's wrong with the world."

She groaned. "You'd think there might be a grace period for fifteen minutes after I wake up, but no! You have to let me know you disapprove of me before I even have my coffee. I got that message a *long* time ago. Now, hand it over."

"Get your own." He nodded to the tin cup resting on the ground next to the coffeepot and ignored her rant. "At least she left us enough supplies to get to town."

She poured herself a cup, then blew away some of

the steam. "I wish she'd left a letter of authentication, as well. 'To whom it may concern. This letter is to verify that in addition to my work as a thief I also dabble in conartistry—'"

"Conartistry?" Sean frowned, which was the closest thing to a smile she'd seen all morning.

She held up one finger and shook her head. "Let me finish. 'I also dabble in *conartistry* by convincing young men and women that I am an adequate chaperone before robbing them blind and leaving them alone in the wilderness. Therefore, let it be known that I exist and testify to my betrayed charges' good character.'"

He watched her carefully. "Do you always talk out of your head in the morning?"

"No, I usually try to talk out of my mouth. However, today there are extenuating circumstances." A quick glance at Sean's nearly smiling lips reminded her of why she'd dictated that letter in the first place. "What are people going to think when we show up without a chaperone?"

His green eyes flickered warily. "Hopefully nothing, but the less time we're alone in the wilderness, the better. It's time to pick up the pace."

Chapter Three

Lorelei paced in front of the Western Union office as she waited for a response to the telegram she'd sent her father. The anticipation she felt knowing she would soon hear from her family confirmed she'd made the right decision about going back to Peppin. Just the thought of seeing her home again suddenly made her so excited she couldn't get herself to sit down. Then again, she'd been sitting down—or rather, sitting *up,* on the back of a horse—for three days, and she wasn't about to do it again if she could help it.

For the past few minutes, she'd been testing out different walks. Originally, her purpose had simply been to stretch her legs. To her fascination, she'd discovered that it didn't matter how many different ways she walked past Sean. He simply would not look up from that piece of wood he'd been shaving with his pocket-knife for the past half hour.

She literally waltzed by his bench. He still didn't notice, but a little girl with beribboned braids stopped to watch. Lorelei winked at her before the child's mother urged her on. The girl looked over her shoulder and beamed, causing Lorelei to do the same. Sean's horse neighed a welcome when she danced toward his hitching post. "Hello, Jericho. You know, you're much friendlier than your owner."

"Lorelei." She jumped at the sound of Sean's voice and turned to see him gesture to the seat beside him on the bench. She reluctantly sat down. He handed her the piece of wood and tucked his knife back in his pocket. "I made this for you."

A miniature replica of her stolen valise sat in her hands complete with tiny handles and a floral pattern. She stared at it blankly, then realized he expected a response. "This is nice."

"Thanks." He leaned back on the bench and covered his face with his Stetson.

She looked at it for another minute, then turned toward him to sharply ask, "Why would you do something this nice?"

"I was bored."

"You should be bored more often," she suggested.

He pushed his hat up slightly to meet her gaze. "Don't let it go to your head."

"Oh, I won't. I hate you. You hate me. Isn't that how this story goes?"

He turned to level her with his sincere green eyes. "I don't hate you."

She stared back at him. She believed him. In fact, she'd known it all along. It was just nice to hear him say it. For a moment she saw all the things that had once made her fall in love with him. She allowed a hint of a smile to reach her lips.

She could almost imagine that he began to lean toward her. The Western Union operator interrupted the tenuous moment by finally calling her into the building. She immediately stood. Sean trailed after her because apparently that's what he did.

"Miss, your father sent the money with a message and special instructions."

"What was the message?"

"I love you and am glad you're safe," he read in a nearly monotone voice.

"Thanks, but I hardly know you," she replied calmly. The man looked up sharply and frowned. Sean turned away with a sudden coughing fit. She smiled weakly. "That was just a little joke."

Sean stepped up beside her again to ask, "What were the instructions?"

"I am to place all of the money in your care, sir. You are instructed to take care of Miss Wilkins's needs and your own from these funds. You are not to let the young lady run off under any circumstances."

"Papa, you didn't," she moaned.

The man surveyed her shrewdly. "He obviously doesn't trust you with the money, Miss Wilkins."

"Smart papa," Sean added with a smile.

She frowned at them both. "Now y'all are just rubbing it in. Sean, get the money from the man and let's get on with this."

"What now?" Sean asked once they left the building.

"We both need a change of clothes, food, a room at the boardinghouse and a train ticket for tomorrow."

Sean realized things had gone too far the moment the words *you hate me* came out of Lorelei's mouth. He'd nearly gotten the picture when she'd questioned why he was being nice, but it wasn't until later that the extent of their poor treatment of each other hit home. He wasn't perfect, but he held himself and others to a very high standard of behavior. Lorelei had failed that standard when she'd inexplicably walked away from their almost romance two years ago and again when she'd impetuously run from the altar and his best friend.

He did have legitimate reasons to dislike her, but *hate* seemed like such an unchristian word. If he'd learned anything by spending countless hours with the woman, it was that she possessed redeeming qualities. She had a funny sense of humor, she hardly ever complained and she didn't fall apart under pressure. He shouldn't discount those things entirely—but neither should he let them skew his view of her completely. Maybe there was a balance. The trouble was that he wasn't sure how to find it.

"Where is everyone?" Lorelei murmured as they waited at the front of the boardinghouse she'd visited before.

Sean glanced around, then spotted the bell on the counter and rang it loudly.

"Mrs. Drake," Lorelei exclaimed as the widow exited the kitchen.

The woman smiled as she glided toward them. "My dear Miss Wilkins, it's good to see you again. I guess you've given up your desire to see your great-aunt in California."

"Yes. I'll be catching the morning train back home." Lorelei gestured to him. "I think you've met Mr. O'Brien."

He nodded respectfully. "Mrs. Drake."

"We were hoping we might be able to stay here tonight."

"Certainly." Mrs. Drake turned to survey her keys. "I assume someone else will be joining you."

Sean tried to act as if he wasn't nervous. "No, ma'am. We'll just take two rooms, please."

"Do you mean that the two of you have been traveling alone?" Mrs. Drake's perplexed look changed to concern. "And for days, by the looks of you. I don't understand how Pastor and Mrs. Brightly would allow such a thing."

"We had a chaperone," Lorelei offered.

Mrs. Drake frowned. "I'd like to talk to her then. She needs to accompany you all the way home, not just part of the way."

"That isn't possible, ma'am." He decided to state the facts honestly and very calmly. "The woman who accompanied us from the Brightlys' camp ran off with all our money."

The woman was quiet for a long moment, then her gaze trailed to the package of new clothing he'd stacked on the counter. Before he could try to explain, her eyes lifted to his again. They boasted a hint of suspicion. "Let me guess. You were sleeping, and you didn't even feel this woman pick your pocket, isn't that right?"

Sean stared at her in amazement. "How could you possibly know that?"

"I've just heard that story somewhere before." The woman transferred her gaze to Lorelei. "Dear, I think you'd at least use a little originality."

Lorelei leaned forward earnestly. "Oh, but it's true this time, too."

"So the parcels in your hand just suddenly appeared?"

"My father wired us money."

"I see." The woman crossed her arms. "What did he have to say about your predicament?"

"I didn't tell him." Lorelei admitted quietly.

Her eyebrows rose. "No, I guess you wouldn't."

Sean felt it was time for him to step in. "Now, hold on. We aren't making this up. The Brightlys saw her leave with us."

She nodded. "Yet, she isn't here now. Do you remember where you left the Brightlys in case I write to them?"

He named the settlement.

Her eyes narrowed. "That's a five-day journey. How long did you actually have this supposed chaperone?"

He cleared his throat. "Really, Mrs. Drake, I appreciate your concern but I think this line of questioning is unnecessary. Chaperone or no chaperone, Miss Wilkins is under protective custody as per her father's request. Now, are you going to rent us two rooms or should we take our business elsewhere?"

The widow surveyed Sean skeptically for a moment. "Miss Wilkins, I'll place you on the second floor. Sheriff, your room will be on the first floor. No gentlemen are allowed upstairs after dinner."

"Thank you," Lorelei said.

Mrs. Drake gave a tight nod, then sent Sean a warning look. "If either of you need anything tonight, remember that my room is directly across from the stairs."

He barely refrained from rolling his eyes but noticed Lorelei gave Mrs. Drake a reassuring smile. He took his key, picked up Lorelei's packages and helped her find her room. As they walked up the stairs, he saw Lorelei bite her lip to keep from laughing. "You think this is funny, do you?"

She allowed her smile to grow. "Actually, yes, it is rather amusing. You made it sound like I was your prisoner. And you really ought to stop acting as though I'm a runaway. I'm much too old to be considered anything but an adult taking a trip, despite what my father or anyone else might say."

He frowned as he followed her around the corner. "When I say 'runaway' I am not describing your legal status."

She glanced at him over her shoulder. "Then what are you describing?"

"Your recent pattern of behavior," he said, then paused as she found her room and tried to unlock the door. "I still think you're just waiting for the first possible moment to get away from me."

"I am, but my efforts aren't doing any good. This door won't open." She turned the knob and banged her hip on the door, then winced. He planted his shoulder into the door and shoved. It groaned as it sprang open. She took her packages from him. "It was my decision to come back with you, remember? I've already told my father that I'm coming home. I won't run away. I give you my word on that."

He leaned against the threshold. "I think we all know what that's worth, don't we?"

It took her a moment to realize he was referring to her engagement with Lawson. When she did, pain flashed across her face. "How dare you? If you want to be mad at me because I left your best friend at the altar, then fine. Be mad, but you should really thank me for doing it."

He scoffed out a laugh. "Why would I thank you? You broke his heart."

She lifted a brow imperviously. "He didn't tell you that."

"He didn't have to. I saw the look on his face. He was stricken."

"He didn't love me, Sean. I know. I asked him. To be honest, I didn't love him the way I should have, either. That's why I didn't marry him." She lifted her gaze to his. "He deserved better than a wife who isn't in love with him. He deserved better than me. Is that what you wanted to hear?"

Yes, but it didn't sound as wonderful as he thought it would. Not with that thread of pain running through the words and the self-deprecating tone in her voice. He met her gaze contritely. "I'm—"

"Save it," she bit out, then slammed the door in his face.

Thankfully the hinge made it close slowly enough that he could jump out of the way. He stared at the thick barrier between them. It always seemed to be there, whether visible or not. If it broke down, he wasn't sure how he'd handle it. It might not change anything, or it might change everything. He allowed his forehead to rest on the cool door for a moment. He couldn't lie to himself. Sometimes he wondered what might have happened if he'd fought for her even a little instead of just surrendering to someone else's claim. He'd never know. Maybe it was best that he didn't.

Sean helped Lorelei down from the train and onto the platform. She was immediately hailed by her parents who pulled her into a long hug. When her father stepped away, Sean handed him Lorelei's new traveling bag. The man gave a nod of appreciation but said nothing more. He seemed too moved at seeing his daughter to speak.

Sean returned his nod. He hesitated for a moment, then went to see about his horse. Once Jericho was secured, he looked for the Wilkinses again. He spotted them walking away. He watched them go, wondering if Lorelei would turn to look at him or make any attempt to say goodbye. She didn't.

They'd both agreed not to lie if asked about the lack of a chaperone, but they weren't going to shout Elmira's deception from the rooftops, either. Lorelei had already told her parents they'd been robbed but hadn't mentioned when or by whom. Sean hoped that by not telling anyone, the subject would become a nonissue. And if that was the case, then this whole convoluted adventure of chasing Lorelei across Texas, bringing her home in spite of all the obstacles, spending every hour in her maddening, exhilarating company would be over. Relegated to the past and forgotten—like it never happened at all.

"What do you mean he hasn't responded?" a man's frustrated voice bellowed, snapping Sean out of his thoughts as he passed the telegraph office that was next door to the railroad station.

Sean stopped to watch the rough-looking older man who stood outside the door. The telegrapher shrugged casually. "I mean what I said. The message was picked up, but no response was given. That's all I know. Now, you can check again tomorrow if you like. Until then, I suggest you stop causing trouble and leave."

The man muttered a few unholy words, kicked the dust and walked away. Sean watched him carefully, then went inside to speak to the telegrapher. "Hello, Peter. What can you tell me about that man?"

"He says his name is Alfred Calhoun. He's been coming by every day for the last week. He sends telegraphs to a Frank Bentley down in Houston. They seem to be trying to coordinate a meeting of some kind. Near as I can tell, that Bentley fellow is coming here."

"I don't guess there's anything wrong with that."

"No. He's an odd one, though. I don't think he has a job. He seems to spend most of his time in the Red Canteen."

Sean nodded thoughtfully. "If you find out anything that concerns you or if you want me to help you handle him, just let me know."

"I will. I've been talking to Jeff about it and I'd planned to tell you when you got back in town. I'm glad you got to see the man in person." Peter finally smiled. "You find that Wilkins girl all right?"

"Yes, she's back with her family now."

"Wish I'd been asked to rescue her." Peter gave him a knowing smile.

"I wish you had been, too," he said with a parting grin. Peter was still laughing when the door closed behind Sean. He let out a sigh. All right, so that wasn't entirely the truth, but it was better to discourage any implication like that before it had a chance to take the form of a rumor. He only hoped that would be enough. The last thing he needed was for people to start asking questions. He planned to let this little episode in his life fade into the obscurity of nothing more than a faint memory. That was for the best. Wasn't it?

Chapter Four

Lorelei pushed the long strips of bacon around her plate with a fork, then glanced up at her parents. Her father sat across from her, hidden behind a copy of the Austin newspaper he'd managed to snag on his last trip to the city. Occasionally, his hand would slip from behind it in search of food. Her mother sat to her right unconcernedly drinking her morning tea as she planned out the day on a piece of notebook paper.

The silence was broken by the crinkle of newspaper. Lorelei tensed as her father folded the paper and set it aside. She braced herself when his gaze met hers. His blue eyes soon dropped to his coffee cup, which he carefully blew on before taking a long drink. She felt her shoulders relax. She lifted the bacon to her lips but could not force herself to eat it. She glanced up once more, feeling tempted to glare at her parents.

It was horrible what they were doing. They hadn't mentioned her running away once since she'd gotten home yesterday. At first, she'd assumed they merely wanted to give her time to rest after her journey. With breakfast nearly over and her father due at the bank in less than a half hour, there'd still been no mention of her actions. She knew that they were of such a magnitude that her parents couldn't and wouldn't leave the subject untouched. Why were they drawing it out? They must know the suspense was killing her.

"Lorelei," her mother began.

Her head shot up, and she prepared herself for battle.

Caroline smiled. "Would you pass me the salt, please?"

"Yes, Mama."

"Thank you, dear."

"You're welcome," Lorelei replied quietly.

Coffee cup drained, Richard stood. "Well, I suppose it's time I get over to the bank."

She watched dumbfounded as her father gathered his dishes and placed them in the sink before returning to the table to kiss her mother goodbye. "Have a wonderful day, you two."

"Shall I send Lorelei with your lunch?"

"That would be nice, if you don't mind, Lorelei," her father said, then leaned across the table to kiss Lorelei on the forehead. His beard and mustache tickled her skin in a familiar sensation.

"I don't mind." Tears pricked her eyes as she watched him turn away and grab his hat. She blinked them away resolutely. He couldn't leave without talking to her. Surely she deserved a lecture or something. She stood. "Papa, where are you going?"

He turned with a perplexed look on his face. "I'm going to the bank."

She gave an exasperated sigh. "I know that. What I mean is…well, I know you two want to talk to me. I'd rather you just say what you need to say now rather than drag it out by waiting until later."

He seemed confused. "What is it you wanted to discuss, Lorelei?"

Her mouth fell opened then closed. "I ran away."

"Yes," he agreed.

"Isn't that something you want to discuss?" she asked.

"Not particularly," her father said.

Lorelei looked to her mother for help, but the woman lifted her delicate brows in confusion. "Well, what would you like us to say, dear?"

She sat down in disbelief. "This is ridiculous. Don't you want to tell me how impractically and irresponsibly I behaved? How dangerous it was for me to travel alone as I did? How flighty it made me appear to everyone? How awful it was of me to leave you two wondering and worrying?"

Her mother took a sip of tea. "Is it necessary?"

She glanced to her husband who looked down at Lorelei thoughtfully. "I don't think so. She seems to have learned her lesson."

Lorelei looked from her mother to her father and back again. With a groan, she buried her face in her hands. "Did I just give myself a lecture?"

"I'm afraid so," her father said with amusement in his voice.

She frowned at him. "You planned this, didn't you?"

He smiled. "Goodbye, Lorelei."

As the door closed behind him, her mother smiled. "Dear, we spared you the lecture because we know you. We know you've already recognized what you did was wrong because you're here. You came back to us.

Don't think for a moment we weren't worried or upset while you were gone, because we were both of those things and more."

"I really am sorry."

"We know that." She reached over to place her hand over Lorelei's. "Why did you leave? What happened that day?"

She sighed. "There I was in a beautiful white dress with one of the best men in the world standing beside me at the altar, and I couldn't do it. I couldn't—even after I spent all that time convincing myself that I could. I knew it wasn't right." She paused to take a deep breath. "It all was my fault because my whole life I was foolish enough to fancy myself in love with the one man who has never cared I existed."

"Sean O'Brien," her mother said softly.

Lorelei stared at her. "You knew. This whole time you knew?"

Her mother laughed. "Of course, I knew. You're my daughter. How could I not know?"

She froze. "Does Papa know?"

At her mother's nod, Lorelei groaned and buried her face in her hands.

Her mother pulled at her hands. "Come now, it isn't that bad."

Lorelei dropped her hands to the table. "That's what I'm afraid of. That everyone knows how I felt about him." *Including Sean.*

"I don't think that's the case. It's common knowledge that you had a crush on him as a girl, but then Lawson began courting you and everyone assumed you let it go."

"I almost convinced myself I had until that day. Suddenly, I realized I couldn't do that to Lawson. I couldn't go into our marriage halfhearted, knowing I couldn't love him as he deserved to be loved. It wouldn't have been right."

"I hope you know how proud I am of you for doing that. It would have been much easier to let things continue as you'd planned," her mother said. "But why did you run away?"

Lorelei shrugged. "I just hated the thought of having to deal with all the gossiping, the speculation, the people whispering behind my back—or saying to my face—that I'm a silly flirt who broke Lawson's heart."

Her mother looked surprised. "Did someone actually say that?"

A long time ago, she thought to herself, and glanced away. "Never mind that. But all of it made the prospect of getting away for a while and starting fresh somewhere new seem awfully tempting. I had everything already packed and ready to go. It…" She smiled weakly. "It seemed like a good idea at the time."

The smile quickly faded as she continued. "But if I thought I could run away from being judged, then I was wrong. Sean tracked me down, and ever since I've had to live with his constant disapproval day in and day out. That's when I realized how foolish I'd been, and decided to come home."

Her mother nodded, then asked, "So where does that leave your feelings toward Sean now?"

Lorelei shook her head. "If I learned anything while I was gone, it's that I'm done with Sean O'Brien. I'm finished waiting for him to look at me with anything more than a frown on his face. I think I've allowed his dislike of me to shape who I've become. That's part of the reason I wanted a new beginning away from here and him."

"I see." Her mother took a sip of her tea thoughtfully. "Perhaps what you are searching for is a new perspective, dear, not an entirely new life."

"Maybe so." Lorelei sighed.

It wouldn't hurt to try, and it was much more practical than any step she'd taken so far. She smiled. A new perspective... That sounded perfect. She had no idea what perspective she needed but whatever it ended up being would be better than the one she had.

Lorelei smiled a greeting at the bank tellers as she breezed through the lobby with her father's lunch basket in tow. Her steps faltered as she neared the open door of the manager's office. Gathering her courage, she knocked lightly. Lawson glanced up from the box he was packing. He paused in surprise at the sight of her before giving her a welcoming smile. "Come on in."

She surveyed him carefully. He didn't seem to be upset with her, but she hadn't seen him since the wedding. She decided to tread lightly as she stepped inside. She placed the basket on his desk, then turned in a slow circle to survey the moderately sized room. The room had been stripped almost completely of his personal items. She turned to face him as the weight of guilt settled on her shoulders. "You're leaving the bank?"

"I resigned a few days after the wedding."

"I'm sorry."

"For what?" he asked curiously.

She crossed her arms and leaned her hip against the desk. "Well, it's my fault you're leaving, isn't it?"

He shook his head. "No. I'm just ready to move on,

that's all. I've been inquiring about a few other jobs. Most of them are out of Peppin."

"I still feel responsible."

"Don't." He closed the box, then met her gaze seriously. "While we're at it, let's get something else straight. You already apologized to me about what happened at the wedding. I'll admit I was hurt but not as deeply as you might have thought because you were right. I didn't love you the way I should have. I knew something was wrong, but I'd made a commitment and I didn't want to be the one to walk away from it. I'm glad you did. It was the right thing for both of us."

She stared at him. "You mean it?"

He nodded. "I hope we can go back to being friends now and that you know if you ever need anything you can call on me."

"Thank you, Lawson. Hearing you say that means so much to me. I hated thinking that I might have hurt you. You've been such a wonderful friend. I wouldn't want to lose that."

"Well, you aren't. You're stuck being my friend so you may as well like it," he teased. Then, looking at her closely, he offered her his handkerchief. "No tears in my office and it's still my office until I take this box out."

She smiled and dabbed her watery eyes before handing it back with her thanks. "I'd better bring Papa his lunch. I guess I'll see you around."

"I'm sure you will for a little while at least."

"Are you all right?" her father asked a few moments later as he cleared his desk to make room for the food. She told him about her conversation with Lawson, and he shook his head. "He's a good man and a good manager. I wonder what sort of work he'll go into next."

"That reminds me," she said as she laid out a plate with her mother's baked chicken, green-bean casserole and corn. "On my way here I stopped to talk to Mrs. Cummings at the millinery shop across the street."

He stared at her in confusion. "How did what I say remind you of hats?"

"She was looking for someone to come in a few hours a week to help her, and I told her I'd like to take the job. Isn't that wonderful, Papa?"

Richard frowned up at her from his dark leather chair. "No, it is not. Why should you want a job, Lorelei? What will my customers think if my own daughter has to work outside the home? I'll tell you what they'll think. They'll think their money isn't safe here."

She lifted an eyebrow and closed the basket. "As if they had anywhere else in town to put it."

He waved his fork. "That is beside the point."

"Well, I don't see why they'd care one way or the other," she reasoned. "Besides, I need something to do besides embroider with Mother."

Hope sprang within her when her father quieted for a moment. "If it's work you want, you are always welcome to work here."

She almost laughed. "Doing what?"

"Why, you could be a teller."

"Papa, I don't want to be a teller."

"I'd much rather you work here."

She grimaced. "I'd much rather not."

"It's a perfectly respectable place. I can watch you," he rationalized.

"It's a perfectly boring place and I don't need to be watched."

He looked at her in wavering contemplation, and

she gave him her best and most pleading look. Finally, he sighed. "I have a feeling this is going to be like the rose garden you tried to start and that bakery idea you tried to get a loan for and the—"

She titled her head. "And the wedding I didn't go through with?"

He stilled. "Now, I didn't say that, did I?"

She fiddled with the lace on her dress and tried to keep the tears from blurring her eyes. "Well, why don't you? Isn't that what you're thinking? I can start something but I don't finish it well, do I?"

"You can do whatever you set your mind to, Lorelei. When you like something well enough, you stick to it. Look at your music lessons. You've been playing the piano—very beautifully—for years. I guess you just try out more things than most and there's nothing wrong with that. If it's all right with your mother, then I don't mind."

"Oh, thank you, Papa." She smiled and slipped around the desk to give him a quick hug. "I'm certain I'll like it, and I'll stick to it no matter what."

"That'll show them." He winked.

She chatted with him for a few more minutes before exiting his office and walking right into a conflict between Mrs. Greene and her father's secretary. Neither party seemed to realize they were blocking the hallway. The man looked positively flustered. "But, ma'am, you don't have an appointment and Mr. Wilkins is having lunch. Why don't I direct you to a teller? I'm sure one of them will be able to help you."

"I'm sure they will *not*." Mrs. Greene's face seemed to grow redder by the moment. "I insist on seeing Mr.

Wilkins right now. I have been entrusted with a letter for him and I aim to see he gets it."

Lorelei spoke up to try to diffuse the situation. "It's all right, Alexander. Father is finished with his lunch. I'm sure he'd be willing to see Mrs. Greene."

The young man stepped aside to let Mrs. Greene pass. The woman's gaze shifted to Lorelei, who smiled pleasantly. Mrs. Greene didn't return the gesture. She just stared with an appraising eye. Lorelei had the strangest feeling that she'd been weighed and found wanting. Mrs. Greene brushed past her to enter her father's office without waiting to be announced. Lorelei grimaced, then glanced at Alexander. He shook his head. "I'd hate to be your father right now. She has one mean bee in that bonnet of hers."

"I'm sure he'll be able to handle it." She said goodbye to him, then waved at the other tellers before she stepped back onto the sidewalk.

It was surprisingly good to be back in Peppin. She hadn't realized how much she'd missed her family and the entire town until she'd returned. Not that she hadn't noticed the curious looks and quiet whispers she garnered. Despite that small discomfort, it was good to be home. She'd decided her mother was right. She needed a new perspective. She was not going to allow herself to be distracted by old desires or thoughts anymore.

"Lorelei." She glanced up into Sean's green eyes as he tipped his Stetson to acknowledge her in passing.

I should have used the alleyways, she thought with an inward groan. She gave a small nod in return. She waited until she crossed the street to glance back for one final look at what never could have been.

Chapter Five

The door to the sheriff's office flew open, banging against the inside wall and allowing a burst of sunlight to paint the room. Sean's hand hopped to his gun. He rose so quickly from behind his desk that he sent his chair toppling to the floor. The door swung closed behind the man who scanned the otherwise empty room. After seeming to establish they were alone, Richard focused on Sean with narrowed eyes.

"Mr. Wilkins, what can I do for you today?"

Richard strode toward him with fire in his eyes. "Sean O'Brien, I ought to tear you limb from limb. No, I ought to lock you up in your own jail cell, scoundrel that you are."

"Hold on just a minute, sir. Those are some pretty strong words." He righted the chair without taking his gaze from the advancing man.

Richard pressed his fist on the top of Sean's desk. The man paused to catch his breath, then his blue eyes locked with Sean's in anger. "Did you think I wouldn't find out? She is my only child. I trusted you. I put her well-being in your hands. You were supposed to protect her but all you did was expose her to slander."

A chill crept down Sean's spine. "I'm not sure what you mean."

Richard's eyes narrowed as his voice turned steely, and he tossed a piece of paper on the desk. "Don't lie to me. You can read it for yourself."

"A letter?"

"Yes, it's from a Mrs. Drake. She writes in stunning detail how the two of you arrived *alone and unchaperoned* at her boardinghouse." He glanced down at the letter. "She says she tried to discover the reasons for this moral gaffe but you were hostile toward her while telling an incredibly dubious and conveniently difficult to disprove tale of being abandoned by your chaperone at some point during your five-day journey to town. She insinuates that you and Lorelei…that you… Well, it is quite obvious what she believes had been going on between you two. I want to believe it isn't true but if it is, so help me…"

"It isn't true." He wavered. "Well, not entirely."

"What does that mean?" Richard took a deep breath and seemed to calm down a bit, though his grim expression didn't change. "Can you prove this woman wrong?"

"Yes. No." Sean swallowed. "Not completely and not immediately. Listen, this can all be explained, but first I think it would be best if Lorelei were present during this conversation."

Richard held Sean's gaze for a long moment, then with a short nod he agreed, "Then send for Lorelei."

Lorelei hurried down the raised wooden planks of Peppin's sidewalk at a pace polite society would frown on. She could already feel herself starting to perspire. She would arrive at the sheriff's office looking flushed and wrung out. Not that she was trying to impress anyone at a time like this. Surely, something must be dreadfully wrong for her father to summon her through a messenger. His tone in the note had been abrupt, almost harsh. It was so unlike him that she was worried that something was seriously amiss. Had he been robbed? Threatened? Attacked? What disaster could have struck that required him to turn to Sean?

Her anxious thoughts hastened her steps the last few feet into the sheriff's office. Surveying the room, she noticed Sean sitting at his desk with her father seated comfortably across from him. Both men stood as she entered but remained oddly silent.

Obviously nothing was wrong with her father's constitution. He even had a bit of color in his cheeks. She paused a moment to catch her breath before venturing farther into the silent room. "Papa, whatever is the matter? I thought something must have happened."

"I'm afraid it did." He looked sterner than she'd ever seen him.

"What did?"

"That." He pointed to the desk.

Her confused gaze lingered on her father a moment before she followed his finger to the object on the desk. "A letter?"

"From Mrs. Drake."

"Mrs. Drake?" she echoed in confusion.

Sean's hand briefly touched her arm, drawing her gaze to his for the first time since she'd entered the room. His eyes were filled with what seemed to be concern and caution. "Lorelei, it seems that Mrs. Drake was concerned about our lack of a chaperone during our trip and decided to write your father about it."

"Oh, no," she breathed before she could stop herself. Her eyes widened as her mind raced through a thousand scenarios of how the next few minutes might play out. Very few of them were good. Her eyes collided with Sean's inscrutable gaze before she turned to her father. "Obviously Mrs. Drake must have misunderstood the nature of my relationship with Sean."

Sean nodded. "I was about to explain that to your father when we decided to send for you. Perhaps it would be best if we all sat down."

Once they all pulled out a chair, a moment of silence echoed through the room as everyone seemed to calm down and collect their thoughts. Her father let out a tired sigh. "Start from the beginning."

Sean leaned forward slightly in his chair, not enough to heighten the mood, but enough to call attention to himself. "Sir, when I finally met up with Lorelei she was traveling with a preacher, his wife and their children. After four days with them, I convinced Lorelei to come home to Peppin with me. The couple took umbrage with our leaving to travel in the wilderness by ourselves for a few days and insisted we find a chaperone. One of the local women offered to chaperone us for a wage, which we agreed upon. We set off with her in good faith, but we were only two days into our trip when she ran off with our money and Lorelei's valise. We considered turning back and rejoining the preacher and his family, but by that point, we thought they'd probably moved on, and that it would be faster to push on to town rather than trying to track them down. We finished the trip alone."

"In the wilderness, alone for a few days, you say?"

"Yes, sir."

The man looked as if he'd aged a few years since entering the office, but he nodded. "I see. Continue."

"Well, that's it."

"What do you mean 'that's it'?"

Sean shrugged. "There's nothing more to tell."

Lorelei pinned her father with her blue gaze and a raised eyebrow. "Were you expecting more, Papa?"

"Don't be smart with me, young lady," he said even as his skin appeared to flush a bit.

"In defense of my honor as a gentleman and Lorelei's as a lady, I would like you to know our behavior was circumspect on the trip home. She slept on one side of the campfire and I slept on the other." He met Richard's gaze. "I mean this as no insult to your daughter's sensibilities, but I want you to know I never touched her."

"All right, I get the point and I appreciate you making it." Richard shook his head. Rising to his feet again, he began to pace. He turned to face them. "I understand what happened wasn't your fault, and I believe you when you say you began the trip with a chaperone. *I* do, but I'm afraid that Mrs. Drake's account…"

"It's embellished, to say the least," Sean said.

"Perhaps so." He agreed. "That isn't the only thing that concerns me. This letter was hand-delivered to me by Mrs. Greene. She is aware of the contents and was quite adamant that I do something to fix the predicament."

"No wonder she glared at me in the bank," Lorelei muttered.

Sean grimaced. Mrs. Greene and his family didn't have the best history. After his parents' death, she'd taken it upon herself to guide their orphaned family on the straight and narrow. Unfortunately, that somehow translated into her being rather harsh and overly critical in her judgment of them. She was hardest on Ellie but wasn't particularly fond of Sean, either. He cleared his throat. "Surely you can just explain to her that there has been a mistake."

Richard shook his head. "I suggested that idea in my office, but she stood by her niece's account and painted a picture of the incident that whipped me into a fury. Sorry about that, Sean."

"It's understandable, sir. I reckon I'd act the same way if I had a daughter."

He stopped pacing to face them. "Even if we could prove your chaperone abandoned you, the fact remains that you traveled alone for days in the wilderness."

"It wasn't our fault," Lorelei insisted.

"No, but can you imagine the scandal? It could easily be construed that you two had some sort of affair only days after you were supposed you marry another man. If word gets around about this…" He shook his head and sat back down.

"Knowing Mrs. Greene," Sean interjected, "she may have already told everyone."

"I asked her to let me deal with this my own way first. She promised she'd keep quiet until I speak to her again but vowed that if I didn't hold you accountable she'd make sure the town would."

Sean clenched his fist. "What does that mean exactly?"

"We don't want to find out." Richard turned to Lorelei. "I need to talk to your mother about this. We'll decide together what to do."

"But, Papa—"

He shook his head. "I think its best that you go on home. I'll be there shortly."

Lorelei watched her father for a long moment, then left without a glance Sean's way.

Richard turned to him. "Come to our house for supper this evening. I'll know what to tell you then."

Without waiting for a response, the man left. Sean stared at the door for a long moment, then sighed. There was nothing left for him to do but straighten the chairs and prepare himself for that evening. Waiting—his least favorite thing to do. He needed something to occupy his time. He glanced around, his gaze landing on the Bible at his desk, and suddenly the choice seemed obvious. He'd read his Bible and maybe even say a little prayer. He could only hope it would help.

"I know we are all anxious to address the issue foremost on all of our minds," Richard Wilkins began, then glanced at her and Sean as if to be sure they were listening before he continued. "I won't keep the two of you in suspense any longer."

Lorelei glanced at Sean to gauge his reaction. His gaze was intent on her father's face as if it might give some hint to the outcome of her parents' decision. Certain she wouldn't be able to swallow another bite of her blueberry pie, Lorelei placed her plate on the small table that rested between Sean's chair and where she sat on the settee. Her mother and father sat side by side in chairs across the room, letting Lorelei know that they were unanimous on whatever decision they had reached.

As if reading her thoughts, Richard said, "My wife and I spent quite a bit of time in thought and prayer about this matter. We ask that you both refrain from commenting on what we say until you have heard us out completely. Is that understood?"

"Yes, sir," Sean agreed.

Lorelei nodded. Settling back in the settee, she clasped her hands nervously in her lap.

"You both have good reputations and I think you know that in a town of this size reputation is everything." Leaning forward, he looked at them intently. "It affects everything from who speaks to you on Sunday to who will do business with you. It's a precious commodity."

Her mother nodded gravely. "I know this will be difficult to hear since the two of you did nothing wrong, but I'm afraid there will be no way to avoid a scandal should any of this come to light. It's in your best interest to try to head that off if possible."

Richard smiled wryly. "I'm afraid I'm not giving either of you much of a choice. I'll not have my daughter's name bandied about as a common trollop. We've already seen with Mrs. Drake that people will turn the facts into whatever sordid scenarios their imaginations lead them to believe. What's worse is that the story would grow with each telling, and, believe me, people would tell."

Lorelei's stomach clenched as her father's gaze narrowed onto Sean. "I'm giving you six weeks."

"Six weeks, sir?"

"Yes." Richard straightened, his jaw firmed. "You have six weeks to court my daughter. At the end of those six weeks, I will expect a proposal."

Chapter Six

Lorelei gasped in shock at her father's ridiculous statement. He couldn't mean it. He just couldn't. "You cannot be serious."

Caroline sent her a warning look. "We certainly are."

Sean leaned forward in his chair. "What about Mrs. Greene?"

Her father shot a glance at his wife. "I think we may have figured out how to handle her. My plan is to try to get the woman on our side in this. We'll thank her for bringing this to our attention, assure her of our intentions to see you two married and ask her to help."

"I think she's done quite enough to help," Lorelei scoffed, feeling her shock give way to anger at the situation. "What else could Mrs. Greene do?"

"Amelia has been a friend of mine for ten years," Caroline said. "I think if I appeal to her sense of decency, she'll help us preserve your reputations by staunching any negative gossip and correcting it with our own messages. From what Richard has told me of his confrontation with her, I believe her concern is to see that the proper thing is done. If the two of you marry, that should satisfy her."

Sean shook his head. "Good luck with that. She doesn't exactly love the O'Briens."

"I think she'll do this favor for me."

"So you want him to propose in six weeks if Mrs. Greene is merciful. I suppose you expect us to fall in love in six weeks, as well." Lorelei shook her head at the hopelessness of their predicament.

"I expect you to try," her father replied. "Whether you do or not should be between you and only you. I want the town to think this is a perfectly normal romance. There will be fewer questions that way." He glanced at Sean. "Do I have your word on that?"

"Before I agree to anything, I have a few questions of my own." Sean shot to his feet and began to pace. "How could people think our courtship is normal when Lorelei was supposed to marry my best friend less than two weeks ago? People might think we'd been carrying on behind his back."

"Your dislike for each other has been rather apparent the past few years. I doubt anyone would believe that."

Sean crossed his arms. "Then why would they believe these silly rumors?"

"They aren't rumors," Caroline answered gently. "We're looking at the facts here. Y'all did spend days alone together in the wilderness."

Mr. Wilkins picked up where his wife left off. "Sean, the two of you could let all of this come to light. If you're right and no one believes the allegation, your reputations might weather the storm. If people do believe it, you'll still end up married because the town would see to that. The only difference is that you'd also be publicly disgraced. My wife and I would like to spare you that, but it means you'll have to cooperate. Will you let us help you?"

Sean met Lorelei's gaze for a long moment. She watched his emotions battle in his eyes until defeat won out. He gave a short nod. Lorelei's fingers bit into her palms. "You're really agreeing to this?"

"I don't want this any more than you do, but it looks like there is no choice."

For him to be that…fatalistic about even the thought of marrying her hurt more than she'd ever admit. She shook her head. "With a proposal like that, how can I say no?"

He sank onto the settee beside her. "I didn't mean for it to sound that way, Lorelei. It's just that this is so much bigger than us. It isn't only my reputation I have to consider—any gossip that's spread about me would reflect badly on my family, too. I can't do that to Ellie or Kate, not when it's my fault for letting this situation occur. I knew the moment Miss Elmira went missing that this had the potential to blow up in our faces. I'd like to control the explosion however I can."

She forced herself to calm her rapid breathing as she tried to make sense of what was happening. Sean was agreeing to marry her. For so many years, she'd longed for a moment like this between them—now she deplored it. It didn't mean that he loved her. It simply meant that he was doing his duty. Logically, it was the best option. Emotionally—it just felt plain awful. At least she didn't love him anymore. That would have sealed the hopelessness of her fate.

A wry smile touched his lips. "You look like you've been assigned a fate worse than death."

She nodded slowly. He seemed to think so. Why shouldn't she? "Maybe I have."

His jaw clenched, and he stared at her for a long minute, then stood. "I think I'd better go. Thank you for dinner, Mrs. Wilkins."

"You're quite welcome."

"Goodbye, Lorelei." He couldn't even seem to make himself look at her before he turned away to search for his hat.

Once the door closed behind him and Caroline rejoined them in the parlor, Lorelei let the silence close in thick around them. Both of her parents were waiting for her reaction. It took a few moments to gather her thoughts. "Maybe I should go to California after all. If I leave, this might all blow over."

"And leave Sean to deal with this alone?" her mother questioned with obvious disapproval.

Richard sat down on the settee beside her and took her hand in both of his. "Running away is what got you into this problem in the first place. It won't solve anything. Besides, didn't you just tell me this morning that you wanted to prove the town wrong about you? This is your chance."

"No, there has to be a way out," she muttered desperately. "We could hire a detective. We could find Miss Elmira."

"To prove that she left you to travel for several days alone?" Caroline shook her head sorrowfully. "Darling, there is no other way."

"No other way," Lorelei breathed, then glanced at the door Sean had walked out of moments before. "He'll hate me for sure now. If not now, then in ten or twenty years."

Richard frowned. "Why would he hate you?"

"I've taken his every chance at happiness, just as he's taken mine. Oh, how will we bear it?" Her parents protested, but she tuned them out with a quick shake of her head and fled to her room. Her desperate gaze flew to her large window. Opening it, a warm breeze washed over her along with the scent of the wild roses that she only bothered to tame when the mood struck her.

She knelt before the window and stared down into the garden. It would be so easy to climb down the trellis, slip into the night and leave her troubles behind—but she'd tried that before. Her father was right. It hadn't worked. In fact, it had only made her problems worse. No, this time she would have to take responsibility for what she had done instead of trying to run from it. Marrying Sean, a man who could never love her, was a high price to pay for her impulsive mistake, but what choice did she have?

She'd show Sean and the whole town. She'd see the courtship and the marriage through to the bitter end, but she wouldn't be foolish about it. She'd keep her wits about her. She wouldn't let any remnants of her childish feelings make her silly enough to love a man who would never love her back. She'd end up chasing after something she'd never be able to catch. The only way to keep her heart safe would be to keep even the slightest fragment of love from taking root. That's exactly what she planned to do.

Sean closed the Wilkinses' gate behind him with a decided thud, then stuffed his hat on his head and clenched his jaw. He just couldn't wrap his mind around the fact that after all this time he was actually going to court Lorelei Wilkins. If this was some sort of divine joke, he didn't find it funny. He shook his head. "This is not part of the plan."

He'd planned to settle down in the next few years but not like this. Not to her. He'd wanted to find a stable, mature, sensible wife he'd be able to count on. Lorelei was flighty, impetuous and a dozen other things he'd wanted to avoid in a life partner. She was the one woman in the world he was sure he could never trust. The woman who'd trampled on his heart and his best friend's. She'd single-handedly managed to take his stable, carefully thought-out life and turn it into complete upheaval. His hands slipped into clenched fists. His heart began to race.

"Sean, where's the fire?"

He stopped short, then whirled toward his friend's voice, feeling a mixture of dread and relief. "Lawson."

Lawson tipped back his Stetson to look at him. "Where have you been? My parents have been out on a doctor's call all day. I got tired of my own company so I went to the café. I was going to rope you into going with me, but I couldn't find you."

"Sorry," he mumbled. Glancing away to survey the town's quiet streets, he debated whether or not to tell Lawson what had happened. How could he not? Lawson had a right to know as his best friend and Lorelei's former fiancé. He swallowed, realizing he might have just gained a wife and lost a best friend. He cleared his throat. "I hope you didn't wait for me. I had dinner with the Wilkins family."

Lawson's mouth dropped open. "You don't say? Well, no wonder you were running like you saw a skunk and looked like you swallowed a porcupine."

Sean shook his head. "Where do you get those sayings?"

"I don't know. They just pop into my head. Are you going to tell me what happened at the Wilkinses' or am I going to have to guess?"

Sean shook his head. "You couldn't guess this. I'll tell you, but I think you'd better sit down."

Lawson frowned curiously then lifted his chin in the direction of the Williamses' house. "Well, come on then. Ma made a pitcher of sweet tea and there are a couple of glasses left. We can sit on the porch."

A few minutes later, Sean clutched the sweating glass of sweet tea tensely as a heavy silence settled between him and his best friend. He'd done his best to explain the circumstances of his predicament and the events that were about to take place. Lawson had listened intently, but his expression remained inscrutably thoughtful. Finally, when he thought Sean couldn't bear the silence another minute, a wry smile pulled at Lawson's lips. "I think your mischievous youth has come back to haunt you."

The glass nearly slipped from Sean's hand. "Is that all you have to say?"

"What did you expect me to say?"

"I had no idea." He set his drink on the table next to him, then slumped in the wicker chair in a strange mixture of relief and confusion. "I thought you might yell at me."

Lawson was the picture of nonchalance as he propped his arm on the back of the wicker bench. "Why would I yell at you?"

Sean sat up in disbelief. "She was your fiancée!"

"Right. She *was* my fiancée."

"If you'd hit me, I would have called it fair. I almost wish you would. I'd hit myself if it were me."

Lawson's smile spread. "Now that would be something to see."

Sean rested his forearms against his knees. "Listen, stop being glib about this. I thought you loved her."

"I thought I did, too…for a while." He rubbed his chin thoughtfully. "Now I think I just loved the idea of being loved by a girl like that. You know what I mean?"

"No," he said dryly.

"Let's just say that when she left me at the altar a little part of me was relieved. I wasn't happy at the time because it was mighty embarrassing for both of us, but if we'd gone through with it…" He shook his head at some imagined outcome, then met Sean's gaze again. "How is Lorelei reacting to all of this?"

"She's no better off than I am." He frowned. "Worse probably and she let me know it."

"That's what I don't get about this whole thing. Lorelei and I never argued. We got along perfectly. I thought that meant we were in love, but now that I know we never were, I'm inclined to think there just weren't any strong feelings there at all. Not even enough to make us bicker." He crossed his arms and tilted his head suspiciously. "You two, on the other hand, can't seem to be in the same room for longer than a minute before you're shooting invisible bullets at each other. It makes me wonder."

Sean narrowed his eyes as he slowly asked, "It makes you wonder what?"

Lawson smiled. "Guess."

Sean's eyes widened. He cleared his throat and looked away. "That's impossible."

"Sure it is," Lawson said sarcastically, then ignored Sean's protests to ask, "When is this courting business supposed to start?"

"I don't remember if Mr. Wilkins gave a specific date besides the engagement, but I'd like to give Lorelei a while to cool down. I could use some time, too." He pulled in a deep breath and rubbed his hand over his face. He groaned. "What am I going to do?"

Lawson shook his head dubiously. "You, my friend, are going to marry *Lorelei Wilkins*—your nemesis since you were ten years old. God help you both."

Sean stared at his friend. "What would I do without your encouragement?"

Lawson shrugged. "I've been wondering that myself, but I figured it would be best if we don't find out. I'll be sure to include it in my letters if I ever find a job out of this town."

"Thanks, Lawson. That would be just dandy." Sean slumped down to rest his head on the back of the chair and stare thoughtfully at the boards of the porch roof. He needed to think practically. If he was going to get married, he needed to find his own place. There was no way he could bring a wife into the one-room cabin he'd rented in town. Just around the corner from his office, the space served him well as a bachelor, but it was no place to start a family.

As if detecting the vein of his thoughts, Lawson cleared his throat. "I know this is supposed to be a secret, but what are you going to tell your family?"

"I don't know," he murmured quietly. "Nothing yet I suppose. I need time to think about this."

His family... His shoulders tensed under the load of a new thought. He was the only one of his siblings who would carry on the family name. With that came the responsibility of continuing his parents' legacy. Theirs had been a love match for sure. He'd wanted that for himself one day, but the way things were shaping up it didn't look as if he was going to get it.

He should have listened to Pastor James. For once, he'd been impulsive and agreed to let Elmira chaperone them even against his better judgment. That decision had gotten them into this mess. If he'd been more patient, he might have managed to convince another parishioner to chaperone them. Or, maybe someone from the next settlement would have gone back with them. He sighed. He'd learned a long time ago that maybes didn't change anything. Only hard work, logic and methodical planning guaranteed results. He'd need all three if he intended to improve anything about the situation he was in.

Lorelei couldn't contain her restlessness any longer. She abruptly set her embroidery on the settee beside her and stood. *If I have to push this needle through that cloth one more time, I'm going to toss this cushion out the nearest window.*

Her gaze landed on the large family Bible sitting on a nearby table. Maybe reading the Psalms would help. She wandered over to the Bible. It opened to the bookmarked page near the back. Before she could turn the page, a verse caught her eye. *"If a man says, I love God, and hates his brother, he is a liar."* She paused for a moment to allow those words to sink in. *"For he that does not love his brother whom he has seen, how can he love God whom he hath not seen? And this is the com-*

mandment have we from him. That he who loves God must love his brother also."

She read the last part of the verse again and frowned. Wasn't there something between love and hate? If there was, God didn't seem to be all that concerned with it. The commandment was pretty simple. Love God. Love your brother.

"Wonderful," she murmured.

Her mother glanced up from her embroidery. "Did you say something, Lorelei?"

She shook her head, then narrowed her eyes thoughtfully. "You can love someone without being in love with them. Right, Mama?"

Caroline shrugged. "Sure you can. Why?"

"Never mind," she said. She wasn't even sure she was ready to go that far when it came to Sean. It was too dangerous to let herself love him in any way, and she just wasn't ready. She smoothed her skirts nervously, then set her shoulders decidedly. "I think I'll take a walk."

Her mother gave a slow nod before glancing toward the window where stylish blue drapes filtered the muted sunlight. "You'd better take an umbrella. It's likely to rain."

Lorelei walked to the curtain and peered outside. "It looks sunny enough to me."

"Nevertheless," her mother said significantly.

Lorelei turned from the window to quickly make her way upstairs. She donned a hat accented with deep blue ribbons and black lace. It perfectly matched her blue dress with the black ribbon detail that ran across her hips before floating artfully down the back of her dress. She hurried back down the stairs and paused just inside the door next to the umbrella stand.

Her hand reached for her father's overly large, overly green umbrella, then strayed to the dainty black parasol just beside it. A quick glance over her shoulder told her that her mother wouldn't notice, so she pulled it from the stand, then she set out on her way with a hurried goodbye. She opened the parasol and set it on her shoulder.

She pulled in a cleansing breath of fresh air as she passed the few remaining houses on the street. Her home had been stifling in the days since her father's alarming edict. She'd hardly allowed herself to think about the impending doom the courtship represented, let alone the man who would help bring it about.

The only bright spot on the horizon was that her mother had somehow convinced Mrs. Greene to agree to the plan they'd devised. Lorelei had listened at the top of the stairs while her mother soothed Mrs. Greene's bluster until the woman promised to help spread the rumors of the new romance, with the caveat that she'd take her niece's story to the judge if the wedding didn't happen as scheduled.

And so, her fate had been sealed over cinnamon scones a week ago. She shook her head in frustration. Sean had not shown up once since that evening or done anything to seek her out. If he didn't want to spend time with her, that was fine. She didn't exactly want to spend time with him, either, especially knowing he was being forced to do so. For that reason, she crossed the street toward the mercantile rather than continuing across the street where she'd have to pass the sheriff's office.

She stopped to peer into the display window of the millinery shop. She saw Miss Cummings speaking to a costumer. The woman had shown her around the shop on Monday when Lorelei had arrived for her first day of work. Since it was only Wednesday and Lorelei was not scheduled to work again until Friday, Miss Cummings only waved at her. She returned the gesture before moving on.

As she passed the seamstress shop, a young gentleman exited the mercantile and caught her gaze before offering an appreciative smile. Lorelei nodded politely but did not stop at the friendly invitation in his gaze. Though she hardly gave the stranger a second thought, his actions somehow reminded her that, despite all of her best efforts, she would be forever bound to a man who could not stand her.

A small cry of dismay escaped her lips, and she glanced around to make sure that no one heard the traitorous sound of her inner turmoil. She searched for something to distract her from her sad thoughts. Her gaze landed on the church's spire not far off of Main Street. Perhaps she would find some relief in the sanctuary.

Her feet began to hasten their steps. She waited for a wagon to pass, then hurried across to the same side of the street as the church. She stepped onto the sidewalk just as the café door opened. Sean stepped out. Her steps faltered when she met his gaze.

Sean watched Lorelei's eyes widen in alarm as he reached out to steady her. Her stormy dark blue eyes turned cold the instant before they dropped from his. She turned to continue on her way. For a moment, he was tempted to let her go. Then with a silent sigh, he turned to follow her. "Lorelei, wait!"

Taking her elbow in his hand, he pulled her to a stop as he stepped in front of her. Her affronted gaze met his as she tilted her head as though in deep concentration. "Is there a particular reason you've decided to cause a scene?"

He didn't have to glance over his shoulder to know he was probably drawing curious stares from the patrons of the glass-fronted café. He leveled her with a quelling look. "As a matter of fact, there is. We need to talk."

"Well, there's no reason for us to stand in the middle of the street to do it." She eyed the café, then took off walking toward the church at a fast pace, leaving him to follow. She glanced up to frown at the large raindrop that landed on her parasol with a definite plop, then transferred her frown to him. "Why now? I don't see how whatever we need to talk about can be any more important today than it was yesterday or the day before that."

Though she ended her speech with a polite smile, Sean easily recognized her dig at his not having approached her before. "I needed time to collect my thoughts."

She glanced up again as the clouds began to steadily drizzle large drops of heavy rain before she turned back to him. "You were avoiding me. Now I wish you'd allow me the same courtesy you gave yourself."

He caught the slight look of hurt in her eyes before she managed to hide it. Lawson's theory about her behavior teased at the back of his mind. Right now, with her deep blue eyes staring back at him, he could almost imagine it was true. "I wasn't avoiding you. I was trying to think this through and come up with a plan."

Her frown turned skeptical. "What kind of a plan?"

He was about to explain when the clouds burst open. The large raindrops turned into a deluge of stinging rain. He glanced around for cover and realized that as he'd been talking to Lorelei, they'd left Main Street and were halfway to the church. He looked over to find she'd stopped to gape at the sky.

She looked rather pitiful. Rain streamed from the corners of her tiny parasol onto her fashionable dress. She seemed unable to decide whether to turn back or go forward. His hand settled pressingly against her waist. "Come on, you're getting soaked."

She followed his lead as they hurried toward the church, but he soon noticed that she'd slowed as they continued their frantic trek. He realized that her heavy skirts were tangling about her legs and restricting her movement. Impulsively, he came to a stop. She glanced at him in confusion. "What's wrong?"

"Hold on to your parasol," he said, then swept her into his arms. Her gasp rent the air. He glanced down at the face close to his own. "Ready?"

He seemed to have taken her completely off guard. She shrank slightly away from him in his arms but gave a small nod.

"Hold on tight," he urged.

Her arm slipped around his shoulder. He took off at a fast clip toward the church. He hid a reluctant smile as her drooping parasol slowly lifted to cover both their heads. It kept the rain from his face, which helped him to see, so he supposed it might have a slight purpose after all. He carefully mounted the church's stairs, pausing at the door only long enough to open it. He stopped just inside the foyer to let Lorelei's feet slide carefully down to the floor, keeping his hold on her waist to make sure she caught her balance.

The sudden silence of the church after the hammering rain rushed around them, stilling them both. He took the moment to survey the woman he was supposed to marry. Her wide dark blue eyes stared back at him framed by thick black lashes that swept downward demurely at his perusal. His gaze followed their movement downward over her angular nose that softened into a rounded tip before his eyes fell to her nearly-too-full-to-be-fashionable lips.

He hadn't allowed himself to notice it in so long that he'd nearly forgotten—Lorelei Wilkins was beautiful. That was why she hadn't been on the Peppin marriage market long before she'd been claimed by his best friend. Sean had thought that claim was going to last forever. Apparently, he'd been wrong. It looked as if he'd be the one to claim her as his own through no real effort of pursuit. It seemed wrong somehow, but it couldn't be helped.

He had to make the most of it, and he'd better start now. He was beginning to realize the task might not be as dreary as he'd once imagined. That meant he needed to be careful. He couldn't allow himself to get confused about his goal. That goal was to convince the town that they were a couple so that they could save their reputations. This courtship needed to go according to plan not only for their sakes but also for their families'. It was his duty to see that it did, and Sean O'Brien never shirked his duties.

Chapter Seven

Lorelei's hand slipped from Sean's shoulder to his chest as she pushed him away. Avoiding his gaze, she shook out her parasol on the church's unfinished floor. She closed it with a snap, then sent him a glare. "Was that perfectly necessary? I would have made it on my own."

"It was 'perfectly necessary' and a thank-you will do just fine."

"Thank you," she muttered, though it was clear she didn't mean it. She turned to glance around the church. The sanctuary doors stood open, but not a sound echoed through the halls of the church beyond their own. "It looks like we have the place to ourselves."

He walked forward to survey the sanctuary, then gestured her inside. "We might as well make ourselves comfortable until the storm moves on."

She averted her gaze knowing she certainly wouldn't be comfortable trapped anywhere with this man. Her grip tightened on her dripping parasol. She wanted to leave and leave now. Realizing that would be impossible, she schooled her features into a neutral expression. "I've never seen so much rain come through so suddenly."

"Well, summer is on its way out, and autumn is coming through like a steam engine. I'm sure we'll see plenty more of these squalls in the next few weeks." He watched her in concern. "You're shivering."

She forced herself to stop. "I'm fine."

"Nonsense. There should be a blanket around here somewhere."

She was cold, so she didn't keep him from leaving to find one. Once he was gone, Lorelei lifted her sodden skirt to step onto the small stage, then dripped toward the piano. She carefully traced her finger along its smooth wood. She'd spent countless hours practicing on the instrument since she was fourteen.

Her parents had donated the piano as a gift to the church with a request that Lorelei be allowed to play the instrument as long as it did not interfere with church functions. Since then, the instrument had provided her with an outlet for her emotions. She suddenly realized how sorely she'd missed playing it the past few weeks.

She heard Sean's boots ring on the wooden floor and stepped down from the platform to meet him in the aisle. She took the blanket he offered her. Wrapping it around her shoulders, she managed to give him a grateful smile and a whisper of thanks through chattering teeth. He grinned. "That wasn't so hard, was it?"

She sent him an ungrateful look.

He chuckled. "It's too late now. You can't take it back."

"I wasn't going to," she said, then settled into one of the pews near the back. She tried to ignore the fact that he took the seat beside her. She scooted a bit farther away under the pretense of fixing her blanket, but he angled his body so that he could see her face. It looked as if he was settling in for a long talk. She sighed. "We should check the weather."

"I just did." He pointed to the small windows that let light flow into the church. "It's still raining."

"Oh."

"No need to worry. We have plenty of time to talk."

She burrowed farther into her blanket. "I'm not worried."

"First off, I'd like to apologize."

Her eyes widened in surprise. "For what?"

He sighed wearily. "All of this is my fault. If I had taken the time to think, I never would have agreed to let Elmira chaperone us. It was a bad decision."

A slight smile teased the corner of her mouth. "Thank you for apologizing, but if I hadn't run away, we would never have needed a chaperone."

Sean seemed to think about this for a minute, then frowned and nodded. "You know what? You're right. It is your fault." He grinned when her mouth fell open, then continued seriously. "However, ultimately it was my responsibility to protect your reputation, and I failed at it. At least this courtship will give me a way to rectify the situation."

She stared at him thoughtfully. "Duty means a lot to you, doesn't it?"

His gaze shot to hers. "I live up to my responsibilities, if that's what you're asking. To do that, I learned I have to think things through and live life deliberately. Perhaps you'd do well to learn a similar lesson."

"You know, you have the oddest talent of saying something nice right before you say something rude."

He frowned. "What did I say that was nice and what did I say that was rude?"

"Never mind," she said, shifting slightly away from him.

He shook his head in confusion. They listened to the drum of the rain on the roof for a few moments before he spoke again. "I've been thinking. We really don't have a lot of time to convince people we're falling in love. I reckon this is as good a start as any."

"Start for what?"

"Our romance."

Dread settled in her stomach. She swallowed and met his gaze. "How do you figure that?"

"I carried you in here, though I doubt anyone saw us, to a rather secluded yet entirely respectable place to find shelter from the storm. It's the perfect starting point for us to further our acquaintance," he said thoughtfully, then nodded. "It makes for a good story."

"It isn't real."

"It certainly isn't a lie. I'll tell people I found myself charmed by your beauty, and you can tell them my unexpected kindness helped you see me in a new light."

"That isn't a lie?" She sent him a doubtful glance, then shook her head. "I don't know about this."

His arm slipped to the back of the pew, and he leaned toward her intently. "You don't know about the story or you don't know if you're ready to play along?"

She shifted away nervously. "Both."

"Listen, we're supposed to make this as believable as possible. That means you have to commit to this. If that's going to be a problem, then maybe we should just come clean and let the town do with us as they please."

"No," she protested. "I said I'd do it and I meant it."

He leveled her with a measuring stare. He nodded

slightly. "All right. We'll take this one step at a time. Just follow my lead and do as I say. We'll be fine."

Her eyes narrowed. "What do you mean 'do as you say'? I hope you know I have no intention of—"

The door to the church opened, and excited chatter erupted from the foyer. She sprang to her feet as Sean rose next to her. They both turned toward the door together. She swallowed as she recognized a few of the women considered to be the pillars of Peppin society. When Mrs. Rachel Stone, Mrs. Amelia Greene and Mrs. Susan Sparks caught sight of them, their chatter slowly died.

Mrs. Stone, the retired sheriff's wife, was the first to speak. "Well, hello, Sean, Lorelei."

Reverend Sparks's wife surveyed them with concern. "Are you two all right?"

Sean glanced down at her and smiled. "Perfectly."

She felt herself blush from the regard his warm smile implied. The warmth in her cheeks only heightened as she caught the women's speculative looks. She was overcome by the need to explain. "I was on my way here and ran into Sean. The rain came pouring down so unexpectedly! We ran in here to find shelter."

The thoughtful quiet that descended on the group was disconcerting. She glanced to Sean for help. He reached down for the blankets they had abandoned. He held them out to Mrs. Sparks. "I'm afraid we soiled your clean blankets, ma'am. We were soaked and cold, so I borrowed them."

Lorelei reached for the blankets. "I'd be happy to have them washed for you."

Mrs. Sparks took her blankets and smiled. "No need. I keep them here for people who find themselves in need of them."

"Thank you," Lorelei said, then sent a sideways glance at Sean. "Well, I suppose I should go."

Mrs. Stone shook her head. "Don't leave on account of us. We just needed to gather a few things from the storage closet."

"We were only waiting the storm out," she said as she began to edge toward the door.

"It's almost over now," Mrs. Sparks added. "Be careful out there. The rain has caused a dreadful amount of mud. I'm practically covered in it."

Mrs. Greene, who had remained quiet the whole time, finally spoke up. "We all are, except you, Ms. Wilkins. How do you reckon that?"

Lorelei realized the ladies' dresses and even Sean's boots were all six inches covered in mud. Her skirt alone remained pristine...if somewhat damp. Her eyes widened. She glanced at Sean who had the gall to look amused. She sent him an impatient glare before turning to face the ladies. She lifted her chin and raised her brows slightly to give just a hint of daring to her words.

"There is actually a very simple explanation. Despite my protests, Sheriff O'Brien was kind enough to carry me into the church. He saved my new skirt," she said, turning to Sean with a half-gracious smile, "which of course leaves me eternally grateful."

A smile pulled at his lips. "As I said before, Miss Wilkins, no thanks is necessary."

Lorelei almost ruined the whole thing with her disbelieving laugh, but she quickly turned it into a delicate set of coughs. Sean stepped closer. "Sounds like you could use a strong cup of tea for that cough."

"You're right. I think I'd better get home." She turned to the women with a smile. "It was wonderful to see you."

They each nodded to her. Mrs. Stone tilted her head as she looked at Sean. "Perhaps you ought to see Miss Wilkins home."

Lorelei shook her head. "That's hardly necessary."

"Now, now," Mrs. Sparks said. "Those mud puddles can be dangerous."

Sean smiled. "Would you mind, Lorelei?"

"I suppose not."

The women moved toward the storage closets, but Mrs. Greene held back to whisper, "I'll take it from here."

They murmured their thanks to her, then made a quick exit. Sean stayed close to her side as they walked across the muddy grass toward the sidewalk. Her heel sank into a deep mud puddle. They had to pause for her to yank her foot out of it. "They weren't kidding about the mud."

Sean smiled wryly. "Mrs. Greene is extremely observant. I'll give her that."

"I can't believe she thought to ask about my skirt."

"It's a good thing she decided to be on our side in this. I don't know how your mother managed that, but I'm grateful." He led her toward the sidewalk. "At least, we won't have to tell people the story of our being at the church alone together. By this afternoon, the entire town will know."

She sighed. "If not the surrounding counties."

"We'll just have to make the most of it," he said.

Dread settled in her stomach. It had begun. There was no turning back now.

But she would be fine. She would! She just needed to maintain her boundaries. She lifted her skirt to step carefully from the dirt to the sidewalk, and his hand supportively caught her arm, then immediately released it. Her gaze met his for a moment. They had barely made it away from the measuring eye of the women in the church, and he'd already slipped back into his normal demeanor. He looked closed off again. Distant. Slightly disapproving. In other words, the same as always. Yes, she'd definitely have to work on keeping up her boundaries. She doubted she'd have to worry about him maintaining his.

Sean intercepted Kate's skeptical gaze as she stood across the churchyard talking with her best friend, Mrs. Stone. He felt a dull heat crawl up his neck and forced himself to refocus on what his brother-in-law was saying. He could easily guess what story Kate was hearing. He didn't have long to wait for a confirmation. Kate walked across the grass to stand beside Nathan. She met Sean's gaze questioningly. "Well, is it true?"

Nathan's arm slipped around Kate's waist. "Is what true?"

She glanced up at her husband, and Sean was grateful to watch her face soften into a smile before she turned to Sean again. "There's a rumor going around that our little brother might be taking an interest in Lorelei Wilkins."

Surprise lit Nathan's eyes even as a cautious smile pulled at his mouth. "Is that right?"

Sean shrugged. He couldn't outright lie to his family, but this wasn't the place to tell them about his true relationship with Lorelei. For the time being, it would be best to talk around it. "You know how unreliable rumors can be."

Kate pinned him with her thoughtful gaze. "So are you saying you aren't interested in her?"

He flew to where Mrs. Greene held court with a

few of her cronies. He swallowed. "No, I'm not saying that exactly."

"I don't understand." Nathan tilted his head skeptically. "What does that mean?"

Sean cast about for something to say that wouldn't be an outright lie. Squaring his shoulders, he settled for a portion of the truth. "It means I've realized that Lorelei Wilkins is a beautiful, intelligent, maddening woman."

Kate exchanged a glance with Nathan before turning back to Sean. "This sounds serious. What are you going to do about it?"

He shifted uncomfortably and glanced around the churchyard until he spotted Lawson joking with a few of their friends. Nathan must have followed his gaze because he quietly asked, "Have you mentioned this to Lawson?"

Sean nodded. "He seemed fine with it."

Kate bit her lip thoughtfully. "Well, it has only been three weeks since the wedding. Maybe it would be best to take it slow."

Suddenly, Ellie appeared at his side. "Take what slow?"

"Sean is thinking about courting Lorelei," Kate supplied.

His little sister's eyes widened for an instant, then she smiled knowingly. "I'm not surprised."

"You're not?" they all asked in various degrees of surprise and confusion.

She eyed Sean as if he'd been living under a rock. "I always thought Lorelei liked you more than she liked Lawson. Don't you remember? When we were children she had an awful crush on you. She always said she was going to marry you when she grew up. Then you were mean to her and she left you alone."

"That's true," Kate agreed.

He frowned. "Sure it is, but that was a long time ago."

She shrugged indifferently. "Maybe so, but then you liked her before she started courting Lawson."

He narrowed his eyes. "What makes you think that?"

"You're my brother," she said as if that explained it all, then added, "Also, I'd catch you staring at her every once in a while and you'd always stand a little taller when she walked in the room."

"I did not," he protested when Kate's eyes flew to Sean's, and she bit her lip to keep from laughing.

"You did." Ellie nodded and continued to stare at him as if concentrating on a puzzle. "Oh, and you were really depressed once she and Lawson starting courting. You tried to hide it, of course, but you were still living with us so I noticed. Right now, your face is turning red. The only reason you'd be embarrassed was if it were true—"

Nathan tried to hide his chuckle as Sean held up a desperate hand. "Ellie, please stop talking. I get it. Thank you."

She sidled closer to him. "I could help you, you know. I'm a very experienced matchmaker."

"Ellie," Kate groaned. "I don't think this family can survive another round of your matchmaking."

"Nonsense! It's because of my matchmaking this family has survived. Need I remind you of how you met Nathan?"

A general groan filled the air.

Ellie took that as a yes. "If I hadn't convinced Sean we needed to mail order a husband for Kate—"

"—and then proceeded to marry us by proxy without my knowledge," Kate reminded with the lift of her chin.

"Y'all never would have had the chance to meet," Ellie continued as if Kate hadn't spoken.

Nathan gazed down at his wife with a smile. "Or fall in love or really get married or have three beautiful children."

Kate grimaced as her shoulders gave a little shiver. "Now, that's a scary thought."

"See?" Ellie poked Sean in the side, causing him to jump. "Don't worry, big brother. I can help you, too."

"Please, don't." He ignored her calculating smile to ask Nathan, "So I have your approval if I decide to court her?"

"I'm not sure you need it, but you have it." Nathan smiled. "You have always been a responsible person. We trust you."

Maybe you shouldn't, he immediately thought. He looked at Ellie, Kate and Nathan. They looked so cautiously hopeful and so unsuspecting of what was really going on. He could tell them now. He *should* tell them now, but he didn't want to utter the words that would shatter their perception of him. He'd spent most of his life convincing everyone that he was the strong, dependable one who had everything figured out. Now he was the one who'd messed up, and there was no way to fix it. Finally, Kate left to round up her children and the moment was lost.

Sean had almost forgotten his offer to help out the telegrapher with his problematic customer when Peter stepped into his office the next afternoon. Sean motioned to the chair across the desk from him. "That fellow giving you trouble again?"

Peter nodded, then shook his head. "Not exactly. I just thought you should know I found out the reason the other fellow hasn't responded to any of Calhoun's telegrams. He was a wanted criminal who was caught and placed in jail. He's been accused of murder and robbery."

Jeff rose from the deputy's desk to join them. "That sounds like your customer is keeping some pretty bad company."

"It sure does. I found out today that the man escaped from jail. That marauder, murderer and outlaw is on the loose, and he already has a contact here. He may be headed this way. You've got to protect the citizens of Peppin."

Sean was quiet for a moment, then he nodded. "That's my priority, Peter. I don't have any jurisdiction outside of this town, so I can't keep that man from traveling toward us on the rail line. Should he come here, I promise I'll arrest him. Unless that happens, the only thing I can do is keep my eyes open."

The man nodded. "I guess that's all I can ask."

"I'd like to see a wanted poster of the outlaw. Can you ask them to send one to me?"

"Certainly."

"Let me know if you come across any other evidence, and I'd be happy to take a look at it."

"Oh, don't you worry." The man grabbed his hat to leave. "I'll let you know the minute I hear anything slightly suspicious."

"Do you think this is serious?" Jeff asked as he took the seat Peter had just vacated.

"I don't know, but we need to treat it as such." Sean went over the notes he'd taken while talking to Peter. "We need to find out more about this Alfred Calhoun fellow. If they were communicating, they might have been trying to coordinate something other than just an escape—especially since Calhoun clearly wasn't expecting his friend to be arrested. Otherwise, he wouldn't have been so angry that his messages had gone unanswered."

Jeff seemed to catch the direction of his thoughts. "I wonder if Calhoun has any other contacts already in town that might be of interest. If he does…"

"Then we may be dealing with a gang." Sean nodded, having already realized the danger. "In that case, there's only one target in town that's big enough to attract an entire band of outlaws."

"The bank," Jeff murmured.

A sober silence permeated the room. Sean leaned back in his chair to think. It made sense. The First Bank of Peppin was also the only bank in Peppin. Even people from the surrounding counties used the bank because Mr. Wilkins had a reputation for fair business practices. A lot of money went in and out of his doors which made it the perfect draw for undesirables. Now that he thought about it, Sean was surprised there hadn't been a threat on it before.

"What's the plan, Sheriff?" Jeff asked.

Sean smiled because Jeff knew he'd already have one. "I'll talk to Mr. Wilkins to find out how we can shore up any of the bank's vulnerabilities. We'll study that wanted poster when it comes in. We'll also keep an eye on Calhoun to see what he's up to."

If someone succeeded in robbing the bank, the community would be devastated and so would the Wilkins family. Oddly enough, the Wilkins family now included him. That made the threat personal. He might not always get along with Lorelei, and he didn't agree with her rather impulsive approach to life, but she was soon to be his wife. He wasn't about to allow anything to happen to her or her parents.

Chapter Eight

Lorelei caught in a short gasp, then let out a loud sneeze that exploded into the silence of the millinery shop. It sent scads of feather particles floating into the air, compounding her problem. She held her breath until the feathers settled back onto the worktable, then cautiously pulled in a small breath. When her nose didn't begin to itch, she turned back to the bonnet in her hands.

She eyed it carefully. Selecting a large peacock feather, she trimmed it down and attached it to the bonnet. A smile lifted her lips. *Perfect.*

She turned the bonnet around in her hands, then frowned. *Or not.* The hat was definitely missing something. As she glanced around the worktable for something to add, she heard the little bell above the door give its cheerful jingle to signal the arrival of a customer. Mrs. Cummings had gone upstairs for lunch, leaving Lorelei to face her first costumer alone.

She set the bonnet aside and dusted away the feathers clinging to her fingertips before hurrying out of the workroom. A cheerful greeting stalled at her lips, and she paused in surprise as she realized the customer was

Sean's youngest sister. Ellie lifted one of the store's most elaborate hats from the shelf for a closer look. Lorelei allowed an amused smile to pull at her lips. She could hardly imagine Ellie wearing such an ornate creation.

Lorelei cleared her throat delicately. "Would you like to try it on?"

Ellie abruptly spun to meet her gaze with wide green eyes. "Oh, no. I wouldn't wear it. I'd like to think I am not as complicated as all that."

Lorelei met Ellie's self-deprecating grin with a smile of her own, then glanced around the shop searchingly. "I can find you something simpler. We have a straw bonnet that I think would suit you perfectly."

Ellie carefully placed the hat back on the shelf. "That's quite all right. You don't have to bother. I heard you started working here, so I just wanted to come in and say hello."

"Oh," she said, then wished she hadn't sounded so surprised when Ellie began to blush. *Honestly, though. What an odd thing for her to do. She's never sought me out before.*

After an awkward moment of silence, Ellie smiled. "You played so well on Sunday. Did it take you very long to learn the music?"

"I already knew most of the hymns from when I practiced as a child."

"I can't imagine." Ellie laughed. "When I was a little girl I never had the patience for anything like that. I was much more likely to be out with the boys finding some way or another to skin my knee."

She gave a cautious smile. "I remember seeing you climb a tree or two now and again."

"I haven't climbed a tree in years! It would hardly be

proper now. I'm sure it would be much harder to manage in long skirts." Even as she said it, Ellie's gaze turned a bit wistful as if she was imagining herself doing that very thing.

Lorelei surveyed the young woman before her in knowing amusement. "I'm sure."

"Well, I'm much less rambunctious now," Ellie proclaimed, but the capricious look in her eye didn't lend her much credibility.

"I can tell."

Ellie laughed. "You aren't the least bit convinced, but never mind that."

The conversation lagged again, and Lorelei began to wonder if she should try to find some way to end it. She was sure Ellie had never said so much to her before. Ellie, Sean and Lawson had been the best of friends, and even when she'd been Lawson's fiancée, Lorelei had never tried to penetrate that bond. As a result, she'd never expected more than a slight acquaintance with Ellie, which was really too bad because she'd always admired the girl's exuberance.

Resolved to end the conversation, Lorelei smiled. "Well, thank you for the compliment about my playing. Are you sure I can't interest you in one of our bonnets?"

"Not this time, I'm afraid," Ellie said, then glanced around the shop for a moment before meeting Lorelei's gaze. "Actually, I did have another purpose for coming here. I've been thinking about having a get-together next Saturday. I was hoping you'd like to come."

"I don't know," Lorelei said in surprise.

Ellie's slim fingers touched her arm. "Please, say yes. I mean, I will understand if you had something else planned."

Lorelei shook her head. "I was just a little surprised you asked, that's all."

Ellie's lashes dropped toward her cheek. "Oh, don't say that."

Lorelei lifted her shoulder in a shrug. "I didn't mean anything by it."

Ellie met her gaze with sincerity. "I know you didn't. It's my own fault, you know. I never went out of my way to be friendly to you before. I'm sorry for that. I hope that we can leave that behind and be friends now."

Why? The question hovered on Lorelei's lips, but she couldn't quite bring herself to ask it. Her eyes widened as she suddenly realized what this must be about.

"I really do appreciate you telling me that, Ellie. I'd like for us to be friends, too." She glanced around the shop. Though it was empty, she leaned forward to slightly lower her voice. "I just don't want you to think that you have to be my friend or invite me places because of how things stand between your brother and I."

"You and my brother," Ellie repeated softly before her eyes widened, and she grinned. "You mean that you're going to let Sean court you?"

"Well, yes," she said slowly. "But—"

Ellie pulled her into a quick hug, then stepped back to meet her gaze. "That's wonderful. Of course we will be friends. There's no reason for us not to be."

Lorelei tilted her head to survey Ellie. She pulled in a slow breath as realization pulled at her mind. "He didn't tell you."

"Well, no. He hadn't told me yet, but he didn't really have to. I knew he was going to ask to court you. Now I really hope you'll come on Saturday. Please, say you will."

"I'll be there. What time?"

"Four o'clock. I'm so glad you're coming," Ellie exclaimed and honored Lorelei with a resplendent smile.

Lorelei returned it with a weak one of her own. *I can't believe he didn't tell them.*

Sean could hardly believe he'd convinced Lorelei to eat lunch with him at the café. Despite her earlier compliance, it was obvious from her cold glare that she had her own agenda for this outing, and it had nothing to do with furthering their pretend courtship. He could tell from the pitying glances he was receiving from those around him that they weren't fooling anyone. Everyone knew he was about to get raked over the coals. He might as well get it over with. "What has your bonnet all in a twist?"

"My bonnet is not in a twist," she said. Her hand lifted toward her pert little hat as though to make sure.

"Then why are you upset?" He lifted a hand to stop her protest. "Oh, I forgot. You normally glare at me like that."

She set her lips into a straight line, then leaned forward with a furious whisper. "You haven't told your family what's really going on. How do you explain that?"

He leaned toward her and tilted his head inquiringly. "How would you know what I have or have not told my family?"

She straightened in her chair. "Ellie visited me at the shop yesterday. It was obvious from our conversation that she didn't know. Why haven't you told them?"

"I plan to."

"When?"

When he found the courage to stomach the disappointment he'd inevitably see in their eyes. He wanted to spare them that. Who was he kidding? He wanted to spare himself. He'd grown up watching first his parents' marriage, then his sister's. Both had been love matches. Both had been filled with incredible tenderness. In short, they were nothing like the distant marriage that beckoned him into a future with the beautiful but almost hostile Lorelei Wilkins.

Even as those thoughts tripped through his mind, Lorelei's hand came to rest gently over his. Instinctively, he turned his hand over to hold it. Her gaze met his as she whispered, "Sean, you need to tell them before they find out like my father did."

Just like that, he read caring in her eyes—but not for him. Her concern was for his family, and he couldn't help but bristle at the accusation, from Lorelei of all people, that he was failing in his responsibility to the people in his life. He sternly lowered his voice. "Leave it alone, Lorelei. I'll tell them when I'm ready."

Her gaze dropped from his eyes to where her hand rested in his. Her face seemed to pale incrementally. He heard her catch her breath. She casually tugged her hand away. "I should go. I'm finished anyway."

"I'll walk you home," he offered.

"There's no need." She tossed him a smile he didn't believe and strode away. The door clanged shut behind her. Ignoring the curious gazes of the busy café, he stared thoughtfully at the vacant chair across from him. What was going on with that woman? She just plain didn't make sense. The way she acted…well, she either loved him or hated him.

If it was the first, he was on shaky ground because if

she ever dropped the act he'd probably like her. Liking her meant he might forget the things she'd done and the choices she'd made that had hurt other people. However, that scenario was rather improbable despite Lawson's opinion. It was far more likely that after everything that had passed between them, Lorelei just didn't like him. He swallowed. He really didn't want to live the rest of his life with a woman who hated him, did he?

He needed to figure out how to have at least an amiable relationship with her. To do that, he needed to figure out Lorelei's true feelings for him. He would have to force her hand, and he knew just how to do it. First, he would walk over to the courthouse and see what had become of the old Hilson place he had his eye on. Then he'd plan a way to let his family know the truth.

Lorelei ignored the startled glances of a few strangers as she rushed down the sidewalk away from the café. She threw a wary glance over her shoulder, then slipped into the narrow alleyway next to her father's bank to wait for Sean to pass so she could continue undisturbed. She couldn't bear the thought of Sean pursuing her or forcing her to explain her abrupt response to him in the café.

She leaned back against the wall to try to catch her breath. It was hopeless to believe that Sean wouldn't have noticed her reaction to holding his hand. Even she was surprised by it. Though she knew it stemmed from nothing more than mere performance, she hadn't known how to react. His derision, impatience and scorn she could easily face without wincing, but she hadn't been prepared for her own weakness.

Oh, how she wished it hadn't affected her. She calmly

reminded herself that holding hands could not cause a resurgence of youthful unrequited love. She knew better now. She'd made a decision to live her life with a new perspective, and nothing was going to change her mind. She nodded, feeling her unease slipping away.

She stepped farther into the shadows of the alleyway as she heard confident steps pound closer on the sidewalk. She watched as Sean passed with a determined look on his face. She waited a few moments to be sure she'd avoided him. The sound of low voices reached her ear from deeper in the alley just as she was about to step back onto the sidewalk. They seemed to be coming from behind the bank.

"Don't tell me there's no back way in. Look! Not a door in sight. What kind of fool built this place?"

Another man snorted. "A fool didn't design this bank. There is only one door in and out. It faces the sheriff's office."

"It'd be a pain to have to blast through these walls. We'd need more power than we have now."

Lorelei stilled a gasp in her throat, then waited to hear the other man's answer.

"No sense in that. Besides, it isn't our way."

"Mighty tempting, though. I bet the safe is right along this wall."

"Let's not waste time. We've had a look at the place. Let's get out of here before someone gets nosy."

Lorelei's eyes widened. She scurried away as silently as possible. With a quick step, she was back on the sidewalk. She was preparing to hurry off when the heel of her boot caught in the seam of a loose wooden board. She tried to tug it out but it wouldn't budge.

Biting her lip, she glanced toward the alley. She saw

a figure round the corner toward her. She leaned down so her hat would momentarily block her face. She hoped beyond anything that the man would just ignore her and step past without questioning her. His pace slowed to a curious tread as he drew nearer. Realizing her skirt hid her other hand from view, she shoved her reticule carefully along the ground. It stopped slightly away from her.

"What have we here?" a deep voice asked.

"Oh." Lorelei glanced up, affecting surprise. She slowly lifted her head to meet the dark eyes of a well-dressed, gentlemanly looking young man. He was not at all the rough drifter she would have expected from the conversation she'd heard.

She let her lips curl into a demure smile she hoped might befuddle his thoughts just enough for him to believe her. "I'm awfully sorry to be blocking your way, but I'm afraid my heel is stuck."

He glanced down at the sidewalk. "I see."

When he didn't say more, she lifted her skirt just enough so that she could see her heel then, endeavored to tug it out again. "I'm sure I'll get it out eventually."

"If you'll allow me?" he asked.

At her nod, he knelt beside her to pull the loose boards farther apart. She pulled her heel free and stepped to the side. "Thank you very much."

He smiled his welcome, then met her gaze with an appraising eye. "You would need to step just so to get caught by that board. Were you in the alley, then?"

"The alley? Why would I be in the alley?" she asked in confusion, then smiled. "I dropped my reticule, that's all."

She stepped to the side and gestured to the ground where her reticule lay. "If you would be so kind, Mr...."

"Smithson," he supplied. Bending down, he picked up her reticule and offered it to her. "You are?"

She took her reticule back, and, though she hated to tell him her name, she was sure he could easily find out some other way. "Miss Wilkins."

His eyes widened briefly. "Are you any relation to the owner of the bank?"

"Yes," she said, lifting her chin. "As a matter fact, I am. Why do you ask?"

He smiled. "No reason, Miss. I was just curious."

"Well, thank you for your help." She smiled again, so he wouldn't think her overly concerned. "Have a good day, Mr. Smithson."

"Same to you."

She gave him a parting nod, then stepped around him to walk along the front of the bank. She glanced sideways at the reflection in the glass to see if he followed her. She saw that he continued to watch her for a moment before he turned and went in the opposite direction.

A breath of relief filtered through her lips. She glanced across the street, debating whether or not to tell Sean what she'd heard. She shook her head. What proof did she have? The men hadn't mentioned any definite plans—but their intention was clear. She spared another quick glance behind her. Satisfied that she wasn't being watched, she walked across the street and entered the sheriff's office.

The last person Sean expected to see when he walked into his office was Lorelei Wilkins. Yet there she sat on the corner of his desk perusing his private files. He eyed her for a moment, then let the door close behind him with a bang. She jumped, and her eyes flew to his, then tracked his Stetson as it sailed through the air to land beside her on the desk. He lowered his chin to stare at her as he approached; tapping the mortgage papers he needed to fill out on his leg. "Where is Jeff?"

"I sent him to lunch. He said I didn't have the authority to do that."

"You don't."

"I know, but he was hungry. I assured him you wouldn't be gone long and if anyone needed anything, I'd send them to the café."

Sean shook his head. "Well, I hope you're here to apologize."

Her delicate brows lifted. "For what?"

He came to a stop in front of her. "Ruining our lunch—unless you can think of something else."

She braced her arms behind her, wrinkling more of his files in the process, and stared back at him. "I'm not here to apologize. I had every right to ask you why you hadn't told your family about us."

"Enough of that," he warned. "If you're not going to apologize, why are you here?"

She placed her hands in her lap and suddenly became serious. "I heard something when I was in the alleyway just now."

He frowned. "What were you doing in an alleyway?"

She shrugged guiltily. "That isn't important. What is important is that I heard two men plotting to rob the bank."

He paused for a moment to take that in. "Are you serious?"

"I wouldn't joke about something like this."

"Then please get off my desk."

She frowned. "That is not the response I was expecting."

His mouth twitched with a suppressed smile. "You're sitting on my notebook."

"Oh," she breathed and finally complied by sitting in the chair he pulled up for her. He grabbed a pencil to carefully record everything she'd heard and seen. Once she finished, he went over the notes he'd taken in silent contemplation. He closed his notebook and set it aside. "Lorelei, think very carefully before you answer the next few questions I ask you. Did he seem like he was suspicious of you?"

She thought for a moment, then nodded slowly. "I tried to ignore it but I definitely got that feeling from him."

"Never ignore your instincts in a situation like that," he advised. "What do you want to do when he contacts you again?"

"*When,* not *if?*"

He nodded and walked around the desk to pull up a chair beside her. "If he's smart, he'll try to figure out how much you really know about what they said. So that means you have two options. The first one is to wait until he approaches you and then play dumb like you did today. If he believes you the second time, you won't have to worry about it again. However, if he figures out that you know too much, you'll be in danger. And I've got to admit, if he didn't believe you this time, then he's probably not going to believe you later, either."

She bit her lip and fiddled with the folds of her skirts. "What's the second option?"

"The second option is to leave town. Visit your great-aunt in California, just like you planned to before. This Mr. Smithson wouldn't be able to go after you, not without delaying his plans for the bank, which he won't want to do. Once he and his friends are in custody, your father can send you word that it's safe to come home."

"No," she said firmly. "I'm not running away—not from this town, or my responsibilities, or bank robbers. Besides, what would Mrs. Greene say if I suddenly up and left?"

"If we explain the circumstances to her, I'm sure she'll understand."

"That's funny. I'm sure she won't."

"No," Sean agreed reluctantly. "She probably won't. But as sheriff of this town, I've taken an oath to protect its citizens—and keeping you safe is more important than keeping Mrs. Greene happy."

"This isn't only about keeping Mrs. Greene happy. If I left town, she'd tell everyone what happened and I might never be able to show my face in this town again. I left this town once, Sean. I know I wouldn't want to stay away forever. Besides, you have to consider your reputation, as well." She lifted her chin determinedly. "No, there has to be another way."

He crossed his arms dubiously. "Such as?"

Sean saw an idea spark in Lorelei's eyes, and his stomach sank as he realized what it meant. She was coming up with another one of her crazy, spontaneous, ridiculous ideas. And he was going to hate it, he was completely sure that whatever it was—

"I could go undercover," she said.

His jaw clenched in frustration. Yep, he hated it, all right.

"Oh, Sean, it would be perfect!" Lorelei continued, practically jumping from her chair to pace the floor in enthusiasm. "I'll pretend that I want to work with them, then they'll tell me all of their plans—I'd then tell *you* those plans, and we'd have the whole group identified and caught in no time."

"No," Sean replied.

She whirled to face him as though somehow surprised by his immediate refusal. "But this idea is the perfect solution and—"

"No."

"I'm sure I'd be able—"

"*No,* Lorelei. It's too dangerous. Don't you understand? It's my duty to keep you safe. This would be the complete opposite of safe."

"It's also your duty to protect the bank, isn't it?" she asked, tilting her head inquiringly. "And don't you think it's my duty, too? It's my town as much as it is yours—and it's my father's bank, which makes this personal. If you'll just trust me, I promise I won't let you down or—"

Sean honestly didn't intend to let the snort of disbelief slip out...but it did, and it stopped Lorelei in her tracks.

"Oh, so that's what this is really about," she said slowly. "You're refusing to let me help because you think I'm too *flighty,* too *insincere* to be trusted, aren't you?"

He shifted uncomfortably in his chair at the change in her voice. In an instant it had switched from that bright, overly enthusiastic tone to one that sounded cold, disappointed and downright...well...hurt. He suddenly felt about six inches tall. He didn't like that feeling at all or the way she suddenly seemed to withdraw into herself. He cleared his throat. "I never said that."

"Didn't you?" she asked pointedly, then perched on his desk a little too close to him for comfort, especially when she peered down at him with that fire in her eyes. "Well, Sheriff O'Brien, I am *not* leaving town and I am *not* going to play dumb the next time I see that man. If you don't trust me enough to let me help, then I suppose I'll have to do things my own way."

She got to her feet, and Sean felt a wave of pure panic wash over him as he grabbed for her arm. "Lorelei, stop! Can't you see that I'm just trying to protect you? Your idea is just too d—"

"Too dangerous—yes, so you said. But tell me, Sean, what would be more dangerous, the two of us coming up with a plan together to put the idea into practice, or me walking out the door right now and doing it all on my own?"

And she would, Sean was certain. Once she decided to act on an impulse, there was no stopping her. She wouldn't even pause to plan things out, either. She'd probably just trust it would all work out if she made things up as she went along. That didn't work in life, and it certainly wouldn't work in this situation. All he could do was try to figure out how to help her, and hopefully protect her.

"You are the most frustrating woman I have ever known," he muttered.

For some reason that made a smile blossom across her lips. She lifted her eyebrows entreatingly. "Does that mean…"

"Yes." He sighed. "You win."

To her credit, she managed to almost completely hide her victorious smile. "You won't regret it."

"I know I won't because we're going to do this together." He smiled ruefully before continuing, "I'll be with you, as you so nicely put it before, 'like fleas.' It also means that you'd have to stay with it until the end. Impulsivity could have no place in this. You'd have to stick to my plan."

He seated himself once more and was relieved to see her settle into her chair, as well. "I can do that, Sean. I know I can and I'm going to prove it."

He nodded. "All right then, Lorelei, I'm trusting you on this, and the whole town will be depending on you. If Smithson approaches you, let him know that you're wise to his plans, then tell me immediately. From then on, we'll take it one step at a time."

Chapter Nine

Sean watched his niece and nephew race across the field. Hope tossed her long dark mane of hair this way and that as she pawed at the ground, playing the role of a wild horse. Timothy was right behind her pretending to swing a rope like a true cowboy. Sean looked back at the picnic Kate had set up for Sunday lunch. Ellie lounged on the blanket beside him and was obviously daydreaming as she slowly finished the apple in her hand. Three-year-old Grace snoozed in Kate's lap, completely unaware of her surroundings while Nathan focused on finishing up a piece of his wife's delicious pound cake.

So this was it. This was the perfect time to tell his family the truth about his relationship with Lorelei. He glanced up at the cloudy blue sky above him to steady his nerves. *Lord, should I?* There was no message spelled out in the clouds, just an overwhelming sense that it was time to do the right thing. He cleared his throat and quietly announced, "There's something I need to tell everyone."

Ellie's eyes lost their dreamy stare as she met his

gaze. Sean looked from her to Kate who watched him curiously. Nathan nodded. "Go ahead. We're listening."

For the first time in a long time, he felt that God was with him. He pulled in a quick breath. "I accidentally have to marry to Lorelei Wilkins."

Shocked silence descended in uncomfortable thickness over his family. Kate recovered first. "Did you just say—"

"What does that even mean?" Ellie exclaimed in confusion.

"I'm really hoping I don't know what that means," Nathan said with a warning glance.

Sean held up a hand. "Hold on. Let me explain myself."

"I think you'd better," Kate urged.

"It started out innocently enough," Sean began, then quickly told them the entire story.

"Oh, Sean," Kate groaned. "What happens now?"

He glanced up to meet their gazes, then cleared his throat to ease the nervous lump that had settled there. "I'm supposed to publicly propose to Lorelei in a few weeks. In the meantime, Mr. Wilkins wants our courtship to appear perfectly normal so that no one else will find out what really happened."

"So that's the real reason you're courting Lorelei?" Nathan asked. "You two don't have feelings for each other?"

He smiled in wry amusement. "The truth is Lorelei can hardly stand me. She just agreed to it because her father didn't give her a choice."

Ellie stared at him. "Are you sure Mrs. Greene is helping you? I mean why would she do that?"

"I haven't seen any evidence to the contrary." He shrugged. "She's doing it for Mrs. Wilkins's sake."

She nodded. "Well, I can guarantee she isn't doing it for yours."

"You and Mrs. Greene need to stop expecting the worst of each other," Kate chided as she brushed a tear off of her cheek. "Sean, what I don't understand is why it took you so long to tell us this."

Nathan shifted closer to his wife to slide his arm around her and pull her into an embrace. "Don't cry, Kate. I'm sure Sean wasn't trying to hurt us."

She nudged him softly with her elbow. "I know that, Nathan."

"Then why are you crying?"

"Never mind," she said. "Let him speak."

Nathan looked as confused by the exchange as Sean felt. With a shrug, Nathan nodded toward Sean. "Go ahead."

"I guess I didn't want you to be disappointed in me."

"Don't be silly," Kate said as she adjusted Grace into a more comfortable position. "We wouldn't have been disappointed in you because of that. You're doing the honorable thing. The only reason I'm disappointed is because you didn't confide in us earlier."

"I'm sorry," he said, then realized something for the first time. "I guess I was disappointed for myself, too."

"Why?" Nathan asked.

"When I was growing up, I saw what a loving, God-centered marriage you guys had. It was the same way with Ma and Pa. I never said much about it, but I've always wanted to have a marriage like that. Now, I don't even have the smallest hope of it." Sean shrugged. "I guess I feel like I failed. I failed to continue Ma and

Pa's legacy. I failed God by not allowing Him to lead me. I failed myself and I've failed Lorelei. That's a lot of failure for one man to admit to even to his own family."

Kate's eyes filled with tears. "Oh, there's so much wrong with that statement I don't know where to start."

Nathan met his gaze evenly. "You know, Sean, sometimes the desires we have in our hearts aren't just our own desires. I believe more than anything that God placed that desire in you to have a loving, God-centered marriage. There is a reason He hasn't taken it away yet."

Sean shook his head skeptically. "It's a sore temptation to give up hope after the mess I've made of everything."

"Never give up hope," Kate said. "No matter how much we might mess up, God never fails. Surrender the situation to Him. Trust Him to work it out and He will."

"That's easier said than done," he countered.

"No, it's the surrendering part that's easier in the long run," she insisted. "We were never created to carry the burdens of our lives alone. That's God's job, Sean."

But wasn't it his job, too? It was his life—shouldn't he take responsibility for it? Shouldn't he be able to come up with a plan to fix things? Surrendering it to God seemed like accepting defeat, admitting that he couldn't handle things on his own. He plucked a blade of grass and twirled it nervously between his fingers. "That seems so passive."

Nathan laughed. "It takes a lot more strength than you might think. Besides, once you are in God's will, He will show you how to be active with your faith."

"I guess that makes sense," he said, mostly because he thought that was what they wanted to hear. It still seemed like a pretty weak way to go about life to him.

Ellie cleared her throat delicately to gain his attention. "One last thing, Sean O'Brien."

He nearly groaned. "Yes, Ellie?"

She arched her brow threateningly. "If you call my brother a failure one more time, I just might have to punch you."

He grinned. "I'll keep that in mind."

"Keep this in mind, too. I don't think you're failing at all."

"What would you call it then?"

She lifted her chin as though preparing for a fight. "I think it's romantic."

"Romantic?" he said with a look that told her exactly how preposterous she was being.

Her lips curved into a mischievous smile. "It certainly has the potential to be. Kate and Nathan didn't start off much better than you and Lorelei. That turned out well, didn't it?"

"What exactly are you suggesting, Ellie?"

"Just because Lorelei is playacting her way through the courtship doesn't mean you have to. We all know she liked you in the past. If she liked you then, what's keeping her from liking you now?" She pointed at him significantly. "Find that out and you could still stand a chance at making her fall in love with you."

He gave a dry laugh. "Not that I think what you're saying is actually right, but even if I did that, it might not bring *me* any closer to falling in love with *her*."

She narrowed her gaze. "Love is a choice, Sean. Don't let anyone tell you otherwise."

Nathan grinned. "She's right."

"Of course I am," she said.

Fine, so maybe love was a choice. But did he want

to choose to love Lorelei? How could he trust her to be someone he could build a life with after all the things she'd done? But on the other hand, if he didn't let himself love her, what kind of life would they have together? Maybe this was a case where he'd have to take a calculated risk.

"Listen, regardless of what I decide to do or not do, y'all can't tell anyone about this. Promise me you'll keep it a secret."

"It isn't our secret to tell," Nathan said.

Kate nodded. "We shouldn't mention it around the children, either. They'd be liable to let something slip without meaning to."

"I won't say a word." Ellie promised.

Kate smiled. "I'm glad you told us."

"So am I." It felt good to finally tell his family the truth. It was even better to realize that after the initial shock wore off, they were more than willing to support and encourage him. But accepting their support meant considering their advice, too. Could he do it? Could he surrender the whole situation to God?

I haven't been doing a great job of taking care of this situation so far, but I'm willing to ask for Your help, Lord. Isn't that the same thing as surrendering? If so, why did it feel as though panic was slowly tying his stomach in tight little knots?

Lorelei stepped down from the buggy without Sean's help and glanced at her surroundings. She couldn't understand why her father had encouraged her to travel unaccompanied with Sean to this abandoned old house just outside of town. Of course, since what the town had perceived as their spat in the café almost a week ago, her parents had been encouraging them to be seen in public more often…without fighting. So far they weren't fighting, but this wasn't exactly public. She pulled her shawl closer around her shoulders. "Why are we here?"

"This is our house, Lorelei."

She stopped walking to stare at him. "Our house?"

He continued looking at the house for a long moment. "Yes. We're going to live here after the ceremony."

She tried to form a coherent sentence, but her mouth would not move. She shook her head. "Are you serious?"

"Sure, I am. You didn't think I'd expect you to live in the one-room cabin I have in town, did you?"

"No," she admitted slowly. No, she hadn't thought that at all. She hadn't allowed herself to think that far.

He mistook her shocked silence for disapproval and turned a critical eye back on the house before he met her gaze. "I suppose you'd rather live in town."

"Yes," she breathed, since he seemed to expect a response.

Concern lowered his brow as he earnestly said, "I can't afford to buy a house in town. I know it isn't what you're used to, but I hope you understand that there is only so much I can offer you."

"My father—"

"He was kind enough to give us a low mortgage on this house. I won't expect anything more from him."

"Sean, don't you think you should have consulted me about this?" she asked incredulously. "Did you take me into consideration at all when you made this decision?"

"How can you ask that? Everything I've done so far has been for you or because of you." He pressed his lips together to keep from saying more. "Why don't we go inside? The house isn't as bad as you think. It will need some work, of course, but the building is sound. There is plenty of room and you'll be able to fix it up however you like."

A resounding "no" begged to dance from her lips.

He seemed to sense it for he lowered his chin to pin her with a look. "Lorelei, I trusted you when you said you'd help me with the bank robbery. Surely, you can trust my judgment enough to at least look at the house."

She let a few awkward moments of thoughtful silence pass between them. He smiled beseechingly. Finally, without a word, she moved forward. She stepped through the front door as he held it open for her, then cautiously walked into the house.

Light dove through the tall front windows to brightly illuminate the empty room. Dust lifted from the wooden boards at her feet and danced in the shafts of sunlight. A brick fireplace was built into the wall on her right. Its chimney stretched up the wall until it disappeared into the tall ceiling that housed the second floor. Sean left the door open behind them, allowing a breeze to filter through and stir the stale air. "This is the sitting room."

"It's a good-size room," she admitted.

"Did you see the fireplace? It will be nice come winter," he offered hesitantly.

She nodded. He seemed satisfied with her response to the sitting room, so he led her through the door into a much smaller space. It had a medium-size window and a small table for two. Sean announced it to be the dining room. She murmured something about it being adequate.

He led her into the kitchen. It had a large oven, but the stove seemed rather outdated. Sean seemed to notice her concern and mentioned something about replacing the stove. Suddenly she realized how like a shy little boy he seemed. He carefully watched her expression and waited for her approval over each feature of the house. She wasn't used to seeing him so unguarded.

She followed him back into the sitting room, then he led her up toward the stairs. As she climbed to the second floor she felt the shock of his announcement begin to wear off. Her feet slowed on the steps. This was going to be her home with this man.

Her heartbeat quickened in her throat. She glanced over the banister to the sitting room where she would probably spend hours in Sean's company. She imagined herself eating at that small table with him. She saw herself standing at the stove with Sean leaning over her shoulder to see what she was cooking, and her knees began to tremble. It was becoming too real.

They came to the landing of the stairs that ended in a wide hallway. Sean opened the door to one of the rooms on the left to let her peer inside of it. She slid through the doorway, careful to leave a few inches of space between herself and Sean. The room was moderately sized and the frames for two mattresses rested in opposite corners, but those could be removed to give Lorelei a nice sewing room or library. She heard the door slide open farther as Sean moved closer, and his voice interrupted her thoughts. "Eventually this would become the children's room."

Children. Her breath stilled in her chest as she realized what that implied. *I hadn't even thought about where we would live; I certainly hadn't considered he might want children. Why would he want to bring children into a relationship like this?*

She turned to find him striding directly across the

hall to another room. He stepped inside and held the door open until she entered. The room was larger than the other with the same high ceiling. Large windows matched those on the lower floor, but drapes concealed the sunlight from their panes and left the room in dark muted tones. Sean turned toward her. His eyes glinted with determination and daring, yet his voice came out gently. "This will be our room, Lorelei."

Lorelei was grateful when Sean's tour ended moments later on the porch. His voice droned on in the background about how he planned to update the house, but she'd stopped listening to his words in the bedroom upstairs when reality had come crashing down around her. She braced her hands on the porch railing and pulled in a deep breath.

Foolish. Foolish. Foolish. I should have known. Of course, he would expect a real marriage and he'd want to have children. What man wouldn't? Why didn't I ever think that far? Why am I even surprised?

The truth was frightening. She'd been living in denial. The world she'd carefully constructed by avoiding her problem and stuffing her feelings as deeply within her as possible was nothing but sham. This was reality. A mirthless smile tilted at her lips.

How ironic that in running from a marriage with a man I couldn't love, I will find myself bound by that same union to a man who will never love me. Every day I'll have to live in his house, eat at his table, be the mother of his children and never know his love. What I spared Lawson in marrying me, I condemned myself to through my own willfulness.

She felt Sean's comforting but fleeting touch on her back and jerked away from him in surprise. He settled his forearms on the railing. "I didn't mean to startle you."

She refused to respond, but the silence worked against her fervent feelings. It lengthened between them until Lorelei felt her shoulders begin to relax and her fingers loosened their anxious clasp on the railing. Sean looked up from his relaxed stance to try to capture her gaze. "I know we said we'd pretend to court. I guess you thought we'd feign a marriage, too."

"I certainly did," she stated unapologetically. "I just don't understand why you'd want to bring children into a situation like this."

"That isn't something we have to decide today or even next year, but I guess I'm just hoping it won't always be like this." He turned to her. "As for feigning a marriage, we may not have much of a choice in this situation but we can choose to go about it the right way or the wrong way. The wrong way is letting this turn our entire lives into a lie."

She turned away from the truth of his statement to stare toward the fields. "What's the right way?"

"The right way is to do our best to fulfill your father's expectations while putting aside our past and trying to create a friendship, if nothing else."

She stilled. "Friendship?"

He stepped closer. "I know we were practically enemies as children, but when we grew up we were friends for a while, weren't we? What happened at the Harvest Dance a few years ago that suddenly changed that?"

She could hardly believe they were having this conversation now after so many years had passed—but wasn't that event what had fueled the last sparks of animosity in their relationship? She shrugged lightly.

"You showed up with another girl. What was I supposed to think?"

"I did it as a favor to Chris. He was sick and didn't want Amy to miss out. Besides, I never thought you'd immediately start courting my best friend."

"You hadn't said anything definite up to that point. I thought it meant you didn't like me after all. Lawson saw that I was upset, though I wouldn't tell him why. He walked me home. He offered to be my beau." She smiled wryly. "Looking back, I think he just offered out of sympathy, but I said yes."

"Why?"

She confronted his intense stare with the truth. "I didn't think you'd care."

"I did."

"You cared." She turned away from his quiet words with a laugh. "Oh, sure."

He caught her arm and gently tugged her so that she faced him again. "Why are you laughing? Don't you believe me?"

"I believe you cared. You cared enough about Lawson to carefully explain all of my faults to him when he told you he wanted to court me."

His eyes narrowed. "Did he tell you that?"

"No, I overheard you. I was supposed to wait in the buggy, but I didn't." She'd wanted to see his face when he heard the news. She'd wanted to know if it would matter to him. He'd answered that question for her pretty quickly.

"You weren't supposed to hear that." His hand loosened on her arm. "I didn't mean it."

She wanted to believe him, but his every action after that moment called him a liar. She let out a sigh and shook her head. "That was ages ago anyway. What does it matter now?"

"You're right," he said seriously. "We're adults now. We should be able to put all of that behind us. Do you think we can?"

She glanced up at him to search his face and found nothing but sincerity. "I suppose we'd better. After all, I'm supposed to marry you and live here with you and possibly have your children. I should probably at least consider you a friend, first."

Relief at her agreement played at his features. He leaned his shoulder onto the porch post and nodded seriously, but a hint of amusement played at his lips. "I know. It's a pretty raw deal, isn't it?"

Was he trying to charm her? It was almost working. She leaned her back against the railing and shook her head in disbelief. "You have to admit it sounds a little crazy."

"It is," he agreed. "But, I think we can do it."

I guess I'll have to try the whole "love your brother" concept. She gave a nod of agreement. He gave her a hopeful smile as if he was truly inviting her into a friendship with him. Her heart gave a rebellious jump. She bit her lip and glanced away with one thought echoing through her mind. *He certainly is* not *my brother.*

Chapter Ten

Sean slid into the chair across from Richard as the man searched through his large mahogany desk. "This should explain all of the safety procedures we use at the bank. I go over this with each of my employees when they begin working for me."

Sean perused the paper he'd been handed. "I see you have information here regarding what to do during a bank robbery."

"Of course, but thankfully, we've never had to use it." Richard watched Sean carefully. "Is there a specific threat to my bank that I should know about?"

"Not at this time," Sean said. He couldn't pass along any specifics because he didn't have any yet. His investigation on Calhoun had only revealed that the man had a penchant for drinking and gambling. The telegrapher hadn't seen hide nor hair of the man since the news of Frank Bentley's escape from jail. There were no indications that the outlaw was heading to Peppin, but Sean continued to be watchful for any man who bore a resemblance to the wanted poster now hanging in his office.

He'd also surreptitiously learned as much as he could

about Smithson after Lorelei's tip. From outward appearances, the man seemed above suspicion. He lived at Bradley's Boardinghouse. He'd seemed to have taken an interest in Bradley's eldest daughter, Amy, and was well liked by the other boarders. So far, there was nothing to connect him to Calhoun besides the fact that they both had rather vague sources of income. No one had mentioned seeing the two of them together, and there was no crime record for either man with the state.

Unfortunately, at this point a general warning was all he could issue. "I'm just asking several of Peppin's businesses to make sure that they have adequate security measures in place to ward off criminals. I don't want people to become complacent just because we haven't had trouble yet."

Richard nodded thoughtfully. "Now that you mention it, with that railroad coming through town, I'm surprised we haven't had more of an increase in crime during the last five years."

"Yes, well, the sheriff's department is always looking for preventative measures we can put in place to deter that kind of activity." He lifted the paper. "May I keep this?"

"Certainly."

He folded the paper and placed it in his pocket just as a knock sounded at the study door. Richard called for the person to come in. Lorelei leaned inside. Her eyes met his for an instant, then she glanced toward her father with a teasing grin. "Are you two going to sit here all afternoon? Sean and I are going to be late if we don't leave soon."

Richard sent Sean a wry smile. "I think that means she's finally ready to go."

Lorelei smiled and lifted one shoulder in a playful

shrug. "Well, a girl has to look just right for her first official evening as part of a couple."

Sean was surprised by the complete lack of sarcasm in her tone. Was she really committing to the friendship they'd agreed to? When she caught his gaze and properly read his surprise, a smile tilted at her lips. Lorelei hardly waited until they left the study to whisper, "Were you talking about the bank? Did you find out some new information?"

He shook his head. "Just safety procedures. Have you heard from Smithson?"

She handed him his Stetson from the hat rack. "No. I would have told you if I had."

He opened the door for her, then followed her out. "Maybe he believed that you hadn't heard anything after all."

"I hope not."

He sent her an exasperated look which only caused her to widen her eyes innocently. He shook his head as he closed the front door behind them. When she turned toward him, he didn't move but inclined his head toward her and looked deep into her eyes, hoping that he might be able to discern some of her emotions. Things between them had been going more smoothly since their truce at the house, but he couldn't let himself get complacent yet. Her behavior could be so hard to predict. He was half waiting for her to suddenly change her mind about their agreement. "Are you sure you're ready for this?"

She lifted her chin. "Entirely. Why? Aren't you?"

He suddenly felt more nervous than he had in a long time. He lifted his shoulders in a shrug and gave a curt nod. "I'm ready."

"Then let's go," she said. She turned away but not before he saw a slightly victorious smile tug at her lips.

He stifled a groan. As long as she cooperated they'd be just fine. Now, if he could only figure out what exactly she thought she'd just won.

Lorelei pulled in a deep breath of country air as the horses in front of her father's buggy trotted along the well-worn road toward the O'Brien farm. A satisfied smile settled at her lips. She'd done it. She had managed to be nice to Sean while being herself. Of course, it hadn't been entirely easy. She'd felt her heart nearly jump out of her chest when she realized he wasn't stepping away outside the front door, but she'd firmly reined in that silly impulse. So there. She could do this after all.

Suddenly Sean pulled off onto the side of the road toward the shade of an oak tree. She clenched the wooden seat in alarm as the wagon bounced over the uneven land. "What are you doing?"

He parked the wagon under the tree, then hopped out and rounded the buggy. "I just thought of something we need to do before we join my family."

"What is it?" she asked as he lifted her from the buggy to settle her on the ground in front of him.

"This." He reached out to take her hand, and she immediately tugged it away. "You always withdraw from me when I touch you."

"I don't *always*," she began, then stopped herself when she realized they both knew he was right.

"We need to be comfortable with each other. People notice when others are on edge. You, Lorelei Wilkins, are definitely on edge. We have to fix that."

He held out both of his hands to her in a silent challenge. She looked at them for a moment, then placed her hands in his. He seemed to wait for her to withdraw. When she didn't, he clasped her hands and let them fall casually between them.

"Much better," he murmured. "By the way, if I happen to say something you think is funny, go ahead and laugh. Or if you're happy, smile. Don't hide what you're feeling from me or others."

"Are you abiding by these rules, too?" she asked, wondering how long he was planning to hold her hands. She was pretty sure this was a test and refused to be the first to pull away.

He winked. "Sure, but you have to say something funny first."

Her heart jumped in her chest at his wink, dislodging an almost reluctant laugh in the process. He nodded in approval at the sound. "You should probably know my family has very little sense of personal distance. They also tend to hug a lot, so expect that."

"It might take me a while to get used to it," she admitted. "My family doesn't particularly emphasize that sort of thing. Neither did Lawson."

"I've noticed that your family is more formal than mine. Lawson has always been that way. I think it has something to do with whatever happened before he came to Peppin." He finally released her hands and stepped back. "Now you reach out to me. You can't hold my hand. We already did that. Do something else."

She stared at him blankly as butterflies began to dance in her stomach. She didn't like this game. She tucked her hands into the pockets of her skirt. "I can't."

"You can." He smiled in what must have been an attempt to put her at ease. It only increased her nervousness. "You're overthinking it."

She pulled in a deep breath. "You said your family hugs a lot."

He nodded.

"All right then," she breathed. Stepping forward, she reached around him to give him a light hug, then immediately stepped back.

He chuckled. "What was that?"

"A hug."

His chuckle changed into a full-grown laugh. "That was the poorest excuse for a hug I've ever experienced."

She stared at him in shocked amusement, then shook her head. "When I see your family I'm going ask them why you're so mean. Just you wait and see if I don't."

"Tut, tut. Friends, remember? Try it again."

She crossed her arms and just looked at him.

He grinned. "I'm sorry for laughing. Show me you forgive me."

She let out a long-suffering sigh as she realized he wasn't going to leave well enough alone until she complied. It had nothing to do with how nice it felt to laugh with him or have him smile at her like that—even if it had scarcely ever happened before. She slipped her hands around his waist, intending only a slightly prolonged repeat of her last hug. But just as she was about to step away, he swept her into his arms, nearly lifting her feet off the ground. She stumbled slightly as he set her back on her feet, then murmured in her ear. "That's what I call a hug."

"For goodness' sake. Do your sisters do that, too?" She threw back her head to see his face. He was already bending down, so they found themselves so close their noses nearly brushed. His eyes captured hers, causing them both to still. She swallowed. She could have sworn his eyes dropped to her lips, then immediately danced away. He released her. "No. Not exactly. We'd better get going. We don't want to be late."

Sean couldn't help stealing a sideways glance at Lorelei as the buggy approached his family's farm. She'd hardly spoken since their hug. Perhaps that was for the best. He wasn't sure what to say, either. He'd wanted to make sure she was comfortable with him before they faced their first test as a couple. He hadn't planned on the sudden vulnerability their closeness unleashed in her eyes. In that moment, he'd wanted to assure her that everything would be all right. That he'd never hurt her. He'd wanted to kiss her.

He pulled in beside the other vehicles and set the brake with a bit more force than necessary. *Keep yourself in check, O'Brien. You can be her friend. You can protect her. You can even marry her, but don't start letting your heart get in the way of your head. Remember who she is and what she's like. If you let yourself care for her too deeply, she'll only let you down.*

Ellie must have spotted them coming because she hurried across the yard toward them. As soon as he helped Lorelei down from the buggy, his little sister embraced her in a hug. "I'm so glad you could make it."

Lorelei managed to give her a decent hug in return. "Thank you! So am I. I hope we aren't late."

Ellie waved away her concern. "Oh, don't worry about that. There is no real time structure to this. We just wanted to give everyone a chance to socialize with each other."

Ellie promptly turned to give his chest a playful little punch in greeting. He absorbed the harmless blow by pulling his sister into his arms for a quick hug. "Is everyone here?"

"No, we're still waiting on a few others to arrive."

Lorelei glanced at Sean then cleared her throat. "Ellie, there is something Sean needs to tell you."

He placed a stilling hand on her shoulder. "It's all right, Lorelei. My family knows the truth about us."

Ellie nodded. "We certainly do. I told him I think it's romantic."

Her gaze flew to him in surprise. "Romantic?"

"There's no accounting for taste," he said with a shrug.

Ellie only smiled in response to their protests. "Lorelei, now that you're practically family, you're welcome to come here anytime you like. There's always plenty to do. We can go riding, wading, anything you like."

"Thank you, Ellie. Maybe I will."

"I hope so."

Sean and Lorelei followed Ellie through the few people who stood outside the house in groups of twos and threes. He felt tension rise in Lorelei's shoulders as they drew nearer to the door. His hand landed in a proprietary touch near the back of her waist. She stiffened for a moment but managed to relax by the time they stepped into the house. He glanced around and was relieved to find that since the house was crowded no one seemed to notice that they entered together. He smiled wryly. *Honestly, did I expect the entire room to stop what they were doing to gasp and stare?*

Someone called Ellie's name. The girl sent them an apologetic smile and promised to return quickly before she set off across the room to a group of young women. It took him a moment to realize that he was practically pushing Lorelei along because she'd stopped moving forward almost completely. He glanced down to find her worrying her bottom lip as she scanned the crowd with a slightly lost look on her face. He pulled her closer to ask at a volume only she could hear, "Are you all right?"

She straightened. "Yes. I just got a little intimidated for a moment. I haven't seen some of these people since the wedding. Now I'm showing up here with you only a month later. What will they think?"

"We can't control that. We can only control what we do. We said we were ready. Now we have to prove it. All right?" He waited until she nodded before he ushered her toward the kitchen. "Come on. Let's find Kate."

Sean immediately spotted his cinnamon-haired older sister laughing with Mrs. Lettie as the two finished preparing the food. He snuck up beside his sister, then darted around her to kiss her cheek. Kate jumped, then grinned at him even as she shook her head in exasperation. "What if I'd accidentally stabbed you with my knife?"

"You would have sewn me right back up. Isn't that right, Mrs. Lettie?"

The doctor's wife who'd been their mother's closest friend barely glanced up from playing with her three-year-old honorary grand-niece. "I learned a long time ago not to get drawn into sibling squabbles."

Kate set aside her knife to welcome Lorelei with a smile. "Lorelei, Ellie told me you were coming. I'd hug you but my hands are a bit messy. I'm glad you came."

"Thank you for inviting me," Lorelei said graciously, then greeted Lawson's adoptive mother, Mrs. Lettie Williams, with an easy familiarity. "Is there anything I can help with?"

"There isn't much left to do, but if you want to wash your hands and put on an apron I certainly won't stop you." Kate nodded over to where a spare apron hung on a hook. "Sean will tie it for you, won't you, Sean?"

Before he could respond his nephew tugged at his

arm. Sean glanced down, then sent Kate a sly grin. He caught the boy by the waist and threw him up into the air before catching him and setting him safely on the ground. The little boy let out a whoop of joy and begged Sean to do it again.

"Later. Right now, I want you to meet someone." Sean looked up from the child to meet Lorelei's gaze. "This is my nephew, Timothy. Say hello, Timothy."

The boy grinned at Lorelei and leaned back onto Sean's leg. "Hello, Timothy."

Lorelei laughed. "Hello, yourself. I'm Lorelei."

Sean poked his nephew slightly in the ribs. "That's Miss Lorelei to you."

He watched as Lorelei tilted her head conspiratorially to capture the boy's dark brown eyes. "How old are you, Timothy?"

"I'm seven," he stated proudly, then pointed across the room at the little girl sitting on Miss Lettie's lap. "That's Baby Grace. She's little."

Lorelei nodded. "I see that. She's your sister, right?"

"Yes, ma'am." The boy stepped away from Sean to get closer to Lorelei. "I have another sister. She's with Pa. Her name's Hope. I think she's four."

Sean placed a hand on Timothy's dark brown hair, and the boy looked up at him. "Hope is five."

"Right," Timothy said then looked back at Lorelei. "Hope is five but I'm seven."

"I remember."

"Do you want to play with me?"

Lorelei hesitated, then glanced at the other adults in the room as though to ask if it was all right. Kate shook her head. "Timothy, Lorelei just got here. Why don't you give her some time to talk to the grown-ups, then maybe she can play with you later?"

"Yes, ma'am," he agreed but whispered loudly to Lorelei, "There's a bunch of us kids outside. You can play with us when you get bored with the grown-ups, all right?"

She nodded seriously. "That sounds like a good plan."

Ellie breezed into the kitchen just as Timothy left. "The girls want to get a closer look at your dress, Lorelei. Will you come with me?"

Lorelei lifted the apron in her hand. "I can't. I promised Kate I'd help with the food."

"Oh, that's all right. You go on." Kate urged, then turned to Sean with twinkling eyes. "I'll make Sean help me. He can wear the apron."

"I'll help but I'm not wearing the apron," he warned as Lorelei and Ellie left. As he washed his hands in the sink, he suddenly became aware of the palpable silence in the room. He glanced over his shoulder to find that Miss Lettie had left him alone with his sister. "What?"

"I like her."

He dried his hands on the apron, then put it away. "I'm glad. That's a slightly different Lorelei than the one I'm used to."

"In what way?"

"She's nicer, friendlier..." He shrugged. "Did you see how well she got along with Timothy? Her eyes just sort of came alive."

She handed him a knife to help her cut up apples. "I noticed that. Maybe she seems different because she's in a different setting. Or, maybe you were just slightly wrong about her."

He spared her a quick glance. "Maybe."

Chapter Eleven

Lorelei deftly tied a wide piece of bright blue ribbon into a dainty bow, then pinned it onto the crown of a wide-brimmed straw bonnet. This hat would be just perfect for Ellie. Lorelei smiled as she thought about the hours she'd spent with Sean's family on Saturday. They'd been so warm and welcoming. By the time she'd left, she'd become much better friends with both of Sean's sisters. She'd taken a tour of the horse ranch from his brother-in-law, Nathan, and even had had time to play with his nieces and nephew.

It made sitting in the back room of the millinery shop seem almost boring by comparison. It was Monday and her day to work, so she needed to stop daydreaming before she fell behind on her quota. She stashed her bright white handkerchief in her dress pocket before she made her way from the workroom to the front of the store. Mrs. Cummings glanced up with a smile when Lorelei entered. "Watch the front, Lorelei. I'm going to make a deposit."

"Yes, ma'am," Lorelei agreed as the woman tucked

a small mound of money into her reticule and hurried out the door.

Lorelei turned her attention to the window display she had been working on. She paused to survey the assortment of hats in the window before she placed the one with the blue ribbon near the middle. Just as she hoped, the bright blue ribbon added color to the display and made the entire window more attention-grabbing.

She smiled, feeling a sense of accomplishment. She'd managed to keep this job for more than a week. That was longer than she'd tended the rose garden. What's more, she was actually good at this, which was why her bakery idea hadn't exactly taken off. She was committed to keeping this job if only to prove that she could.

The bell above the door chimed, and Amy Bradley walked in on the arm of none other than Mr. Smithson. Lorelei steeled herself with a smile as she welcomed the young woman who had been her good friend in school. Though the two had drifted slightly apart since then due to Amy's responsibilities at her family's boarding-house, they tried to maintain their friendly ties whenever it was convenient. After inquiring about Lorelei's parents, Amy introduced her to Mr. Smithson. The man greeted her politely before recognition sparked a gleam of curiosity in his brown eyes. "Miss Wilkins and I have already met."

Amy sent Lorelei a confused glance. "You have?"

"Well, yes," Lorelei said blithely. "He helped me free my heel from that broken piece of sidewalk by the bank. I didn't know he was your Mr. Smithson at the time."

Amy blushed mightily and gave a subtle shake of her head. Lorelei quickly turned the conversation to another subject entirely. "As you can see, we sell a large variety of ready-made hats for men and women. However, we do encourage that you personalize the hat to better reflect your personality. We can do that by making subtle changes to the ready-made hats or we can help you design your own."

"That sounds fun."

"It really is." She glanced at Mr. Smithson, who was studying her intently. "We don't offer to design hats for men, but we do have a specialty catalog you can look through if you'd like. With the railroad coming through town, shipping is quick once we take the measurements and send out the orders."

He agreed to look at the catalog while Amy attempted to try on nearly every item in the store. Lorelei attended to her, sensing the young woman might actually be looking to buy something. Every now and then Lorelei would glance back over to where Mr. Smithson stood and find him already looking at her in that unnerving way of his. If his attentions were any indication, he had not been convinced by her act outside the alley. That meant she had to take control of the situation, just as she and Sean had planned.

She didn't have much time. Mrs. Cummings would be back from the bank in a few minutes. She needed to do something now. Amy was having trouble deciding between two hats, so Lorelei left her alone to think and moved closer to Mr. Smithson. She gathered her courage to set her plan into motion. "Is there anything I can help you with?"

"Perhaps," he said without looking up. "I think you know more than you're letting on."

She swallowed. "About men's hats?"

He glanced up in amusement but said nothing more.

Lord, help me to do this right. She glanced nervously at Amy who was busy trying on a third hat in one of the store's mirrors. She gave Mr. Smithson a significant look and hoped the right words would follow. "As a matter of fact, I do tend to see and hear more on some subjects than you would imagine. With my father being the president of Peppin's bank, hearing something about that would draw my interest."

"I thought so." He shot a glance toward Amy as the young woman moseyed over.

Lorelei smiled at her, then turned her attention back to Mr. Smithson. Feeling more in control of herself and the conversation, she continued, "I think fashion, especially hats, communicate a lot about a person."

"What do you mean, Lorelei?" Amy asked with a curious tilt of her head.

"Take, for instance, the bowler hat Mr. Smithson came in wearing." She dared to lift it from where it rested on the countertop to survey it carefully. "It's different from the Stetson most men around here wear, so it tells others that he's a stranger. It also shows that he's a businessman." She tilted her head thoughtfully. "You're a man with a plan, aren't you, Mr. Smithson? I'd bet the plan is going to involve a lot of money."

He sent Amy an amused glance that hardened when he looked at Lorelei. "You saw that in my hat, too, did you?"

"Certainly," she said. "It was easy to tell that from the quality of the hat."

Amy shook her head. "Lorelei, you're a wonder. Tell her, Silas. She's exactly right, isn't she? Mr. Smithson is an investor."

"Really? What sort of investing are you doing in our

little town? We hardly have much to offer other than land. You're rather late to invest in that. I'm afraid the railroad already passed through, and those who had land along the rail line cashed in long ago."

"I work for the railroad."

"Oh, a railroad investor," she said, challenging the legitimacy of his statement more for Amy's sake than anything else. "What exactly does a railroad investor do?"

"Really, miss. I'm just passing through." He turned to Amy. "Are you about done here?"

"Yes, Silas."

"I'll wait for you outside."

He brushed past Lorelei. They watched him walk outside, then Amy turned to Lorelei with a glare. "Honestly, Lorelei. What were you trying to do?"

She lifted one shoulder in a shrug. "Well, I wasn't trying to chase him away."

"That's for sure," Amy huffed.

She stiffened. "What do you mean by that?"

"Nothing," Amy said then amended, "It's just that if I didn't have it on good authority you and Sean were courting, I'd think you were trying to show me up with Silas."

"Goodness, no! I'm not the least bit interested in Mr. Smithson."

"Good," she said with a huff, then frowned. "Well, if you weren't flirting, what in heaven's name were you doing?"

"I was just letting him know that someone is watching out for you." She almost said "this town" but caught herself in time. "I don't trust him, Amy. Be careful."

"That's a fine thing to say about someone you only

just met. Perhaps I'd better go." Amy placed the hat on the counter and hurried to the door. She stopped in the door to give Lorelei a wave that said they were parting as friends before she turned and almost ran into Mrs. Cummings.

Mrs. Cummings watched the girl leave before eying the bonnet Amy left on the counter. "What was that all about?"

"A difference in opinions," Lorelei said as she turned to walk into the workroom. She eyed the table strewn with feathers and ribbon, then closed her eyes. Smithson knew that she was wise to him. That much was obvious. She wished she'd been able to gain a clearer idea of what he was going to do about it.

Lorelei sat down and tried to sort the supplies into some sort of order. Feathers began floating in the air. She pulled out her handkerchief to cover her irritated nose from that onslaught when something fell from her pocket onto the floor. She reached for the folded piece of paper. Unfolding it, she stared at the words printed neatly on a scrap torn from a page in the catalog. She smoothed the folds out of the paper as she read it just above a whisper. "Say nothing. Do nothing. I'll contact you."

Sean slipped the scrap of catalog paper Lorelei had given him during her lunch break into an envelope. He sealed it, then placed in it the slim file he'd collected on the investigation. He knew Silas Smithson was up to no good, but Lorelei hadn't been able to provide any description of the other man in the alleyway that day. Sean was sure it must have been Calhoun. Unfortunately, he couldn't prove that or anything else about this investigation. Hence the nearly empty file.

He locked the file in his equally empty bottom desk drawer and frowned. Regardless of the lack of evidence, Sean couldn't get rid of the uneasy feeling in the pit of his stomach. He was running out of ideas, and he was running out of time. Lorelei was his only chance to break open the case. So far she'd done admirably well. He hated to ask more of her or place her in any more danger, but it was beginning to look as if that might be necessary.

Lawson provided a welcome distraction when he stepped into the sheriff's office. Sean stood to greet his friend and eyed the man's large suitcase. "I'd ask how it's going but I think the better question might be *where* are you going?"

Lawson set the suitcase down on a nearby chair. "I'm going to Austin. Nathan talked to one of his contacts with the Rangers and they're giving me a chance at a job."

Sean took a moment to process this, then gave a low whistle. "The Rangers? That's a great opportunity, but are you sure you want to go?"

He chuckled. "Would I be leaving if I wasn't sure?"

"Guess not." He leaned back onto his desk and crossed his arms. "How long are you planning to be gone?"

"At least a couple of months. I'll try to come back whenever I get a break." He smiled sheepishly. "Look at me talking like I already have the job."

"You'll get it," he said with quiet certainty.

"Thanks for that." Lawson shifted uncomfortably,

then met Sean's gaze and held out a hand. "Seriously, thanks for everything."

Sean shook his hand. "You're welcome, but that sounds a little too final to me."

He shrugged. "Well, I've said all of my goodbyes, so I guess this is it."

"Have you seen Lorelei?"

"Yes, she wished me the best."

"So do I."

"I told her what I'll tell you." He grinned slyly. "I'd wish the same to you, but you already have the best. You're just too stubborn to see it. You know I think she made the right choice, ending things between us. I hope you don't hold a grudge for my sake."

Sean made a noncommittal sound in reply. He wasn't quite ready to let go of that grudge yet, and he didn't want to lie to his best friend. Lawson shook his head at him but seemed to accept that. "I also made a deal with her," he continued. "One I'd like to make with you, too. I'll pray for you if you pray for me. How about it, Sean?"

"It's a deal." He held out his hand, and Lawson shook it firmly.

"I'd better go so I won't miss my train. Doc and Mrs. Lettie are waiting to see me off."

Sean nodded. "I know you'll do us proud but you're always welcome home."

"I'll make y'all proud." Lawson hefted his duffle bag onto his shoulder and paused at the door to tip his Stetson. Then he was gone.

Lorelei opened the door to the boardinghouse a few days later with a bouquet of yellow roses to make amends with Amy for their little misunderstanding at the millinery shop. She was also prepared to deal with Silas Smithson should she happen to run into him. She glanced around the large two-story's foyer for some sort of direction.

She followed a sign's instructions to ring the bell at the front desk for service. Amy appeared from around the corner. "Lorelei!"

"Hello, Amy. I'm sorry to bother you, but I wanted to bring by some of my roses. I hope you'll forgive me for the way I behaved in the millinery."

Amy took the flowers Lorelei extended to her with a smile. "Of course, I forgive you, silly. I thought we'd cleared up that misunderstanding already. Thank you for the flowers. They're beautiful. Now, I don't mean to be rude, but a whole bunch of new boarders just checked in and I've got to help Ma."

"Don't let me keep you." Lorelei received Amy's hug before the girl hurried off to do her chores. She opened the door and nearly ran into someone who was entering. She glanced up directly into the eyes of Silas Smithson. "Oh, excuse me."

His surprise gave way to a pleased grin. "Miss Wilkins, how fortunate. I was just thinking that I should visit you in the millinery and here you are practically on my doorstep."

Lord, help me to do this right if it's Your will, she prayed, though trepidation sent her pulse jumping. He followed her down the steps. She pulled in a deep breath. "What did you want to discuss?"

He tilted his hat to another boarder who passed them. "A present for Amy, of course. Don't let me hold you up. I can walk with you a ways."

She glanced at him in wry amusement. "Was that a joke? 'Don't let me hold you up.'"

He held her gaze, then looked around before steering her toward the quieter area of town by the courthouse. "Since you obviously know what I want, why don't you tell me what you want? I assume you want something. Otherwise, you would have already alerted the sheriff."

All right, Lord, here goes. She braced herself. "I want in."

"You want in," he repeated incredulously. "Tell me why you, of all people, would want anything to do with this."

She tried to dredge up some of the desperation she'd felt weeks ago. She found it really wasn't that hard, especially since she'd rehearsed it in front of her mirror. "I'm tired of the memories, the murmurs and the men. I want out of this town. This is going to pay for my ticket and my new life."

He scoffed. "Why not just ask your dear old papa for the money you need? He obviously has plenty of it."

"You really are new to this town, aren't you?" She laughed, then slowly transformed her face to a scowl. "I ran away from this town a few weeks ago. I got as far as the Texas border before 'dear old papa' got the sheriff to drag me back here kicking and screaming. He's not suddenly going to have a change of heart."

He gave her a skeptical glance. "Ah, yes. I heard you're on pretty good terms now with that same sheriff who brought you home kicking and screaming."

She sighed. "I'm just keeping Papa happy until I can make my move."

"You're willing to rob your own father for a ticket out of this quaint little place?"

She glared at him. "I'm not planning to rob him. You are. I see no reason why you can't cut me a small take of that big Peppin safe in exchange for some information."

That caught his attention just as she and Sean had thought it would. "You'd sell me information?"

She nodded as she tried to maintain her composure when she could hardly believe what she was proposing. She swallowed. She'd gone too far with this to back down now. "Yes, for the right price."

"What if I refuse?"

She stopped to look at him. "Well, Silas. Let me put it this way. I'm prepared to make this process easy for you or I'm prepared to make it a lot more complicated. There is no in-between."

He lifted a brow coldly. "I could kill you and be done with it."

Sean had thought of that, too. She was ready with an answer. "Sure, but that wouldn't get you any closer to robbing that bank. Besides, this is too small a town for you to get away with something like that. Are you willing to exchange bankrolls for a murder charge?"

"They'd probably just think you ran away again. No one would even look for you."

"Of course they would. Besides, I thought you were a gentleman. I doubt you'd want a lady's death on your conscience," she said. *If he has a conscience, which I can't be entirely sure of,* she realized but continued confidently, "Really, why go through all that trouble when having me on your side would make things so much easier?"

"All right. You're in at three percent. You won't get a penny more, so don't ask for it. You'll keep quiet and do as I say. Don't ask questions. I'll tell you what you need to know. Is that clear?"

She hid a frown at his command not to ask questions since her job was to do exactly that. However, she decided it was best not to push him on their first meeting. She nodded. "Completely."

He shook his head as if he couldn't believe he was agreeing to it, then he smiled. "Welcome aboard, Miss Wilkins. It's going to be quite a ride. I'll contact you again soon. Be ready."

"Be careful how and when you contact me, Mr. Smithson. I have a reputation to uphold," she reminded him. He nodded, then tipped his hat and left her to circle back toward the boardinghouse. She continued toward Main Street alone. She paused across the street from the bank to stare at it while she gathered her thoughts. She shook her head and whispered, "Well, I did it, Lord. Now what?"

Chapter Twelve

A satisfied smile tilted Lorelei's lips as she followed Ellie through the woods the next day. Her spur-of-the-moment decision to take Ellie up on her invitation to visit anytime had resulted in a wonderful day and an exciting new friendship. She glanced down to survey herself and shook her head. "If my mother could see me now, she'd faint."

Ellie glanced back at her curiously. "What? Why?"

"Just look at me." She stopped to exhibit herself. "My hands are red from washing clothes. My fingernails are stained purple from picking blackberries. I have a bruise on my arm from falling off a horse. I'm drenched from head to toe because you pushed me in when we went wading."

Ellie rolled her eyes unsympathetically. "You tripped and fell in. That's hardly my fault."

"That's your story and you're sticking to it, but I'm not buying what you're selling."

Ellie wrinkled her nose at Lorelei, then lifted her chin to curb a smile. "You may as well admit it, Lorelei. You…had…fun!"

"I certainly did." She exchanged a grin with Ellie, then looked more closely at the young woman and sing-songed, "You've been eating berries. Your teeth are purple."

Ellie's eyes widened as she guiltily pressed her lips together. "Well, don't look so smug, Miss Wilkins, so are yours."

"What?" She covered her mouth with her hand and groaned. "It's getting worse by the minute."

Ellie giggled. "Do you know what will make it better? A race."

Lorelei laughed. "You didn't even give me time to ask."

"First one to the house without spilling their berries gets to freshen up first."

"I don't know, Ellie— *Go!*" She rushed through the woods toward the house, keeping a careful eye on her bucket.

"Cheaters never win!" Ellie yelled from a few paces behind her. Lorelei lengthened the distance between them in long, smooth strides. She rounded the corner of the barn and stopped abruptly when she came face-to-face with Sean.

"Lorelei," he said in startled amusement.

She began to respond, then remembered to clench her lips together at the last second. She slowly became aware of the awful picture she must make. Suddenly Ellie shot past them with a triumphant laugh. The race! Lorelei sprang into motion once more with nothing more than a backward glance at her befuddled husband-to-be. She burst into the kitchen only seconds behind Ellie. Kate glanced up from her mending at their abrupt entrance but otherwise didn't bat an eye at their appearance. Apparently, this sort of thing wasn't un-usual around the O'Brien house.

"I won!" Ellie declared.

"No fair. I ran into Sean."

"You certainly did," Ellie said with a teasing pur-ple smile.

Lorelei laughed. "At least I remembered not to smile. I guess that means you get first dibs on freshening up."

Ellie shrugged. "That's all right. I'm used to the grime. You go on. Anything in my wardrobe is fair game. Just keep in mind that you'll probably get dirty again."

She frowned. "I don't see how."

"Ellie seems to attract messes, so you can't go by her. Although it is good advice with three children running around here," Kate suggested. "Besides, you'll want to be comfortable at dinner."

"Oh, I wasn't planning to stay. I mean I don't want to put y'all out. I've been here most of the day already."

Kate set aside her mending to check on the stew she was cooking. "Don't be silly. Now hurry upstairs unless you want Sean to get a better look at you."

It wasn't long before she'd cleaned up and changed into a simple blue blouse and navy skirt. She helped Hope set the table while Kate put the finishing touches on dinner and Ellie kept three-year-old Grace occu-pied. Nathan, Timothy and Sean soon filed inside. Sean washed his hands, then nonchalantly meandered over to take the seat beside her. "I was surprised to see you here but Nathan says you've been here most of the day and even helped him with the horses."

She fiddled with her napkin. "I thought you were working."

"Today is my day off. I always come home for dinner."

Lorelei glanced from him to his sister. "Ellie didn't tell me that."

"No," he said with a chuckle. "She wouldn't."

Ellie pretended not to hear them, though she would've had to have been deaf not to as she slid into a chair across from them. "We just keep adding more chairs to the table."

"And more table to the table," Nathan added as he took his seat at the head of the table. "That's a good thing."

"It certainly is." Kate made sure her children were settled, then glanced at Sean. "Let's say grace."

Sean bowed his head. "Lord, thank You for the food and those who prepared it. We especially want to thank You for our unexpected company. Amen."

"Amen," Lorelei echoed along with everyone else, then glanced up at him. He smiled and handed her the mashed potatoes as dishes of food began circling the table. "What were y'all saying about chairs? I didn't quite understand."

Kate's gaze swept around the table. "When our parents died they left two empty chairs at the table. Nathan filled one when he came. Lawson filled the other while he lived with us. Since then we've been adding chairs. One each for Timothy, Hope, Grace, and now there's one for you."

It took a moment for her to gather her voice. "Thank you. I'm honored."

"I wish my parents could have known you," Sean said without looking up from his plate.

"They would have liked you," Kate said, but Lorelei couldn't glance away from Sean when he finally met her gaze.

"I wish I could have known your parents, too." she said softly.

Ellie smiled. "It's all right. You'll meet them one day."

Lorelei nodded, then sat back to watch the O'Brien family interact with each other and Sean. He seemed to drop the mantle of responsibility just enough to enjoy dinner with his family, but she could still sense his tension. Or, maybe that was from her being there. She glanced around the table, then looked down at her food to hide her rising emotions. She'd never imagined his family would be so open, kind and accepting. They all knew the truth about her relationship with Sean but they didn't seem to care.

Sean's left hand strayed behind her to give a comforting rub to her back without his family's notice. She glanced at him in surprise, then looked away as he drew his hand back. Who was this man? He was more relaxed. More gentle. More himself? She was starting to like him. That was fine. Like was a long way from love. Wasn't it?

The stars stretched across the expansive Texas sky above where Sean settled on the thick, moist grass an hour later. His hands cushioned the back of his head. He could hear the soft undistinguishable murmur of Ellie's voice as she talked to Hope and Timothy a good distance away. Lorelei stirred beside him. Her hand lifted, tracing out patterns he'd shown her in the constellations before she let it drop to her chest. He turned his head to look at her. "How long have you been here exactly?"

"My father dropped me off this afternoon. He was going to pick me up in an hour, but Nathan insisted he'd take me home when I was ready and that was the end of that," she answered softly. "I like it here. It's peaceful, simple, uncomplicated. Do you think the sky will look this big from our place?"

"It should." He turned to look at the sky again. He just couldn't get over how well she fit into his family. The children loved her because she played with them. Kate seemed to appreciate the way Lorelei was always willing to help out. Nathan obviously liked being able to explain his business and talk about his horses to someone who hadn't heard him say it all a thousand times already. Ellie seemed to have found a new best friend. As for him, well, he wasn't sure what he thought about it yet. He wasn't sure what he thought about her anymore for that matter.

"Sean?"

"Yes."

"I talked to Silas yesterday."

He smiled. "I know. I saw you in the courtyard out my office window."

"Oh." She sat up and hugged her legs to her chest. "I told him I wanted in. He let me on the team—"

"Into the gang," he corrected with a smile.

"—under the condition that I help out and keep quiet," she finished. "I convinced him that I wanted in for an opportunity to get out of this town. He believed me."

"That's funny. I would have believed it, too," he said as he sat up. "In fact it sounds—"

"Strangely familiar, I know." She smiled almost cheekily in the moonlight. "That's why it worked so well. Oh! The funniest part is that I told him you were just a pawn in my scheme to keep Papa happy."

"Oh, yeah. That's really funny."

She smothered her mirth but not before a laugh slipped out. "I'm sorry."

"You should be, but I don't think you are."

"He said he'd contact me soon."

"I figured." He heaved out a sigh. "Well, it's pretty obvious that you have to continue. Don't look so excited. You're going to have to abide by my ground rules since this is an official investigation. You'll have to let me know when he contacts you and the specifics of what is said. If he threatens you, you will let me know immediately. I reserve the right to pull you off the investigation at any time but especially if I feel you're in danger. Is that understood?"

"Yes."

"If you happen to think of this as a lark or a game or anything other than a life-and-death situation, you should shed those notions right now. We aren't entirely sure who or what we're dealing with, but we do know that Smithson is dangerous. You could get hurt or killed."

She met his gaze soberly. "I understand that."

He surveyed her for any sign of fear but didn't find any. He nodded. "Good. When you meet with him, there is certain information you can give and certain information you need to try to get."

"Shouldn't I write this down?"

"No. I want you to memorize it." He placed his elbows on his knees and leaned toward her. "If Smithson is working with someone else, and we know he is, then I can arrest him and his partner or partners before they ever set foot in the bank on the charge of conspiracy to commit an armed robbery. That means they agreed to carry out the robbery, then took some action toward doing so. We're looking for evidence in the form of things like layouts of the bank, the date the robbery is going to take place, getaway plans, anything like that. You can draw that material out by advising them on all of it."

She frowned. "But should I really tell the truth about that? What if they actually get away with it?"

"They won't because we won't let them," he said seriously. "Tell them the truth. We don't know how much information they already have, and we don't want to let them think you're double-crossing them in any way. We'll have to see how deep they let you into their plans. So far you've been pretty clever about all of this. Keep your wits about you, and I think you'll do all right."

She leaned back, bracing her hands behind her, and tilted her head. "Was that a vote of confidence I just heard?"

"It certainly was."

"My, oh, my. What an unusual day this has been. Maybe it's time for me to go home. I don't know how much of this I can take."

Neither do I, he thought at the sight of her smiling like that with the backdrop of a million twinkling stars. "I'll get the horses."

Chapter Thirteen

Lorelei became intensely aware of the hand Sean had tucked into the crook of his arm when Mrs. Greene's gaze landed there. Rather than pass them on the sidewalk, Mrs. Greene stopped to smile at them. "You two seem to be holding up admirably well. I'm sure this must be quite a strain on you to pretend feelings you don't have."

Lorelei's eyes widened, and she glanced around to make sure no one was in hearing distance. Relieved that no one was, she realized she had no idea how to respond to the woman's statement. She was grateful when Sean changed the subject. "We'd both like to thank you again for being so considerate about this."

"Well, as Mrs. Wilkins said, there's no way to prove you did wrong just like there is no way to prove you did right. I love telling a good story as much as the next person, but I'm not out to ruin anyone's reputation needlessly." She dabbed her handkerchief across her brow. "I'm still holding y'all to the wedding ceremony. If you don't go through with it, the deal is off."

"We know," Lorelei said quietly.

"Your courtship is getting more believable, but something is still a little peculiar. I'd know that even if folks weren't telling me. You'd better fix that or people might start asking questions and I might not catch myself before answering." The woman's eyes strayed back to Lorelei's hand before she nodded a farewell. "Y'all have a good day now."

As soon as the woman passed, Lorelei released her hand from Sean's arm under the pretense of staring into the display window of Sew Wonderful Tailoring. She caught a glimpse of her reflection in the store's window and carefully smoothed a lock of hair back into place. Her moment of respite came to an abrupt end when Sean stepped up beside her. "I don't know what else to do to make this more believable."

"Neither do I."

"I'll think of something," he said before they continued on.

He'd invited her on this walk. In the spirit of their new, tentative state of truce, she had agreed, but she'd hoped Sean would make this a short venture. She didn't like the feeling of being on display. A sideways glance at his expression almost made her sigh in discouragement. He looked perfectly content to mosey along hardly making any progress. His slow pace might actually convince someone he wanted to spend every moment he could with her. She knew it was only part of the show. She just wished that fact didn't bother her so much. He touched her waist to indicate they should cross the street. "Have you had any contact with Smithson?"

"I haven't seen nor heard a word from him since last week. He's making me nervous. What do you think he's waiting for?"

"It could be any number of things," he said as he led her to the gazebo the town had built halfway between the church and the schoolyard. "He could be waiting for someone to arrive. He could have decided against going through with it, though that is highly unlikely. He could be waiting to see if you're serious enough to contact him again."

They slowly mounted the stairs to the empty gazebo. "So what do I do?"

"Give him a little while longer. We'll try to stick to our original plan, and if he doesn't come through, we'll figure something else out." He sat near the end of the wooden bench that followed the curve of the gazebo. His gaze strayed from hers to rest on the schoolhouse. "You've made quite an impression on my family. Almost a week has passed, and they're still talking about you, especially Timothy."

An unbidden smile rose to her lips. "They were sweet and Timothy was adorable."

"You seem to make a good impression on children, Lorelei."

"I guess I do," she said, thinking about her rapport with the Brightly children. "I can't for the life of me figure out why."

He frowned at her self-derisive comment. "I don't think it's too hard to figure out. You let down your guard when you're with them."

Her eyes flashed to his suspiciously. "What does that mean?"

"You're different somehow. Maybe it's because you know they won't hurt you. I've watched you. You suddenly become more charming and clever and interesting. Your eyes even start to twinkle."

She crossed her arms. "I think I should be offended by that comment."

"Don't be."

"Why are you telling me this?"

"Because I'm beginning to think you aren't exactly who you've presented yourself to be—at least, not to me."

She couldn't look away for a long breathless moment. Finally, she stood and turned away from him to lean against the gazebo railing that looked out toward the schoolhouse. She could almost see herself as a child slipping away from her friends in the playground to confidently tell the boy she loved that she'd marry him one day. It hadn't even crossed her mind that he wouldn't feel the same way. His disgust had taken her aback, and the schoolchildren's incessant teasing for weeks had kept the wound from healing as it should.

She'd learned a valuable lesson. Love wasn't something that should be boldly exposed but rather hidden away for protection. Somehow in hiding that she'd hidden away so much more. She'd hidden part of herself.

She suddenly realized Sean had joined her. He caught her arm to guide her away from the railing, so she faced him. He looked searchingly over her features. "I think I figured out what's missing from our courtship, Lorelei. It's you, isn't it?"

She allowed her gaze to drop to their feet.

He sighed. "Maybe that's for the best."

She glanced up in sharp inquiry.

He shrugged. "The woman I glimpsed playing with my nephew, having dinner with my family and racing across the barnyard with my sister wasn't just downright beautiful. She was practically irresistible. I don't think either of us are ready to handle that, are we?"

She tensed and stepped back. "No."

He picked up the Stetson from where he'd dropped it on the gazebo bench. "I think I'd better get you home."

* * *

Lorelei desperately tried to focus on her job to put yesterday's conversation with Sean out of her mind, but she'd discovered a problem. She couldn't breathe. At least, she couldn't breathe normally. She concentrated on pulling even breaths through her lips as she placed one hat aside to look at the request for another. Orders for hats had come rushing in after a few of her designs had been seen around Peppin. Lorelei took special care in designing the hats so they would live up to the expectations of the new customers. But it was hard to concentrate on sartorial brilliance when she could barely breathe. Mainly, she just wanted to live past her shift.

She glanced around the lonely workroom and sighed. "Lord, I so wanted to prove that I could stick to something, but this is just awful. The feathers are simply everywhere—in the air, on the table. I even find them in my hair when I get home. I don't understand. Really, I don't. They just seem to multiply."

She opened her eyes to stare at the fragments of feathers lying on the table. She had hoped that her body would get use to them after a while. Instead of getting better, she seemed to be getting worse. She hadn't noticed how much worse until this morning. She closed her eyes a moment to gather herself. "Well, so much for that."

Tucking her handkerchief back into her pocket, she marched the few feet to Mrs. Cummings's office. Mrs. Cummings glanced up from her books. "Yes, Lorelei?"

Lorelei opened the door farther and stepped in the room.

The woman's eyes widened. "Your face is remarkably red."

She reached up a hand to touch her warm cheek. "Is it?"

"Are you all right?"

"No. I'm afraid not. I can't tell you how sorry I am. I will have to leave early today." She took a moment to gather her breath, then shook her head. "I appreciate this opportunity, but I will not be coming back."

"I was expecting that."

"You were?"

"This is your last check." Mrs. Cummings took an envelope from her desk and handed it to Lorelei. "I was going to let you go at the end of the day."

"Oh," Lorelei breathed.

"Child, I've never heard anyone sneeze so much in my life." The woman gave a firm nod. "As wonderful as your work has been, I, for one, am glad you came to your senses. Promise me you'll go see Doc Williams right away."

"Yes, ma'am, I will." She didn't bother to smile. She gathered her hat and reticule from the workroom before hurrying out the door. It slammed shut behind her with a plaintive ring of its bell. She'd hoped the fresh air would help, but the air was humid and she felt even more uncomfortable.

"Lorelei!"

She glanced up from her boots at the sound of someone cheerily calling her name. She lifted her lips into a weak smile as Ellie fell in step beside her. "Ellie, I'm sorry. I've got to get to Doc's."

Ellie's large green eyes widened as they traced Lorelei's features. "Heavens, you look as if you might faint."

Lorelei shook her head. "I'll be fine. I'm just allergic to the feathers I've been working with."

"At least wait a minute to catch your breath." She

pulled Lorelei to a stop, then glanced around in a mix of frustration and concern. "Now, where did Sean go? There he is."

"Please," Lorelei said as kindly as she could while she removed Ellie's detaining hand and tried not to panic. She continued on by herself for a moment before a strong arm slipped beneath hers to offer support. She glanced up into Sean's concerned gaze.

"Let me carry you to Doc's."

She immediately shook her head. "It isn't that bad."

Ellie stepped up to the other side of her. "Please, Lorelei. We don't know what's wrong, but we want to help. Let him carry you. You'll get there faster."

She glanced toward the bank. "If Father sees—"

"He won't," Sean promised. "I know a back way that's shorter."

She nodded, then followed Sean off the sidewalk to the narrow alleyway behind the businesses with Ellie at her side. Sean immediately lifted her into his arms. Her arms instinctively went around his shoulders while embarrassment caused her to turn her face into his neck. She caught her breath enough to murmur, "I don't think this is necessary."

"A lot of things aren't necessary in life, Lorelei," he said quietly. "That doesn't mean you should do without them."

"Things like allowing others to care for you when you're in need," Ellie said firmly. Glancing over her shoulder at the two of them, she smiled. "And things like love. It may not be as necessary as the air you breathe or the water you drink, but a life without love is hardly worth living."

Lorelei lowered her brow in confusion.

"Ellie, this is not the time," Sean said with a bit of

exasperation. "Run ahead and tell Doc we're coming, will you?"

Ellie's eyes flashed Sean a silent message Lorelei couldn't quite decipher before she lifted her skirts to run down the alley.

"We're almost there. Just relax."

Lorelei closed her eyes and tried to do exactly that. It felt like the longest few minutes of her life. The tension in her chest refused to ease as she attempted to take easy breaths. Thinking about breathing seemed to make it more difficult, so she tried to think of something else. She lifted her face from Sean's chest to see if they were attracting any attention. Thankfully, they were now the only ones in the alleyway.

She slowly became conscious of the rapid thundering of Sean's heart beneath her fingers and swallowed. When exactly had her free hand slid over his heart? She stared at it for a long moment. Sean shifted her closer. She readjusted her arm around his shoulder. *Lord, please help me. I really can't breathe.*

Sean glanced down, distracting her with a rueful smile. "This is beginning to become a habit with us, isn't it?"

She lifted her shoulder in a hapless shrug. "Don't get—used to it."

He chuckled quietly. "No, I suppose not."

She closed her eyes as he turned a corner, then mounted the steps to Doc Williams's office. Ellie threw the door open for them. Doc led them down a hallway and into an examining room, then promptly commanded Sean to leave. One quick encouraging look later, Sean was gone. Lorelei glanced over at the doctor who had turned away to prepare her treatment.

"From what I've heard, you are having trouble breathing, is that right?"

"Yes," she exhaled.

"Runny nose, watery eyes, itchy nose and eyes," he rattled off as he examined her. "You, my dear, have a severe case of hay fever. Try breathing through your mouth calmly instead of gasping for breath. If you keep overcompensating, you'll hyperventilate. There's nothing to worry about. I'll give you some medicine and keep an eye on you for a while."

"It isn't serious?" she asked in disbelief. "But…"

"But what?"

But…when Sean held me I couldn't breathe. She swallowed. "Nothing, Doc. It was nothing."

Sean's thumb tapped a frantic rhythm on his denim-covered knee while he waited for Doc and Lorelei to emerge from the examining room. Ellie's hand covered his. He squeezed it gently, then glanced up at her. Her smile was reassuring. He leaned back in his chair and let out a pent-up breath.

"Don't be so worried. She's with Doc. If anyone can make her better, he can," Ellie said.

He glanced at her. "I know that. I've just never been good at waiting."

Her lips curved into a smile. "You're really starting to care for Lorelei, aren't you, Sean?"

The question settled into the air like the smell of kerosene at an explosion site. Sean grunted. Let it settle all it liked, he wasn't about to answer. "Do you really want to ask that question, knowing what you know?"

She winked. He shot her a glare. She gave him a saccharine-sweet smile, then picked up a catalog from a table. He sighed, then walked the window for some time alone.

"Lord, I can't make heads or tails of anything lately," he muttered in a barely audible voice to keep Ellie from hearing. "I don't know if it's me messing up my life or if You're trying to teach me something, but I've never been so lost or confused. Please help me out here."

He stood in quiet anticipation in the stillness interrupted only by Ellie's intermittent page turning. He waited for peace to overtake him, but instead panic filled his chest. His heart began to beat faster. His hands clenched into fists. He wanted to take it back. Those words he'd spoken were good in theory, but they came a bit too close to surrender. He wanted to believe that he could fix it on his own. Perhaps if he just tried a little harder to do…something.…

The truth was he'd become so invested in his relationship with Lorelei that it was making him a little crazy. The more he thought about it and the more he played along, the more he really began to hate this game of pretend he and Lorelei were involved in. He hated wondering if the town would find his proposal too sudden and start asking questions he wouldn't want answered. But most of all, he hated the way he wasn't sure himself how real their courtship was, for him or for her. They'd been getting along so much better recently, but was the new cordiality real, or was Lorelei just keeping up appearances? And what about him? Were his feelings for her truly growing?

He probably shouldn't have told her that he found her irresistible when she wasn't acting like someone she wasn't. It was true though. He realized that they'd finally been able to create a friendship. But it wasn't enough. She wasn't the type of person he'd planned on spending his life with, but they were getting married. That meant he needed to do something that would start them on a path that would eventually lead to love. But would he end up on that path alone?

He closed his eyes against the dizziness and heard a door open down the hall. Grateful for the distraction, Sean glanced up to see Doc Williams walking toward him. "How is she?"

"She should be fine. I'm going to watch her for a while to make sure the treatment is working. She asked me to take her home after that."

Ellie slipped up to Sean and nudged him softly in the ribs. "I guess that's our cue to leave."

"I guess so." He reached down to grab his Stetson.

"Tell her we'll be praying for her," Ellie urged.

"I'll do that," Doc promised.

Ellie stepped up to press a kiss on Doc's cheek. "Bye, Doc."

Sean shook Doc's hand. When he would have let go, Doc held on. He glanced up to find the man looking at him carefully. "Actually, Ellie, I'd like to speak with Sean alone."

Ellie nodded. "I'll wait at your office, Sean."

Before Sean had a chance to respond, Doc released his hand and turned back down the hallway he'd just walked. Sean followed him in confusion. Doc motioned Sean into an empty examination room. "Sit down, Sean."

"What's wrong?"

Doc took the chair across from him, pulled out a notepad and looked him in the eye. "How long have you been having this panic problem?"

Shock stilled his rapidly beating heart for a moment before it resumed its quick pace. He shifted in his chair, then stared at the door. So that's what these episodes were called. He wasn't sure if he was more alarmed or relieved to know what they were. His gaze shot back to Doc's. "How did you know?"

"I felt your racing heart during our rather moist handshake, you seem short of breath and if the look in your eyes tells me anything, you are feeling an unexplained sense of terror or lack of control right now." He didn't wait for Sean's confirmation. "Do any other symptoms usually occur along with or instead of these?"

He swallowed. "Dizziness."

Doc marked it down, then nodded for him to continue. "When did you first begin to have these episodes?"

"After my parents' deaths."

Doc put down his pencil. "I'm not surprised, but I am concerned that you have not mentioned this to me before. Does your family know?"

"Should they?"

Doc smiled slightly. "It isn't fatal, if that's what you're asking. Telling them is up to you."

"Is there a cure?"

"That depends. Do you know what triggers them?"

Sean was thoughtful for a long moment. "Thinking about certain things like situations I can't control."

"A loss of control due to outside pressures," Doc muttered as he wrote in his tablet. He glanced up. "In that case, I would suggest you find someone to confide in. Talking about what's wrong rather than internalizing it, will probably help. Also, how often during those moments do you pray and surrender the situation to God?"

"I pray…sometimes." He swallowed.

"I see." Doc leaned forward. "In medicine we have vaccines. That means to keep someone from contracting diseases such as smallpox we give them smallpox in a little dose. Once the body builds defenses against the small dose, it can fight off a stronger infection. In my opinion, the best vaccine for the panic you feel when giving up control is to give up control in small ways until you can do it comfortably in large ways."

Sean's smile was wry. "So to treat panic I need to panic."

Doc laughed. "Yes, because the point is to learn how to deal with that panic."

"If I do that, will I finally be able to overcome this?"

"With time, I hope that you will."

He wanted to overcome this, and if that meant he needed to give up a little bit of control, then maybe he could do that. The biggest source of stress for him was his relationship with Lorelei. What had he thought earlier? He needed to start them on a path toward love. That meant taking a chance. That was a form of giving up control, wasn't it? Perhaps it was time to be honest with himself and with Lorelei. He was tired of playing pretend. He wanted a real relationship with her. For once, he'd take a risk. He'd approach Lorelei and ask her to let him court her for real. Maybe, just maybe, she'd say yes. Perhaps that would help him shake this panic once and for all.

Chapter Fourteen

Sitting on the wooden bench of her parents' back lawn the next afternoon, Lorelei placed her pencil back onto the paper. It was the first time she'd ventured out of the house since Doc had helped her drowsily inside. Whatever medicine he'd given her had been enough to fell a horse. She'd slept her way past the effects of the allergy and the medication to awaken feeling healthy and strong again. Now that she didn't have a job and Silas Smithson hadn't contacted her, she figured she might as well try a new hobby. Obviously drawing wasn't going to be it. She drew line after line with her pencil, but no matter how many lines she drew, she couldn't come up with a flower.

A shadow suddenly covered her drawing pad. She frowned and glanced up at the sky for the offending cloud only to meet the shimmering deep green eyes of Sean O'Brien. She jumped. Her drawing pad tottered violently before diving into the grass. Glancing back up at Sean, she uttered a single slightly disappointed word. "Oh."

His lips stretched slowly into an amused grin. "That isn't exactly the kind of hello a man dreams about."

She couldn't help but return his smile. He watched her for a moment before he knelt in the grass to retrieve her things. She took them from him, then carefully swung her feet down and scooted to one side to make room for him on the bench. He sat beside her but angled himself so he could see her face. She shrugged in a delayed response to his statement. "Maybe not, but do you realize that I've seen you nearly every day this week?"

He angled his chin down and leveled her with a teasingly suspicious look. "Are you complaining?"

She lifted her shoulders while innocently placing a hand on her chest. "Complaining? Oh, no. I was just commenting about it, that's all."

He gave her an easy grin. "Yeah, well, I'm afraid you're going to have to get used to it, darlin'."

She narrowed her eyes, ready to tell him just who he wouldn't be calling darling. He unnerved her into silence by sliding his arm across the back of the bench and leaning toward her. She forgot to breathe when he met her gaze. He gestured toward the drawing pad. "What's this?"

"My failed attempts at drawing." She shoved the drawing pad toward him. He seemed to take the hint because he took the pad and moved closer to his side of the bench. She watched him look over her drawings.

"These aren't so bad." He held his hand out for the pencil.

She handed it to him, glad to see him engrossed in something other than staring at her, even if it was correcting her mistakes. She smoothed down the wrinkles in her dress. Finally, she grew impatient. "Don't tell me you came all the way over here just to look at my awful drawings."

"I might have troubled myself to walk all of those three long blocks between our houses just to look at your drawings, if I'd known ahead of time you were drawing, but I didn't." He flourished one last stroke of the pencil, then handed the drawing pad back to her. "They weren't awful."

She stared down at the paper in astonishment. "You fixed them."

"I moved a few lines."

"You must have." She brushed away a clump of small scarlet flowers that fell onto the page from the crape myrtle branches that stretched above them. "How did you learn to draw?"

"I sketch the designs for the furniture and wood carvings I make now and then. It's just a hobby." He shifted to face her. "Lorelei, I came here to say something, so I may as well say it. I want to court you for real."

She stared at him for a long moment. His words just didn't make any sense. She frowned at him and shook her head in confusion. "Whatever for?"

"Aren't you tired of putting on an act, Lorelei? If we were really courting, we wouldn't have to do that anymore. We would just have to live."

"What's wrong with acting?" she asked, setting her drawing pad and the pencil on the grass.

"Besides the facts that it's slightly deceptive and that neither of us are very good at it?" He laughed. "Well, I hate to tell you this, but I don't think we can even come close to convincing the town we're really a couple if we don't make this courtship legitimate. Remember what Mrs. Greene said?"

Leaning back into the corner of the bench, she sighed. "I remember."

"Peppin is too small to hide anything. How long do you think we can keep up a ruse like this before someone finds out? This way we may have to act like our relationship is progressing faster than it really is, but at least there would be a genuine relationship."

She could feel her heartbeat drumming through her veins. He was threatening to out-reason her. She couldn't let that happen. "I really don't think this is a good idea."

"Just forget about the town for a minute. Forget that we're pretending. Forget everything else and think about this." He took her left hand in his right and looked her straight in the eye. "We're getting married, Lorelei. We've already established that we're going to have a real marriage. Shouldn't we also have a real courtship?"

"No," she whispered as she removed her hand from his. "I don't want it to be real."

"Why not?"

"I just don't," she said urgently.

He dropped his head for a moment, then quietly asked, "Do you really dislike me that much?"

"Dislike you?" she asked in a breathless exclamation. She turned away from his disconcerting scrutiny to try to control her emotions. She had suppressed them for so long that they refused to be contained any longer. She stood. Pressing her lips together, she turned to face him. Once the words finally came out, she couldn't seem to stop the rest that followed.

"I never disliked you, Sean. I loved you once, or at

least I thought I did. I let all of those silly emotions go. I moved on. I was even going to find a new life for myself in California, then you had the nerve follow me. Now, after everything I've gone through, you say that you want to court me for real because that will make things easier on you."

Her breath was coming in short gasps. She paused to catch her breath and tried to remember why she was telling him all this. *Oh, yes.*

"The answer to your question is no. No, Sean. I don't dislike you. Well, maybe I do just a little for good reason, but that's not why I don't want you to court me. It will just confuse everything and take the focus off what we're supposed to be doing—fooling the town into thinking we're falling in love."

She waited for shame and fear to follow that statement, but it didn't. Instead, she felt a burden lift from her soul only to be replaced by peace. There. She'd said it. She'd told him exactly how she felt and now she felt free. Finally, free from the secret that had weighed her down for years. It felt wonderful. It also left her feeling exposed.

Sean slowly stood and stepped directly in front of her. As the moment lengthened, curiosity eventually drew her eyes to his. What she saw there wasn't at all what she expected. She had no idea what emotions glimmered from those depths, but there was no trace of mocking or disgust. It wasn't until a slow half amused, half confused smile pulled at his lips that she knew she was in trouble.

Sean watched the blush in Lorelei's cheeks heighten incrementally. His amused smile grew even as he tilted his head to survey her in confusion. "Wait a minute! Did I just hear you say you love me?"

If possible, her eyes widened even more, and she shook her head. "No, you didn't. You heard me say 'I loved you.'"

He frowned, not seeing the difference.

"It was past tense," she carefully explained.

"Oh, I see." He nodded. "It was very clumsy of me to make that kind of a mistake. There is a very large difference in loving someone and having loved someone."

She frowned with a trace of suspicion. "I should say so."

"Then I take it back. You are an extremely good actress. I had no idea."

Her lips parted in surprise, though her brows lowered in suspicion. "You really couldn't tell? Not even when we were younger?"

He shook his head. She looked at him carefully as if trying to discern the truth of his statement. Obviously finding something wanting, she tilted her head and pinned him with a look before slowly asking, "Then why don't you look more surprised?"

For the first time during their exchange, he felt slightly uncomfortable. "Lawson recently guessed you might feel that way."

"Lawson guessed," she repeated thoughtfully, then shook her head. "Well, now you know he was right. I hope you also understand that I've refused to let you court me."

"Hold on. I think you've got something wrong. I'm not *asking* you to let me court you for real. I'm *telling* you. I'm going to court you for real."

Her mouth dropped open, then she narrowed her eyes. "You can't do that."

He hadn't planned on it—and even now he could feel an edge of panic deep inside at the thought of committing himself to a courtship when she wasn't willing to meet him halfway—but it was obvious that there would be no other way to end this standoff. He could see them thirty years down the road still at the same impasse. One of them was going to have to risk getting hurt, and since it clearly wasn't going to be her, it would have to be him.

He was going to romance this woman whether she liked it or not because he didn't know what else to do. Surely God would take it from there. He had to. There was no other way this would work. It was with that knowledge that he stepped out in faith. "I can and I will."

"I don't understand. You don't even like me. Why would you want to court me?"

He frowned. "I thought we went over that."

"Yes, and we agreed to be *friends*."

"We are friends, aren't we?"

She was quiet for a long moment—too long of a moment. She just stared at him skeptically with those large blue eyes of hers. She was making him uncomfortable on purpose, and they both knew it. A smile tipped his lips, causing her to try to hide one of her own. She glanced away. Her tone spoke of her long-suffering patience. "I guess."

"Think of this as the next step then."

"The next step to what?" She crossed her arms. "You aren't going to make me fall in love with you. You know that, right?"

He didn't want to examine why those tentative words cut right to his heart, but they did until he remembered. "You fell in love with me once before."

"Yes, but I've resolved not to be that foolish again," she said stubbornly.

He frowned. "What's foolish about loving someone?"

She straightened. "Well, everything! You're giving someone the power to hurt you by becoming completely vulnerable."

"I don't want to hurt you, Lorelei," he said in frustration. "I just want to court you."

"Oh, no, you don't. You're like every other normal man. You want a wife who loves you, but that's hardly fair in this case."

"Why isn't it fair?"

"Because you aren't going to love me back!" She let those uncomfortable words settle between them for a moment before she continued passionately. "Oh, you may start to care for me, but as soon as you do you're going to think about Lawson and what I did to him. You're going to think about the Harvest Dance when I ignored you because I thought you betrayed me. Then you're going to remind yourself of all the little things you don't like about me—"

He gently clutched her arms. "Stop it, Lorelei."

"It's true. Tell me it isn't," she challenged. He couldn't and she knew it. She glanced down, but not before he saw the tears in her eyes.

"Lorelei," he began, but she shook her head.

"That's quite all right, Sean, because I'd be doing the same thing. You want this to be real, so fine. For you, it's real. But, I won't do it. I'll just keep acting." She gathered her things and headed inside. "Say hello to my parents before you leave. They love your visits. I'll be in my room if they need me."

She was right. He realized it then and there. She was right about him, and she always had been. He did tend to focus on her faults, but that was only so he wouldn't have to focus on all the things he liked about her. She'd been his best friend's girl for so long that disqualifying her had become a necessary habit. There. He'd admitted it to himself. His heart always had had a weakness for Lorelei, and he'd never allowed himself to give in to it. Doing so would have meant betraying a friend.

Things could be different now if they let it. They needed their relationship to work now, not just in the long run. He would continue with his plan to woo her because it was all he knew to do. Hopefully along the way they'd both be able to set aside the past.

Lorelei picked up the large serving spoon covered in melted cheese and hefted a portion of casserole onto her plate. She wasn't sure who'd brought the dish to the church's potluck picnic, but it looked delicious. She was only vaguely aware of someone stepping up beside her in line before a low voice murmured in a teasing tone, "You're a hard woman to get a hold of these days, Miss Wilkins."

Lorelei carefully placed the spoon back in its place before she glanced up into the eyes of the man beside her. She smiled politely to hide her relief that he was finally making contact. "Hello, Mr. Smithson."

"Please, call me Silas." He returned her smile as they progressed down the line. "I was sorry to hear you quit your job at the millinery."

Lorelei exchanged a smile with one of the church ladies overseeing the buffet table. She carefully placed a sweet roll onto her plate. "I'm afraid it couldn't be avoided. It was literally making me sick."

He paused to take a large piece of her mother's pie. "I heard it had something to do with that. I hope that won't prevent you from helping me."

"I see no reason why it should." She glanced around at all of the innocent churchgoers milling about in groups.

"I thought you might say that." Silas led her farther away from the table where they were less likely to be overheard. "I hate to mention this, but your illness might have caused a problem. How am I supposed to contact you without raising suspicion?"

Her lips tilted upward in amusement. "You'd be doing fine now if you weren't frowning."

"How can you say that?"

"What's wrong with us meeting here?"

"It's a church, isn't it?"

She laughed. Maybe God had a purpose in allowing her to get sick after all. "Don't tell me you came to church just to talk to me?"

He glared at her.

"Did you have to sit through the whole sermon?"

"Yes, I did. I don't understand why you're so amused by it."

She shrugged. "I just thought it might have done you some good, that's all."

"Like it did you good? Just imagine what these people would think if they found out what you were really like."

She bristled at his tone but found his words achingly true. She was trying to deceive the town just as he was, only not with the same intentions. He wanted to steal the town's livelihood. She was just trying to protect her reputation. She glanced back at Mr. Smithson and realized he expected a reply, so she shrugged nonchalantly. "They'd never believe it."

"Well, it doesn't matter. I have to talk to you about something serious. Our old plans have been delayed, so we're creating a new plan. I'm going to need you to produce on that information you promised me."

"What do you need?"

He shook his head. "Not now."

"When?"

"Meet me Tuesday evening at 7:30 in the alley where we first met. We have a lot of planning to do."

She returned his nod as they went their separate ways. A few minutes later, Lorelei leaned across her mother's brightly colored quilt to snag a sliver of Mrs. Greene's famous cornbread from one of the three plates stationed in the middle. A few crumbs managed to drop from the moist cornbread before she captured it in her mouth.

Her father grinned at her from where he sat to her left. "Is it good?"

"Delicious," she said, finishing off the rest of the piece.

"Lorelei," her mother called softly. "I think you have a visitor."

She glanced up in confusion to see her parents smiling. Following their gazes, she turned around to see three-year-old Grace standing at the edge of the quilt. She held her hands behind the skirt of her blue-and-white dress while she watched Lorelei shyly. Lorelei's lips lifted into an amused smile. "Grace. Hello."

"'Lo." The girl smiled impishly, then pulled a bouquet of wildflowers from behind her back. "Yours."

Lorelei stared at the bouquet in surprise. "Are you sure?"

The little girl nodded so adamantly that a little red curl slipped from its place to dance around her shoulder. Lorelei heard her parents chuckle. She shot a helpless glance at them before she turned back to the girl.

"Thank you so much." She took the flowers from the girl. "They're beautiful."

The girl grinned, her blue eyes sparkling. She dropped to her knees and placed her hands on her lap as though ready for a long chat.

"Did you pick these flowers all by yourself?"

Grace shook her head. "No."

"Did someone tell you to give them to me then?"

A smile blossomed on the girl's face. Her brow lowered earnestly as she said something that sounded almost unintelligibly like, "Unca."

"Uncle." Her eyes instinctively swept the picnic blankets laid out against the green lawn, searching for Sean. A moment later, her suspicious gaze connected with his. He was kneeling on one of the O'Brien family's picnic blankets, obviously having just sent off his little emissary. He caught her watching him, and a slow smile spread across his face. She shook her head slightly even as a reluctant smile teased her lips.

"Yes, I see," she murmured.

His smile and gaze were completely genuine, which meant he was really going through with his misguided attempt to court her. That didn't mean she was going to make things easy on him. Oh, no. If she had her way, things were going to become very interesting.

He was trying a new strategy on her, but he had no idea she had a strategy of her own. She was no longer an insecure child half-afraid of the attention she might arouse. She was going to guard her heart, but she was also ready to fight fire with fire. She glanced back to Grace. "I think I'm supposed to take you back to dear old Uncle."

The little girl gave a careless shrug and pointed to the flowers. "I like those."

Lorelei laughed. "Which one is your favorite?"

The girl pointed to a bright yellow one. Lorelei pulled it from the bouquet and deftly shortened the stem before tucking it into the girl's hair. "There."

Grace beamed and carefully lifted her hair to touch the flower. "Pretty."

"Very pretty," she said as she stood, then glanced down at her parents. "I've been summoned."

"Go ahead, dear," Caroline said. "We're almost through here anyway."

Her father scooped up Lorelei's abandoned plate and winked at her. "More pie for me."

Lorelei pulled in a deep breath, then stood and extended her hand to Grace. "Let's go see Uncle Sean."

Instead of grasping Lorelei's fingers, Grace extended both arms upward in a sign that she wanted to be carried. She swept the girl onto her hip as she approached the other blanket and sent Sean a grin. "Look what I found."

"I knew I'd left her someplace." He stood to greet them with a smile.

Grace lurched forward and placed her hand on Sean's cheek in order to get his attention. "I did it."

"Yes, you did. You are such a good girl." He leaned

forward to kiss her forehead. "I think your mama was looking for you."

Lorelei set Grace down, then watched as she raced the few yards to where Kate was talking to a few other women. "I talked to Silas."

"I know. I saw you. What did he say?" He listened as she explained about the meeting before frowning. "You did well, though ideally you should have tried to arrange it for a public place in daylight. That's my fault for not instructing you to do that. We'll go over what you need to say again before you meet him. I'll be present, but you won't see me. Do your best to act like I'm not there."

"Yes, sir," she dutifully agreed.

"By the way, did you like the surprise I sent you?"

Impulsively, she stepped forward onto her tiptoes to place a quick kiss on his cheek. "I did. Thank you. It was an adorable surprise, and the flowers were lovely."

She had the pleasure of watching him blush. He cleared his throat, then raised a brow. "That almost sounded sincere."

"I think it almost was," she said teasingly.

A suspicious smile played at his lips. "Why, Miss Wilkins, I haven't the slightest idea what you're up to, but I think I like this side of you."

She felt a pink warmth steal across her cheeks even as her heart gave a decided thump. For goodness' sake, what was wrong with her? It wasn't as if she'd never flirted before. Of course she had. She'd just never flirted with Sean. She covered the sense of panic bursting through her by tilting her head and sending him a mischievous look. "What makes you think I'm up to something?"

"Aren't you?"

She'd hoped to somehow even the playing field by unnerving him. It was the only way she could think of defending her heart from the onslaught of his unfeigned courtship. Perhaps she was overestimating her abilities. She'd hardly seen more than a fleeting flash of attraction in Sean's eyes. Still, it was too early to concede defeat yet. She swallowed. "So what if I am?"

"Nothing," he said as he casually stepped closer to her. "Just do me a favor, will you?"

She lifted her gaze to his questioningly.

He dipped his chin to capture her gaze more completely, then grinned slowly. "Don't stop."

Her breath stilled in her throat. Then again, there was the possibility that she was in *way* over her head.

Chapter Fifteen

Sean's fingers carefully followed the curving wood of the headboard for the bed he was making. As soon as he finished this, he would start on a set of new kitchen cabinets for Lorelei. The ones in his new place were hardly worth looking at. He was also planning another project. A wardrobe that he hoped might interest Mr. Johansen at the mercantile. It was a wild idea, but it might give him another source of income besides what the town allotted him.

He glanced up at the sound of the barn door swinging open and met Ellie's gaze with a welcoming grin. "Hey, I thought you were helping Kate with the mending."

She carefully settled on a chair he'd made for the kitchen. "We finished, so I thought I'd come out here to spend some time with my big brother. I can hand you tools or something."

Right. He shot her a wry glance. "What's on your mind?"

She froze in surprise for a moment before her green eyes began to sparkle and her lips pulled into an annoyed pout. "You think you're so smart. What if I had actually come out here to help you?"

He laughed. "Then you wouldn't have settled onto that chair like you were ready for a good, long chat." He grabbed a nearby chair and straddled it. "I'm ready for a break, so shoot. Just try not to make it fatal."

She rewarded his jest with a smile before she leaned back onto the chair and met his gaze seriously. "I was just wondering how things were progressing between you and Lorelei."

Glancing away, he shrugged. "I don't know, Ellie. I think we've made a lot of progress in some ways, but we're still at a stalemate."

"What kind of stalemate?" she asked gently.

He met her gaze. "As best I can figure, she doesn't want to love me because she doesn't want to get hurt."

"What about you?"

"What about me?" He rubbed his hands together to rid them of the dust from the wood. "I'm trying to love her—"

"Trying to love her?" she asked in amused derision. "No woman would want to hear a man say he is 'trying to love her.' What does that even mean? It sounds like you're telling her that despite her best efforts, you haven't been able to make yourself actually fall in love. That's just awful."

He sighed and crossed his arms over the back of the chair. "Well, Ellie. Would it sound any better if I said that there are lots of things that make her easy to love— but lots of reasons why it doesn't seem like a good idea? I've had a whole list of reasons why I shouldn't fall for Lorelei for years now. Even now that I want to move on and care for her, how can I just let go of that?"

A compassionate smile pulled at her lips. "Well, I think you should stop trying so hard to love Lorelei and just love her."

"That doesn't make sense."

"Sure, it does. I don't have to think about loving you, Sean. I just do." She glanced up to the rafters of the barn as if the words she sought were just out of reach. "It's like when you're trying to breathe. If you just sit there and think about it, you become so aware of it that it's harder to do. You just kind of have to surrender to it. You just have to trust that it will happen without you trying. Then it does. Don't worry about the reasons why you should or shouldn't fall in love with her. Just let it happen naturally."

He stared at his sister for a moment before letting out a short, low whistle. "That's a little too deep for me, Ellie."

She sent him an exasperated look. "I'm being serious."

"I guess you're right."

"I know I'm right," she said earnestly. "Sooner or later you'll figure it out."

He rolled his eyes. "So that's it? You just came out to impart wisdom, and now you're going to leave?"

She lifted her eyebrows. "As if you'd actually let me touch one of your projects anyway."

He grinned, knowing he usually didn't. "Get out of here."

She wiggled her fingers in a little wave, then flounced out the door. He shook his head. All right, so she made some good points. He'd made some progress so far by deciding to court Lorelei for real. She'd dropped the cool, unemotional act. The problem was she'd picked up another. Suddenly she was being warm and friendly. She'd even gone so far as to flirt with him more than once. He couldn't tell where the act ended and her real feelings and personality started. She wasn't playing fair anymore, but it didn't matter. He wasn't giving up on her or himself. Meanwhile, he'd do his best to ignore that whisper of fear—the one that told him it would be far easier to convince himself to love Lorelei than it would be to convince her to love him back.

Lorelei grasped her hat by its black ribbons and held it tightly in her hand as she stepped from the house onto the porch. She cast a careful glance to where her parents sat together on the porch swing. Her mother was the picture of peaceful contentment as she sat within the circle of Richard's arm. Her father lifted his book closer to his face to compensate for the rapidly fading light. Lorelei knew better than to attempt to sneak off, but she wanted to make her leaving seem as natural as possible. She breezed past them with a quick smile on her way to the porch stairs. "I'm going to meet Sean. I'll see you two later."

"Just a minute, Lorelei," her father's strong voice called out.

She tried not wince before turning around with an innocent expression. "Yes, Papa?"

"I just wanted to say that I'm proud of the way you're dealing with this courtship. You're handling it well. What's more, you actually seem to be giving Sean a chance. That shows great strength of character."

"Thank you. That means a lot. Our relationship has improved, but I'm still not interested in falling in love with him. That hasn't changed. He hurt me once before. I may have moved on, but I haven't forgotten."

Caroline sighed. "I hope one day you'll be able to, dear."

"Well, try to have a good time and enjoy yourself," Richard said. "If you come back after dark, make sure he walks you home."

"Yes, sir."

A few minutes later, she waited in the alleyway beside the bank for Silas to join her. She heard a sound in the alleyway and turned abruptly only to see Mr. Smithson making his way toward her. Her heart rate ratcheted up a notch from nervousness, but his grin was actually rather calming. "Well, what do you know? You're here."

"I told you I would come." A cool wind blew through the alley, sending chills across her skin.

"That you did." He stepped farther back into the alley. "Follow me around the corner. I've got a place all set up for this meeting."

Hoping Sean would be able to see her from wherever he was hiding, she followed him farther into the alley. Sure enough, as she turned the corner she saw a barrel set up against the back wall of The Barber & Bath House. A shadow opposite the barrel moved as she approached. Her steps slowed as she met the gaze of the stranger who straightened from where he'd been leaning against the wall. Silas stepped forward to shake the man's hand. "I didn't know you'd decided to come. How are you holding up, Calhoun?"

The man shook his head. "This waiting is bad business."

Mr. Smithson nodded. "Don't I know it? Calhoun,

this is Miss Wilkins. She's going to help us make our wait as strategic as possible."

Lorelei stepped forward with a polite nod. "Mr. Calhoun, how do you do?"

Mr. Calhoun looked her up and down, then met her gaze for a long moment before he grinned. "It looks like we've got a real live lady present. I haven't talked to one of them in a long time. It sure is a pleasure. Evening, Miss."

She hid her smile, then glanced at Mr. Smithson for direction. He stepped forward, then lifted her carefully onto the barrel before she had a chance to react. Pulling a small pad and pencil from his pocket, he glanced at them. "Let's get to work. Lorelei, you may as well know I'm giving you information as needed. I'm guessing you'll do the same with us. The first thing we need to know is the location of the safe."

"Do you have a layout of the bank building?"

Calhoun handed her a piece of paper.

She looked at it for a minute, then frowned. "Is this it? It's just a big square with little notches for the tellers."

Calhoun grimaced. "We couldn't get past the lobby."

"I'll draw a better one for you." She took a pencil from her reticule, then turned the paper over and found herself staring at a telegram. On my way STOP Do not do anything stupid STOP. She glanced up at the men. "Does anyone have a blank sheet of paper?"

Silas took a small notebook from his coat pocket and tore out a piece for her. She folded the telegram and held it under the closed notebook he gave her to write on. She carefully drew a diagram of the bank complete with the back offices and hallways. She drew an X near the back wall. "The safe is all the way back here."

"Who knows the combination to the safe and where do they sit?" Calhoun asked with a greedy gleam in his eyes.

"Only my father and the manager."

Silas smiled knowingly. "Yes, but your former fiancé has left town so there is no manager."

Lorelei rolled her eyes at him. "This town talks too much. I can't wait to get my ticket out of here. Speaking of which, how am I going to get my share of the money?"

"I'll stick around a few days after the robbery to keep from looking suspicious. I'll get you the money."

Calhoun edged toward her. "You two can figure that out later. Tell us about the safe, Miss Wilkins."

"The new manager is coming in from out of town. He'll be a good target because he'll be too new to care about anything other than not getting hurt. His office is right here. He won't get here for a week, though. Is that going to be a problem?"

"Not the way things are going with the boss," Calhoun said dryly.

She handed them the new layout and the notebook while nonchalantly tucking the pencil and the telegram in her reticule. "What else do you need to know?"

Sean couldn't help feeling a bit proud as he shifted into a more comfortable position to watch Lorelei act her way through the meeting. If he didn't know better, he might even believe Lorelei was really in league with the possible bank robbers for a percentage of the safe and a quick ticket out of Peppin. Trusting her to handle her part of the plan hadn't been a mistake after all.

Of course, they'd gone over her role in this a hundred times, leaving no chance of a mistake, but she'd taken his instruction with relative complacency and already given him a big break in the case.

Calhoun was involved just as he'd suspected. Just from listening to their conversation, he almost had enough to charge both Calhoun and Smithson with conspiracy to commit armed robbery. He'd been planning on that very thing until Calhoun uttered one word that changed everything. *Boss*—their boss wasn't here yet.

That proved his suspicion that these two men weren't acting alone but as part of a larger gang that had set its sight on Peppin. Smithson seemed the highest ranked of the two men, but when it came down to it they were muscle men. If he wanted to keep this from happening to Peppin again or to another less suspecting town, he needed to go after the top. That made things infinitely more complicated.

Twenty minutes went by. It felt like an eternity, especially once the mosquitoes discovered his hiding place and tried to give him away. Finally, Calhoun slunk down the alley toward the saloon, leaving Lorelei alone with Silas. The two continued talking for a few minutes until Silas set her on her feet and walked off. Lorelei seemed to wait until she was sure the fellow was gone before she smiled, lifted her skirts and took off half running, half skipping down the alley away from Sean and toward their meet-up point.

He grinned at her obvious excitement at a job well done. He rose to his feet to leave, then immediately sank back into his hiding place when Calhoun appeared again. The man scanned the alley and seemed to catch sight of Lorelei's fluttering hem as she disappeared around the corner. The rough drifter started following her at a leisurely pace.

Sean surged to his feet and rounded the corner back onto Main Street. He had to catch up with Lorelei before Calhoun did and before Lorelei could find him absent, start calling out for him and give them both away. He saw Silas had nearly reached the boardinghouse and hoped the man wouldn't turn around to see him running down the sidewalk or at least wouldn't draw the connection from him to Lorelei. There were only a few folks on the street he had to avoid so Sean was certain he was making better time than Lorelei and Calhoun.

He rounded the hotel and slipped back into the alleyway skirting around the tall wooden fence that sectioned off the expansive garden of the hotel. Lorelei ought to come along at any moment now with Calhoun not far behind her. Sean tugged at the thin fence door that led from the alleyway into the garden. It opened easily. Relief filled him. He'd told Mr. Martin a dozen times if he'd told him once not to leave this gate open to the alley. Thankfully he hadn't listened. It would provide the perfect getaway if he could manage it.

The lanterns in the garden cast golden shards through the slats in the fence to warm up the murky twilight as he stalked silently along the fence. He positioned himself so he'd be within easy reaching distance of Lorelei once she turned the corner. He heard her accelerated strides as they approached. He timed it perfectly so that as soon as she turned the corner, his arm went around her waist and his hand silenced her startled scream. Her eyes were wide with alarm. They widened more as recognition filtered through them.

"Quiet," he whispered, then ushered her through the

open gate mere feet away. He closed it and locked it behind them. She began to speak but he shook his head abruptly. He grabbed her arm to urge her to hide behind some tall bushes in case Calhoun got a notion to peer through the fence slats. They knelt together. Her eyes met his in confusion. A minute passed between them in silence until it was filled by quick uneven footsteps. They went past the fence gate then slowed to a stop. Calhoun rattled the locked gate, then a quiet curse punctuated the air. "Lost her. Fool woman."

Sean and Lorelei waited as the footsteps faded away. He helped Lorelei stand. She held on to his arm, tensely whispering, "He's gone?"

"I think so," he whispered back but wasted no time in paving a way through the bushes to distance them from the fence.

"Why was he following me?"

"Perhaps to see if you'd meet up with me." He jumped down the steep grade to the garden path, then reached up to lift her down.

She didn't seem to notice. Instead, she glanced at her reticule thoughtfully. "Maybe he wants his telegram back."

"You took his telegram?"

She met his gaze with a triumphant lift of her chin. "It has a rough layout of the bank on the back. I thought you might want it."

"Lorelei…" he began. Apprehension filled her eyes. He caught her waist, lifted her in the air and waited until she looked him in the eye before continuing. "You're a wonder."

Her eyes never left his once her feet made it safely to the ground. She seemed to be trying to determine his sincerity. She must have been satisfied for she tilted her head in acknowledgment of the compliment, and the most unguarded smile he'd seen yet slowly blossomed on her lips. She finally turned away to begin walking along the winding garden path. She came to an abrupt stop. "Where are we exactly?"

"The far reaches of the hotel garden." He placed a hand near her waist to guide her forward. "I think you're going the right way. It's easy to get lost in here, so stay close."

"Yes, I think that's the point," she murmured.

They ignored a few forks in the path that probably would have taken them deeper into the heart of the garden. Even so, it was a while before the path widened then abruptly opened into the main area. He glanced at Lorelei sharply when she gasped. "Look at this. Isn't it lovely?"

A long rectangular pond with a fountain stood in the center of the garden. Upon its raised stone border sat small glowing lamps. They dispelled the darkness just enough to cast golden light on everything without penetrating the feeling of seclusion. It was nice, but he was more interested in the evidence Lorelei had for him. "It sure is. How about letting me have a look at the telegram?"

She sent him a hopeless look as she dug it out of her reticule and handed it to him. "Sean, you have no sense of romance."

He carefully studied the telegram. *Wait. Did Lorelei use the word* romance *in the same sentence with my name?*

He tried to recall the comment he'd automatically dismissed as a quip. Yes, she'd used his name in the same sentence as *romance* if only to point out his lack of it. He took a second look at his setting and situation.

He couldn't go shooting himself in the foot when it came to courting Lorelei. He ought to take advantage of this situation, but how? It would probably be a good start to put the telegram away.

Lorelei had wandered toward the pond. She glanced back to find him watching and smiled as she hugged her arms to her waist. "Oh, I don't think I've ever felt so wonderful! Wait. Yes, I have. Right before you found me with the Brightlys and I almost drowned. Isn't it exhilarating?"

He chuckled. "Drowning?"

"No!" She laughed. "This. Preventing crime. Protecting the people you love. No wonder you're a sheriff. You get to do this every day."

He meandered closer. "It's mostly paperwork. This is really unusual for Peppin."

"Yes, but it's important paperwork."

He considered this thoughtfully for a minute, then shook his head. "No, usually it's pretty bor—"

She stepped forward to place a stilling hand on his chest. "Sean, do me a favor. Just let me have this moment. All right?"

"Whatever you say," he murmured. Her knees suddenly seemed to give out, and he had to catch her before she slipped to the ground. "Lorelei, what happened? Can you hear me?"

She closed her eyes as though dizzy. "I don't know. I must have had a moment of delusion. I thought you said, 'whatever you say.'"

"I did," he said, then froze when she opened one mischievous eye. He released her. "I should have let you fall."

She began laughing, then couldn't seem to stop. He

finally shook his head at her and headed for the hotel porch. She caught his arm to try to pull him to a stop. "I'm sorry, Sean. I'd just never heard those words come out of your mouth before."

He turned toward her but kept walking backward. "Your apology would be a lot more effective if you weren't laughing."

That finally quieted her laughter. She peered up at him as though trying to discern his facial expression in the low light. "You aren't really upset, are you?"

He tugged her closer, bringing them both to a stop. "What do you think?"

The moment lengthened after his quiet question. Her gaze searched his face, then his eyes. That close, he could watch as she raised her guard. "I think I'd better go home."

Disappointment filled him, but he nodded, realizing it wouldn't do well to push her too much, too fast. "I need to think about our next step anyway."

Her eyes widened. "Another step?"

"With the robbery," he explained when he realized she thought he was talking about their courtship. "I'd better walk you home."

"But Calhoun—"

"—is exactly why I want to walk home with you. You disappeared fifteen minutes ago. What you've done during that time is anyone's guess. If you show up with me, the only thing he'll know for sure is that we're courting. Everyone knows that." He offered her his arm. "Let's make it convincing."

"Lorelei, is that you?" her mother called from the kitchen a few minutes later.

"Yes, I'm home." She walked to the kitchen to watch her mother pour herself a cup of tea.

"Did you have a good time?"

"Yes."

"What did you do?"

Lorelei glanced up at her mother. The woman offered her a cup of tea by lifting an empty cup. Lorelei shook her head. "We went for a walk in the hotel gardens."

"That's sounds lovely."

"It was wonderful." At her mother's knowing look, Lorelei dropped the smile she hadn't known was on her face. She said good-night, then walked up the stairs to her room and closed the door behind her. She set her reticule down and pulled the hairpins from her hair. She had to admit—it had been exhilarating. She'd held her own with those outlaws and Sean had seen it all.

She wandered to the window and peered out at the stars as she brushed her hair. She had to admit, it wasn't until Sean lifted her in his arms, looked her in the eye and called her a "wonder" that all of those emotions were released. It wasn't because she was falling in love. No, she wouldn't let it be that. It was just that, after all those years of receiving his disapproval, she'd finally done something right in his eyes.

This afterglow was only the result of finally being able to create a friendship and a fledgling partnership with him. She was perfectly content with both and hoped that Sean would be, too. Surely he'd give up on this courtship once he realized he was wasting his time and efforts. Then maybe they'd be able to settle down into a warm friendship with no heartache involved. She just had to wait him out.

Chapter Sixteen

Sean lifted the open-style kitchen shelves into place and somehow managed to settle a nail into the pre-drilled hole in the back of the unit. He banged the nail through the hole into the wall, then frowned. Perhaps he should have waited for Nathan's help on this one. He was almost done fixing up the kitchen in his new place and hadn't wanted to wait. He was too far along to stop now, so he slid to the other side of the unit.

"This is not the same kitchen." The sound of Lorelei's voice made him nearly drop his hammer.

He peered over his shoulder at her. "What are you doing here? Never mind. Come over here and help me hold this shelf in place. It isn't heavy."

She set her reticule on the new kitchen table to join him near the stove. "Where did all this furniture come from?"

"I made it." With his newly freed hand, he was able to set the nails and hammer them through the wall in just a few seconds.

Lorelei hesitantly let the shelf unit go. Once it stayed in place, she turned to him in confusion. "Wait. You made the furniture? All of it? Even that cupboard over there?"

He glanced at the large piece of furniture standing by the window. "Is something wrong with the cupboard?"

She walked over to run her fingers over it. "Nothing is wrong with it. That's my point. I knew you whittled and you've talked about designing furniture, but I didn't realize you were such an accomplished carpenter."

He shrugged. "I'm not a carpenter. I just like to make furniture now and then. It's a hobby."

She shook her head in awe. "I wish I had a hobby like that."

"You do." He crossed his arms. "You're a pianist. You're dedicated to it. It's the one thing that's held your interest for years. You should focus on it and stop trying to force yourself to do other things you're only half-interested in."

"Maybe, but I like doing new things." She tried out one of the kitchen chairs. "I don't want to interrupt your carpentry. Ellie asked me to show her around. I'm sure she won't be long."

"It's no interruption. I was just doing this while I waited for Ellie." He smiled as he repeated Lorelei's exact words. "'She wanted me to show her around.'"

"What?" she breathed in confusion.

"Ellie has been overly confident in her skills as a matchmaker since she was about ten years old. If this is one of her latest escapades, she might not show up at all."

"I don't believe it. She sounded like she really wanted to see the house. I still think she's just running late."

"If you say so," he said doubtfully. Fifteen minutes later, with no sign of Ellie, they both thought it prudent to give up. "No use wasting a trip out here. I can at least show you the rest of the property. Let's walk."

Lorelei kept up with Sean's steady pace as they explored the different areas of the farm from the barn and chicken coop to the empty fields and pastures for the animals. He told her of his plans for the future of the farm. She listened intently and even smiled now and again when he was particularly enthusiastic about something. He let out a sigh of relief. Her reaction to the farm was much better than it had been the first time. Perhaps she was beginning to see the value in the land that he did. Finally, he announced, "There's only one more thing I want to show you. It's on the way back."

If she didn't fall in love with the farm after this, there would be no hope for her. The trees began to thin out until they stepped into a clearing. One large oak tree stood by itself. The trunk had to be more than seven feet in diameter. Three thick offshoots rose from the trunk high into the air while one seemed to mosey out sideways for at least ten feet before it also contributed to the maze of large branches hovering above the ground. He glanced at Lorelei when he heard her gasp.

"It's so beautiful! I've never seen anything like it." She shook her head in wonder.

Sean followed her gaze to the large wooden swing attached to the branch that hovered over the ground. He gently bumped her arm with his. "Want to try it out?"

"Of course I want to try it out." She tugged at his arm, pulling him forward with her.

"Are you ready?" he asked a moment later.

She caught the ropes on either side of the seat. "Ready."

His hands settled on the ropes below hers as he pulled

the swing back, then let it go. She swung higher each time he pushed her while the wind teased and pulled at her hair, trying to work it free from the pins. The swing was starting to get pretty high off the ground. It was now or never.

"Slide to one side," Sean warned.

Lorelei quickly did as he directed then gasped as he took hold of the ropes and lifted himself onto the seat beside her. He balanced on the swing in a hunched position for a moment before he managed to lift himself into the correct position. The swing tottered along its usual path until Sean pumped his legs enough to straighten it out. Finally, he looked at her with a grin. She stared back at him in amused exasperation. "That could have ended badly. You know that, right?"

He laughed. "No, I had it all planned out. I knew it would work."

Her dark blue eyes narrowed thoughtfully. "Do you realize you do that constantly?"

His confused look must have told her that he had no idea what she was talking about.

"You plan constantly," she said. "Every time we come upon a situation that holds the least bit of uncertainty you rush in to save the day. You plan the problem away in a matter of minutes. Then you make sure every little part of the plan is carried out successfully."

"I guess I do, don't I?" He flashed a grin. "You're welcome."

She rolled her eyes. "I'm not thanking you, Sean. I'm asking you why you do it."

He felt tension begin to build in his shoulders. He tried to shrug it away. "I don't know. I guess I'm trying to control everything so it will turn out all right."

"That explains a lot."

"Like what exactly?"

She shifted in her seat to face him a bit more directly. "It explains why you bought this house without even asking my opinion. I guess it's also why you told me you were going to court me regardless of how I felt about it. And—"

"I understand."

She lifted her brow and stared back at him inquiringly. "So you realize that God is the only one who could possibly control everything in your life? That the only way any of your plans will come out right is if you surrender them to Him?"

He definitely didn't want to talk about this. What was going on with everyone lately? Was he doing such a bad job of managing his life that everyone felt he needed to listen to their advice? He was glad that Lorelei wanted to talk about spiritual things. It signified a deepening in their relationship. But, why this? Why now, when he was finally getting things in hand? He cleared his throat. "That's a lot to take in."

She left it at that to glance up at the sky thoughtfully. He should probably have done the same, but he noticed a long hairpin working its way loose from her fashionable chignon. "Your pin is falling out."

She found it but couldn't seem to fix it with only one hand free, so he reached over to do it for her. He barely touched the silly thing before it wobbled and fell from her hair. Lorelei gasped, then turned her head toward him abruptly, sending her long brown curls spilling over her shoulders. "Thank you so much for helping."

"Anytime." He grinned as the wind took complete control of her hair, tossing it across her face and teasing his cheek. At its fleeting touch, the tension immediately fled. He caught his breath. *How is that possible?*

He brushed her hair out of her face, then allowed his hand to stray into her curls. They were soft and full and like nothing he'd ever felt before. He met her wide blue eyes. Suddenly, he recognized the girl he'd known at eighteen when past tension seemed easily buried and new possibilities were at hand. He saw the future they could have had if a misunderstanding and childish pride hadn't stood in the way. He saw the woman she was now. The woman he was beginning to care for. It scared him, and he was tempted to bring the past between them again but he didn't want to. He wanted for one day, one moment to let his guard down enough to see her as she really was—the woman he'd always longed for.

It was in that moment that he knew he was going to do something crazy, but he didn't try to stop himself. He kissed her. He kissed her gently, testing, half expecting her to send him flying off the swing for his gall. She would have had every right to do so. For that reason, he ended it nearly as quickly as it began.

Her dark lashes swept down to hide her stormy blue eyes. They were both quiet for a long moment as the swing settled into nothing more than a gentle sway. Finally, she glanced up at him again. The anger in her eyes told him he was in for a sudden squall.

Lorelei set her boots on the ground to bring the swing to an abrupt halt and pinned Sean with a glare. "I don't want to be just another one of your plans, Sean O'Brien."

He had the nerve to look confused. "What are you talking about?"

"If you made our courtship real just so you can go through the motions and check things off your list, you can just stop this silliness right now." She twisted her hair back into its normal style and used the only remaining pin in her curls to keep it in place. She stood to look around for her missing hairpins. "At least when I'm acting for the town, you still know exactly where you stand with me. Sean, the only person you're really fooling now is you."

"You don't know what you're talking about," he growled as he stood to help her look in the grass.

"Do you really think if you just plan it out and follow all of the steps, you can schedule yourself into loving me?" She took the hairpin he offered her and shifted it into place. "Buy a house. Check. First outing as a couple. Check. First kiss. Check. Check. Check. I refuse to add to that checklist you have in your head."

"Will you hush for half a minute?" He caught her arms and pulled her toward him. "I don't have a checklist, but I will admit that I planned to court you. Why is that wrong? I told you I would."

She braced her hand against his chest to push herself away, but he wouldn't release her. She forced herself to ignore the warmth that spread across her hand as it flexed against his chest. "It's wrong because you aren't telling the whole truth."

His gaze was unflinching. "What truth am I not telling you?"

Why wouldn't he just let her go? She shook her head. "The truth is you don't want to court me any more than you wanted to kiss me."

He stared at her in what seemed to be amazement. "How could you possibly think that?"

"A woman can tell when a man wants to kiss her and when he doesn't."

"Apparently not."

"Just admit it, Sean. That kiss was just like you—controlled and lacking any true emotion."

His jaw tightened, though his stare held disbelief. "Did you ever think I was just trying to be a gentleman?"

"If you were a gentleman, you wouldn't have tried to steal a kiss in the first place," she reasoned passionately. He seemed to lack the ability to respond to her well-argued logic. He would cave any second now. He'd give in and tell the truth, then she'd know she couldn't trust him with her heart.

She'd be able to weed out every little seed of hope that had taken root inside of her. She would get back to the peaceful life she'd led before he'd stormed in attempting to take control of her affections. A slight feeling of unease shifted through her. She almost questioned if that would be the best choice. She pushed the feeling away and tried again to make him admit the truth. "I could have seemed more sincere than that just by acting."

He stared at her in deep contemplation for a moment. She could feel her victory coming. His jaw flexed again, then he lifted a brow and said exactly what she would never have expected him to say. "Prove it."

She stared at him. "What?"

"I said prove it." He released her but didn't step away. "Prove that you can give me a more genuine kiss by acting than I was able to give you a minute ago when I wasn't acting."

When he says it like that it sounds crazy, she admitted to herself as she tried to think. She thought about calling on the Lord for help, but she'd gotten herself into this mess. She had a funny feeling that He wouldn't get her out of it. In fact, she had an uncanny sense that He was as interested in seeing how this might play out as Sean seemed to be.

Drat. What had she been thinking? A small flicker of a fire seemed to light his eyes with gold as he stared back at her, daring her to continue. She immediately began to doubt herself. After all, pretending to rob a bank was nothing like pretending to kiss somebody. She really didn't even have that much experience to draw from. She couldn't remember the last time Lawson had kissed her. Their relationship hadn't had much of a physical aspect to it. It hadn't had much of anything else, either.

Sean's arms slipped around her waist. Suddenly, she realized this wasn't a game because Sean wasn't playing. He was serious—really serious. She froze. "I get where this is going. I know what you're trying to prove, but I'm pretty sure that it won't work."

"I think you're just afraid it will."

Since when did he know her well enough to read her thoughts? Since now, apparently. She could make this easier on herself by stepping away from him. Of course, she didn't.

"It's time you realized something, Lorelei Wilkins." He pulled her slightly closer. "I've never hated you. I don't dislike you. I'm sorry that we've wasted so much time at each other's throats. I think it's the only way we knew how to fight against this."

"Fight against what?" she whispered.

"These feelings that have always been there and

never seem to go away. I, for one, am tired of fighting against them and you. I want to see where this goes."

She stared into his sincere green eyes, but she couldn't quite believe the words he was saying. His face blurred with her tears, and she tried to blink them away. It didn't do any good. He saw her tears and wrapped his arms around her until she surrendered to his embrace by hesitantly resting her forehead on his chest. He shook his head. "I'm so sorry we've hurt each other. I do care about you, and I'm trying to show it, as unsophisticated as I may be at it."

"Sean," she breathed for lack of anything better to say. She finally glanced up to meet his gaze. "Do you really mean it—about being sorry?"

He nodded solemnly.

"Thank you." Impulsively, she rose on her tiptoes to kiss him gently.

He stared down at her in surprise. Slowly, a smile tipped his lips, and he shook his head. "We just can't get our timing right on this. Are you ready?"

"Yes." Yet, even as she spoke, his head dropped toward hers. His lips hovered over hers for an achingly eternal second before they captured hers. She could feel the sun shining down on those infernal seeds of hope inside of her, and at the moment she didn't care a whit.

He could have gone on kissing Lorelei all day, but somehow he managed to set her away from him. Only the self-control gifted to him by the Holy Spirit kept him from hauling her into his arms and doing it all over again when he caught sight of Lorelei's dazed expression. His voice came out at least half an octave lower than it normally was. "Were you acting?"

"No."

He set her away from him. "In that case, we'd better not make a habit of that just yet."

She blushed. He winked at her, then caught her hand in his to lead her through the woods back toward the house. She dragged a bit behind him. He glanced back but found her gaze already on him. He sent her an inquiring look, and she glanced away.

"You're going to be incorrigible after this. I can already tell," she muttered.

He grinned as they stepped out of the woods and walked to the front of the house. He felt like singing, but he knew better than to try. They still had a long way to go, but they'd definitely made progress. He paused at the sight of Ellie waiting for them on the porch steps. She bounced up to her feet with a smile. "I'm sorry I'm so late. Kate has been feeling poorly and everything that could delay me did. I've been waiting here about fifteen minutes. I figured you two would make it back eventually."

Ellie paused to take a breath. When no one responded, she gazed at them curiously. Her eyes widened at the sight of their joined hands. Lorelei seemed to notice at the same time because she abruptly jerked her hand from his and tucked it into her skirt pocket. Ellie tilted her head thoughtfully. A curious smile curved her lips as she sent him a questioning look. He shrugged.

"Well," she said briskly before a mischievous smile graced her lips. "It looks like you two have been having a lot of fun without me."

Chapter Seventeen

"'This is what I command you: that you love one another.'"

Lorelei sighed at the message she couldn't seem to get away from.

Reverend Sparks closed his Bible and set it on the pulpit. He looked at the congregation. "This is probably going to be the hardest thing I've had to do in my ministry."

Lorelei watched in confusion as Reverend Sparks looked at his wife who sat in the front row. The woman rose to her feet and went to stand by his side. He turned to face the congregation again. He straightened his shoulders. "Today I'd like to announce that I am stepping down as the reverend of this church."

A gasp rang through the church, leaving only silence in its wake.

"I'm still going to live in Peppin. I will still be involved in this church. I even promise to preach the occasional sermon. However, the time for me to shepherd this flock is over. God has made that abundantly clear to me and to my wife."

He smiled peacefully. "In fact, just as I was seriously thinking of stepping down, I received a letter out of the nowhere from someone whom I would eventually regard as a son. Someone whom I am fully convinced is being called to this town."

Lorelei shifted in her seat along with half of the congregation who now craned their necks to watch the proceedings.

"I received the first letter a few weeks ago. We've been corresponding regularly since then. I have gotten to know this man and his family through the letters. He is a traveling preacher who has been looking for a place to settle down with his wife and five children."

Lorelei stopped breathing. Her eyes narrowed. *Impossible.* Lorelei frowned and shot a glance over her shoulder to Sean. He met her gaze to share a look of suspicion. Reverend Sparks's voice drew her gaze back to him.

"He heard about our little town and felt compelled to write to the church to find out if there were any open positions on staff. I told him there might be a position opening up. The rest, as they say, is history." He grinned. "James Brightly and his family will arrive in Peppin in two weeks."

"Oh," she breathed in alarm. Thankfully no one noticed because everyone started talking at once. *This is not good. If they mention anything about what happened with Miss Elmira—even accidentally—everything Sean and I have been doing will have been for nothing.*

"I hope to make the transition a very smooth one," she heard Reverend Sparks say, but the rest of his words faded into mumbles.

The congregation began dispersing, but Lorelei

didn't move. She glanced up to find her mother hovering over her. "Are you all right, Lorelei? You look so pale."

She looked from her mother's concerned face to her father's. They didn't know. They didn't recognize the name, and she didn't have the strength to tell them. She shook her head. "I'm fine."

The words weren't true, but they needed to be. This was not the time to cause a scene. *Sean. Where is Sean?* She turned in search of him just as he appeared at her side. He looked just as bewildered as she felt. She saw his gaze slip to her parents and the moment he realized they didn't know that a crisis could be at hand. He slid into the pew next to her. "Mr. and Mrs. Wilkins, would you mind if I had a moment alone with Lorelei?"

Richard frowned. "I don't know. She looks like she had a fainting spell. She needs to go home."

She sent him a pleading look. "Please, Papa. I need to talk to him. He'll take care of me."

She watched indecision war across his features before he nodded. "Come on, Caroline."

Once her parents left, they had the sanctuary to themselves. Sean's arm stretched across the back of the pew, and she turned toward him. She finally felt the color begin to return to her cheeks. "I can't believe it."

"We should have told them we hated this place."

She let out a nervous laugh. She glanced up at him as amusement overcame her dread. "We should have told them how muddy the sidewalks get. How you can hear the noise from the saloon three blocks away because everything else is so quiet. How frightening it is to hear the train whistle when you least expect it."

His shook his head. "Lorelei Wilkins, we have a major problem on our hands. What are we going to do?"

"You're the one who always has the plans."

He quirked a smile at her. "I thought you hated my plans."

He coaxed an answering smile from her as she widened her eyes innocently. "Oh, no. I love your plans. They are always extremely well thought-out."

"Sure you do."

She looked him over with a measuring glance. "Are you trying to tell me that you don't have a plan?"

He shook his head slowly. "Don't tempt me. I'm trying to reform."

She sent him an unappreciative look.

"Hey, you should be proud that you made your point so well."

"I don't see how it's doing me any good."

"Where's your faith? 'None of your plans will turn out right if you don't surrender them to God,'" he parroted.

"Do you really believe that now?"

His gaze turned serious. "I don't know. I'm trying."

"Maybe our first step is to pray."

"We can do that." He caught her hand in his. They both bowed their heads as Sean began to pray. He asked God to lead them and give them wisdom in how to respond to this new challenge. Lorelei was feeling much calmer by the end of the prayer. Her mind spun with possible answers to their problem. "We should write the Brightlys a letter."

Sean pulled her to her feet but didn't move out of the aisle. He seemed to be assessing her steadiness. "What would we say?"

"We could explain everything," she said as he guided her out to the aisle and they walked toward the exit. "We can tell them that we're planning to get married. We could ask them to keep what happened to themselves."

"It might be worth a shot." He stayed close to her as they walked through the small foyer.

She glanced over her shoulder at him. "I'm not going to collapse."

He ignored her as he opened the door for her to step outside. She surveyed the milling groups of people who were gathered around either the Reverend or his wife. She gasped. Sean was instantly beside her with his hand supportively catching her arm. She turned to meet his gaze. "Forget the Brightlys. What if they told the Sparkses?"

"I'd better talk to the reverend."

"I'd better talk to his wife."

They split apart, and Lorelei managed to get close enough to Mrs. Sparks's conversation to hear what they were talking about.

"I hate to see you two step down," Mrs. Williams said. "There's a time for everything, though."

"Yes, I'm actually very pleased about it. This move has been coming for a long time. I'm especially glad that such a nice family will be taking our place."

Mrs. Stone smiled as she resettled her baby on her hip. "It's just amazing that he happened to write you at just the right time."

"It looks like Peppin is the talk of Texas," Mrs. Bradley said. "I wonder who might have told them about us."

Mrs. Sparks's gaze connected with Lorelei's. "I think we have Lorelei to thank for that."

Lorelei glanced around at the large group of women who now focused entirely on her. The question lingered in the air so loudly she wondered why someone didn't just say it. "I met the Brightlys when I ran away."

Mrs. Greene leaned forward as though she couldn't help herself despite their agreement. "Where did you have your sights set on going again?"

Her smile felt rather stiff, but she offered it anyway. "California. I have a great-aunt who lives there."

Mrs. Lettie touched her arm. "Well, what is your take on our new pastor?"

Grateful for the well-timed subject change, she met the kind eyes of the woman who had almost been her mother-in-law to concede, "He and his wife and children are wonderful."

Mrs. Lettie nodded as if that settled it. "The family should be a good addition to our town."

Lorelei stayed in the circle a few more minutes until she was satisfied that the conversation had completely moved on. She stepped away and began looking for her parents. Her mother waved at her. She wound her way through the crowd toward them.

"Miss Wilkins."

She turned to see Silas at her side. "Silas, I'm sorry but I really can't talk right now."

"When?"

She tried to think quickly. "Tomorrow at one. I'll be dropping a letter off at the post office at that time. You can meet me then."

He nodded, then slipped away.

A moment later, she met her parents. They insisted on escorting her right home, and she let them. She needed to talk to them privately anyway. It would be unfair of her to keep this from them. Yes, she'd tell them, then write one very important letter.

* * *

Lorelei held the sealed envelope tightly in her hand as she stepped onto the wooden sidewalk that ran alongside the boardinghouse. Two men stood on the sidewalk just ahead of her. One of them noticed her coming and made the others move out of the way for her. "Good afternoon, miss."

She nodded politely and tried to ignore their stares as she passed. She stiffened as one of them let out a low whistle. They made no attempt to hide their conversation from her. "I've never seen so many pretty women in one place."

"It makes me glad we'll be here a few days," the other responded.

She tried to step out onto the street, but a wagon abruptly turned in front of her so she had to step back.

"What do you think my chances are with that one?"

Lorelei dashed a glance toward them. They were still watching her. She gave them a cold stare, then lifted her chin. "Nonexistent, and I'll thank you to keep your comments to yourself."

That left them dumbfounded enough to allow her to escape across the street before their hoots of laughter echoed behind her. She stepped onto the sidewalk, then looked up to meet Silas's brown eyes. He took her arm, then speared the men on the other side of the street with a quelling glare. "Did they say something uncouth?"

"No, they were just overly outgoing," she said as she pulled her arm from his grasp. "I hope they aren't staying at Bradleys'. I would assume Mr. Bradley would be more cautious than that with his daughters working there."

"They aren't staying at the boardinghouse. They're

just a couple of fools making a nuisance of themselves," he said with a bit of aggravation, then smiled politely. "I see you have a letter to mail. I was heading in that direction myself. Mind if I join you?"

"Not at all," she said as they walked. When he didn't immediately begin a conversation, she figured he must think they'd be too easily overheard on the bustling sidewalk. "How is Amy?"

His face seemed to turn pensive. "She's well."

"Are you two still spending time together?"

He nodded but wouldn't meet her gaze.

She lowered her voice, so only he could hear her. "You're going to break her heart."

He pinned her with a piercing gaze. "What about you and your sheriff? I hear you two seem to be getting pretty serious. How do you feel about breaking his heart?"

"Not nearly as bad as you feel about breaking Amy's," she guessed.

The color heightened in his face. "Leave it alone, Lorelei. We need to focus on getting the job done."

"Fine," she said as they passed the seamstress's shop. "Has that new manager come in yet?"

"He's here."

"Good. I need you to meet me Thursday at two o'clock outside of the courthouse. We'll go over a few last-minute things, and I'll let you know when we'll be ready to move." He tipped his hat and was gone almost as quickly he appeared.

He has to be one of the strangest people I know, she thought to herself as she stood behind the only other person in line at the post office. *He sure doesn't seem like a hardened criminal. Maybe he's new to the job. He needs to get rid of some of that politeness if he wants to make it as a bank robber. He seemed truly upset that those men were bothering me. I would believe those men were criminals before I would believe Silas was.*

This was not the time to worry about Silas she realized as she stared at the letter in her hand. She bowed her head and prayed, her lips barely moving along with her entreaty. *Please, God. Let the Brightlys want to help us by keeping quiet about the whole thing for now. Please—*

"Miss Wilkins, did you want to mail something?" the young man behind the counter asked.

She glanced up to see she was now the only one in line so she stepped up to the counter. "Yes, I'm sorry. I was thinking about something. How fast do you think this will get to where it needs to go?"

He took the letter and stared thoughtfully at the address. "Reverend Sparks usually hears back from this fellow in a couple of days."

"Am I sending it to the right address, then?" She handed him the money for postage.

"Yes, ma'am." He postmarked it and placed it into the mailbag behind him. "Just check back in a few days."

"Thank you." With a parting smile, she turned away breathing quietly, "Your will be done."

"Thanks, Maddie," Sean said as Maddie slid the cup of lemonade he'd requested onto the table.

"Sure thing." She straightened, then paused to peer out the window. "Why didn't you tell me Lorelei was coming?"

"She isn't."

"Sure, she is. She's right there. Aren't you going to have lunch with her?"

He followed her gaze to see Lorelei crossing the street toward the café. "I wasn't planning on it."

Maddie placed a hand on her slim hip. "Well, here's your chance. Go get her. Tell her I'll have a slice of my pecan pie waiting. That girl hasn't been in here in ages."

"Yes, ma'am," he agreed as he slipped past Maddie.

Lorelei had just passed the door by the time he made it out. She was only a few feet away so he called out, "Hey, beautiful! Where are you going?"

She slowly turned around. Then, narrowing her eyes, she tilted her head at him. "I assume that means you want me to stop and talk to you."

He grinned. "Have you eaten yet?"

"No."

"Would you like to have lunch with me?"

"No."

"Lorelei."

Her dark blue eyes filled with mirth. A smile tugged at her lips, and she shook her head as she approached him. "You realize that half the people in the café have their faces pressed against the glass, don't you?"

He frowned. "What happened to the other half?"

"They already had front-row seats."

"Have lunch with me," he repeated.

She looked over his shoulder toward the café thoughtfully. "Why?"

"You're here. You're hungry. I'm here. I'm hungry. It seems like a good idea."

Her gaze lifted to meet his. "Silas said that people think we're getting serious about each other."

"That's good," he said, feeling his stomach rumble

in protest of the delay. Then his eyes narrowed, and he looked at Lorelei closely. "When did he say that?"

She tugged on his arm and stepped past him. "Let's eat."

"Lorelei," he protested, but she had already walked into the café.

Her gaze met his, then danced away as Maddie showed her to his table. Maddie took Lorelei's drink order but didn't leave to fill it immediately. Instead, the woman grinned. "That was quite a hello you received."

Sean looked at Maddie in amazement. Now, how had she heard that? Perhaps the door hadn't closed behind him before he'd said it. Lorelei laughed. "I'm getting used to it. That wasn't the first time I was hallooed today."

He frowned. "It wasn't?"

She shook her head. "I think it was the third."

"Oh, my." Maddie laughed. "Sean, it looks like you may have some competition."

"Let me at them," he growled and more people in the café than just Maddie laughed.

He shook his head. That was one of the perils of living in a small town where everyone was so interconnected. There wasn't enough room to mind your own business, so you often ended up minding others'. No wonder Mr. Wilkins had been so adamant that he marry Lorelei.

"Now, what can I get you two to eat?"

They both ordered the special. After Lorelei received her drink, they were left alone for a while. Lorelei glanced up at him with a smile. "Do you know what I did today?"

Everyone seemed to go back to their own meals, but

he leaned forward and lowered his voice slightly just to be safe. "You mean besides meeting Silas Smithson without so much as a word to me?"

She shook her head. "No, besides that."

"I have no idea."

"I mailed the letter to the Brightlys," she said softly. "I feel optimistic about it. After all, they're good people. They shouldn't mind helping us, should they?"

"I guess we'll find out soon enough."

She nodded. "The postmaster said it should only be a few days until I hear back."

They both stopped talking as Maddie made her way toward them with their food. After they said grace, Sean gave Lorelei a few minutes of uninterrupted eating before he pinned her with the question she should have answered long ago. "So why didn't you tell me you were meeting with him?"

She glanced up at him, then back at her food. "We arranged it yesterday at church. I told him I couldn't talk to him then, so he asked to meet me today. My parents wanted me to leave right after that, so I didn't have time to tell you."

He nodded. "I see why you didn't tell me then. Why didn't you tell me earlier today?"

She lowered her fork, admitting, "I was working on the letter but I did follow your advice. We met in a public place in the daytime just like you said we should."

"I'm glad to hear it, but next time you have to let me know so I can at least be in the general area. I mean it, Lorelei. If something happens, I need to be able to help you."

"I'm meeting him Thursday at two o'clock in front of the courthouse. He wants to go over some final details. You are more than welcome to be in the general area then."

"Thursday at two." He chewed thoughtfully for a moment. "What happens at the bank around that time?"

She glanced up curiously. "Nothing. It's usually pretty quiet."

"That's what I thought."

"You mean?"

"I mean I have a lot to do."

"*We* have a lot to do."

"That, too." He needed to go over Lorelei's role in this, but as soon as they finished, he'd head over to the courthouse and talk to the judge about swearing in as many temporary deputies as he could find. He'd put Jeff on watch at the train station. Most important, he also needed to prepare Mr. Wilkins and the new manager now that the threat seemed imminent.

His whole plan hinged on being prepared in advance. That's why Lorelei's information was so valuable. He wanted to have the tellers and the deputies lying in wait for the gang so they'd have the benefit of surprise, not the other way around. He was pretty sure he'd be able to find a lot of eager volunteer deputies. This was Peppin, after all. They wouldn't go down without a fight because they plain refused to go down at all.

Lorelei did her level best to pay attention to the book she was pretending to read and not try to scan the courtyard for Sean. He'd told her he would be in the vicinity but refused to tell her where. She sighed. *Very comforting, Sean.*

She'd been instructed to act as though she was totally oblivious to the fact the robbery might actually be happening today. She could act that way, but just the possibility of the holdup becoming a reality had her body strumming with nervousness. The waiting wasn't helping, either. *Where in the world is Silas, anyway? I've been waiting at least ten minutes already.*

She made it through the next few pages of her book before she realized someone was approaching. Silas strolled toward her bench as if he didn't have a care in the world. She closed her book and offered him a smile. "Hello, Silas."

He carefully returned her smile. "Lorelei, it's a beautiful day for a walk. Join me."

"Certainly." She slipped her arm into his, then glanced at him curiously when he pinned it to his side. She surveyed his expression carefully. He seemed uncharacteristically lacking in emotion. "Is something wrong?"

He shook his head. "No. Everything is going according to schedule."

She allowed him to continue to lead her along the sidewalk away from the center of town. "Do you have some information you want to share with me then? Perhaps a final date so that I can be ready?"

He watched her for a long moment. A strange mix of emotions settled in his eyes. They were filled with pity, amusement and a bit of derision if she wasn't mistaken. "No, I'm afraid not."

"I don't understand. Why did you insist on meeting me today?" The sidewalk abruptly ended, causing her to stumble.

Silas caught her arms in his hands until she regained her footing, then pinned her with his stare. "You're going to cooperate, aren't you, Lorelei?"

Her eyes widened. "Yes, of course. I told you I would."

He seemed much more like the Silas she knew when he smiled his approval. "Good. Follow me."

She had little choice since he kept his grasp firmly on her arm and pulled her behind the courthouse. The rail yard stretched behind a big iron fence to the right. The sight of the large bay stallion tethered to the fence caught her attention. Waves of dread slowly filtered through her stomach as Silas made a beeline toward it. "Get on the horse, Lorelei."

She swallowed nervously. "Why?"

His voice was calm. His eyes were deadly. "If you don't, I'm going to have to kill you."

"You wouldn't—" She bit her lip as she suddenly found herself staring down the barrel of his gun. Her heart pounded in her chest. She daringly lifted one eyebrow and shrugged nonchalantly. "No need to be nasty about it. Put that thing away and give me a boost."

He put his gun away, but not before she saw a flicker of respect in his eyes. She waited until he met her gaze again. "It's happening today, isn't it?"

He gave her a hard stare, then cupped his hands for her boot. "We don't have time for this. Drape your skirt across the saddle horn and sit sidesaddle."

She did as he said. He untethered the horse and swung up behind her before turning the horse abruptly. As they rode out of town, Lorelei didn't dare look behind her to see if Sean might be following. Instead, she closed her eyes. *Lord, I've been trying to do the right thing. Please, protect me and the rest of the town. Show me how I can stop this before someone gets hurt.*

* * *

Sean waited until he felt he had a good sense of the direction Lorelei and Silas Smithson were heading before he cut through the alleyway toward the livery. Joshua Stone and Jeff Bridger looked up questioningly as Sean stepped out of the alley into the doorway of the livery. Sean gave them an abrupt nod. "Today is the day just like we thought."

"Your mount is saddled and waiting like you asked," Mr. Stone said.

"Thank you. Jeff, gather the others and get into position. Mr. Stone, notify Mr. Wilkins. Make sure everyone is armed and ready."

Jeff frowned. "Where are you going?"

He swung onto his mount, then glanced down at the two men he knew he could count on to carry on without him. "They took Lorelei. I'm going to get her back."

As he rode out of town, he muttered a prayer. "All right, Lord, I know I haven't been the best at asking for help or advice. I reckon You must not hate my plans entirely since You let me think of them, but this one is too important for me to do by myself. The town needs You, Lorelei needs You and I need You to see to it that this plan goes off without a hitch. I'm surrendering this to You, Lord. Please, protect us all."

Chapter Eighteen

The ride was shorter than she expected. Silas reined in his horse about a quarter mile outside of town. They stopped in front of a small railroad supply shed that had obviously been built and abandoned five years ago when the railroad swept through town. She eyed the building dubiously. Silas helped her dismount before grabbing her arm in that tight grip of his and forcing her inside the shed.

Despite the bright sunlight outside, the inside of the small building was dim. The only square of sunlight in the room burst through a busted window along the back wall. Once her eyes adjusted, she met Calhoun's gaze with a smile she didn't feel. "It looks like your waiting is over, Mr. Calhoun."

He grunted around the pipe in his mouth and said nothing else at first. He just continued to watch her. It was only when she glanced away that he spoke to Silas in that rough voice of his. "The others should be here any minute."

"What others? I thought you were just waiting for your boss."

Mr. Calhoun grinned slowly. "The boss and rest of the gang, Missy."

"The rest of the gang," she echoed, wondering how many that meant. She hoped Sean was prepared for more than they'd planned. He'd refused to tell her anything about his role and what he'd done to prepare for it, so that if questioned, she could honestly say she didn't know.

Silas moved past her to stand by the window. The air suddenly filled with the sound of horse hooves and strange wild yips. Mr. Calhoun stood from where he sat on an old crate and walked toward the door muttering, "Bunch o' wild ne'er-do-wells, the lot of them."

He stood outlined in the door for a long minute while the whoops and yelps grew louder. Finally, he yelled, "All right, all right. We know you're here. Shut your traps."

The sounds only increased in volume until the first man burst through the door. She immediately recognized him as one of the men who'd pestered her on the way to mail the letter to the Brightlys. "Calhoun, you old coot, you're cranky as always, I see. Remind me why the boss keeps you around."

"Because I've got more sense than the rest of y'all put together," he said wryly, then glanced behind him. "Except for maybe Smithson here."

She knew the instant the younger man caught sight of her because he gave a slow whistle. "Who's that?"

Another man burst into the shed. He took one look at Lorelei and stopped short. A lecherous grin tipped his mouth, and he elbowed the other man. "Lookee there. You see what I see, Jake?"

Jake looked her over slowly. "Looks like a woman to me, Owen."

She straightened her shoulders and sent them a haughty glare meant to put them in their place. "That's funny. From here it looks like two fools."

Jake grinned. "You can call me whatever you want, honey, as long as I get to look at you."

Owen pinned her with his lazy smile as he sank onto a nearby crate. "Look all you want. Just don't touch her. I claimed that little gal when I saw her on the sidewalk. Ain't that right, Miss Wilkins?"

She ignored him and turned toward Silas, who was still staring out the window. "It looks like there's a lot you didn't tell me, Silas."

Calhoun hooted. "Now that's the truth."

She lifted her brows inquiringly. "Are there any other surprises, gentlemen?"

Silas suddenly turned to face her. His eyes were dark, hard and unflinching. His mocking smile sent chills through her body. "You might be surprised to know that I didn't believe your little act for a moment. I will congratulate you on your valiant effort, though."

Chills tripped down her arms. She swallowed. "What are you talking about?"

"The only reason I kept you around was to get the layouts of the bank and feed the wrong information to that sheriff of yours." He stepped toward her threateningly. "Do you really think that I wanted your help?"

"So the plans we made…"

Calhoun grinned. "That was funny. You planned a nice little robbery all by yourself, didn't you? We might have to use that plan on the next town we hit."

"I see," she said thoughtfully, then frantically tried

to think of a way to get herself out of this mess. She tilted her head and gave a dry laugh. "Well, you had me fooled. I almost thought you were a gentleman."

"You thought Silas was a gentleman?" Jake laughed in disbelief. "He's just like the rest of us only he wears fancier clothes because we send him in to scout places out. I always say, you can dress up a donkey so he looks like a horse but inside he's still—"

"Shut up, Jake," Silas growled.

Jake rolled his eyes, then sat down on a crate with a thud.

"When is the boss getting here?" Owen asked.

"He's riding over now," Calhoun said from where he leaned next to the door.

Lorelei hated to bring the focus back to herself, but she needed to know what she might be up against. "If you don't mind me asking, what are you planning to do with me?"

Owen leaned forward with a leer. "Now, there's a question I'd like to answer."

She sent him a scathing glare. "I wouldn't care to know that answer. Besides, I was asking you, Silas. After all, you could have just let me remain oblivious to all this. I wouldn't have been able to tell anyone anything about your real plans. What's the point of taking me captive?"

A new man entered the shed. All of the others sat up in attention. The mood immediately became more serious as he took stock of everyone. He was tall and thin but about as well dressed as Silas. His hands rested at his holster. His light brown gaze stopped when it met hers. "You're our insurance. Your pa owns the bank. He'll be much more cooperative if he knows we've got you."

He turned to address his men. "I've been thinking. We'd better not take her with us at first. We don't want the locals to get any ideas about saving her before everything is done. Someone will need to stay behind with her, then join the rest of us in about twenty minutes. By that time, we should have what we need."

"How will he believe we have her if she isn't with us?" Silas asked.

"We'll take proof."

Calhoun frowned. "What kind of proof?"

"Something she's wearing," Jake offered.

"Her dress," Owen quietly suggested with a smirk.

"You don't have time for that," she said to the boss as she removed her hat. "You can take this. Papa knows it's mine."

He wavered for a moment, as though unwilling to accept her direction. Suddenly snatching the hat from her hand, he bellowed, "Everyone mount up. I'll go over assignments outside."

The door closed behind the last man with a bang. Lorelei knew they'd probably send Silas back in to guard her, but she didn't plan to sit around and wait while her father's bank was robbed. Her hand strayed to the small derringer Sean had insisted she strap to her leg. She sank onto a nearby crate and hid the gun beneath the folds of her skirt while she waited for her guard to come back in.

"Lord, please help me get out of here," she whispered to herself as she heard the others' horses ride away.

The door opened slowly, then closed with a decided slam. She glanced up. Instead of meeting Silas's dark eyes, she was confronted with Owen's lecherous grin.

She stared back at him. She slowly rose to her feet, hiding the derringer behind her. "Where is Silas?"

Owen leaned back against the door to watch her. "The boss wanted him to go with the gang since he knows his way around town. I guess that just leaves you and me."

"Unfortunately," she murmured.

He threw his hat on a nearby crate and began to pace measured steps toward her. "The way I figure it, we've got about fifteen minutes all to ourselves. What do you reckon we could do in fifteen minutes?"

"I plan to sit right here and wait until it's time to leave," she said as her hand tightened around the gun.

"That's too bad because I'm planning on having a little bit of fun," he said, reaching toward her.

She jerked away from him, pulled the derringer from behind her back and pointed it straight at his heart. "Stay where you are or I'll pull the trigger."

He pulled his gun with a lighting-quick speed that took her breath away. Her little derringer looked awfully harmless compared to his Colt. The amusement on his face told her just how serious he was taking her threat. "That's a nice little pistol you have there, Miss Wilkins. Hold it out to the side so I can get a good look at it."

She braced herself, then squeezed the trigger. Light exploded off the end of her gun. He roared as the bullet ripped across his left shoulder. She darted past him. A sharp cry of pain rent from her lips as he grabbed her arm and twisted it behind her body. The gun slipped from her hand. He shoved her against the wall. "I'll teach you not to fool with me."

She gasped for breath as she struggled against him to

no avail. *Dear God in heaven have mercy,* she thought frantically just before his filthy laugh sounded in her ear.

Sean rushed toward the shed as a gunshot rang out. He prayed he wasn't too late. Lorelei's sharp cry of pain sounded inside. He pushed through the door and saw a man pin her against the wall. Fury filled his stomach. He drew his gun.

His finger twitched over the trigger, then stalled. He flipped the gun over to hold the barrel. The man's putrid laughter filled the air as Sean walked up behind him. Without hesitation, he lifted the gun and crashed the handle onto the man's head. He dropped like a boulder in a river. Sean eyed him to make sure he was really knocked out before he glanced at Lorelei. She was still staring at the man in disbelief. Slowly, her gaze lifted to his.

Her dark blue eyes were wild and stunned. They filled with tears an instant before she launched herself into his arms. He caught her tightly to his chest. That's when he knew why he'd been fighting so hard to win the heart of a woman so reluctant to give it. He loved her. He'd been intrigued since that moment ten years ago when she'd announced their fates were intertwined. He'd hated watching her court Lawson until he'd resigned himself to it. He'd done a pretty good job of burying his feelings over the years, but they'd always been there waiting to be unearthed. With her in his arms, he lacked the will and the desire to deny their existence any longer.

"Just like breathing," he murmured.

"What?"

He glanced down at her and shook his head. He

couldn't tell her. She wouldn't believe him anyway. It was best to keep his discovery to himself for now. He lifted her over the prone man to settle onto a crate close to the door with her in his lap. Her whole body seemed to tremble. Her arms clung tightly around his neck, which was fine with him because he wasn't about to let her go. He pressed a kiss against her hair. "Did they hurt you?"

She shook her head against his shoulder. "Not yet."

"I wish I could have slugged him."

She leaned back to look up at him. "Oh, Sean. It was awful. Silas knew I was pretending the whole time."

Sean placed a stilling finger on her lips. "Do you hear that?"

She was quiet for a long moment as the sound of approaching horses' hooves filled the shed. Her eyes widened. She whispered, "Someone is coming."

They hurriedly stood to their feet. Sean drew his gun again, then motioned to her. "Get behind me."

She brushed the tears from her cheek. "Don't be ridiculous. I'm not going to hide from these brutes."

"Lorelei," he chastened in frustration.

"This is my battle, too." She sent him a hard look, then picked up what he recognized as her derringer off of the ground. She spread her boots apart just enough to find her stance. Pursing her lips in concentration, she trained her gun toward the door.

They quieted in time to hear the hoofbeats come to a stop outside the shed. Someone dismounted. He tried not to let himself tense as the footsteps neared. The moment the door opened and the man stepped inside Sean commanded, "Hands in the air where I can see them!"

Silas's hands crept cautiously toward the ceiling with his right hand already holding a gun. The man's gaze swept the room quickly before returning to Sean. "What's going on here?"

"First, throw your weapon outside nice and easy. Don't give me a chance to shoot you because I'd sure like to," he said calmly.

Silas followed his directions, then lifted his hand to the ceiling again. "Is Owen dead?"

Sean shook his head. "I haven't checked but I'd say he's just unconscious for now."

"He tried to accost me," Lorelei interjected.

Silas lowered his head slightly. "I'm sorry, Lorelei. I was coming back to help you."

Sean narrowed his gaze. "Why do that after putting her in danger in the first place?"

"I had to in order to finish the job. You see, we're all on the same side here."

Lorelei shook her head. "Oh, no, we aren't."

"Yes, we are. I'm an undercover Texas Ranger."

"Prove it," Sean demanded over Lorelei's gasp.

"I have to get the papers out of my boot." At Sean's nod, he leaned over and pulled off his shoe. Using a knife he pulled from his pocket, the man wedged the heel open and removed a folded piece of paper. He dropped the knife on the ground away from him, then held out the paper for Sean to take.

Sean glanced at Lorelei. She nodded and kept her gun trained on Silas as Sean holstered his and examined the paper in his hand. He glanced up at Silas. "It looks legitimate."

"It *is* legitimate," he said as he tucked the paper in his pocket. "I've been working with this gang for almost five months. I gained their trust so I could gather the evidence I needed. As soon as they get the money from the bank, I'll be ready to arrest them. I allowed Lorelei to become involved because she would have botched the whole thing otherwise."

"Thanks a lot," she said wryly.

"I was trying to keep you safe." He stomped his foot back into his shoe.

"You left her at the mercy of one of your gang members," Sean objected. "I don't think that qualifies as keeping her safe."

Silas's gaze was defiant. "My priority was to finish the job. She involved herself in this. If something had happened, it would have been as much her fault as mine."

Sean grasped him by the front of the shirt and stared down at him. "Let's get this straight. You could have told Lorelei no in the beginning. You could have come to me, the local law enforcement, to explain your assignment. Instead, you allowed this to progress until you placed her in a position where she could have been hurt or killed. If something had happened to her, it would have been as a result of your negligence, not your duty. Do you understand?"

Silas glared back at Sean for a long moment, then shoved himself away. "I've got work to do."

"I hope that means saving my papa's bank from being robbed," Lorelei said pointedly.

"It does," he said. They followed him outside as he picked up his weapons. He stopped beside his horse. "Sheriff, you can ride along with me if you like. I'm sure I could use your help rounding up all of those outlaws."

Sean nodded. "I'll deal with the one here, then Lorelei and I will follow you into town. You and I probably won't need to do much. The whole town decided to pitch in to catch the bank robbers. We've probably got them outnumbered three to one."

Just as Sean had predicted, all of the outlaws had been bound and gagged by the time he arrived at the bank. He walked inside and was immediately met by Jeff. "It all went according to your plan."

"Anyone hurt?"

"No. Not a single gun was fired." Jeff grinned. "I wish you could have seen the look on those outlaws' faces when they burst in with their guns waving only to find themselves surrounded by half the town's arsenal. I doubt Judge Hendricks will ever swear in so many temporary deputies again."

"Where is Mr. Wilkins?"

"He's in his office with Doc. He was looking pretty pale when those good-for-nothings came in holding Lorelei's hat like a medal of honor."

Sean headed to the back of the bank and walked into Richard's office. The man stood from his chair as soon as he caught sight of Sean. "Lorelei. Is she—?"

"Fine, Mr. Wilkins. She stopped for a minute outside to talk to Amy, but I can assure you that she is perfectly fine."

Richard sank back into his chair and let out a relieved breath. "Thank God."

"Deputy Bridger tells me everything went as planned."

Richard nodded. "They hardly got past the door."

"Good," he said. "I'd better make sure those men are officially taken into custody."

Richard waved him away. Sean had barely taken a few steps out of Richard's office when Silas approached him. "I'd like to transfer these men to the jail now. They shouldn't be there long. I'll wire headquarters immediately."

"Good. I'll open the jail for you." He was walking out the door when Lorelei stepped inside.

No one could miss the glare she sent to the outlaws lined up against the wall. She grabbed her hat from where it sat on the counter, then walked over to Sean. "Is Papa in his office?"

He nodded. "He'll be glad to see you."

She glanced around, then, with half the town watching, she rose on her tiptoes to place a soft kiss on his cheek. Pausing to meet his eyes meaningfully, she whispered, "Thank you."

He might have returned her gesture with a bit more gusto if she hadn't quickly stepped past him to hurry toward her father's office. The sly knowing looks he received from the other men in the bank told him they thought he was falling hard. He smiled wryly. Lord, help him. They weren't half-wrong.

Lorelei gave a parting smile to her parents as they stopped to talk to their friends. She continued through the crowd toward the gazebo where the main Founder's Day activities would take place. It looked as if most of Peppin's citizens had turned out for the event that would begin with a picnic and end with a dance late that evening. Usually Lorelei anticipated this day for weeks, but her mind had been so preoccupied by other things lately that she'd hardly given it a second thought.

She spotted Ellie a few yards in front of her and wound her way through the crowd toward her. As she neared, Ellie caught her gaze with a smile. "Lorelei, I was just looking for you. Where are your parents?"

"They stopped to talk to Doc and Mrs. Williams," she explained, then leaned around Ellie to wave at Kate and Nathan. "Kate, how are you? Ellie told me you were feeling poorly last week."

"Just fine." Kate shared a smile with Nathan, then leaned toward Lorelei to whisper, "I told the rest of the family, so I guess I should tell you, too. Nathan and I are going to have another baby."

Lorelei's eyes widened. "Congratulations! That's wonderful."

Nathan grinned. "It certainly is. I think it's going to be another boy this time. We need to even things up."

Judge Hendricks stepped forward on the platform of the gazebo and raised his hands to get everyone's attention. "Quiet down, folks. Quiet down."

Ellie nudged Lorelei and whispered, "Did you hear that Sean is getting an award for stopping the bank robbery?"

"Yes, I know," she returned quietly. Sean had tried to convince her to let the town know about her part in apprehending the criminals, but she'd been more than appalled at the idea. Actually, she'd been more than appalled at the thought of what her father might have to say if he knew the extent of her involvement. Having caught the outlaws red-handed, there was no need for her to testify. As far as she was concerned, her foray into undercover work would remain a secret until no one cared to hear about it.

Judge Hendricks cleared his throat. "As one of the town's founders, I would like to welcome you all to the fifth annual Founder's Day celebration."

Lorelei glanced back to look for her parents, hoping they wouldn't miss the judge's speech as the hundreds of people around her cheered, whistled and clapped. She saw her parents edging forward at the back of the crowd. Richard smiled when she met his gaze and gave her a little wave. She turned back in time to see the judge hold up his hand to indicate he was ready to speak again. The cheers died down, so he continued.

"We have set this day aside to come together to show our commitment to each other and this town. We come together to remind ourselves of the ideals our town was founded upon. We come together to express our thankfulness to God for seeing our town through another year and to pray that His will is accomplished in the next.

"As we do, we remember the faith, dedication and perseverance that took us through the first fifteen years. Those same qualities will sustain us through the next one hundred and fifteen."

Lorelei joined in with the thunderous applause that interrupted the judge.

"Reverend Sparks will begin the day with a prayer. After he does, I would like to invite retired Sheriff Hawkins, who served this town for fifteen years, to come up and help me with a special announcement."

"This is it," Ellie whispered proudly a few minutes later.

Lorelei smiled as the tall but slightly stoop-shouldered sheriff from her childhood stepped forward. Judge Hendricks shook the man's hand, then turned back to the crowd. "The citizens of Peppin have long been interested in finding a way to express their appreciation to outstanding members of the community. It is my pleasure to announce that we finally figured something out."

Chuckles rang through the crowd as the judge continued, "From now on we will recognize citizens who show admirable courage, self-sacrifice, fortitude, so on and so forth by awarding them with the Peppin Award of Honor.

"I'm sure all of you have heard by now, a gang of outlaws tried to rob the First Bank of Peppin a few days ago. If they had succeeded, our celebration today would not have been quite as joyful. As it was, members of this town came together to help defend the bank and managed to put those outlaws right where they belong—in jail. Today the town would like to recognize Sheriff Sean O'Brien for his outstanding leadership in coordinating this effort and for his service to the community."

Sean stepped forward as Mr. Hawkins presented him with a fancy-looking box and everyone clapped. He faced the crowd, then held up his hand as Judge Hendricks had done. He managed to keep the applause short. "I am very grateful to all of you for finding me worthy of this award. However, this award really belongs to this town and not to me. I especially think we should recognize those who were sworn in as temporary deputies to help in the effort.

"There are about ten of you, so I didn't want to forget anyone." He grinned, then pulled out a piece of paper to read off their names. After everyone cheered for the temporary deputies, Sean put the piece of paper back in his pocket. "There is another person from our town we should thank. This person has chosen to remain anonymous but provided vital information necessary to the success of our efforts. I hope this person knows how much I truly appreciated their help."

He gave a self-deprecating smile. "Now, I think I've said about enough, so I'll leave y'all to enjoy the day."

"He did a good job," she whispered to Ellie.

Ellie nodded but tilted her head toward the gazebo with a confused look on her face. She glanced back at the gazebo to see Judge Hendricks holding his hand up to keep the people from clapping just yet. "Hold on there, Sean. I thought there was something else you were planning to say."

Even twenty feet away she could see Sean begin to redden. He whispered something to the judge, but the man just grinned. "Don't be shy, now. If a man has something to say, he ought to just go ahead and say it. Right, folks?"

Several teasing remarks rang from the crowd urging Sean to speak. Lorelei smiled and exchanged a glance with Ellie. "What in the world?"

Ellie shrugged, then cupped her hand by her lips to yell. "Speak, Sean. Speak!"

Sean laughed. "Fine. I wasn't planning to do this, but while I was waiting to come up here I realized the opportunity had presented itself."

"That and this town is too nosy to let him leave the stage without saying something interesting," Ellie whispered to Lorelei.

She giggled and nudged Ellie with her arm but had to admit, "That's the truth."

The crowd waited as Sean took the paper from his pocket and flipped it over. He read whatever was on the back of it then slipped it into his pocket. He glanced at the chortling judge and shrugged. "A man has to get this sort of thing right."

A ribbon of suspicion began to flutter in her mind about the same time that Sean's gaze met hers. His voice was loud and clear as he called out, "Lorelei Wilkins, will you come here for a minute?"

Chapter Nineteen

Her eyes widened as she felt the entire town turn to look at her. Her breath stilled in her throat. She shook her head no, but she was urged forward by Ellie and pretty much everyone else. She made it to the base of the gazebo.

"You are the most wonderful, beautiful and captivating woman I have ever met." He held his hand out to guide her up the stairs of the gazebo. A playful smile flashed at his lips for an instant, and she realized he was pulling her into their own little secret before he continued. "I have had no choice but to fall in love with you."

She covered her mouth with her hand in a gesture that appeared to be of amazement but was really meant to hold in the laughter that begged to spill from her lips. Everyone had backed away to give them their space. Now, the crowd shifted to get a better view as Sean knelt before her.

"I would be honored to spend the rest of my life with you," he said with a sincerity that might have sobered her if that playful gleam hadn't returned so quickly. "Will you marry me?"

She gave herself a moment to gather her thoughts. Slowly, she managed to lower her hand from her mouth. A smile pulled at her lips. She nodded, then realized not everyone could see that.

"Yes," she said loudly, then bit her lip to keep from laughing at the ridiculousness of the entire situation. "Yes, Sean O'Brien, I'll marry you."

The town erupted in cheers so loud she could hardly think. Sean shot to his feet and pulled her into a warm embrace. She pulled back to meet his gaze with her mirth-filled one. She shook her head. Knowing the crowd would think she was teasing him about the proposal, she swayed toward him to whisper beneath the crowd noise. "You are such a liar!"

"Is that any way to speak to your fiancé?"

The cheers were just beginning to calm down when Ellie called out, "Give her a kiss."

Lorelei shot a glance at her soon-to-be mischief-maker-in-law as other people encouraged Sean to do the same. Turning back to Sean, she felt a blush begin to color her cheeks. He looked at her with mock seriousness. "We'd better give the people what they want. It's my job to keep the peace around here, and they might riot if we don't."

"We wouldn't want that," she breathed.

His kiss tempted her to forget all about the people watching them until he stepped away to slip the ring on her finger. She waved it at the crowd, hoping they would take the hint and move on with the festivities. She followed Sean down the steps toward his family.

Judge Hendricks regained the attention of the crowd. "That's the most exciting thing that has happened on Founder's Day yet. I hope we make it a tradition. Well, folks. That's all of the ceremonial stuff. You are free to go have fun. Enjoy each other and the festivities planned for today."

Lorelei spent the next few minutes accepting congratulations from the town as people began to disperse. The more congratulations she received, the harder it was to keep the smile from slipping off her face. Finally, her parents joined her where she stood with the O'Briens. Her father shook Sean's hand with a firm clasp. "Well done on that proposal, son."

"Thank you, sir."

Mrs. Greene stepped forward to congratulate them, but before she left she also added, "I'll be at the wedding. Don't you forget it."

Lorelei grimaced as the woman walked away, but her mother was beaming. "Why don't y'all come over to our house after lunch for dessert? I made ice cream. We can celebrate and make plans for the wedding."

Sean's family quickly agreed. Lorelei glanced around the happy faces of the two families in disbelief. *This entire thing is nothing but a farce, and they know it. How can they possibly be so genuinely happy about this?*

Sean's hand grazed her back, and she glanced up to meet his questioning gaze. "Is something wrong?"

She shook her head. "I'm fine."

It wasn't long before they were all gathered on her parents' front porch with their bowls of creamy vanilla ice cream in hand. The children sat on the porch steps in raptures at the treat. Lorelei slid onto the end of the bench where Kate and Ellie sat. Sean took a chair next to her. Her mother and father sat beside him. Nathan completed the familial circle by sitting between her father and Kate.

"Now," Caroline announced as they were all finishing with their desserts. "I think we ought to decide on a wedding date."

Lorelei's eyes widened in alarm. "So soon? I was hoping things might be able to slow down now. After all, you only gave us a deadline for the proposal."

Her father shook his head. "The sooner the better, Lorelei. Everything will settle down once you're married. Anyway, we promised Mrs. Greene."

"I guess you're right," she agreed, then bit her lip.

"How soon were you thinking, Mr. Wilkins?" Sean asked.

"I think I'll have to defer to the women on an exact time frame, but I think it should be done as soon as possible," he said with a glance toward her mother and Kate.

Kate's gaze turned thoughtful. "Ellie and I would be willing to help in whatever way we can, Mrs. Wilkins. How long do you think it will take to get everything ready?"

"Well, Lorelei already has a dress, so that should help cut down on the time considerably. I'd have to see when the church would be available."

"I'd rather not have another wedding in the church," Lorelei said. "We can have it here, if Sean doesn't mind."

"Fine by me."

"I'd like to keep things small and simple."

"Well, if that's what you want, darling," Caroline said. "That would make things easier on us. We can have a small ceremony at home. You could always have a reception later and invite more of the town. If we keep it under thirty guests, I see no reason why we can't have everything ready in two weeks."

Richard nodded his approval for the plan. "We'll set

the date for two weeks from today. Now, why don't we go back to the Founder's Day activities? I hear there is going to be a bazaar this year."

"There certainly is," Nathan said as everyone began to stand. "I brought several of my horses out for exhibition."

Lorelei let out a resigned sigh as everyone began putting the chairs back inside where they belonged. She helped gather the ice cream bowls and set them in the sink to soak before going back to the front porch to meet the others. Her breath stalled in her throat as she realized they had departed, leaving her alone with Sean. "Where did everyone go?"

"I asked them to go on ahead so we could have a moment alone," he said quietly.

"Why?" she asked, then lifted her gaze to his threateningly. "Sean, if you say 'we need to talk,' I won't be liable for my actions."

A slow smile stretched across his lips. He reached toward her, but she stepped back to avoid his touch. His hand dropped to his side as he watched her in concern. "I won't say that, but I would like to know why you're so upset with me."

She felt the tension in her shoulders ease. "I'm sorry, Sean. I shouldn't have been so harsh. I guess our marriage is just becoming more of a reality."

He frowned in confusion. "I know the proposal was a bit of a surprise, but we knew this day was coming all along."

"Yes, but I never thought you would do it so soon. We had nearly a full week before Papa's deadline. Why didn't you wait?"

She could hardly believe it, but he actually blushed.

"Honestly, I didn't plan it. I think I got a little carried away in the moment."

"Oh, that's just fine," she breathed and shook her head. "The one time you do something impulsive it's this."

He frowned at her sarcasm. "Your father wanted the proposal to be public, didn't he? What does it matter? It would have happened anyway."

"I know." She shrugged and gave him a conciliatory smile. "I guess I was just counting on a few more days of freedom."

Sean stared at Lorelei. His lips pressed together with the same agitation that filled his stomach. "Freedom? You make our marriage sound like you're going to be forced into a fate worse than death."

Her gaze dropped from his haltingly. "That isn't what I meant."

He stepped forward, then lifted her chin so that he could read the emotion on her face. "No, but it's how you feel, isn't it?"

"I don't know." She broke away from his hold but didn't step away.

Disappointment battled with panic. He'd known all along he might be faced with this moment—the moment when he knew for certain that he was in love alone. That didn't make it any easier to bear. He had to fix this. He had to prove to her and himself that the situation wasn't as hopeless as it appeared. He shook his head. "Maybe our relationship isn't ideal for two people who just got engaged, but I thought we were making progress."

"Progress?" she asked as her eyes filled with tears of frustration. "How have we made progress? We aren't any closer to loving each other than we were when we started out."

"How can you say that?" he asked in disbelief. "I thought if nothing else that kiss showed you—"

"Showed me what? That isn't love, Sean. That's nothing more than—"

"Don't," he said harshly. "Don't cheapen that moment or what we feel for each other by calling it nothing more than lust. That couldn't be further from the truth and you know it."

"Nothing has changed, Sean," she replied quietly. "We're still in the same situation that we've always been in."

He stared into her dark blue eyes. "A lot has changed. I think you're just too afraid to admit it because that means you'd have to actually allow yourself to feel something for once. That's why you're so willing to demean these feeling between us. You don't really want them to be meaningful, do you?"

She arched a brow coldly. "Are you done?"

He stepped back. "Yes, I'm done. I'm done trying to talk about love with someone who refuses to ever feel that emotion."

He started to walk away. It felt good to leave her standing there until he realized it wouldn't do for him to return to town without his fiancée in tow. He let out a deep breath, then turned to face her. "We have to go back together."

A tense moment passed between them. He almost thought she would refuse when she stepped up beside him and slipped her hand onto his arm. He met her gaze, but she immediately looked away. He narrowed his eyes as an idea came to mind. She wanted to believe that nothing had changed between them. Well, he'd just have to show her the difference.

The toe of Lorelei's kid leather boot rhythmically measured out the beats of the music as the melody coursed from the instruments in the gazebo into the heavy evening air. The sun would soon finish setting and bring a close to the endless stream of Founder's Day activities. She could hardly wait.

As soon as Sean had walked her back to the flurry of activity, they had separated. He had spent the next few hours with his nieces and nephew. She had spent the rest of the day with Ellie, Amy Bradley and Sophia Johansen. Now she was alone because they were all dancing and enjoying themselves immensely, as far as she could tell. Sean had not approached her for a dance. In fact, he hadn't approached her at all since their argument. Didn't he realize people would think it strange if he didn't even acknowledge his fiancée after proposing to her earlier that day?

"Apparently not," she mumbled to herself. She glanced over to where he stood talking with a few other men. *I'm not going to stand around waiting for him to notice me like that awkward child I once was.*

She began to thread through the crowd in an effort to find her parents so she could let them know she was going home. She heard someone call her name and turned to find Mrs. Sparks walking toward her. "Lorelei, wait just a moment."

She looked at the reverend's wife curiously. "Is something wrong, Mrs. Sparks?"

"No, no. I just wanted to give you this," she said, handing Lorelei a letter. "The postmaster accidentally put it in with our mail. I guess he saw the Brightlys sent it and assumed it was for us. I've been meaning to give it to you."

"Oh, thank you. I've been waiting for this." Lorelei glanced down thoughtfully at the letter in her hand, then back up at Mrs. Sparks. "I've been wondering something. Did the Brightlys ever mention anything about me or Sean in their letters to you?"

Mrs. Sparks smiled kindly. "One thing my husband and I have learned while in the ministry is the benefit of staying out of others' affairs unless they directly impact the ability of the church to operate as it should. Whatever the Brightlys communicated to us was private. It will stay private." Mrs. Sparks gave Lorelei's hand a gentle squeeze. "Does that answer your question, dear?"

Lorelei blinked away the tears that threatened to fill her eyes at the woman's kindness. "Yes, it does. Thank you."

"You're welcome," she said before walking away.

Lorelei slid her finger under the flap of the envelope, then stopped halfway through. She glanced over to where she'd last seen Sean. He had just as much of a right to know the contents of the letter as she did. Squaring her shoulders, she made her way through the crowd toward him. The town's blacksmith saw her first and gave her a welcoming grin. "Here comes the bride, gentlemen."

"Hello, Rhett." She flashed a smile at him, but it was Sean's gaze she sought. "I'd like to steal my fiancé away for a few minutes, if you don't mind."

"By all means, we won't miss him," Rhett said teasingly.

Sean shot him a wry look. "Thanks a lot."

She waited until they were out of the earshot of Sean's laughing friends before she said, "Let's find a place a bit more private so we can talk."

He sent her a questioning glance but agreed. She felt his warm hand settle at the back of her waist to guide her through the maze of people. Her arm brushed his chest as they walked between a particularly dense part of the crowd, and she felt that touch way more than she should have.

She bit her lip. She hated to admit it, but he was right. She was attracted to him, but her feelings went much deeper than that. She had grown so used to being with him, laughing with him, sharing secrets with him. She hadn't planned on it, but somehow between all of their squabbles he had managed to become her closest friend. That was definitely not something she'd been expecting. Sean settled onto the church step, then glanced up at her. "Is this private enough?"

"I'd say so," she said, glancing back at the hundred or so people who talked, laughed and danced. She opened the envelope and carefully removed the letter. "Mrs. Sparks gave this to me. It's our response from the Brightlys. She said it got mixed up in her mail."

He stilled. "What does it say?"

"I don't know," she said quietly. "I thought we should read it together."

He gestured to the stairs. She carefully settled onto the step beside him. He shifted toward her and placed his arm behind her to brace himself. Awareness rushed over her. She felt the warmth emanating from his chest just inches away from her shoulder.

She glanced up toward where the moon hovered in the sky, eagerly awaiting the sun's departure as she tried to reason with herself. She didn't want to give in to the seductive feeling of hope that stirred in her chest. She didn't want to acknowledge whatever emotion spread warmly through her soul. It couldn't be love. She knew better than to give in to that, so there was no reason for her to react this way. She scooted farther away from him, then held out the letter. "You'd better read it."

He looked at her curiously but took the letter without comment. He scanned it carefully. "They say they can't promise the children won't slip and mention something, but they are willing to stay silent about it since we'll be married in a few weeks anyway. They are excited to see us again. They hope we will meet them at the train station."

"That's it?" she asked in confusion. "I wasn't expecting it to be that easy."

"That's it." He smiled as he refolded the letter. "You didn't need to be nervous after all. Now, we just have to get ready for the wedding."

She nodded slowly. "That shouldn't be too hard. It sounds like we're going to have a lot of help."

He grinned. "My sisters are going to pour themselves into it."

"So will my mother," she said with a smile. "Our families seem to get along pretty well, don't they?"

"A sight better than we do." He glanced away but not before she saw a shadow of pain in his eyes. She hated that she'd put it there. She also hated the change that seemed to have taken place in their relationship since their argument. Sean seemed less open and less like himself around her. She half expected him to get up and leave her as he'd tried to do earlier that day. Surprisingly, he seemed just as content to stay with her as she was to stay with him.

Above their silence, music from the quartet drifted softly toward them. She realized they were playing slower songs to calm folks down before the festivities came to an end. Only a few couples danced in the open field. It was hard to distinguish the identities of the couples from their silhouettes, but it looked as though her parents were out there dancing. She smiled as she watched them twirling slowly to the music. A new song started. It was just as slow as the last one.

"You've never asked me to dance," she blurted out.

He looked at her carefully. "I didn't think you would want me to."

She shrugged lightly, as though it didn't matter.

He broke the lingering tension between them with one slow, teasing, heart-stopping grin. "You want to dance with me. Don't you, Lorelei?"

She tried not to smile, but it didn't work so she met his gaze defiantly. "So what if I do?"

"Come on," he said with an enticing wink.

"We'll never make it before the song is over," she protested, even as she allowed him to pull her to her feet.

"Sure we will." He tugged her down the stairs. Instead of leading her across the field, he pulled her into his arms, then began to dance. Her gaze darted to the other couples. No one seemed to have noticed them. She wondered why he hadn't tried to move into the open where everyone would see them. She bit her lip as she was suddenly reminded of all the times he'd told her that he was no longer just pretending to court her.

Now, for the first time, she was willing to believe it. She wanted to know how it felt to be courted by the man she'd loved without endeavoring to push him away or silence her own feelings. She just wanted to enjoy the moment without worrying about what would come next or if she would get hurt or anything else. She was here with him. Perhaps that was all that mattered.

He dipped his head just enough to whisper into her ear. "I missed you today, Lorelei."

She pulled back enough to look up at him. "Then why did you stay away?"

The corner of his mouth pulled into a half smile just guilty enough to tell her he had been up to no good. "I almost wish I hadn't because I missed spending the day of our engagement with you."

She tilted her head suspiciously to repeat in a whisper, "Then why did you stay away?"

He met her gaze seriously. "I wanted to prove something."

"What?"

He stared down at her for a moment. His green eyes deepened in color, then he pulled her closer until their dancing became little more than a simple sway. She hardly noticed when they stopped dancing all together. She was more aware of the way Sean's arms slipped around her waist, the rough fabric of his shirt beneath her cheek and the way her heart seemed to respond to his. She was about to prod him for an answer when his voice rushed past her ear in a firm statement. "Lorelei Wilkins, this isn't 'nothing.'"

She let those words settle around her for a long moment as she acknowledged the truth behind them.

"I know, Sean," she agreed softly. *Yes, I know. I know, and it scares me to pieces.*

Chapter Twenty

Sean had never imagined such a large family could travel with so few pieces of luggage. He set the last large trunk onto the wagon where it joined its partner and only two other suitcases. He exchanged a look with James Brightly.

James shrugged in amusement. "It doesn't look like much to start out with, does it?"

"You couldn't carry much in that traveling wagon," Sean replied. "You should have plenty of room to spread out in the parsonage." He grinned and slapped the harried-looking man on the back. "It sure is good to see y'all."

"I feel the same way. I'm sure Marissa and the children appreciate seeing familiar faces in this new environment." James grinned. "I have a really good feeling about this town, Sean."

He laughed. "Well, don't burst your buttons yet, Preacher. This is just the railroad station."

With everyone helping, it only took a few minutes to get the Brightly family settled into the wagon. Sean gave James directions to the parsonage, then promised to meet them there to help with the unloading. The children waved at them until the wagon turned the corner. Lorelei waved back at them as they began to follow the wagon. "I thought I'd never see them again."

"They were certainly happy to see you."

"The children thought I was going to be their nanny again." She glanced away and toyed with the strap of her reticule. "I told them I couldn't because I was going to marry you."

"I hope you didn't sound that depressed when you said it."

He glanced down in time to see her press her lips together. This was not good. The closer they got to the wedding, the tenser she seemed to become. He wished he knew what to do. He'd thought about telling her the truth about his feelings for her but he was pretty sure it would just make things worse. She might even get a notion into her head to save him from a loveless marriage like she had with Lawson. At least this way she thought it was fair because they were on a level playing field.

He wanted to reassure her that everything would work out for them. He wanted to tell her that he'd be good to her. That he'd be kind and understanding while she adjusted to farm life and that he was sorry it was all he could offer her. He wanted to banish all of her fears so that she would look forward to their wedding day with joy. But who was he kidding? He hadn't been able to banish his own fears since he was ten. How could he possibly banish hers?

Lorelei slid onto the piano bench and gently brushed her fingers over the smooth keys. After helping the Brightly family unload their luggage, Sean had gone back to work while she'd slipped away to let the family settle in. She hadn't gone far. She needed the respite that the sanctuary offered. She stared at her engagement ring.

The nine days since the proposal had rushed by in a whirlwind of preparation for the wedding, leaving her breathless. Less than a week remained before she would officially become Lorelei O'Brien. She sighed. She'd just have to make the most of it. Wasn't that what people always said when they were faced with doing something they knew they would probably fail at?

A burst of sound filled the air as her fingers tripped through the scales. What had happened to that fearless girl who'd jumped on a train willing to ride all the way to California in search of a new life? She guessed that girl hadn't been running to something as much as she had been running from it. *What had Sean said? I'm afraid to allow myself to feel something for once.*

Her fingers paused abruptly. "What does he know anyway?"

Resettling her fingers on the piano, she began to play Beethoven's "Moonlight Sonata." The soft melody slowly built until she lost herself in it completely. The piece ended as softly as it began, leaving the last notes to fade into the stillness of the silent sanctuary. She valiantly tried to blink away the tears that clung to her lashes, but a few renegade drops tumbled down her cheeks. She didn't bother to brush them away. Instead she stared at the tear-blurred keys. The sound of movement in the sanctuary made her jerk to attention. She felt heat gather in her cheeks.

"Pastor James," she breathed in quiet alarm.

He stood from where he sat on one of the back pews

to offer her an apologetic smile. "I didn't mean to intrude. I heard you playing and couldn't stop listening. Mrs. Sparks said you played on Sundays, but I had no idea you were so accomplished."

"Thank you," she said, grateful that he was giving her time to recover her wits. "Reverend Sparks and his wife were gracious enough to let me practice on the piano whenever it didn't interfere with church functions."

He sat on the front row. "I hope you will continue to do that."

"I probably won't be able to come as often as I used to." She smiled briefly. "I'm getting married, you know."

"Well, I hope you'll come in and practice whenever you have the time."

She was surprised that he didn't question her about her obviously precarious emotional state. He seemed to recognize her confusion and smiled. "I am your pastor now, Lorelei. Well, maybe it isn't quite official yet, but it will be on Sunday. I hope if you ever need to talk to me or my wife, you won't hesitate to do so."

She bit her lip as she considered whether or not to ask the question that her heart begged to know. "Now that you mention it, there is something that I would like your opinion on."

He leaned forward and clasped his hands together. "Go right ahead."

"You and Marissa know more about my true history with Sean than most of the people in this town. What you may not know is that I was in love with Sean for a long time. I never told him, until recently—and at that point, I made it very clear that my feelings for him were all in the past. I carried the pain of my silly, childish broken heart for a long time." She smiled ruefully. "I've managed to forgive him and myself. Now, I think I'm falling in love with him again."

He surveyed her in careful concern. "Why do I get the feeling you think that is a bad thing?"

She bit her lip. "I had gotten to the point where I was fine without love. Now, I'm so afraid of being hurt, I think I'd rather just not feel anything at all. I don't know what to do."

He frowned thoughtfully. "I think you have the wrong idea about love, Lorelei."

"I think so, too." She turned on the piano bench so she could face him, then clasped her hands in her lap. "What is the right idea?"

"I don't mean to offend you, but the type of love you're talking about seems almost like a selfish sort of love. You're concerned with how accepting love from others will affect *you* when you should be concerned with how giving love to others will affect *them*."

"I'm not sure I understand."

"Lorelei, even if you are the only person in the world who can do without love, that doesn't mean others can. Love others as you wished to be loved. I'm not saying that you won't get hurt. We all have our failings and often end up hurting others intentionally or unintentionally. Regardless of that, we still need each other."

She glanced down and smiled ruefully. "If that's true, then it does seem like I've been rather self-preoccupied, doesn't it?"

"You were confused, hurt and trying to protect yourself. I completely understand that. It's just…" He paused for a moment as if searching for the right words. His eyes landed on something behind her, and she followed his gaze to the large wooden cross at the front of the church. She glanced back to see him step onto the platform. "We have to put it in the perspective of the cross. Wouldn't you agree that Jesus' sacrifice on the cross was the purest act of love the world has ever seen?"

She glanced up at the cross. "Yes, I would."

"Jesus was the Son of God. It was within his power to protect himself." James turned to face her and thoughtfully spread his arms out to mimic the shape of the cross. "This is how he died, Lorelei. There is nothing defensive about this position. In fact, it's probably the most exposed position a person can take. He opened up his heart. He stretched his arms wide and became completely vulnerable to show us what true love looks like."

He dropped his arms, then turned to look up at the cross. "A lot of times we only see love as beautiful and healing and restorative. Yet, sometimes love is purest when it's bruised and aching. Whatever form it takes, Lorelei, the cross proves that one thing never changes. Love is always, *always* giving."

She didn't even realize she was crying until a quiet sob caught at her throat. She covered her lips with her hand. James seemed to sense that she needed a few minutes alone because he quietly slipped away. Left with nothing but the visual reminder of his words, she allowed the tears to flow freely from her eyes. They were tears that had been held back for far too long.

Minutes later, she wiped the tears from her face. She was stronger than her fears. With God's help, she would face the future. Resolve filled her being. She was ready for her wedding.

* * *

Lorelei pulled in a deep, bracing breath as she glanced down at the clinging bodice of her wedding dress. She had made a few changes to the design since she'd last worn it, but the white satin stretched across her hips with familiar ease. She waited as her mother attached the veil to the back of her hair, then straightened it. Setting her shoulders in determination, she met her mother's gaze.

Caroline smiled as she carefully tamed one of Lorelei's wayward curls. She stepped back to survey Lorelei and nodded her approval. "You look beautiful, dear. Are you ready to head downstairs?"

"I think I'd like a few minutes alone first."

"I'll let everyone know that we're almost ready to begin."

"Thanks, Mama." She waited until her mother slipped out the door and closed it quietly behind her before she turned to face the image of a bride staring back at her in the mirror. The breeze from the open window stirred her veil and filled the room with the scent of roses.

This was it. This was the moment she had alternately hoped for and dreaded. The moment she said "I do" she would be making herself completely vulnerable. She was going to promise to love, honor and keep Sean for the rest of her life—and she was going to mean it. Despite her talk with James, traces of fear swirled through her mind.

"Perfect love casts out fear," she breathed. She'd learned a lot about love since her talk with James by studying what the Bible said about it. She opened the large family Bible that had taken up residence on her night table and flipped through the pages until she reached the verse that had been bothering her. Her finger trailed across the page. "'Love does not rejoice in iniquity, but rejoices in the truth.'"

Truth. She swallowed at the thought of all of the guests waiting downstairs. What would their reaction be to the truth?

Sean barely refrained from pulling at the high neck of his fancy white button-down shirt. He fiddled with the cuff links on his black Western-style jacket before stuffing his hand in the pocket of his black pants. He stood in the front of the parlor where the ceremony would take place and tried to make small talk with Judge Hendricks.

He glanced around the parlor at the thirty people who had managed to fit inside while still somehow leaving space for a center aisle. Some of the men stood around the perimeter to give the ladies room to sit. Judge Hendricks stepped aside to have a word with the violinist who would provide the music for Lorelei to walk down the aisle, leaving Sean to fend off his nerves by himself.

He glanced to the back of the room in time to see Caroline step in from the hall to wait with her husband. That meant no one was with Lorelei. He spotted Ellie talking to Caroline, then managed to catch his sister's attention and discreetly summon her. "What's the hold up, Ellie? I thought the ceremony was supposed to have started already."

"Goodness, you look nervous," she said in amusement. "Lorelei just wanted a few minutes to herself. That's all. Calm down."

He froze, but his heart began to race. "How long has it been since anyone talked to her?"

"A few minutes, maybe. I don't know, Sean. No one is timing it," she said distractedly. At his sharp intake of breath, she looked at him more carefully. Suddenly her eyes widened. "You don't think…" She bit her lips as if afraid to continue.

He sent her a glance that told her exactly what he thought. He tried to appear calm as he passed under Mrs. Greene's watchful eye to walk toward the Wilkinses. He met their curiosity with tempered alarm. "Did Lorelei come down these stairs?" he asked in a low voice that didn't carry past the two of them.

"Of course not," Richard said.

"She is still in her room," Caroline offered. "She just wanted a few minutes by herself."

I bet she did. He glanced up at the stairs. "Her room has a window, doesn't it?"

Caroline nodded. "Yes, it overlooks the backyard."

"Excuse me," he breathed as he stepped past them.

He walked out to the backyard, then glanced up at her open window. He expected to see a sheet hanging down the side of the house, but it wasn't there. He must have anticipated her. Any minute now he would probably see her satchel tumble to the ground beside the yellow rose bushes. Or perhaps she'd step out onto that tree branch next to her window. It was plenty close enough to afford an escape. He crossed his arms, bracing himself to wait. He heard the back door of the Wilkinses' house open and glanced over to see Caroline staring at him in confusion. "Sean, come inside."

He shook his head, then turned back to the window. "Just a minute, Mrs. Wilkins."

The woman went back inside, leaving him staring at the open window. The ground beneath him began to sway. He braced himself. He began to consider the possibility that he was too late. He should have thought of this. He should have had a plan. He'd just been so sure that she was dedicated to getting married. His only concern had been securing her love. He'd felt her tension. Why hadn't thought of making sure she was prepared to walk down the aisle? He should have planned better.

His chest began to tighten. She'd run from Lawson. Why wouldn't she run from him? It wasn't as though she loved him. She'd made that clear plenty of times. He'd thought she wouldn't want to sentence him to a loveless marriage. Maybe she didn't want to sentence herself.

He closed his eyes and tried to slow his racing thoughts. It felt as though they were swirling around just above his head. He couldn't grasp any of them. Was he going crazy? He needed to think. He needed to sit down. Maybe that would stop the swaying. He needed to pray.

His low words were interrupted by his rapid breaths. "Lord, I've been holding on to the most important pieces of life as though I could take better care of them than You. All of my plans couldn't help me hold on to the piece that meant the most to me. She's gone, but finally I'm giving my life entirely to You."

His breathing began to steady as the pressure on his chest loosened. "Your will isn't my backup plan anymore. From now on, it's my only plan. I don't just want You to be my Partner in life. I need You to be my Guide from here on out. Amen."

The swaying beneath his feet began to lessen. His mind stopped reeling enough for him to sit down on the bench beneath the crape myrtle. He buried his face in his hands and propped his elbows on his knees. A weight gradually began to lift from his shoulders.

"I thought we were getting married in the parlor." Lorelei's gently teasing voice drifted from right behind him. He froze. *Delusions? Doc never mentioned delusions.*

There was a whisper of movement, then a light touch on his back. "Doc said I might want to check on you. Ellie told me why."

The tension eased from his shoulders even as he growled. "Ellie."

She laughed. "Don't blame her entirely. I could tell she knew, so I begged it out of her. I'm pretty sure I know why you haven't told me."

"Why is that?" He managed to ask as he let his hands fall from his face so he could stare at the ground.

"You don't like showing weakness. You want me to see you as strong, dependable and controlled. Well, I've always known you were strong and dependable. Sometimes I think you're a bit too controlled. For instance, you have to be dying to see what I look like today but you're staring at that leaf so hard you're going to tear it in two."

A smile pulled at his lips, but he didn't move.

"You're building up all of that tension inside of you when turning around and sharing that moment with me would get rid of a lot of that stress. We're getting married, Sean. I need you to share your load with me and allow me to control my share of the reins. I need to know that you aren't always strong so that I have permission to be weak once in a while, too. That's the only way this is going to work."

He pulled in a deep breath. He slowly stood and turned toward her, then couldn't help staring. Her hands rested delicately on her hips, accentuating her curves, which were already embellished by the cut of the brilliant white dress. Her hair was partially pulled back from her face and gathered beneath the wreath of delicate blue flowers that crowned her head. The rest of her dark hair spilled down her back in rich curls that begged to be touched. She took his breath away, which, combined with what had just happened, left his voice sounding nothing like it usually did. "Lorelei."

Her lips curved into a tempting smile. "Better, right?"

"Much better."

"Remember that." She lifted her skirts carefully as she stepped through the grass to meet him.

"I will." She hadn't run the other way in the face of his weakness, but could he dare to upset the delicate balance of their relationship any further? He swallowed. How could he not? "Lorelei, before we do this, there is something I need to say—"

"Stop everything!' They both jumped at the sound of Mrs. Greene's voice. She burst out of the house with Richard and Caroline right behind her. "I can't make you do it."

"What?" Lorelei asked in an echo of his own confusion.

The woman fanned her brightening cheeks as she came to a stop in front of them. "Pastor Brightly called on me yesterday. We talked and he pointed a few scriptures out to me about meddling and gossip. Oh, he was gentle about it, but I got the message. I tried to ignore it, telling myself over and over again that I was in the right but seeing everyone all dressed up and ready to go…"

"You're releasing them from their promise, aren't you, Amelia?" Caroline asked as she stepped forward to place a gentle hand on her friend's arm.

"Yes. Yes, I am."

Sean's gaze shot to Lorelei. Her mouth dropped open as she looked to her father for guidance. Richard shook his head thoughtfully. "There is still the chance that all of this could be discovered. However, since there isn't an imminent danger, I think it's time we let you two decide your own fate. I believe you're fully aware of the consequences of either choice. We'll leave you to make your decision."

The relief that lowered Lorelei's shoulders told him more than he wanted to know. He turned away to gather his emotions as he heard the door close softly behind Mrs. Greene and Lorelei's parents. He shook the tension from his hands to keep them from clenching into fists. He was supposed to have surrendered his plans to God. Maybe he'd better act like it for once.

He turned to face Lorelei, then leaned back against the ashy trunk of the crape myrtle to offer a smile he didn't feel. "I guess it really is bad luck to see the bride before the wedding."

Chapter Twenty-One

Lorelei wasn't sure how she'd expected Sean to react to this news, but a careless smile wasn't it. She searched his gaze for the tension she'd seen earlier but lost sight of it in the swirl of unfathomable emotions in his green eyes. Silence hovered between them. She sat down on the bench as she tried to grasp the implications of what just happened. She shook her head. What were they going to do? They had a house full of guests waiting for a wedding. She did not want to be the one to walk away from another wedding. Who was she fooling? She didn't want to be the one to walk away from *this* wedding. She met Sean's gaze, and one thought echoed in her mind.

Love rejoices in the truth.

The truth. Her breath stilled in her throat. *The truth is I love him.*

Her heart began to thunder in her chest. With each beat came the knowledge that if she was ever going to overcome this, it would have to be now. She suddenly realized her choice would determine much more than if she said those three little words. It would determine how she would spend the rest of her life. Either she would trust God to protect her heart as she gave of it freely in obedience to His will, or she would continue on a path that would bring momentary security and lasting unhappiness. There was only one real choice.

Her heart begged to speak the truth that she'd refused to allow cross her lips. Rather than deny its request, she finally allowed the words to roll off her tongue and rest softly between them. "Sean, I love you."

That got his attention. He straightened his shoulders and stared down at her with his penetrating eyes. Some of her courage fled. She swallowed. She dropped her gaze to the tips of her white bridal boots, then forced herself to continue. "I don't think I ever really stopped. I know you probably don't return my feelings. I just thought you should know in case you are ever able—"

Lorelei was barely even aware that Sean had erased the distance between them until he guided her face upward and kissed her with a gentle reverence. Her lashes flew open to meet his gaze. He knelt in the grass in front of her with a relieved smile. "I love you, too. Now let's get married."

He began to stand, but she reached forward and grabbed his hand before he could get away. "Wait!"

"What?"

She stared at him in wide-eyed disbelief. "This is not going to be the story we tell our children, Sean O'Brien."

A confused smile tilted his lip. "What are you talking about?"

"I just said I love you—present tense, mind you." She tugged his hand until he knelt before her again, then looked at him hopefully. "Don't you have anything else to say besides 'I love you, too? Now let's get married'?"

"Should I?" At her emphatic nod, his doubtful look turned into one of understanding. "Well, I told you everything I felt when I proposed. I meant what I said."

"You did?" She dared to ask, "What did you say?"

His shoulders slumped as though severely disappointed. "You don't remember my proposal."

She bit her lip and shrugged innocently. "I remember you proposed. Everything else is kind of blurry. There were a lot of people around and I didn't know you meant it. You acted like it was all a joke."

"I knew if I did otherwise you might not be able to say yes." He squeezed her hand. "That's all right. I remember it. It went something like this."

He cleared his throat and became all seriousness and sincerity as he captured her gaze. "Lorelei Wilkins, you are the most wonderful, beautiful and captivating woman I have ever met. I didn't fall in love with you to fulfill my plans. I fell in love with you because, as you informed me nearly ten years ago, 'We belong together. We'll always belong together. I don't know how I know it, but one day you're going to marry me and we're going to be happier than anyone who's ever lived.'"

Lorelei laughed as tears filled her eyes, and she shook her head in slow disbelief. "You remember that?"

He smiled slowly. "I never forgot it...or you. Now—" he stood and pulled her to her feet along with him "—will you *please* prove yourself right and marry me already?"

"Absolutely. I think we've left everyone waiting long enough—including each other."

They stepped inside the house a moment later to find both of their families standing in the hallway outside the parlor. Everyone waited with bated breath. Lorelei glanced at Sean. He drew out the moment by surveying each family member carefully. Finally, he spoke. "Well, what's everybody standing around here for? Someone tell them to start the music."

The hallway echoed with celebration, causing a few of the guests to peer around the corner to see what all the commotion was about. Lorelei hardly noticed. She leaned into Sean as he slipped his arm around her waist, then grinned at their families' enthusiasm. Ellie presented Lorelei with her wedding bouquet. "Hallelujah! There's going to be a wedding. Everyone get to your places and I'll tell them we're ready."

Sean was amazed at how quickly everyone was ready to go. He pulled at his choking collar and let out a relieved breath when the music began. A moment later, Lorelei started down the aisle on her father's arm. The peaceful smile on her face lasted until she was halfway down the aisle. She bit her lip. He could literally hear their family and friends sit forward in their chairs. Her steps became more halting. Her gaze met his in desperation.

Sean held out a hand to Lorelei, willing her to take it. She quickly kissed her father on the cheek, then slid her hand into his. They turned to face the judge. He could almost hear the guests let out a breath of relief behind them. Lorelei tugged at his hand as if she wanted to say something. He leaned down to incline his ear toward her. As the judge welcomed the guests to the wedding, her whisper filled his ear. "I have ants in my shoe."

He glanced at the pained expression on her face. "Which one?"

She tapped the shoe nearest him against his boot. He

threw a cursory glance over his shoulder, then quickly knelt on the floor and slipped his hand under the hem of her dress. The judge abruptly stopped speaking. A gasp rent through the air.

Bracing herself with a hand on his shoulder, Lorelei used her other hand to lift her skirt. He finally found her boot and ripped it off. He brushed a few ants off of her foot, then turned the shoe over to bang it on the floor. He met her gaze thoughtfully. "You'd better take off the other one."

Her foot disappeared back under her skirt. A second later, the last shoe slid from under the white satin. He gathered the boots in his hand, then gave them to Caroline who stepped forward to collect them. Sean stood. Lorelei slipped her hand back into his. He nodded at the judge to continue.

The judge cleared his throat. "As I was saying, if anyone has just cause why these two should not be married, let them speak now or forever hold their piece."

He couldn't help it. He glanced back at Mrs. Greene. The woman caught his gaze and smiled her approval. A weight lifted from his shoulders. Once blessed silence reigned through the parlor, the judge instructed them to face each other. "Sean, will you take this woman to be your wedded wife, to live together after God's ordinance in the holy state of matrimony? Will you love her, comfort her, honor and keep her, in sickness and in health: forsaking all others, keeping only unto her so long as you both shall live?"

"I will."

"Lorelei, will you take this man to be thy wedded husband, to live together after God's ordinance in the holy estate of matrimony? Will you love, honor and keep him, in sickness and in health: forsaking all others, keeping only unto him so long as you both shall live?"

"I will," she said with calm assurance.

Judge Hendricks beckoned for the rings to be presented. "Sean, repeat after me as you place this ring on Lorelei's finger."

He took the ring, then met Lorelei's gaze sincerely as he repeated his vows. "I give you this ring as a symbol of my love." He waited for the judge to continue, then spoke. "With all that I am and all that I have, I honor you…" He slid the ring onto her finger. "In the name of the Father, and of the Son, and of the Holy Spirit."

"Lorelei, repeat after me as you place this ring onto Sean's finger."

"I give you this ring as a symbol of my love," she said confidently as she slid the ring onto his finger. Then as she glanced up to meet his gaze, she smiled. "With all that I am and all that I have, I honor you…in the name of the Father, and of the Son, and of the Holy Spirit."

"Those whom God has joined together, let no man put asunder. By the power vested in me by the state of Texas, I now pronounce you husband and wife. You may seal your union with a kiss."

Sean wasted no time in doing exactly that.

Epilogue

"**P**aging Mr. and Mrs. Sean O'Brien. Paging Mr. and Mrs. Sean O'Brien."

Lorelei raised her hand to attract the porter's attention before Sean even had a chance. She sent him a meaningful look as she answered the porter's call. "We're Mr. and Mrs. Sean O'Brien."

Sean grinned at her. "Sounds good, doesn't it?"

"Mmm-hmm," she agreed with an answering grin.

The porter arrived at their seats, clutching a basket of fruit. "Please accept this gift as a token of our deepest apologies."

"Well, thanks," Sean said as he took the basket. "But why are you apologizing?"

"There was a mix-up, sir. You two should have been shown to a private car in first-class when you boarded. If you'll follow me, please, your luggage has already been transferred."

Lorelei shook her head. "We didn't pay for a private car in first-class. I think we'd better stay here."

"The car has been paid for, ma'am, by a Mr. Richard Wilkins and a Mr. Nathan Rutledge."

Sean's gaze met Lorelei. "How do you like that? Our families treated us."

"I like it. Let's go."

It only took a few moments to gather their things and follow the porter up the aisle toward first-class. As they walked, a familiar flash of color caught Lorelei's eyes. She stopped abruptly. Sean ran directly into her.

"Hey," he protested, but she hardly noticed.

She narrowed her eyes, then slowly turned around. "Back up."

He watched her in confusion but walked backward as she commanded—not that he had much choice with her hand on his chest. She stopped again to stare at the traveling bag sitting abandoned on an empty seat. "That's my bag."

"What?"

She lifted the bag to look for her initials on the right handle. She found it. She turned to Sean. "This is my traveling bag. The one Elmira stole. Look, my initials are still here—*L.W.*"

He surveyed it closely. His eyes widened in recognition, but he shook his head. "Your initials are *L.O.*"

She sent him an exasperated look. "*L.W.O.* Thank you very much."

"Excuse me, ma'am," a deep voice said. Lorelei turned to find the young couple seated across the aisle was watching them closely. The man frowned. "You must be mistaken. That bag belongs to our chaperone."

She exchanged a look with Sean, who stepped toward the man. "I'm sorry, did you say your *chaperone?*"

"Yes," the young woman answered. "She just stepped out for a minute, but she'll be back and I'm sure she'll want her bag."

"*My* bag. I'm sure she'll want *my* bag. She probably stepped out as soon as she heard the porter calling us. Well, we'll wait right here until Miss Elmira comes back."

The dark-haired young man shook his head. "See? You're mistaken. Our chaperone's name is Lorrie Wilson."

"Lorrie Wilson... Lorelei Wilkins," Lorelei repeated, then looked at Sean. "She stole my name! Don't laugh at me. Do something."

Sean leaned his arm on the back of the empty seat to survey the couple. "You two seem like nice people. I guess you deserve a fair warning. Miss Lorrie Wilson was our chaperone, only back then she went by the name of Elmira Shrute. That *is* my wife's bag. Miss Elmira stole it along with my wallet. Notice I said '*my wife.*'" He lifted Lorelei's left hand and displayed it as proof. "That's just the kind of chaperone Miss Elmira is."

"Oh, heavens," the young woman breathed.

Sean grinned. "Yes, ma'am. Hiring her was the best mistake I ever made."

Their eyes met, and Lorelei smiled until he put her bag back on the seat and ushered her down the aisle. "Aren't we going to wait for Miss Elmira?"

"Nope." He took the key from the porter, who was waiting by their open door. "We certainly aren't."

"You can't be serious." She let him guide her into their room as she protested. "What about my bag?"

He closed the door and leaned against it. "You have a new one."

She tilted her head entreatingly. "My honor?"

He held up his left hand to show his wedding ring. "Protected."

She caught his hand in both of hers. "My pride?"

"Well, now." He lifted her hand to his cheek, then pressed a kiss into her palm. "That's something you'll have to take care of yourself."

She frowned. "I will. If you would be so kind as to move out of the way?"

He crossed his arms. "That isn't going to happen."

"Really? We'll see about that." She tried to reach behind him in a valiant effort to open the door. He stopped her every attempt. "Let me give her a piece of my mind!"

"No. You're not going out there. You have to let this go." He held her off with one hand and locked the door with the other, then slipped the key under the door into the hallway.

She gasped. Her eyes flew back and forth between floor and him until she met his gaze. "Do you think that's perfectly necessary?"

"Perfectly." He leaned forward to peck her on the lips.

Well, it was hopeless. She wasn't getting out. Miss Elmira was going to get away. She let out a loud disappointed sigh and caught Sean grinning at her antics before he turned away to hide it. She smiled, then crossed her arms to watch him unpack his trunk. "That's just fine. What are we going to do when we really need to get out of here?"

He had the nerve to glance around the room as though another door would suddenly appear. "There's always the window."

She laughed. "You first!"

"I am perfectly content to stay exactly where I am."

"I bet."

He caught her sly look and lifted a brow. "You ought not to insinuate such things, Mrs. O'Brien."

"Oughtn't I?"

He closed his trunk and sat on the top of it. "Come here for a minute, will you?"

Once she stood in front of him, he guided her to sit on his knee. She placed her arm around his shoulder as his went around her waist. "Lorelei, I can't let you go after Miss Elmira because she did us a favor. If she hadn't abandoned us I might never have married you."

"I know." She sighed. "It's just that every once in a while I'd think to myself that if I ever got my hands on that Elmira Shrute—"

"You'd what?"

"Well, I never got that far—probably nothing," she admitted then smiled. "You're right, though. I am thankful for everything that happened."

"Are you sure?"

She looked at him more closely. Did he honestly doubt her? "Of course, I'm sure. I love you. I wouldn't trade what we have for a thousand reckonings with Miss Elmira."

"In that case…" He reached into his pocket to pull out the key.

Her mouth dropped open. "You had it the whole time!"

He laughed. "You didn't think I'd want to be trapped in here with you for the whole trip, did you?"

She pushed away from his chest, but he wouldn't let her go. "You're a scoundrel. That's what you are."

"And you're trouble." He waited until she stopped

struggling to continue, "I knew it from the moment I held you soaking wet to my side and you laughed when James threatened to kill me."

She gave him her most innocent look. "Well, it was funny."

He dipped her backward and kissed her until her arms went around his neck. When he pulled away slightly, she glanced up at him with dancing eyes but kept the tone of her breathless voice serious. "Sean, do you know what the best part of running away was?"

He shook his head. "What?"

"Getting caught."

His warm emerald eyes searched her face, then he grinned a slow heartfelt grin and she knew she was right.

* * * * *

"Get back!"

Definitely a female voice, from the other side of the barn. He walked around the barn. If someone had asked him to guess what he might find there, he wouldn't in a hundred years have guessed correctly.

A young Amish woman—Plain dress, apron, *kapp*—was holding a feed bucket in one hand and a rake in the other, attempting to fend off a rooster. At the moment, the bird was trying to peck the woman's feet.

"What did you do to him?" Daniel asked.

Her eyes widened. The rooster made a swipe at her left foot. The woman once again thrust the feed bucket toward the rooster. "Don't just stand there. This beast won't let me pass."

Daniel knew better than to laugh. He'd been raised with four sisters and a strong-willed mother. So he snatched the rooster up from behind, pinning its wings down with his right arm.

"Where do you want him?"

"His name is Carl, and I want him in the oven if you must know the truth." She dropped the feed bucket and swiped at the golden-blond hair that was spilling out of her *kapp*. "Over there. In the pen."

Daniel dropped the rooster inside and turned to face the woman. She was probably five and a half feet tall, and looked to be around twenty years old. Blue eyes the color of forget-me-nots assessed him.

She was also beautiful in the way of Plain women, without adornment. The sight of her reminded him of yet another reason why he'd left Pennsylvania. Why couldn't his neighbors have been an old couple in their nineties?

"You must be the new neighbor. I'm Becca Schwartz—not Rebecca, just Becca, because my *mamm* decided to do things alphabetically. We thought you might introduce yourself, but I guess you've been busy. Mamm would want me to invite you to dinner, but I warn you, I have seven younger siblings, so it's usually a somewhat chaotic affair."

Becca not Rebecca stepped closer.

"Didn't catch your name."

"Daniel...Daniel Glick."

"We didn't even know the place had sold until last week. Most people are leery of farms where the fields are covered with rocks and the house is falling down. I see you haven't done anything to remedy either of those situations."

"I only moved in yesterday."

"Had time to get a horse, though. Get it from Old Tim?"

Before he could answer, a dinner bell rang. "Sounds like dinner's ready. Care to meet the folks?"

"Another time. I have some...um...unpacking to do."

Becca shrugged her shoulders. "Guess I'll be seeing you, then."

"Yeah, I guess."

He'd hoped for peace and solitude.

Instead, he had half a barn, a cantankerous rooster and a pretty neighbor who was a little nosy.

He'd come to Indiana to forget women and to lose himself in making something good from something that was broken.

He'd moved to Indiana because he wanted to be left alone.

Don't miss
The Amish Christmas Secret *by Vannetta Chapman,*
available October 2020 wherever
Love Inspired books and ebooks are sold.

LoveInspired.com

*Heartfelt or suspenseful,
inspiring or passionate, Harlequin
has your happily-ever-after.*

With new books published
every month, you are sure to find the
satisfying escape you know you deserve.